AN ENDURING UNION

Nancy Dane

AN ENDURING UNION

BOOK FOUR

NANCY DANE

TATE PUBLISHING
AND ENTERPRISES, LLC

Published by Tate Publishing & Enterprises, LLC
127 E. Trade Center Terrace | Mustang, Oklahoma 73064 USA
1.888.361.9473 | www.tatepublishing.com

Tate Publishing is committed to excellence in the publishing industry. The company reflects the philosophy established by the founders, based on Psalm 68:11,
"The Lord gave the word and great was the company of those who published it."

Published in the United States of America

ISBN: 978-1-62024-696-2
1. Fiction / Historical
2. Fiction / Romance / Historical
12.05.17

Books by Nancy Dane

Tattered Glory
Where the Road Begins
A Difference of Opinion
A Long Way to Go

Dedication

To the memory of Mama and Daddy.
They would have been so proud.

A WORD FROM THE AUTHOR

As the *Tattered Glory* series draws to a close, I have conflicting emotions—elation that a twenty-year project is completed (I researched for years before starting the novels) and sorrow to part with these characters. They are real to me. Can you tell?

There are a few new characters in this novel. One is a young orphan girl. When I read an official report about orphans at Fort Smith during the war, I felt this was an element that should be included in the novels, and so I created young Sarah. She would be about six years old and an orphan whose parents had been killed by bushwhackers. Later she would be a refugee on a steamship named the Chippewa.

I then developed a giant case of writer's block. In frustration one morning, I decided to do away with Sarah's story line and try a different one. For some reason, after prayer, I sat down at the computer and did a web search of Civil War orphans in Fort Smith. Much to my amazement I found a news clip, an interview with the curator of the Old Jail Museum in Greenwood Arkansas, asking for information about—you guessed it—a six year old Civil War orphan named Sarah whose parents had been killed by bushwhackers and who had been placed on a steamship and sent to an orphanage in Illinois.

Now my Sarah was real, and she had a last name. Campbell. It is a fascinating story, and I hope to help solve the mystery of what happened to Sarah and if she ever returned to Arkansas. If anyone has any information, please contact the museum at Greenwood.

As always, I have many to thank for assistance in research and editing. Thank you, Professor Tom Wing for the private tour of the

Drennen-Scott House in Van Buren. You are a treasure trove of valuable information. Chris Kennedy, thank you for another beautiful cover shot. Thanks to my friends, readers, and editors, Sheree Niece, Nancy Cook, Jackie Guccione, and Les Howard. You guys do a great job! Special thanks to Karen Brown and Jill Marr, busy people who read the manuscript and gave gracious endorsements. Thank you, Jan Townshend and Diane Walters, for all you do.

To my readers, thank you. Without you it wouldn't matter. I love hearing from you. Email me via my website: nancydane.com. Also on the contact page, click on the link to join me on Facebook!

HEADQUARTERS,
Clarksville, Ark., January 22, 1865 - 11.50 a. m.

Major General J. J. REYNOLDS,
Little Rock, Ark.:

SIR: The steamers Ad. Hines and Lotus will leave here today for Little Rock. The Chippewa was captured and burned, and the Annie Jacobs is eighteen miles above here on this shore with machinery damaged, but being repaired. She is guarded with part of my force. The rebels attacked the boats with artillery and a force said to be 1,500 strong. The Jacobs received eighteen shell and solid shot through her, but was saved by the coolness and daring of Colonel T. M. Bowen, Thirteenth Kansas Volunteers, who was on the hurricane deck during the whole engagement, directing the pilot. He was on leave of absence, but assumed command when the enemy approached.

I am, sir, very respectfully, your obedient servant,

W. R. JUDSON,

Colonel Sixth Kansas Cav., Commanding 3rd Brigadier, 1st Div., 7th Army Corps.

Official Records War of the Rebellion Series I VOL 48 PART I PG 14-16

CHAPTER 1 ⚘

Allen looked over his shoulder and frowned. Gentle valleys, now muted in evening shadows, fell away from the green hills shielding Fayetteville. He hated leaving Nelda alone and unprotected. Then he grinned, imagining her reaction to such thoughts. Apt as not, she'd flail him with a tongue-lashing. Meekness was not Nelda's strong suit.

He relived their parting. The urge was strong then to turn the gelding around and gallop back. Instead, he drew a deep breath, pulled his hat brim low, and hunkered deeper into the ragged jacket. In spite of the numerous holes, it felt good against cold wind ruffling tall wheat-colored grass alongside the wagon road.

It was wise to put distance between himself and the Union garrison. If he rode hard, he could make a few more miles before dark. He nudged the black's flank with the heel of a run-down boot, cut across country, and headed south.

As the sun slipped low, the sky changed minute by minute from pink to coral and every shade in between, highlighting the golden hickory and blood-red, black gum trees dotting the hillsides. He wished for Nelda to share the beauty. She always commented on every sunrise and sunset. With a shake of his head, he admitted life without her seemed dull already.

After several miles of rough trail, he made camp in a secluded valley. Wind soughing through tall pines on the ridges did not reach into the hollow where a transparent stream rushed over gray rocks and eddied into deep pools holding the promise of perch and brownie.

Too bad I don't have a hook and line, he thought.

Barely enough light remained to locate pine knots and deadfalls for a campfire. This far off the main road, he felt safe having a fire. All too often in the past two years he'd made cold camp. It might be wiser tonight, considering his proximity to the Union garrison. Nonetheless, he built a small fire and then sat near to eat a can of beans. As Nelda's face danced in the flames, he turned his back and climbed into the bedroll.

"Reckon she'll haunt me now like a dang ghost," he muttered, staring at the clear starlit sky. After sunset, the sharp wind had lain. For now the extra blanket was folded back, but he figured to need it before morning. Such a clear night would produce a cold dawn.

He listened to the black cropping grass close by. In the valley beyond, a pack of coyotes yipped, and then a dog barked. The sound was deceptively near on the night air.

As usual, his thoughts turned to Nelda. The first time he had noticed her, she was sixteen and the only girl at the dance who was more interested in politics than dancing. While the men discussed the state of the nation, she stood behind her pa, taking notes fast and furious for her pa's newspaper. Even then he'd realized she was different… special. On more than one occasion, she had led him a merry chase. Little spitfire Southern Yankee! All in all, he figured she was more than worth the aggravation.

All those months of having to deceive her had rankled. Oh, even then, he had never out and out lied to her. Nonetheless, he had felt villainous all the while he gathered information from her to pass along to the Confederate forces. It was a crying shame they had to be on different sides in this conflict.

His mouth curved into a smile. He remembered another dance and a long ride home, her hair shimmering in moonlight. Then his jaw hardened as the image changed to her battered and bruised, a hostage of that damned Jess and his cutthroat gang of bushwhackers. That was the first time he had known he loved her. He had struggled against blinding rage, all the while knowing it would take cool wits to back down a blackguard like Jess. Allen had been one gun against a gang— but he had gotten Nelda back.

But nothing could compare to the hell he'd endured watching her life hang by a thread when she took a bullet meant for him. He still broke into a cold sweat just thinking about it. Had she jumped into that fray out of love…or mere instinct? It was still a mystery. The long weeks on the trail together had given him hope. And the kiss. Yes, there was no doubt about that.

A small creature rustled dead leaves on the ground and the horse blew. Allen rearranged the stiff makeshift pillow of saddlebags and rolled over.

After a while, his mind went to his brothers—two gone west, the rest in the Confederate Army…except for Seamus. Allen's mouth drew down. He'd like to give that young whelp a whipping. Why in the world had he…

On second thought, it was typical. Seamus had always been hard to figure. He was as rough and tumble as any of the Matthers clan, often joining in the fun but keeping his deepest thoughts to himself.

"Pot calling the kettle black," muttered Allen, admitting he was somewhat that way himself.

With a grunt, he reached under the blanket and dislodged a pebble gouging his shoulder. Soon his breaths were deep and even.

As the hint of pearly dawn streaked the horizon, Allen was in the saddle. He had no coffee beans and no desire for breakfast yet, so he left the small hollow. With caution, he entered a wider valley bordered by steep, timber-covered hills. He had been here before. Back then, this glen had been well watered, lush with grass, and filled with horses and fat cattle. Now, except for a lone doe that flashed a white tail and bounded away at his approach, it was empty.

Avoiding the main roads would mean a longer route, but he could ill afford to meet Union patrols. Too many federals knew him by sight. It was pure luck he wasn't recognized at Fayetteville. He'd expected any second to hear a shout announcing his duplicity. It had happened before, he recalled with a quick chuckle. At Helena when Nelda had given the alarm, he'd almost gotten his neck stretched. Back then she would have been glad.

He rubbed his chin. He reckoned in that respect circumstances had changed. Although in the bright light of day, his doubts returned. It was true she did not hate him now. And she had taken a bullet meant for him. Apt as not, she'd have done the same for anyone. Nelda was prone to jumping into situations without considering the consequences. He pursed his lips in thought. *Then again, she had returned his kiss.*

He scratched his chin again. He needed a shave. Most men wore a beard these days, but he'd never cottoned to one. He had enough red hair on the top of his head without having a chin covered in it, too. As soon as he was in friendly territory, he'd have a shave and hopefully a hot bath—a luxury he cherished.

Allen looked up. The sky looked a thousand miles high, clear and vividly blue. It was a beautiful October day—a day that should be spent harvesting corn or hunting game, the kind of day that made a fellow curse war. He let out a deep breath. But this war was a reality, and he still had a part to play. He kneed the horse and rode on.

The black stepped out briskly, making good time heading out of the hills and down toward the river valley. Allen wanted more information before riding too far. He was looking for Marmaduke's or Cabell's cavalry. The last he'd heard, they were in Little Rock. Of course, by now, they were somewhere else. The Yankees had captured that city. Fort Smith was also firmly in Union hands. He wondered if Clarksville had suffered the same fate. If not, maybe John Hill and his company of home guards were still around. They might know the cavalry's whereabouts. Allen headed through a gap in the hills and pointed the black in that direction.

Two days later, he stopped in a thicket a few miles from town with the sun directly overhead. Smoke curled from the mud and dab chimney of a cabin just beyond a wide creek. Things looked peaceful, but Allen was taking no chances. Just then, he saw a flicker in the trees near the water's edge. Eyes narrowed, he peered through the brush until he made out the shape of a boy squirming to get a better perch in a gnarled oak shading both creek and trail.

"Isaac, that you?" he called and then chuckled as the boy almost fell from the limb. He nudged the black forward, lifting his boots a bit as water rose high on the gelding's legs.

"Damnation, Mr. Allen! You 'most made me fall out on my noggin." But the boy's tone was friendly as he slipped from the tree and landed barefooted onto the ground. In the wide smile, a small gap separated the prominent white front teeth. Fair hair, long on his neck, touched a ragged collar.

"Pa was just talkin' about you the other day. He said the Union caught ya at Helena and hung ya. I was awful sorry to hear it, and so was Ma." The youth squinted up at him. "How'd you get away?"

"It's a long story, Isaac." He glanced at the cabin. "Your ma cooking dinner?"

"Yep, she's cookin' all right. I got a mess of squirrels this morning, and she's frying 'em."

"Reckon there's enough for me?" asked Allen with a smile, already knowing the answer. Even if there was not enough Carrie Hackett would stretch to make do.

"Sure! I'll run tell her you're comin'." The boy ran a few steps and then called back, "Put yer horse in the barn lot."

Allen was not surprised when lanky Roy Hackett arrived in the barnyard along with Isaac. He had suspected the older Hackett might be home when he first saw Isaac guarding the trail. With the river just a stone's throw away, it paid to be watchful. Army patrols often rode the river trail.

Roy stuck out a calloused hand and shook Allen's.

"Matthers, sure is good to see you." He slapped Allen's broad back. "Appears we've been grieving for nothing," he added with a grin, the gap between his front teeth identical to Isaac's. "Heard you got yourself hung for spying at Helena. The general and the rest of us fellows moped around for days."

Allen stripped the saddle from the black. "Caught but not hung," he said. "Glad to see you made it through the battle in one piece."

Roy nodded. "That one and a few more since. Never much boredom riding with John Marmaduke."

"I figured as much from the bits and pieces of news I've been hearing. Since I've been out of pocket lately, I need to catch up on what's been going on."

"Come on inside. Such as it is, Carrie has dinner on the table. We can jaw while we eat."

Allen strode forward gratefully. Carrie Hackett was a good cook. It had been a while since he'd eaten a good meal.

Carrie, her plain, wide face all smiles, greeted him with a big hug. "Allen Matthers, I knew it would take more than a few thousand Yankees to best you. Did you bring yer fiddle?" she quickly asked.

He shook his head sadly. "I knew I'd be traveling, so I left it in safekeeping with some friends near Fayetteville. Sure do miss it, though."

Isaac spoke up. "I got one that Ma's cousin give me. But it ain't much good," he said as his face fell.

"After dinner, I'll give it a look-see. Might just need tuning," encouraged Allen. He sniffed the air. Then he winked at Isaac. "Carrie, is that fried squirrel I smell?"

"Sure is. Along with hot cornbread and fresh milk."

Allen's eyebrows rose. "How'd you manage to keep a cow from the foragers and bushwhackers?"

"We keep her tethered in the woods. Isaac moves her around every day. So far so good. Sit down," she said while filling the glass sitting near the pewter plate with creamy milk.

The cabin was small but neat. In the fire crackling in the fireplace, tongues of blue flame darted among the yellow.

When Carrie was seated, Allen glanced around the table. Every head was bowed. Seldom had he encountered the practice of saying grace. At the Matthers' table, when Kate yelled, "Come and get it," it had been every man for himself. Now, while he breathed in the aroma of fried meat, he bowed and hoped Roy's prayer was not as long-winded as Preacher Simon's.

"Amen," said Roy and then reached for the platter heaped with cornbread. He crumbled a piece into a glass half filled with milk.

Allen split open a steaming piece and watched with his mouth watering as the generous pat of rich, yellow butter melted. He took a bite and savored it before asking, "Any Yankees here abouts?"

Roy nodded towards Carrie. "The wife says a company marched through coming from Fort Smith about a month ago. They went on downriver. None here now that I know of, but I reckon you heard about Little Rock?"

Allen talked around a mouthful of crisp, fried squirrel. "No particulars—just that the Yankees have it, and that Price pulled back south."

Roy nodded. "We got away by the skin of our teeth. Price headed for Arkadelphia."

"Marmaduke still with him?"

"Naw. Him and General Price ain't exactly on good terms just now. The real trouble started back at Helena. Walker never supported us like he was supposed to, and Marmaduke's had a burr under his saddle ever since."

He went on, "Before the Little Rock fracas, Price had ordered him and Walker to join forces at Brownsville to guard the roads in that direction. The Yankees pressed us hard there, and we had to fall back toward Little Rock. Later on, Marmaduke and Walker got into it, hot and heavy. General Marmaduke called Walker a coward." Roy stopped to take a bite. He talked around the mouthful before swallowing. "Walker challenged him to a duel. Price heard about it and sent orders to call it off and for each 'em to stay at their own headquarters. I reckon old John was just too steamed up. Next mornin', they met with pistols, and he killed Walker stone cold dead. O' course, Price was madder than a wet hen—him with Yankees breathin' down his neck and now one of his generals dead by the hand of his other. I figure Price wanted to shoot Marmaduke himself, but he needed him too bad."

Roy went on, "We were the rear guard coverin' Price's retreat. When Marmaduke's command got ordered to Rockport, he gave a few of us leave to go home and he'p with the corn harvest." Roy frowned. "Not that there's much to harvest. Women and kids can't grow crops. What of us the Yankees don't kill, I reckon they'll starve out."

"Anybody I know get killed since I left?"

Roy scratched his bearded chin. "Let me see…yeah, that youngest Morrison boy from Clarksville—Drew I think his name was. He got both hands shot off at Helena. Omer said it was the most pitiful sight he ever seen—"

This was not news to Allen. Nelda had told him about Drew. However, he had reason to be interested in Omer. Omer could get him into a world of trouble.

He quickly looked up from bending over his plate. "So old Omer is all right?"

"Odd thing about Omer," said Roy. "On the retreat from Helena, he just disappeared."

"Deserted?" asked Allen with a keen look.

Roy shrugged. "No one knows. I heard he was guardin' some Yankee—a woman spy, and they both took off. Since Omer ain't no ladies man, I figure she must have got his gun and forced him to go along. I wouldn't doubt but what she killed him. She must've had help—least ways there was horse tracks leavin' camp, but the mules and the wagon was all still right there. Curry tracked 'em a ways but lost 'em at the White."

Allen looked back down and took a mouthful. So Curry had kept his word. He had half expected Curry to tell Marmaduke it was he who helped Nelda escape. It could yet be a problem. He swallowed and took another bite.

I'll cross that bridge when I come to it. For now, it's enough that Nelda's safe and not in a Confederate prison.

He chewed for a minute, enjoying the golden-crusted cornbread as he wondered what had happened to Omer.

"You aiming to go back to scouting for Marmaduke?" asked Roy.

"I figured to."

"I'll be going back in a few days. Need to get up plenty of firewood first."

"I'm a fair hand at chopping," offered Allen.

"Good," said Roy. "Then we can ride together. It's safer than a lone man traveling these days."

Allen took a long drink of milk. It was cold, a testament to Carrie's thick-walled, rock springhouse fed by an artisan spring. He wiped his mouth with the back of his hand.

"Sounds good to me. You need any help with gathering that corn?"

Isaac's face lit. "We sure do!"

Both men laughed. "Son, that sounds as if you'd be glad to let Allen do your part."

That evening after supper, Isaac got his fiddle. "Like I told ya, it ain't much account. Don't reckon you've ever played on one this sorry." He reluctantly handed Allen the battered instrument and a bow with stray hairs.

"You're wrong," Allen said as he took the fiddle and then caressed it. He plucked the strings and began tuning. After he had pulled the stray hairs from the bow and rosined it, he drew it across the strings. He spoke with the fiddle tucked under his chin. "You could use some new strings, but this fiddle is fine."

After a few random notes, he began to play a lively rill. Carrie's face beamed. "Now ain't that fine!"

They all laughed as Roy tousled Isaac's hair and said, "Close your mouth, son. You're catching flies."

Isaac stared with worshipful eyes. "Mr. Allen, could you teach me to play like that?"

He handed the fiddle to Isaac. "I was just about your size when a good neighbor of mine, Caleb Tanner, taught me."

Isaac's mouth dropped again. "Why it was him give me this here fiddle."

Allen's eyes twinkled. "I recognized it. It's the very one I learned on."

Carrie spoke up. "Upon my word! Why, Caleb is my kin! His ma, Granny Tanner, is my great aunt— o'course, we call her Aunt Bitty— cause she's so tiny."

"She's one of my favorites," acknowledged Allen.

"Mine too," agreed Carrie. "I don't reckon it's much exaggeratin' to say— betwixt me and Roy together—we're kin to half of Johnson County."

"Isaac, I'll show you some chords," he said. "But the rest is up to you. It takes a heap of determination and practice. When I was your age, I played so much my ma threatened to strap me for neglecting my chores." He grinned. "Of course, she never did."

In a week, the corn was gathered and enough firewood cut to provide the Hackett family for the coming months. Roy said he must get back before the general declared him a deserter.

In the morning mists, Allen mounted the black. "You're coming right along with that fiddle, Isaac. Keep it up, and you'll be a first rate musician."

"I aim to keep practicing ever' minute I can," avowed Isaac.

While Roy bid his family goodbye, Allen sat in the saddle and waited. Abruptly he lowered his eyes. It was a mournful thing—watching a man bid his loved-ones goodbye. Fog hid the brilliant autumn foliage and cloaked the nearby creek. Allen's keen ears heard acorns dropping through the branches. He had enjoyed the respite from war and travel, although the farm labor had invoked bittersweet memories. With pa dead and ma migrated to Texas and his brothers only heaven knew where, he knew the happy times at home were gone forever.

Roy ceased hugging Carrie and, with a final squeeze for Isaac's shoulder, gathered the reins and mounted. With a regretful look back, he turned the blazed-faced mare into the trail. Allen also glanced back. With hand raised and face tear-streaked, Carrie, a brown shawl draped around her shoulder, stood in the mists alongside a woebegone Isaac and watched until the trees hid them from sight.

*A woman's tender eyes...*Along with that thought came the image of Nelda.

"She's a fine wife," said Roy. "And the boy..." He swallowed. "Well, I'm blessed to have the both of 'em."

"Sure are," agreed Allen. "Isaac is a fine boy— sharp as a tack, and I'm already missing Carrie's vittles."

He chewed his jaw. Try as he would, he couldn't imagine Nelda keeping house. Even she had admitted she couldn't cook. Then he shrugged. He could cook—not as good as ma, but good enough. Of course, they had more to overcome than that little obstacle. Nelda was cultured, educated, strongly pro-Union, and he, Confederate to the bone, was from a rowdy clan known for distilling good moonshine. Not much in common there. It was crazy to hope she would ever want to marry him.

More than likely, after the war, she'll want to start a newspaper, he thought and then drew his mind back to the present.

At first they headed west and then, near the little settlement of Roseville, crossed the Arkansas on a small steamer. The mists had almost disappeared. A few wisps still hugged the low grassy inlets fronting the river. Elsewhere, sun sparkled on the water.

The loquacious captain, known to Roy, shared the latest news and rumors.

"Don't know all the particulars, but, a few weeks back, there was a fierce battle in Georgia—a place called Chickamaga or somethin' or other. We pushed the Yanks back, but it wasn't pretty. Hard to believe, but they say in just two days of fighting there was more than four thousand dead and more than twenty thousand wounded."

Allen shook his head, and Roy whistled.

The captain went on, "Things closer to home ain't so good. Price is still down yonder in Arkadelphia, licking his wounds."

"Any news of Marmaduke moving out of Rockport?"

"Not that I've heard. But Shelby is back raiding in Missouri."

"Really?" asked Roy in surprise. "With so many Yankees around, I figured Price would keep all the cavalry on a short leash for a while."

The hawk-nosed man shrugged. "Well, you know Joe Shelby. He never was one to wait around twiddling his thumbs."

Allen pondered the news. It seemed every time the Confederate Army in Arkansas was given up for dead, it somehow resurrected itself. Preacher Simon would call it a miracle.

Then, Allen's lips quirked. On second thought, since Simon was a Union man, he'd more likely call it the Devil's own work.

The captain nosed the boat close to shore and threw the mooring rope to a black-skinned man on the dock. "Tie her up tight, Tobe." He lowered the gangplank and turned to shake hands with Roy and then Allen. "You boys go careful. Lots of Union patrols coming and going these days."

"Well, I'll be damned!" With raised eyebrows, General John Marmaduke rose from a chair pulled up to a polished desk in the parlor and strode quickly across the room. On his narrow face, a neatly trimmed beard framed his even teeth. Longish dark hair touched his collar, but his tall forehead bordered a sharply receding hairline. He stuck out a slender hand, and after giving Allen's hand a firm shake, he slapped him on the back.

"We heard they hanged you."

"They wanted to, but I had other notions."

Marmaduke laughed. His eyes were keen with interest. "I surmise there must be some cracked Yankee skulls back in Helena?"

Allen flashed a grin. "A few."

Abruptly, the general was all business. "Your coming just now is providential. I need your talents. He motioned to the orderly to shut the door and dropped his voice. "I'm planning an action against the garrison at Pine Bluff and would feel much better knowing their actual strength. Can you get in there?"

Allen rubbed a bristled jaw. Lately there had been no time for shaving. "Don't suppose I'm known by many in that neck of the woods." He pondered for a long moment. "Guess I could try that stevedore stunt I used at Helena. Hope it works better this time," he said grimly, without adding that this time there would be no pretty little Unionist to give him away. "Since the water is up, likely they'll be moving cotton down to the Mississippi and then north. I could ask for work on one of the boats upriver without arousing suspicion."

Marmaduke frowned. "I think it's risky trying the same thing again. No, I have a better idea. This time, you're a gentleman farmer from upriver with cotton to sell to the greedy Union Army." He turned toward the desk and picked up some papers and studied them. "I'll need a troop count and an exact count of artillery and location. Powell Clayton is no fool. Even though we'll outnumber him, I'd feel better having all the facts." He crossed the room and summoned the orderly.

"Locate a wagon and load it with cotton bales. Find a nice suit of civilian clothing for Mr. Matthers."

The orderly sized up Allen's big frame. "The cotton and wagon will be no trouble a'tall; but begging your pardon, General, where in the hell will I find a nice suit of clothes in this rag-tag army—let alone one big enough for Goliath."

The general raised a brow. "I've seen your resourcefulness, McCloskey. No doubt you'll come up with something."

The orderly left abruptly, grumbling under his breath. Allen looked at the map on the wall and then traced the Princeton Road to Pine Bluff with his finger. "You know I can't arrive from the south. That would look suspicious."

"Exactly. We'll get you across the river at an inconspicuous place. You can head north and then circle back south and cross the river again at the bluffs.

Allen turned back. "How long will I have?"

"I'd like the information by the end of the week."

Allen pursed his lips. It was Sunday. "It'll take some doing," he said, "and lots of luck—but I was born lucky."

As Allen left the room, the general sat back down. His pleasure took the form of a softly whistled tune. Matthers possessed an amazing ability to garner information, and in spite of his bulk, to blend into surroundings without exciting notice. Yes, the general felt much better about the upcoming assault on Powell Clayton's stronghold.

CHAPTER 2 ❧

A week later, in the morning sun, a flock of gray doves rose from the roadside. One straggler walked along the road, bobbing its head with every step. As horses approached, it too flew. Allen pulled rein on his saddle horse and sat quietly. His sashay into Pine Bluff had come off without a hitch, and he had gleaned enough information to let General Marmaduke know the coming battle—if it turned into one—would not be a Sunday picnic.

Now, his gun hand rested on his thigh, handy to either the pistol at his hip or the rifle in the saddle sheath. Straight ahead, a Union patrol halted. Into the tense silence came the mournful call of a dove. The Yankee lieutenant eyed the confederate white flag with skepticism. Allen could hardly blame him. Only a few minutes earlier someone had fired an unauthorized shot.

The rebel officer alongside Allen spoke first. "Sir, I insist on being allowed to pass forward with this dispatch for your commanding officer."

The young lieutenant's eyes narrowed. "Considering you already fired on us once—no. But I will send one of my men back with any message. He should get there and back in half an hour."

"I insist on taking the message myself. It's a dispatch from General Mamaduke, demanding surrender of the post."

The lieutenant shifted in his saddle and then toyed with the reins for a second. At first there was biting humor in his words. "Colonel Clayton never surrenders. But he's always anxious for you to come and take him."

Allen grinned to himself. He admired grit in a man no matter what color the uniform.

Then the lieutenant's humor vanished. "Now, get back to your command, or I'll order my men to fire on you, white flag and all."

They had barely pulled back when the skirmish began. Allen ducked as a bullet whined past and clipped a bough arching the trail. As lead poured into the thicket, the sharp scent of pine filled the air. The black gelding suddenly leaped and snorted in terror. Allen let him run until they had pulled away from the melee. Then he pulled up under cover of thick trees to examine the animal. A bullet had gashed one hip, but the wound was not deep.

"You're all right, old fellow." He patted the sleek, trembling neck. "Reckon we were both lucky this time."

He had not gone far before encountering Marmaduke's men riding forward. After a hurried confab, Allen turned the black and headed back toward the firing. Although his job was civilian scout—with a bit of spying thrown in—he sometimes joined in the shooting if the need arose. Judging from what he'd seen in town, he figured Marmaduke would need every gun.

The general had ordered the assault carried out in three columns. Allen rode with the center.

The pleasant day had just a nip of fall in the air. The seasoned soldiers did not appear nervous, but Allen noticed the smooth-faced private alongside him looked green.

He ought to be squirrel hunting instead of facing this, Allen thought sadly. This war can't end soon enough to suit me—though it sure galls that the Yankees are winning. Even if we drive them away from town today, he silently admitted, likely they'll just come back stronger than ever.

"Mister, you been in battle before?" The boy appeared about sixteen, with big, dark eyes in a slender, tanned face.

"A few."

"Did you feel sort of sick to your stomach the first time?"

Allen flashed him a quick grin. "Everyone does. See that big sandy-haired fellow up there?" He pointed ahead.

"Jameson?"

"Yep. Jameson puked all over his boots and mine right before Prairie Grove."

"Really? I never figured he was scared of anything," said the amazed youth.

"No man alive doesn't fear something. The thing that separates a man from a boy is a man faces up to it and does his duty anyway. A boy runs from it."

The boy swallowed. "To be honest, I'm not sure if I'm a man or a boy."

"Just admitting that shows you're more man than boy," said Allen. "You'll do fine. Just keep your head down and listen to Sergeant Murray. Advance when he says advance and retreat if he says retreat. That's all you have to worry about."

The boy nodded. "I'll try," he said, but worry was plain in his eyes.

"What's your name, son?"

"Jacob Montgomery. My folks live close to Lewisburg. Ever been there?"

Allen's mind flashed to his last time at Lewisburg. He had died by inches there watching Nelda fight for her life.

"Sure have," he said. "Spent several weeks once at the Markham Inn."

"You must be rich," said Jacob. "I've seen the inn but we never could afford to even eat there. There's eight of us children and not much money to go around."

Allen chuckled. "I'm not rich. I worked for my keep while I was there." He changed the subject. "That's a right-fine horse you're riding."

"She is," agreed Jacob with a fond look at the chestnut mare. "When I turned sixteen, I was bound and determined to join up. Pa knows General Marmaduke, so he got me in with the cavalry." He paused and then swallowed again. There was a slight tremor in his voice. "Pa says a man's life depends on a good horse, so he gave me the best he had."

"You the oldest?" guessed Allen.

Jacob nodded.

"Me, too," declared Allen.

Jacob studied the trail ahead. The firing had ceased for a time. Now it began again and closer. "Five brothers and two sisters," he said.

"I've got five brothers, too," said Allen. "No sisters, though."

"Halt." The men stopped and then obeyed the order to dismount. Allen glanced over. Jacob licked his lips.

"The first few minutes are the worst. After that, you sort of get into the fray and forget about anything except trying to win."

Jacob nodded his thanks.

"March. On the double quick," barked Sergeant Murray, a tall man with a large hooked nose and dark eyes that missed nothing.

Allen surged forward staying alongside Jacob. He wasn't worried for himself, but his fatherly concern for the youth surprised him. With a silent chuckle, he admitted he was getting soft or old…or both.

As a musket ball whizzed to bury in the dirt near his right foot, he raised his rifle. He fired. The sniper jerked back behind the tree. Allen felt fairly certain he had nicked him. Almost immediately the man mounted and joined other pickets galloping back toward town.

"Come on," yelled the sergeant. "We got the bastards on the run."

Without slowing, the column poured down the road until rooftops came into view. Then, as the sergeant strung out the line, pointing men into position, the first cannon shell erupted in a blast that rocked the ground and splintered the tree directly in front of Jacob into a million fragments.

"You hit?" asked Allen.

Jacob, eyes wide and face pale, wiped a smear of blood from his neck. "Naw, just a splinter in my neck is all."

Another shell exploded. Dirt and rocks flew into the air. A hail of bullets riddled tree limbs all around. The Confederate ranks headed steadily forward, advancing through thick pines emitting a strong and pungent odor. Allen had always loved the piney smell, but now, mingled with gunpowder and nervous sweating bodies, it was revolting.

"Loud, ain't it?" he called with an encouraging grin for Jacob.

Just then, a soldier marching nearby was knocked to the ground. Headless, he did not rise. As blood pooled onto the ground, Jacob eyed the gore, bent, and vomited. Then he wiped his mouth with the back of a hand and kept advancing, Allen gave an approving nod. The boy would do fine. Jacob had seen about the worst and stayed the course. Yes, he would do fine. After that, Allen focused on the battle. He was an excellent shot and snipers were decimating their ranks.

Steady firing rattled the trees. It sounded like hailstones pinging the roof shakes at home. Straight ahead was the bell tower of a church. The line halted a short way from the building. From their rear, a battery thundered past. The horses stopped across the road in back of the church. Allen sprinted forward to hunker in the trees near the artillerymen rushing to get guns into firing position.

Beyond the church lay the town square, hemmed in by walls of cotton bales, which were even now rising higher. He was close enough to see scores of black men frantically rolling more heavy square bales from the warehouse. All along the ridge, civilians ran pell-mell toward the river. Old men, women, and children with terror-filled eyes plunged down the hill. Others hugged the bank. Some civilians fled toward their lines and were hurriedly ushered toward the rear.

Just as an artilleryman collapsed across the cannon, Allen noticed a puff of smoke in the church tower. Taking a steady bead, he squeezed the trigger. A body crumpled in the tower.

While keeping his eyes on the scene ahead, he tore a paper cartridge with his teeth. Sweat and gunpowder were salty on his tongue. He rammed the load into the musket barrel. He raised the gun and then abruptly lowered it. A woman sprinted past the church, fleeing toward the river. Tall and as slender as Nelda, she had auburn hair, just the shade of Nelda's, drawn back into a heavy knot. He held his breath, willing her to safety. He groaned when she jerked and grabbed the back of her head. The knot of hair at the nape of her neck suddenly hung down crazily, still attached to her head by only a few strands.

"Well I'll be," he muttered. A smile curved his powder-caked lips when the tall woman whirled and shook her fist at them.

"You heathen, rebel scum shot the bun clean off my head! Damn you all to hell!"

He chuckled aloud. "Spunky like Nelda, too."

"Hold your fire," yelled the sergeant. "Let the lady pass to the river."

While a hot breeze ruffled the clipped tresses, she gathered her long skirts, and with head high and shoulders ramrod stiff, walked down the hill and out of sight. Abruptly, the lull vanished inside a storm of bullets.

The sun inched up the sky. Allen licked dry lips. He drank from his canteen and passed it to Jacob.

"Thank you, sir. I was getting dry as powder and I forgot to get my canteen. It's back yonder still on my saddle."

The morning wore on. Snipers firing from the second story windows took constant toll on the Confederate ranks. All along the line, men fell. Even more were maimed and bloodied. A miniball grazed Allen's forearm. He barely slowed from loading and firing.

The lanky sergeant nodded toward a line of two-story frame houses. "We've got to stop those damned snipers."

Allen watched him squint at the sun overhead. Then he turned as a captain rode near.

"Cap'n," called the sergeant. "Things aren't going near as well as we'd hoped. We outnumber the bastards double. But they're well fixed behind those cotton bales. Unless we do something, they'll just out-wait us."

The captain scowled and took a deep breath. "I fear you're right, sergeant."

Sergeant Murray suggested, "If we set fires, it'll drive out the snipers. If the cotton bales catch, it'll be all over for them."

The captain was thoughtful. "Yes, I'll consult the major." He returned shortly. "Get some torches ready."

Sergeant Murray nodded vigorously. "Begging your pardon, sir, you don't look none too happy."

The captain stared toward the besieged town. "No, Sergeant, I'm not. The third white house on the left is mine." Shoulders sagging, the middle-aged captain turned away.

"Poor bastard," muttered Allen under his breath.

"From the looks of that smoke yonder, someone else had the same idea." Jacob pointed to trails of smoke rutting the sky.

Sergeant Murray pursed his lips. "We've not gotten close enough to fire those bales. Their own guns must have started it. They'll have the devil's own time putting it out. We best get busy giving them some more worries." He turned to bark orders. "Light some pine torches!"

Allen was glad the sergeant did not assign him torch duty. He had no fear; but he detested the cruel waste, the tearing down of what men and women had fought to build. Since the beginning of this war, each time the order came to destroy crops, cattle, or homes, there was a knot in the pit of his stomach. Since he was a scout, he rarely carried out such orders. But he had often seen it done.

Just then he threw up his head. From the Union barriers surged scores of Negro men, some carrying buckets and a few clutching rifles. In spite of sudden galling fire, with amazing rapidity and order, they formed a line down the steep hill to the river. Suddenly a bucket dropped and a man fell backwards. Others scattered, still clutching sloshing buckets. Rifle fire peppered their ranks and two more fell. Then, as the Negroes with weapons returned fire, the company of Rebel troops advancing along the bank fell back. Allen watched with admiration as the scattered bucket brigade reformed and began passing water up the hill.

"Look there."

He turned to see that Jacob had moved closer and now hunkered behind the next tree. The boy pointed toward the bank.

"Those black men are rolling bales down to block us from sneaking up the river. They're mighty brave, aren't they?"

"Yep." Allen agreed. "Matter of fact, if they stay hooked like this, they could cost us the battle. If those barriers hold—"

"Fire!"

Allen covered his ear.

When the thunder had passed, Jacob shook his head and coughed. "Never knew a cannon could be so loud. It sure shakes the ground. A fellow can hardly breath for all the smoke."

Sergeant Murray rejoined them. He hunkered and wiped sweat from running into his eyes. "I need volunteers to torch those buildings and the mule barns yonder and the warehouses."

He plugged his ears just as the battery commander again yelled, "Fire!"

When the roar abated, Jacob stared toward the line of determined black men. Even before the boy opened tight lips, Allen knew what he was going to say.

"I'll do it, sir."

Allen stifled a protest. It was the boy's right—even if he didn't survive the valiant gesture. Allen felt a fool. He silently argued with himself and stood anyway. "Hell, Sam, I'll go, too."

The sergeant nodded. "Torches are lit. You two fire that barn over yonder. Turn the horses and mules out and head 'em this way. We can use some more horseflesh."

After getting the torch, Allen handed it to Jacob. "For now, you carry both torches," he said, "I'll cover us. But don't move out until I give the nod."

White-lipped, Jacob nodded.

They moved forward warily in a crouching run to halt often behind trees, houses, and outbuildings until sturdy corrals loomed ahead. As Allen darted forward, a puff of dust exploded near his left boot. He ducked behind a dilapidated wagon and held up a warning hand to Jacob.

"Stay put. There's a sniper in the barn loft "

Jacob nodded and hunkered lower behind a protecting tree. He jerked when a bullet splattered bark into his face. At the same instant Allen leveled the rifle and fired. A rifle clattered from the loft. He waved Jacob onward and in a low run, reached the corral gate and pulled it open. It stuck on the ground, and he jerked it free. With Jacob in tow, he circled the milling livestock, frenzied now by shouts and shelling. Together they herded the horses and mules toward the gate. The first horse was almost through the opening when a soldier in blue spied them and sprinted forward.

He fired, missing Allen by inches. "Hyaah!" he shouted and waved the empty rifle. But the horses thundered through the gate. In the chaos Allen and Jacob ducked into the barn. Allen squinted through the dust beginning to settle in the corral and took aim. The soldier, however, using the running livestock as a shield, disappeared behind a building.

The barn interior was dim. Only a few mote-filled shafts of light filtered through cracks between the rough boards. It was a tall barn with numerous stalls and a hayloft overhead filled with mounds of loose hay.

"Start at the back and set the fires," ordered Allen. "I'll keep watch."

Under Jacob's torches, mounds of hay smoldered and crackled and then began disappearing into blackened cinders. Flickers lit the dim recesses. Along with the musty scent of horses and mules, acrid smoke soon filled Allen's nostrils.

Suddenly shrill neighs echoed.

"Oh no!" yelled Jacob. "There are horses back here in some stalls."

"Bridle a couple and lead them up here," called Allen. "Turn the rest loose."

He peered through the door at a dozen blue-coated men rapidly closing in on the barnyard. "Where the hell is Murray?" he muttered and fired. One soldier stumbled. The rest scattered behind barriers. Allen ducked behind the door. Bullets pattered the barn like wind-lashed raindrops. With gaze focused outside, he reloaded the rifle by feel, drew a pistol from his belt, checked the cylinder, and then holstered it again. In a shaft of sun coming through the door, his gun powder smoke mingled with the burning hay smoke.

When the terrified horses plunged past, he fired again and then drew the pistol and fired twice. This time, an advancing soldier pitched backwards. It slowed the others. But Allen knew they'd be waiting with rifles aimed.

"Mr. Allen, here's two bridled but I didn't take time to saddle them."

Allen gave a quick, appreciative nod. The boy was no greenhorn. He had removed his shirt and draped it over the head of one plunging, snorting horse. A saddle blanket draped the head of the other. In spite of being lifted off his feet by the rearing animals, Jacob hung stubbornly to the reins while sweat ran in rivulets on his smoke-blackened face. Allen took the reins.

"We ready to make a run for it?" asked Jacob, squinting back at angry smoke filling the room.

Allen held the horses with a steel grip. "In just a bit. I want to make sure the fire is going good enough they won't be able to put it out."

Jacob's voice held a slight tremor. "They'll know we're coming."

"Yep."

In a few moments Jacob began to cough. Smoke stung Allen's eyes. He glanced back. A dozen separate blazes popped, cracked, and leaped high. Even with his iron grip the frenzied rearing horses almost broke free. He hauled them down again and nodded to Jacob. "Climb on, then I'll uncover his head. Lay low as you can. Try heading toward our battery."

At the same instant Allen uncovered the horse's head, he also jerked the blanket from his horse and leaped onto its back. Jacob's crazed mount bolted out the door with Allen's only inches behind.

Withering rifle fire instantly sprayed them. Jacob's horse, ignoring the gate, leaped the fence. Allen's sped through the opening. The horse stumbled. Then it lunged onward. After a few staggering bounds, it collapsed. Allen jumped. He tried rolling free, but his leg stayed penned. While blood splayed from the struggling animal onto his leg, he drew the pistol and fired. The closest Yankee ducked back, minus the lobe of his left ear. Allen was near enough to hear him curse.

Using the free boot, he shoved with all his might and dislodged his leg. Although it wasn't broken, it throbbed. He eyed the long space across open ground to the nearest tree. For now, with the dead horse as a shield, he'd stay put. The rifle had fallen only two yards out of reach. But with vicious bullets peppering the ground, it might as well be miles away. He looked through the haze. Dead bodies littered the ground where advancing Confederates had been felled.

The Confederate battery was out of sight beyond the trees. Any minute, though, Allen expected another wave of Sergeant Murray's men to come boiling forward.

Cannon fire trembled the earth. Like a hot knife through butter, the shot split the wall of a nearby building. In the midst of dusty, smoking debris, men clutching rifles poured out. Towers of black smoke roiled from the town. Even amidst the hailstorm of musket fire and exploding cannon balls, the bucket brigade ran to and fro in a brave but futile attempt to douse the flames devouring the town.

Allen quickly turned in time to see, far to his right, an advancing wave of gray. They halted in the edge of the trees. Then his eyes widened. He wanted to cry out, to tell the boy to go back. But that would alert the Yankees. Jacob was already racing toward him remounted on his own chestnut mare. To give the boy cover, Allen leveled the pistol, firing again and again. He jerked out the empty cylinder, yanked a fresh one from his pocket and popped it into the gun. Jacob, only rods away, lay low on the horse's back. It was running hard. Allen crouched and then sprang, swinging into the saddle behind the boy. He kept up a steady firing while Jacob jerked the reins and turned the mare. Livid Yankees boiled from cover and returned fire. They were almost out of range. Allen turned for a last shot.

Jacob laughed, a boyish exuberant laugh. "We sure fooled them, didn't—".

He slumped and the reins went slack. Allen grabbed to keep him from falling. Blood wet his hands.

"Jacob," he said. But there was no answer. He was stunned. How had the bullet missed him and hit the boy? With the enemy behind them now, his big body should have shielded Jacob from enemy fire.

The mare galloped into the trees. The reins trailed on the ground. Still holding to Jacob, Allen leaned forward, patted her neck, and spoke gentle and coaxing. Finally, she stopped, her flesh quivering.

Allen slid from her back. He lifted Jacob's limp body and gently laid him onto pine needle-covered ground. Blood still poured from a gaping hole in his neck. The once shining eyes were glazed and dull. The bullet must have come from their own ranks. Tragic though it was, it happened in battle. It had happened to General Jackson.

Allen dropped his head and groaned. He had meant to protect the boy. Instead he had caused his death. He swallowed hot bile rising in his throat. Not for years had the sight and smell of battle physically sickened him. For a moment, he shut his eyes. Then he opened them. After taking the handkerchief from his pocket, he wiped his hands and gently shut the boy's staring eyes.

The mare blew and sidestepped. Allen caught her reins and tied her to a nearby tree.

"Fall back men!"

Allen looked over to see shadowy figures hurrying through hazy, black, powder smoke, men falling back from the battle. Mixed in were horses, mules, and a frantic cluster of civilians, black and white.

Blood-curdling screams rent the smoky air. Allen turned. A warehouse was ablaze. Even as he watched, the roof sagged, and then, in a sea of flame, it caved, shooting sparks high into the billowing smoke. Abruptly, the horrible screams ceased.

Sergeant Murray stepped around a shaggy cedar. His mouth drew down as he looked at Jacob's body.

"Pity," he said with a sad shake of the head. "He was a brave lad."

Allen swallowed. "So we're falling back?" he asked.

Murray expelled a deep breath. "Another pity, but yes. We drove them all back to the square behind their barriers. But storming those breastworks is foolhardy. The general decided against it."

Marmaduke was correct. It was a good decision. Eventually they'd have broken through, but they would have been cut to ribbons doing it. It was better to retreat.

"We stung 'em," said the sergeant. "And we took a passel of livestock and contraband."

Allen frowned. They had been stung, too. He lifted Jacob's body from the ground.

Sergeant Murray looked perplexed. "Best to leave the dead. You'll travel faster. Besides, it's a mite warm for toting bodies. It ain't as hot as July, but he'll still mortify quick enough in this sunshine."

"I'm not leaving him."

Murray shrugged. "Suit yourself." He jerked his thumb backwards. "But he'd have plenty of company right here. There's at least a hundred of us dead back there. I figure the Yankees will give a decent burial."

"I'm taking him and his horse home. I can make it quick in a hard ride."

Murray eyed the horse. "That's a prime piece of horseflesh," he said. "A shame to turn it over to some farmer when we're in such need."

Without a word, Allen untied the reins of his own horse, gathered the chestnut's reins, mounted, and headed west.

CHAPTER 3 ❧

Nelda pulled the shawl tight. It was spring, but the air in Fayetteville had a bite like November. She supposed it was dogwood winter.

April in Arkansas, she thought with a cynical smile. About the time a person puts away wraps and shawls and picks up a fan, along comes another nasty spell.

She had not intended to go to headquarters today. She had been there yesterday. But Mrs. Lowell's constant chatter had worn her nerves thin. The elderly woman was a sweet soul, but her habit of re-telling stories was as nerve-racking as a squeaky door. In the past months, Nelda figured she had heard the same tales at least a hundred times. Besides, she was anxious for news from Clarksville. Colonel Harrison had sent a scout in that direction.

She passed the town square, now a huddle of mostly empty shops. The greening landscape—dotted with tiny blossoms of blue Jacob's Ladder and pink, downy phlox—did little to brighten the spectacle of the blackened ruins of nearby buildings, a token of the last rebel attack. It had happened a year ago this month, long before her arrival. But Nelda knew all about the battle. It was Mrs. Lowell's favorite narrative, especially the miraculous escape of the women and children huddled in the Baxter house cellar. If the Confederate shell had not landed in a pot of lye that extinguished the fuse, all would have perished. According to Mrs. Lowell, since she lived next door, she too would have died.

Only the valiant heroics of Colonel Harrison and his men had held the garrison against the Rebel force led by Colonel William Cabell. Nelda had once seen Old Tige—as his men affectionately called the popular colonel. Even Mrs. Lowell grudgingly admitted, perhaps Fayetteville owed him a bit of gratitude. He could have fired the town but did not. Before the words were hardly out, she recanted and said, more than likely, he was just protecting the homes of his men and officers. With down-turned mouth, she had added, "There are as many families of Cabell's men living here as there are of Colonel Harrison's. I declare it gets confusing—a battle between the First Arkansas Cavalry and the First Arkansas Cavalry, one Union and the other Rebel. If a woman tells me her man is with the First Arkansas Cavalry, I don't know whether to smile or glare."

Nelda had sympathized. It was the same in Clarksville. Divided loyalties and divided families. Even though almost a year had passed since she fled from home to carry the warning of Price's intention to attack Helena, it was still not safe for her to return. Thinking about it now, she shook her head and walked on.

Busy, orange-breasted robins covered the Headquarters lawn. They barely fluttered as Nelda passed. She nodded at the young sentry on duty. He let her pass unchallenged. After climbing the porch steps of the neat, white house, she paused. It was not news from Clarksville she craved. There was nothing of consequence there now. Papa was dead. Mama too. Allen was likely elsewhere. Yes—she admitted with warm cheeks—she would welcome news of him. She put a hand on the nearest white column. She had been standing just here when he kissed her. For weeks, she had chided herself for returning the kiss. They were as different and as far apart as the sun and the moon. It had been absurd to encourage such familiarity. She must stop such foolishness!

With a sigh, she smoothed thick, auburn hair back into the snood and then opened the door.

Colonel Harrison rose to greet her. "Good morning, Miss Horton. The nippy air has painted roses in your cheeks."

"It certainly is nippy," she acknowledged while taking the chair that he offered, drawn near a small stove radiating pleasing warmth.

He remained standing. "What brings you out today?"

"I was anxious to hear if your scout had arrived from Clarksville."

Harrison frowned. For a moment, he drew aside a heavy brocade drape and stared out the window before turning to face her. "He made it back last night. The news isn't exactly to my liking." He shook his head to answer her question. "No, the town is still in Union control. But it's tenuous. Bushwhackers and guerrillas are wreaking havoc."

She wondered if Allen was a participant.

The colonel went on, "We can't keep the telegraph up. As fast as our men string wire, along comes someone to tear it down. Wilson said three dead repairmen were brought in while he was there." The colonel paused a moment and then added, "Ordinarily I'd spare you the details, but I've come to know, as a newspaper woman, you prefer the whole story."

"Please go on," she encouraged.

"They'd been horribly tortured and mutilated. Death was a great relief, I'm sure."

They were both silent for a while.

Nelda sighed. "I've been toying with the idea of going back. There's really nothing for me here—"

He interrupted, "I strongly advise against that. Here's a recent dispatch from Colonel Judson at Fort Smith. This part concerns Clarksville."

He handed her a paper. She quickly read where he pointed.

"Clarksville most in danger. Ordered them to barricade the streets, take possession of the houses, loophole the valleys, and defend it to the last."

Harrison went on, "According to the scout, there's already been a hard-fought engagement. We held the town, but who knows for how long. If the Rebels do gain control, your Union activities won't be forgotten." He gave a crooked grin. "Don't forget, if anything happens to you, Major General Prentiss is holding me personally responsible."

She gave a brief smile. "Well, I'm tired of doing nothing." She had almost lost her wits from months of inactivity. The most she had done since coming here was to write letters for a few illiterate soldiers.

"That's understandable," he acknowledged. "Just this morning something came to my attention, and I thought of you."

She sat up taller. "Go on."

"I know a chaplain named Springer. He recently helped start a Union newspaper at Fort Smith. He might give you a job—at least until things calm down a bit at Clarksville."

Nelda's eyes lit. Writing articles for Papa's newspaper had been the most fulfilling thing she'd ever done. Yes, this would be work to her liking.

"I'll do it," she said. "When do I leave?"

Colonel Harrison's hearty laugh rang out. "Miss Horton, I like your spunk."

She imagined the jovial attitude was due more to relief of getting rid of her.

He looked at a dispatch lying on his desk. "I have a scout going that way next week. I'll see about making accommodations for you to go along."

Just then, a soldier knocked on the office door. Although he lowered his voice, Nelda overheard.

"Colonel, four rebel guerrillas were just brought in. They killed some of our men who were a short way out of town guarding the horses. About twenty of the rebs were dressed in Union uniforms, pretending to be 14th Kansas. Our men were completely thrown off guard. Eight of them were killed. An old fellow named Brown who lived nearby was also murdered."

Harrison swore. "Bring the rabble in. I want to question them, find out how they got those uniforms." He faced Nelda. "Please excuse me, Miss Horton. I'll get word to you about the travel plans."

Nelda quickly stood and thanked him. She was halfway down the hall when the front door opened. Manacled and prodded forward at gunpoint, four men stepped inside. None looked older than twenty. Three had hard, bitter eyes. The youngest—his blue uniform ill fitting and dirty—merely looked terrified.

Two weeks later, Nelda stood in a tiny office in Fort Smith, the head-quarters of the New Era Newspaper. The tall, slender gentleman standing before her squinted at the written introduction from Colonel Harrison. The sunken cheeks were stern. But the eyes lined with dark circles were not unkind as his mouth drew into a frown.

"Highly irregular of Colonel Harrison to send you along without informing me…not even inquiring ahead of time to see if I need an assistant."

Her heart sank. Then she drew a deep breath. "I'm well-qualified. I often wrote articles for my father's newspaper."

He laid down the colonel's letter. "This paper is small. I do most of the writing myself. I don't think we can afford more staff."

Nelda had not come all the long miles in a jolting army wagon to be swept aside so casually. "Reverend Springer, if you don't mind me saying so, you look as if you've been ill."

He nodded. "Recovering from a nasty bout of typhoid," he admitted.

"While you're getting back your strength, I could relieve your work load," she pointed out, "and I'll pay for my wages by soliciting new ads and subscriptions. I was very good at that for my papa's newspaper."

For the first time, there was a spark of interest in the reverend's eyes. "Hmm." He stroked his chin. "On my last trip back to Kansas, my wife pointed out the paper's lack of items for the ladies. Perhaps you could do something to interest females."

Nelda hid a frown. She was politically minded. Ribbons and lace held no interest. However, she did want the job, so she kept silent.

"All right, Miss Horton," he decided. "I'll give you a trial. But remember, it is just that—a trial." He went on, "One thing I need to caution you about," he said gravely. "Loyalties are divided in Fort Smith.

There are traitors who wear cloaks of respectability, but, in heart, they are in complete sympathy with the Rebels. Be on guard. If in the course of newsgathering you learn anything of importance, be sure to come straight to me or go to Colonel Judson, the post commander. Trust no one else."

It was good advice. But Nelda did not even trust the reverend. She had learned that valuable lesson from Allen Matthers.

He handed her a paper. "Read today's editorial, and you'll see what I mean."

She scanned the article.

> There have been several meetings of traitors held in rebel houses in this city of late, at which, under cover of night, males and females have met and exulted over their prospects of re-capturing this city—sending off letters to the rebel army and entertaining spies. The testimony against some of them is clear and unquestionable, and they will be made to feel the consequences ere long. Let them be arrested irrespective of their sex! Precisely our fix here in Fort Smith.

When she looked up, the reverend added, "It's incomprehensible how anyone can be traitor to such a great country as ours." He shook his head. "War-makers—void of loyalty and wanting to enslave an entire race! They're beyond reason."

Nelda had seen a different viewpoint through Allen's eyes. He—as well as many Confederates—was not in favor of slavery. But now was not the time to argue with Reverend Springer, not while his brows were drawn together and beetled like a righteous, angry prophet. Instead she shook his hand and thanked him.

"Do you have a place to stay?" he asked. "No? Then might I recommend Mrs. Hanover's rooming house. It is clean and reasonably priced."

With a light step, she left the office and squinted in the bright sun. With a hand she shaded her eyes. Along Garrison Avenue snaked a long train of wagons with tops of tattered canvas flapping in the breeze.

The numerous hooves and wagon wheels sent trails of dust upward to fall on sweaty arms and faces. The occupants were as threadbare and pitiful as any refugees Nelda had seen. She wondered where they were from and where they were heading.

A gaggle of soldiers, civilians, blanketed Indians, and conveyances of every sort shared the wide street. She wondered why Garrison Avenue was so wide. Ten wagons could travel abreast without being crowded. It seemed an odd waste of city property.

Across the way rose the impressive, two-story, brick and stone edifices of the Union fort surrounded by high stone walls. In the midst of the courtyard, the Stars and Stripes rose high and regal into the clear, blue sky atop the tallest flagpole she had ever seen. A city of tents dotted the distance. It appeared most of the Union Army lived outside the stone walls.

She stepped aside as a young boy of about twelve years old with straw-colored hair ran down the sidewalk, almost knocking her down as he bolted for the door.

"'Scuse me, ma'am," he called, rushing past and gripping a flat crowned hat on his head.

A soldier standing near the door chuckled. "Slow down, Will. Something on fire?" he asked with twinkling eyes.

"Naw," the boy called back. "I need to tell the preacher about those folks from Texas yonder. They're 'most starved to death."

The soldier's eyes sobered as he looked at the train.

"It's a big train," said Nelda.

The private frowned. "And all of them need supplies. We've had hundreds come through since the weather warmed, most of them loyal farmers driven away by the Rebels and the bushwhackers. Country is swarming with them."

"Why," she asked, "was the boy so anxious to see Reverend Springer?"

"Oh, William there is one of the Reverend's orphans. Poor kids. There's plenty of them at the fort. The chaplain mothers 'em like an old setting hen." He nodded toward the wagons. "And when folks like those show up, he's always the first to help."

"He must be a good man," she noted.

"He is that," agreed the soldier. Then he grinned. "But he's fire and brimstone against the Rebels."

Her eyebrows rose. "So I noticed," she said.

The soldier tipped his forage cap and passed on. Nelda weaved her way through the traffic, slowly retracing her steps down the dusty road as she followed Reverend Springer's directions to a quiet, shady street. The old white boarding house with a wide front porch had seen better days but was still homey and comfortable. Mrs. Hanover, the motherly, full-busted proprietress with a strong Mississippi accent, had a tongue not loose at both ends. Nelda welcomed the peace and quiet.

"Miss Nelda?" The voice was incredulous. "What in the world you doin' here?"

Nelda shielded the sun from her eyes and looked up at the soldier on horseback. The blue eyes made her heart skip a beat and then slow with disappointment. The eyes were very like Allen's and so was the coppery shade of hair. But the hair was too long and the shoulders a bit too narrow. Although Seamus Matthers was a young giant with even, white teeth and a wide friendly smile, he had only the shadow of Allen's magnetism.

"Hello, Seamus. I might ask you the same question." She eyed the blue uniform. "What are you doing here?"

He chuckled. "Playin' soldier," he said with a wry grin.

She smiled and held up a tablet. "I'm playing newspaper correspondent."

He leaned over the saddle horn. "Can you take time out for a glass of lemonade? Believe it or not, my friend Tom says they still have some over at Judson's Ice Cream Parlor. The lemonade is a mite tart, but Tom says it's still tasty."

"I'd love some."

Seamus dismounted and walked alongside her leading the horse. "How long you been here?"

"About two months. And you?"

"Several months…I've about lost count." He slowed. "You seen Allen lately?"

She shook her head. "Not since last fall." She turned to face him. "Have you—"

"Naw. I've not seen him since before that." Holding the reins loosely, he chewed his lip and looked at the ground. "Don't reckon he wants to see me—maybe never again. I seen Dillon a few months back, and he said Allen was mad as a hornet when he found I'd gone Union."

Seamus's sorrowful face tugged at her heart.

"When we discussed it, he didn't seem upset," she said.

"Really?"

"Really," she reassured.

His face beamed. "That's good." Then he sobered. He began walking again but slower. His boots clinked on the wooden sidewalk. "They might not know it, but I reckon I care a lot for all my brothers—still and all, there's something special about Allen. I always looked up to him. Always wanted to please him—even more than I wanted to please Pa." He suddenly looked embarrassed. "Rattling on like a dumb kid. Next thing you know I'll start blubbering."

She put a hand on his arm. "I know what a special bond your family has. It's a beautiful thing. I'm sure after the war…" The words died as she realized what she was about to say could never be. They would not all be together again. Not ever. Red Matthers was dead. Kate was gone to Texas. They might never be reunited.

Seamus drew a deep breath. "With Pa gone now, it'll never be the same. I sure miss him." His forehead puckered. With a scowl, he let the matter drop.

"Here's the ice cream parlor. Hope it's cooler inside." He wiped sweat from his brow. After tying the horse to the hitching rail, he held the heavy door for Nelda.

It was cooler inside. Nelda welcomed the pleasant interior. She was tired and it felt good to sit and enjoy the pleasant atmosphere of six small tables covered with white linen cloths. Each had four burgundy velvet padded chairs drawn near. She had heard of ice cream parlors but this was the first she'd ever seen.

There were no other patrons. A slender old man with bushy white eyebrows looked up from wiping the counter and immediately came to take their order.

"What will you folks have?"

Seamus squinted at the menu, a single sheet of heavy paper, cream-colored, and decorated with tiny lithographs of Europe. Nelda recognized the ruins of the Coliseum of Rome.

The man smiled at them. "Menu won't do you much good today. We still have ice from the icehouse, but not enough sugar for ice cream. Used the last I had this morning for a jug of lemonade. Lucky to have lemons. Got them off the last boat that came upriver. Captain said he sold me the last dozen he had…and, let me tell you, the price was dear."

Seamus looked uncomfortable. "Just how dear is a glass of—?"

Nelda interrupted, "I'd rather have ice water. I've not had a sip since last winter and somehow ice water in winter just isn't the same as ice water in July."

"Coming right up." The old man smiled not seeming to mind that the order would be a cheap one.

As they sipped the sweating glasses of ice water, Nelda told how she had come here hoping to work for Reverend Springer at the newspaper. Then she listened as Seamus related how he'd followed his best friend James Loring into the Union Army. He admitted to misgivings when he learned his brothers had joined the Confederacy.

"Allen was so closed mouth. I never even knowed he'd joined. Patrick and Mack headed out west not too long after the ruckus started. Dillon and Shawn stayed hid out most of the time, tryin' to keep out of the way of those conscript men." He shook his head. "With Ma gone, there was no reason to hang around. I miss her…"

He drew a deep breath. "Oh well, no use cryin' over spilt milk. "Tis what 'tis and now I'm on one side and they're on the other."

"But aren't you proud that you're helping keep the Union together?" she quickly asked.

He quirked an eyebrow the way Allen sometimes did. "Not particular, Miss Nelda. I ain't high on the politicians in Washington City. Have to admit, though, I am proud to be fightin' against slavery. Those boys in the First Kansas Colored is smart troops in any man's army. Matter of fact, all the colored troops I've knowed have fought hard and smart."

He went on, "I don't cotton to one man owning another. But truth to tell, that ain't what got me into this fracas. I was riled up over some confederate killing Pa. Mostly, I just wanted to fight and didn't much care who." He gave a dry laugh. "Like Pa used to say, there's just no cure for stupid.

"Trouble is most all I've done since I got here is drill and drill some more, pull guard duty, and throw up fortifications. We've dug enough trenches and cut down enough timber to fill up the Arkansas River. It's hard work but it's better than sittin' around camp. A body goes crazy from the lonesomeness and havin' nothing to do. I've even gone to church a time er two. Chaplain Springer gives a right good sermon. He uses fancier words than Preacher Simon back home. Other than that he makes a right good talk."

He gave a crooked grin and his blue eyes sparkled. "Don't you never tell Allen, but I've even took up playing euchre. It ain't as good a card game as poker, but some of the fellers like it better, so I took it up, too."

Nelda smiled. She had heard euchre was a popular game among the men. She'd never learned any card games. Along with most of the women she knew, Ma had considered them wicked.

Seamus took a sip of water. "This is right refreshing. The army doesn't serve ice water, but they feed us—if the ships run and the supply trains get through. That's been slim at this place. I've et enough wild hog to make me oink and only half rations of weevily hard tack more times than not. Some of the men are in bad shape, and we lose mules every day."

His eyes clouded. "If we want to eat regular, we got to take it from some poor farmer. That's the part I hate most. I don't mind pulling corn out of fields on those big plantations along the river when the folks have already lit out South. But it galls me raw to go foraging and steal from old men and women and kids who'll starve after we take what little they have. Every time we head out with empty wagons and orders to fill 'em up, I get plum sick to my stomach."

Nelda nodded. "I've been the victim. Before I left Clarksville, Drew Morrison and his men took almost all I had."

"Them damned Morrisons," he muttered.

"Drew and his pa are dead," said Nelda, "I don't know about the others."

"Good," Seamus shot out with venom. "I never liked none of 'um. If what Chaplain Springer says is true, I reckon I come close enough to hating Bo to put me in danger of hell's fire. I figure it was him killed Pa. If I ever get the chance, reckon I'll kill that bastard." Then he fidgeted with his drink, his big fists looking awkward on the delicate glass.

"I once felt that way about someone," said Nelda softly. "But a wise woman told me that hate only poisons the person doing the hating. No grudge is worth that."

He nodded. "I reckon yer right," he admitted.

She changed the subject. "Have you been in any battles?"

"Only fight I seen was when General Thayer marched us off to meet up with Curtis near Camden. We got our tail feathers singed in that deal. Lots of men killed. James Loring took a bullet. Last I heared of him, he was in a house gettin' took care of by some women who was tendin' Reb and Union wounded alike. Plenty of our boys weren't that lucky. Rebs wouldn't let us go out and tend our wounded ner bury our dead."

His eyes shadowed. "Almost starved on that retreat. We was three days without a bite to eat, all the while the Rebs nipping at our heels like mad dogs, and us slogging through the rain."

Nelda read much into that short narrative as Seamus gave an involuntary shudder.

He tossed back the last swallow of water like a shot of whisky and sat the glass back onto the wet circle it had made on the table. "It's getting late. I gotta get back." He brightened. "Hey, there's gonna be big doings at the fort next week to celebrate the Fourth."

Nelda nodded. "I plan to be there. Reverend Springer is to read the Declaration of Independence."

"As I recall," he said, "you like to dance."

With a smile, she said, "Yes."

"There'll be entertainment that evenin' for the officers and their wives at the officer's quarters. I'm playing guitar and maybe some harmonica. Might even sing a tune," he added with a grin. "Would you like to come?"

"I'd love to, but are you sure it's all right?"

"Yes, the musicians can bring someone. Where you stayin'? I'll rent a buggy and pick you up."

"There's no need. It's within easy walking distance."

In her bedroom, Nelda leaned near the lamp to critically eye what she had written. It was a good piece. However, it was doubtful if Reverend Springer would be pleased. He had made it plain such articles were not what he intended, but for the last few days, she had racked her brain to no avail to craft an article of interest to the ladies.

"Well," she muttered, "even ladies will be interested to know this!"

Quiet by accident that evening at dinner, she had overheard Mrs. Hanover's guest, a gregarious officer, relating news to the landlady. He claimed that General Buford at Helena had launched a letter-writing campaign, calling for the Federal abandonment of the interior of

Arkansas. When Mrs. Hanover had pressed him for specifics, he had produced a copy of the general's letter and allowed Nelda to peruse it as well. If the general's suggestion was heeded, Federal troops would be withdrawn from Fort Smith. Nelda had quickly scribbled notes.

"Why do we continue to occupy the interior of Arkansas?" Buford had written. "What good has arisen from the occupation?" He then went on to list the cost such occupation had already cost the Union—and according to him—with almost insignificant results; three gunboats, several transports, three regiments of men, seven hundred wagons, four thousand mules, two thousand cavalry horses, six pieces of artillery, and a million cartridges.

Nelda did not doubt the general's numbers. She did, however, disagree with his conclusion, and penned a strong rebuttal. If Arkansas's interior was abandoned, the Rebels would be emboldened to press against Union posts along the Mississippi. Even Helena would be susceptible to attack again.

She put down the pencil and stared out the window into the black, starless night. With a shudder, she envisioned the unthinkable suffering such abandonment would unleash on loyal families. With firm set jaws, she picked up the pencil and began writing again. It was after midnight when she finally blew out the lamp. Undoubtedly, she owed Mrs. Hanover extra rent for the valuable lamp oil she had just used.

Reverend Springer glanced up when she entered. He nodded to a curved back wooden chair and then returned to the letter he was reading. Nelda sat down on the hard seat to wait.

The reverend sighed and removed his glasses to pinch his nose where the spectacles had set. "So much discouraging news," he lamented. "Colonel Judson just shared this report from your friend Colonel Harrison in Fayetteville. It seems he has recently been forced to burn three gristmills. He says they were being used by guerrillas. I find that ironic, since guarding those mills was part of his duties." He went on,

"But he does have an idea that bears investigation. Harrison has begun some colony farms. He's settled fifty loyal families on Rebel lands with enough able-bodied men to serve as home guards. It just might work. Heaven knows we need producing farms in this state!"

"Do you think Colonel Judson might try the same thing here?" she asked, at once intrigued with the idea.

"He might." Then Springer frowned. "Although to be honest, I doubt it would work. No one is safe from guerrillas even a mile from any of our posts, but the River Valley is especially infested. This morning, while I was in the colonel's office, an officer of the Second Kansas Colored rode in, returning from Dardanelle. He reported carnage all along the way. Just a few days ago, several union citizens were hanged between here and there. Just a few miles from here, a farmer was murdered and his yoke of cattle killed. Any such colony would require many armed men."

Nelda nodded. She held out the editorial. "Soon there might not be many armed men left in this district."

The reverend's brows drew together. He put his glasses on and began reading. His face remained impassive. Nelda wondered what he was thinking. She sat stiff in the chair until he laid the paper on his desk.

"How did you come by these facts?" he asked.

As she related the circumstances, he tented his fingers to stare at her over his spectacles.

"Miss Horton, in war time one has to be extremely careful not to aid the enemy. Printing this would very likely do just that. After reading this, they might even step up attacks, intending to discourage opponents of General Buford's plan. Besides, such an article would prematurely create chaos in the civilian population. There will be time enough for such news when and if his proposals are implemented." He pierced her with a stern look. "Therefore, I strongly suggest you restrict your writing to entertaining our female readership, rather than filling them with panic."

With a sinking heart, she swallowed and quickly stood. "Yes, sir. I understand completely."

Boom! The horrific explosion awakened Nelda. Windows rattled and the house shook. She jumped from the bed. Then with a tiny laugh, she lay back down and settled onto the pillow. It was only the beginning of the celebration, a cannon salute to Independence Day. Since she did not have to work today—at least not until there were notes to take at the ceremony, she decided to go back to sleep.

After a few more cannon blasts, she gave up and began dressing. The light blue muslin was the prettiest gown she owned. Mrs. Lowell had made it last winter from cloth in her attic trunk, taking tiny stitches—and great pains to smarten her up. The dress was also the only one wide enough for the hoops Mrs. Lowell insisted on giving her. Nelda detested hoops. However, it might be best today to be smartened up. She would be meeting important dignitaries.

Humidity made her heavy auburn hair curl stubbornly, the tiny ringlets around her face escaping the snood. She studied her wavy reflection in the flawed vanity mirror, frowned, and jerked the black net free and began again. After the third try, she gave up and let the curls triumph.

After a breakfast of course grits sweetened with honey from Mrs. Hanover's coveted stash—brought forth today in honor of the holiday—Nelda leisurely strolled to the fort. From the cottonwood, oak, and willow trees along the river, rose the predictable chorus of cicadas, often punctuated by shotgun blasts, gunpowder hammered on anvils, and cannon fire. Some cannon blasts were faint and far away, floating on the hot breeze from Rebel territory. Nelda assumed the Rebels were saluting their own Independence.

She was impressed with the fort. High stone walls surrounded the military grounds, spaced with four large gates where armed sentinels stood guard. At one corner, spreading green vines clung to a beautiful, rustic stone building that was the commissary.

The grounds were well tended and green. A wide gravel drive circled the parade ground. In the center of the circle rose the one hundred foot high flagstaff. Outside the circle was the enlisted men's barracks, a tall building of red brick trimmed with pristine white. Across the parade ground, stood the officers' quarters—twin buildings, elegant and two storied, with white posts and generous porches.

Vegetable gardens of lush vegetation sprawled behind the dwellings, its rows of sweet corn tasseled and tall, protected from looting gangs by the high stone walls beyond. The prosperous appearance of the grounds could not mask the emaciated state of the army's horses and mules. Some were in fair condition, but others Nelda had seen were little more than skeletons.

Today, a large crowd had already congregated, including many ladies, all dressed in their best—albeit ragged—and carrying parasols against the sun. Most were already seated on benches and chairs placed near the podium, a wooden platform recently erected near the parade ground. Nelda made her way to a seat near the back and sat down, holding her tablet and pencil ready.

Just then Reverend Springer made his way to the platform and the buzz of conversation stilled. He cleared his throat.

"I have a sad announcement to make. An accident occurred this morning. While firing the National salute, Mr. Ford, the gunner, was withdrawing the rammer. There was a premature discharge of the piece, which tore off his left hand—as well as the thumb and finger of his right. The incident was caused by bad powder and the chamber of the gun being in such a condition that it could not be thoroughly cleaned. There is no blame attached to any person." He waited a moment until the sympathetic mummer died.

"Mr. Ford belongs to Co. H, Thirteenth Kan. Infantry. Of course, the occurrence has greatly marred the enjoyment of the day for his company. However, he is being well taken care of and is doing fine. He is expected to recover. Remember him in your prayers.

"Now please stand for the invocation. Let us pray."

After numerous amens had echoed the close of the sincere prayer, he unfolded a page and began to read.

"When in the course of human events, it becomes necessary for one people to dissolve the political bands which have connected them with another, and to assume among the powers of the earth, the separate and equal station to which the laws of nature and of nature's God entitle them, a decent respect to the opinions of mankind requires that they should declare the causes which impel them to the separation."

Before Nelda could read, Papa had taught her a love of the document. The eloquent words never failed to stir her.

"We hold these truths to be self-evident, that all men are created equal, that they are endowed by their Creator with certain unalienable rights, that among these are life, liberty and the pursuit of happiness."

She recalled it was these very words that had ultimately led Papa into Union sympathies. With the memory, tears sprang to her eyes.

"That to secure these rights, governments are instituted among men, deriving their just powers from the consent of the governed. That whenever any form of government becomes destructive of these ends, it is the right of the people to alter or abolish it, and to institute new government—"

Just then a shouted amen rang through the bars of the guardhouse. Obviously, one of the Rebel prisoners wanted to make a point. A few days ago, Nelda had seen chained, manacled prisoners being led to the guardhouse. They were the same young men she had seen at Fayetteville, the rebels disguised as Union troops who had killed Federal soldiers.

Looking vexed, the chaplain continued.

"—laying its foundation on such principles and organizing its powers in such form, as to them shall seem most likely to effect their safety and happiness. Prudence, indeed, will dictate that governments long established should not be changed for light and transient causes; and accordingly all experience hath shewn, that mankind are more disposed to suffer, while evils are sufferable, than to right themselves by abolishing the forms to which they are accustomed. But when a long train of abuses and usurpations, pursuing invariably the same object evinces a design to reduce them under absolute despotism, it is their right, it is their duty, to throw off such government, and to provide new guards for their future security…"

While Nelda chewed her pencil and ruminated on these principles, her mind wandered away from the long lists of grievances against King George. Allen Matthers did not consider the South's grievances to be light and transient causes. How differently good, intelligent people could view a situation! That difference had led to this heinous war. Finally, with an almost imperceptible shake of head, she began listening once again.

When the last speech was finished, Nelda wondered if the Rebel's ears were burning. Lieutenant Hover had left no doubt of his contempt for the southern cause. His scathing hostility toward anything rebel had drawn enthusiastic applause.

The rest of the festive day was filled with noise and color. Regiment after regiment paraded to the fife and drum of regimental bands. Some were fine brass bands playing rousing patriotic tunes. Stocky farm boys from Kansas marched in unison with Indian troops whose brown faces were stern, their eyes forward and heads high, appearing almost disdainful of the onlookers.

Of particular interest to Nelda were the smart ranks of the First Kansas Colored. She scanned the face of each marching man. Her friend Gideon was in the Second Arkansas Colored, but men were sometimes reassigned. She wondered how Gideon and Della were. The baby would be a few months old if everything had gone well. Nelda's friend and servant Della had looked terrible the last time she had seen her right after the Battle of Helena.

In the hottest part of the afternoon, Nelda returned to her room. After carefully hanging the blue muslin on a hook, she pulled the curtains and lay down for a nap. When she awakened, it was late afternoon. She had to hurry to meet Seamus on time.

The sun slanting through the trees was bright against the river, but a strong breeze rippling the water had cooled the scorching July heat just enough to make the evening bearable. Ladies strolling on the lawn arm in arm with uniformed officers seemed oblivious to the added warmth of layers of starched petticoats and skirts; however, occasionally an officer wiped moisture from his brow with a white handkerchief. As far as Nelda could tell, the only enlisted men present were the musicians. The army band was playing martial music at the moment, so Seamus joined her in a stroll.

When a bugle blew, the crowd stilled, awaiting the lowering of the colors. Every eye turned to the fluttering banner as the ground shook and a cannon boomed salute. Each morning and evening, Nelda had heard the salute, but she'd never seen the ceremony. Chills laced her arms.

"Sort of makes a body get a lump in the throat," said Seamus.

"It certainly does," she agreed.

As they walked on, Nelda glanced at the guardhouse where a lone man looked out through the bars. In the twilight, his wide, beardless face looked exceedingly young and sad.

"Poor bastard," muttered Seamus, taking her arm and steering her away. "Guess you heard they're to face a firing squad in a few days."

She nodded. "I was at headquarters in Fayetteville when they were arrested. I suppose those stolen uniforms cost them their lives."

"Yep. I doubt they'd be getting shot if they'd had on their own," agreed Seamus. "As it is, they're considered marauders."

"How did Rebels get our uniforms?"

"Oh, they have plenty of our uniforms," said Seamus. "I don't especially fault them—but I damn sure do fault our officers for making it easy to get 'em."

She listened with interest until Seamus changed the subject.

"Look, they're tuning up. I better get on over to the bandstand." He smiled at her. "You look mighty pretty this evening. I doubt you'll have to sit out one dance."

When the dancing began, she was seldom without a partner. Seamus sent merry looks her way as he strummed the guitar. Later, he exchanged the guitar for a harmonica.

While a thickset soldier with clumsy hands fumbled his way through guitar cords, Seamus managed to join her for a dance. In spite of the grating music, Nelda enjoyed the dance. It was a relief, however, when another man, an officer, stepped up, and amid friendly laughter, took the guitar from the sweating soldier.

"Seamus, I noticed you keep staring at the girl in the light green dress. She keeps looking back. Don't you think you ought to ask her to dance?"

He grinned. "I'd love to…if you don't mind?"

She chuckled. "I don't mind at all."

Opposites attract, she thought, viewing the smiling girl in Seamus's huge, muscled arms. She was a porcelain doll, small-boned and tiny, with curling brown ringlets framing a heart-shaped face. After three dances, the girl seemed as disappointed as Seamus when he answered the summons to return to the musicians.

Nelda danced every dance, but never with the same partner. Lonely soldiers far from home were prone to instant infatuation. She wanted no young officer getting the wrong idea. However, late in the evening, she made an exception for one young captain named Daniel Tory. She did not consider him more charming than the rest. Her interest piqued upon learning his uncle owned a newspaper in New York. He had even suggested she might send some articles to him.

He bowed low over her hand. "Would you do me the honor again?" he asked with twinkling brown eyes. "You're by far the best conversationalist and the best dancer here."

She smiled and accepted his outstretched hand. He smelled faintly of a good cigar. "Captain, tell me more about your uncle's newspaper."

He thought for a moment and then said, "It's small but respectable and gives an accurate account of the news." A grin revealed even white teeth. "You might say dangerously accurate."

Her eyebrows were a question mark.

"Last year during the draft riots, he printed the whole story in all its sordidness. His readership plummeted."

Nelda knew President Lincoln had many detractors in the north. She had read about the riots, how angry thousands had taken to the streets, burning and plundering and murdering to protest the new law passed by Congress to institute a draft. The main objection, if her memory was correct, was the exemption of anyone able to pay three hundred dollars, a vast sum for any but the wealthy. She recalled the term, "Rich man's war, poor man's fight."

"Didn't people want the truth?" she asked.

"Absolutely not. Especially, not when he editorialized the shameful burning of the orphan asylum."

Nelda was incredulous. "Why on earth did they burn an orphan asylum?"

He gave a dry snort. "Because it housed about eight hundred colored orphans and they blame the war on the Negro race."

She stopped dancing. "How could men—"

"It wasn't all men," he said. His eyes went cold with the memory. "Uncle Cecil said the mob of more than two thousand was filled with women and even children. He personally talked to Chief Engineer Decker who tried to quell the uprising. Mr. Decker stamped out the blazes as fast as they were set until finally he was surrounded by the mob and threatened. Even then he stood on the front steps and begged them to do nothing so disgraceful as to burn a benevolent institution. He warned it would be a lasting disgrace to them and to the city of New York."

Captain Tory sadly shook his head. "It had no effect. They overpowered him and lit more fires. Uncle Cecil said if not for the heroics of the men of the fire engine company they would have killed Decker and even the children might have come to harm. As it was, they were frightened out of their wits by the threats to wring the necks of damned little Lincolnites." He turned fiery red. "Beg your pardon, ma'am. I got worked up and forgot I was talking to a lady."

She waved aside his embarrassed apology. "Captain Tory, I'm a newspaper woman and prone to listening in on male conversations about politics. Believe me—I've heard far worse." Her lips pursed. "Odd," she added.

His eyebrows rose.

"Rather, I should say unbelievable," she corrected, "that it took place in the north—horrible anywhere, but not as unbelievable if it had happened here." Nelda, lost in thought, managed to make several missteps and was glad when the dance ended.

The only time the dancing ceased was when Seamus lowered the harmonica and filled the soft night with his fine tenor and the mournful strains of an old Irish Ballad, The Foggy Dew. The last stanza echoed through evening mists rising from the river.

> And the world did gaze in deep amaze
> At those fearless men and true
> Who bore the fight that freedom's light
> Might shine through the foggy dew

It was another place and a different war, and yet Nelda suspected the emotion sweeping the crowd was the same as had swept Celtic hearts long ago when the song was new.

She recalled the Matthers' cabin on a moonlit night two years ago. Seamus had sung that night as well. But Allen's face was the one now pictured in her mind's eye. A pang of loneliness stole joy from the evening. How much she missed him!

The soft breeze stirring sheer white curtains at the bedroom window held sweet perfume. Nelda took a deep appreciative breath. Then remembering the lilacs that grew near the back door at home, she fought a depressing wave of nostalgia.

She chewed the pencil held in her teeth. Mama had hated the habit, but it seemed to help when ideas were brewing. After a rueful look at the tooth marks, she put it down on the desk.

In the weeks since her arrival, the mundane articles she had been forced to write had almost dried up her love of writing. If not for the charity work of helping the refugees and orphans, she thought she would go mad. Now, however, she was working on an article of her own choosing. It might get her fired. If it did, she would just look for another job.

Her brow furrowed as she tried to recall every detail she'd learned from Seamus about the rebels obtaining Federal uniforms. Some officers—if not complicit with the rebels—were at least negligent about recruitments. According to Seamus, known rebels were allowed to enlist. Apparently, some officers were more interested in quotas than in a soldier's true allegiance. Often, the rebels received uniforms by joining and then deserting the Union Army. This was costing Union lives. Using such uniforms to masquerade in an attack was becoming a common occurrence. Nelda hoped to shed light on the practice. Reverend Springer might not print the article. If he did, he might not want her name attached. It was not the sort of writing he expected of her. But she hoped to dissuade him of that.

She reread what she had just written:

"Capt. Ross of Van Buren, who only lately returned from the rebel army, took the oath of allegiance and joined the Third Wisconsin cavalry, bringing along seven men. He recently deserted taking along nine men, two more than he originally brought into the Federal ranks. All the men had been issued a complete outfit of arms and clothing. There is little doubt these provisions will be used by the enemy army."

Picking up the pencil again she wrote three more paragraphs, which ended with a warning.

"Even now our guardhouse holds prisoners who, disguised in Union uniforms, deceived loyal soldiers at Fayetteville and then killed them. The cavalier bestowing of the Oath of Allegiance is not only foolish but criminal."

Nelda blew out the lamp and went to bed. Tomorrow she would beard the lion in his den and hopefully win him over. If she had to write one more line about the latest styles back east—about hats, gloves, and bonnets—she'd scream. The articles were silly anyway. Across Arkansas, women were starving and wearing old rags. It was ludicrous to print such trivialities.

Nelda thought she was dreaming. The tapping on the window was the maple tree blowing against the bedroom window at home. Then she sat up, coming fully awake. Someone was knocking on the window glass. Katydids rasped in the darkness.

"Nelda," the call came again, but softly. "Don't strike a light."

She jerked on a robe and drew back the curtain. The moonlight was faint but the outline standing near the open window was a big man.

"Allen!" she whispered. Her heart pounded. "What are you doing here? How on earth did you find me?"

He leaned on the sill and his teeth shown white in the darkness. "To answer the first question—I came for a kiss." When she stayed silent, he chuckled low in his throat. "Didn't figure that would pass muster." He went on, "To answer the second—now Nelda, me love, you know I have sources."

"Stop joking and tell me what this is all about." She hoped she sounded calmer than she felt.

His voice grew grave. "I want you to leave town and soon. Go back to Fayetteville, and, please, this time stay there."

"Why?" she asked.

"That I can't tell you, and I'm asking you not to say a word to anyone."

"So there's to be an attack," she surmised.

She did not expect him to answer. For a moment she chewed her lip. "The town is full of refugees and orphans. What will happen to them?"

He shrugged. "A little diversion just might help some of them to slip off and head south without being followed."

Perhaps Seamus was Allen's source. She sucked in a breath.

"Your brother Seamus is here. I saw him just yesterday, riding out of town. I was on the sidewalk. He came over and spoke for a few minutes. He's in a detail heading out on the prairie to guard livestock. Are you going to warn him, too?" she asked.

"He'll get no warning from me."

She was surprised at the bitterness in his tone. Her brows rose. "As I recall, when we discussed it before, you didn't seem too upset about him being on the opposite side."

"Well, I am," he said. "We Matthers are clannish. We fight everyone else at the drop of a hat. This is the first time one of us has ever sided against the rest. None of us are happy about it."

"I wondered about that," she said softly, as she recalled the happy, boisterous family.

There was hurt and disappointment peeking through Allen's bitterness. "Seamus wasn't high on the Confederacy after Pa got killed by someone conscripting for the army. But that's no reason to take sides against the rest of us."

"Allen, don't be bitter at Seamus. When he joined, he didn't know the rest of you were in the Confederate Army."

For a second, he turned away and looked into the night. The moon had come out of the clouds and bathed the yard with soft light. Then he turned back and abruptly changed the subject.

"How have you been making out?"

"I'm fine," she said. "I stay busy. I like that. I almost lost my mind at Fayetteville with nothing to do. Here, I'm helping with the refugees. There are so many. Most have nothing. They've been driven from their homes by bushwhackers or guerrillas or the regular army foraging. Oh, Allen, the children are so thin and ragged. The women have such haunted, scared eyes. Even though I'm not a teacher, I've been holding classes for the children down by the river. They love it." She gave a wry grin. "Except for a few boys who would rather be fishing. Even they seem to enjoy the stories, and the mothers are very grateful."

"Teaching agrees with you. You look good."

"My landlady insists on fattening me up. I feel guilty when I think about the refugees."

He reached a strong thumb to smooth her cheek. "You're beautiful with your hair down and wavy on your shoulders."

Her heart jumped. For the first time, she was glad there was no mosquito netting on the window. What was she thinking? She must not encourage him!

She frowned and drew back.

For a brief, unguarded moment, there was hurt in his eyes. Then, brusque, he asked, "You going to leave?"

"No. I've been through attacks before. But I truly do appreciate the warning."

He nodded and turned away.

"Allen," she called softly, "take care of yourself."

When he didn't answer, tears slipped down her cheeks. Once again he'd put his life in peril for her and once again she'd hurt him.

CHAPTER 4 ⌘

The sun baked the hills and hazy heat blurred the prairie spread out below. It was hot even in the shade where Allen looked over the general's shoulder to study the map spread out on a rock. The attack plan appeared sound to him. However, there was a lot of open ground to cross; and he'd learned from hard experience that things had a way of going wrong in battle. General Gano was known to be a fine officer, one of Morgan's most trusted. Allen had never before ridden with the Texas officer, but so far he was impressed with the man. Gano had listened to his reports and suggestions with the deference due a knowledgeable scout. Allen figured the Feds were in for a big surprise in the morning.

Gano pointed at the map and then winced a bit. Allen figured the arm wound the general had gotten a few weeks ago was still tender.

"Colonel Folsom, since your division is so much smaller than I'd anticipated, we'll have to change General Cooper's plan. Instead of attacking that cavalry encamped at Caldwell's on the Jenny Lind Road, you'll join us in the attack on the grove. We'll hit them from three angles—I'll head up the attack on the right. Folsom, you hit the left. Colonel Wells, you will strike the Federal center. This scout tells me,"— he nodded to Allen—"along with the Sixth Kansas, there are about one hundred Arkansas Feds camped just across this small stream." He glanced back at Allen. "Matthers, you'll stick close to me in case I have any questions about the lay of the land."

Allen frowned, wondering if Seamus would be with the Union right flank. He wished he'd asked Marmaduke to send him elsewhere. Of course, the general might have sent him anyway. He did know this land like the back of his own hand. But he should have asked for another assignment. Nelda hadn't heeded the warning anyway.

Then he scoffed. No use fooling himself. He'd have come anyway. He wanted to see her again. She did look mighty pretty with her hair down—even though she had made it plain she wanted no part of his lovemaking.

The general went on, "Colonel McCurtain, your orders will stay the same. You'll prepare an ambush here at the west end of Devil's Backbone in case we are forced to retreat and the Federals pursue." While nods of agreement ensued, the general rolled up the map.

They made small supper fires and only a few. Folsom's Choctaws and Colbert's company of Chickasaws stayed to themselves, silent and stone-faced. Allen had been introduced to one tall Choctaw. The man intrigued him. Somehow he'd never envisioned an Indian preacher. He wondered if Tiok-homma and Preacher Simon from back home had the same doctrine. Probably not. Folks had a heap of differing ideas about the Good Book.

Nearby, the Texas troops played cards. Others wrote letters. It was always that way before a battle. Allen supposed he ought to write Ma, but he had no idea if she was still at Uncle Clyde's down in Texas. The roads were thick with people fleeing Texas. Besides she couldn't read anyway.

Then he envisioned the land he'd recently scouted— the rolling grass-covered prairie with rugged mountain ridges visible in the distance. The rippling creek tucked like a desert oasis in the center of a few pleasant shady hills covered with thick oak, hickory, and cottonwood perfumed with honeysuckle. It was a shame to blow all that peace to hell tomorrow.

He spread his bedroll on a clear piece of ground, and, in spite of shrill katydids and crickets and a pain in his heart that wasn't physical, he was soon asleep.

There was no bugle call, merely a nudge in the side or a shaken shoulder to rouse the troops. Allen sat the blackened pot back on the grate covering the campfire and took a sip of bitter cornbran coffee. It had been a muggy, mosquito-filled night. Mourning doves cooed while he watched the sky pale and lighten. Heaviness weighted his chest. He would be a fool to keep hoping. But Nelda had so consumed his thoughts, it would take some getting used to. The red ball of sun promised a scorching day. He turned away from the breakfast fire and ambled over to hear the confab at the edge of camp.

"They'll see us comin' two miles off. I don't cotton to the ider' of chargin' acrost no prairie into Yankee Sharps. Ain't no doubt about hit—them thar' Sharps rifles can outshoot my old musket two ways to Sundee."

"Hell, Texas, you ain't liked nothin' you've been ordered to do since this fight commenced."

The furrow-faced, short man squinted up at the younger man. "That's a fact. I ain't likin' takin' orders from no Injun-lover." He scowled toward the Indian troops. "I ain't likin' fightin' alongside of no redskins." His words were loud, but if the coppery-skinned men heard him, they gave no sign. "I fi't them savages down in Texas. Don't make no sense to me to give 'em guns. Mark my words, jest as soon as this here ruckus is over and done, they'll use 'em ag'in us."

Tiok-homma swallowed cornbran coffee and then stood. He pinned the Texan with keen dark eyes. "A house divided against itself cannot stand. It is better we stand together today, or we will fall separately."

Allen gave a small grin and walked on. The Indian chaplain had wisdom just like Preacher Simon.

When the order to mount was given, he eased his foot into the stirrup of a tall sorrel. The black gelding had pulled up lame. He'd always preferred a sorrel anyway, and this was a fine animal. It reminded him of his favorite horse that was probably being ridden by some Union officer now. It had an easy swinging gate that ate up the miles effortlessly but ran like lightning if the need arose. Today would be one of those times.

That was a wide stretch of prairie for a cavalry charge. He patted the horse's neck and glanced down the ranks of mounted men. Five hundred strong, they were an impressive sight. But Allen was not foolhardy—the old Texan was right. Yankee Sharps were better than many of the shotguns and old muskets here. The Yankees were good shots.

They made their way, slowly, cautiously, to the edge of the flats then halted. Like the surreal calm in the eye of a storm, a strange hush descended. General Gano raised a hand. When it dropped, they charged forward like rushing wind.

Exhilaration pumped in Allen's chest. For a short, glorious while, he gave himself to the feel of the strong horse beneath him and the rolling prairie flashing by, trampled by a thousand hooves.

Across the expanse rose the first glimpse of the low wooded hills of the Union camp, and, in between, what at first appeared to be small dots. The shapes grew into horses with manes and tails flying. It was the Union herd stampeding. A handful of blue-garbed soldiers gave up trying to turn the herd and sped back toward camp.

Through the rapid blaze of gunfire, at first the Union lines held. Surprised men, some with suspenders still dangling, knelt and emptied rifles and six-shooters at the charging waves of gray. Then the human wall began to crumble as soldier after soldier was forced back. Some were cut down. As others gave ground, men stopped to reload and fire again. These soldiers were gritty, just as others he'd faced. It had been ages since Allen had heard the braggadocios claim that Yankees didn't stand a chance against Southern guts and guns.

Under scathing fire, he and the men alongside him obeyed orders and fell back, but only momentarily. After reloading, they charged again. The man on Allen's right toppled from the saddle. He heard the zing of lead as a ball passed near his own ear.

It took three attempts before the Union right finally broke. Bluecoated soldiers scattered like chickens in the shadow of a hawk. Allen kneed the sorrel and went pounding after men stumbling and running across uneven brushy ground and then onto the open prairie. Some turned back to fire. Others ran without a backward glance. Most were soon overtaken. Up ahead in a dusty melee of sweaty horseflesh and grim-jawed men stood prisoners with hands raised.

From the corner of his eye, Allen saw a rifle poke from a brushy knoll. It was leveled at General Gano. Allen spun and fired. The big man fell, but tried to crawl away. As Allen rode near, the man lay still, his Sharps rifle nearby.

Never taking his eyes from the soldier, Allen dismounted. After drawing his pistol, he approached with caution. There was a hole in the blue blouse and a blood puddle on the ground. He thought the man was mortally hit, but he'd been fooled before. Keeping him covered, Allen eased the Sharps away with his boot before kneeling to turn the body. The soldier's longish red hair fell away from his face.

Allen went cold to the marrow of his bones. On legs without strength, he sank onto the grass and stared into Seamus's glazed blue eyes.

A booted toe finally nudged Allen. He had no idea how long he had sat there. "Hey, didn't you hear the order? We're pulling back."

He gave no thought to the distant gunfire tattooing the heat-shimmered air. Nor did he pause to acknowledge the soldier who asked what he was doing. In a daze of anguish, he caught the trailing reins of a nearby gray horse and tied it short to a low limb. Then he hefted Seamus's big girth onto the shying animal's back as it pranced, blew, and sidestepped.

At first, there were disgruntled mutterings about why the hell he was moving a damned Yankee's carcass. Then a voice hushed the protests.

"Leave him be. Look at that red hair. They're bound to be kin."

Iron-jawed, Allen untied the reins, mounted his own horse, and loped back toward the low line of hills. In the July heat, he couldn't take Seamus home to the pine tree bordered cemetery edging Piney.

He could at least bury him deep and careful and mark the spot with a rock, so someday Ma could come and place a bunch of prairie flowers.

He rode until all the troops were out of sight and only stopped at camp long enough to get a shovel. Without looking at the body, he remounted and rode until he was alone in the blowing grass. Finally, he stopped. It was a fair place, a low rise near a tree line covered with grass and yellow wild flowers. He climbed down and began digging. After only a few shovels full, he bowed his head and leaned on the handle. Then, with hard jawed determination he began digging again.

When the grave was done, he stripped the saddle from his sorrel and got the blanket. Tenderly, he lowered Seamus from the gray horse onto the blanket. Although it was a chest wound, blood had dripped onto his face. Taking a canteen, Allen wet a handkerchief and carefully wiped the face gently, as if he were a baby.

He stared with dread. He ought to go through the pockets for Ma. There might be something she would treasure. He bent and, gritting his teeth, reached inside the blue shirt pocket. His fingers closed over cold metal. It was Seamus's harmonica.

Allen crumpled from his knees onto the ground. Great racking sobs shook his big frame. He had not cried since he was eight years old, the day his favorite colt had died—not even when Pa had died. But nothing had ever pierced his soul like this.

"Oh, God! I can't stand it!" he silently cried. "Why didn't you let him kill me instead?"

Finally, he drew a ragged breath and raised his head. Slowly, he got to his knees. He smoothed Seamus's red hair.

"No," he gently said. "I wouldn't have you suffer this, little brother. Being dead is better." He stood. "I reckon you know how much I loved you."

Tears streamed down his face, but they were not violent now, merely slow and steady.

CHAPTER 5 ～

While fanning away humid heat with a fresh copy of the New Era Newspaper, Nelda made her way to a shady spot near the river. The ink smell still clung to the thin paper. A butterfly, yellow-gold with brown lace edging, fluttered away after gathering nectar from a cluster of orange milkweed. It was a rare touch of beauty in the dismal camp near the river where hundreds of refugee families struggled against starvation and sickness, and the ragged-topped wagons looked no worse than the people who called them home.

"Here comes teacher!" Little girls with sweet smiles and faces ran to meet her. The boys barely slowed the game of mumbly peg.

Nelda sat on the chair some thoughtful person had provided. Before, she had always sat on a big rock only partially shaded by the huge elm tree.

"Come on, boys," she called. "I only have a few minutes to read before I have to get back to work."

There was muttering as jackknives went back into trouser pockets, but they complied and were soon seated on the grassy bluff overlooking the lazy river far below.

"Stop pinching!" complained pudgy Henry Jordon as he pushed on William's shoulder.

William took a grass stem from his mouth. "I never pinched nobody," he denied, looking as innocent as an angel.

Nelda raised an eyebrow. William could look angelic, and, although there was no real meanness in the child, he was full of mischief.

"Boys, settle down," she admonished.

When ragged, dirty Matilda Herman scratched her head through tangled, matted brown hair, Nelda resisted the urge to scratch her own head. Although she had never been infested with lice, the mere thought of the vermin made her scalp crawl.

She began the lesson, "We've been discussing different types of literature. What types can you remember?" she asked. Several hands rose. Nelda pointed to pretty, six-year-old, Sarah Campbell with hair as black as midnight and intelligent, dark eyes that sparkled liked stars.

None of the children wore attractive clothes. But Nelda thought Sarah's the worst. A woman's black brocade dress had been poorly remade to cover the small frame. Although the long skirt had been shortened and hemmed, it dragged the ground. The wide, exaggerated width at the elbows had been chopped off and gathered into narrow cuffs that were still much too large for the tiny wrists.

With a stammer, Sarah shyly answered, "S-some are sc-schoolbooks that teach things like m-m-math and s-science and geography. S-some are for fun, like the st-storybook you read us last week."

"Very good," said Nelda. "Today we're going to learn about another type of literature and the powerful way it can affect our lives. Can anyone tell me the name of the newspaper here in Fort Smith?"

While the other intent faces were blank, William stood, drew up tall, and stuck out his chest. "It's the New Era, and Preacher Springer is the editor."

"That's correct," began Nelda.

She paused as a soldier approached on horseback. He drew to a stop a few feet away, sat still a moment, and then dismounted. Nelda's brows drew together. It was Daniel Tory, the young officer she had danced with at the party. He had been very sweet and polite. Now his face looked drawn and troubled.

"Ma'am," he said. "I'm sorry to interrupt, but I've been looking for you all over. I have news…" His voice trailed away, and, not meeting her eyes, he looked past her at the river.

"Children," she said, "we'll finish our lesson at another time."

She and Daniel stood silent until the last child had scurried away. "What is it, Captain?" she asked, steeling herself for bad news.

He toyed with the reins a moment, looked at the ground, and then drew a deep breath. "It's bad news, ma'am, about your friend Seamus Matthers."

Nelda sucked in a quick breath. She had of course heard about the battle—how Union soldiers had been driven across Massard Prairie by several charges of Rebel Cavalry. Many Union soldiers had been killed. Others were surrounded and captured and a great number of horses and arms had been taken. It was a total defeat. She had worried about Seamus...and about Allen.

"He was killed yesterday in that skirmish out on the prairie." He hesitated and then added, "At least an eyewitness said he was. We haven't recovered the body, but the lieutenant said he saw him shot, and he was certain he was dead."

Nelda put a hand over her mouth and quickly sat back down on the chair. "No body?" she asked dazed.

Daniel looked miserable. "Well, ma'am, sometimes all the dead aren't recovered. There were Indians with this bunch, and you never can tell what they'll—" He left the words hanging. After a few moments, he asked, "Can I escort you back to town?"

"Poor, poor Seamus." She looked up through tears. "Captain, is there a list of the Confederate dead...I mean were any of them identified?"

He was perplexed. "Well, ma'am, the only one I know of for sure was some big Choctaw chief. I forget his Indian name, but the whites called him William Cass. There was a big stink at headquarters because some of our Cherokees scalped some of the Confederate dead. I think Cass was one of them."

When she gripped the side of the chair and groaned, he grew red and flustered. "I apologize. I should never have told you that."

"That's quite all right, captain. As you know, I'm a newspaper woman. I'm used to hearing indelicate facts." Her knuckles grew whiter on the side of the chair seat. "I know you'll find this question odd but..."—she drew a shaky breath— "were any of the Confederate dead…were any of the scalps coppery red?"

Shock knit his brows. "Not that I know of. Do you have relatives in the Confederate ranks?" he guessed.

"A very dear friend," she said.

With sympathetic eyes, he nodded. "May I escort you back to town?" He asked again.

"Thank you, but I'd like to just sit here for a while."

He nodded. After turning to mount he looked back. "I'll check with the burial detail, and I'll let you know if I find out there was such a man. I think the rebs lost about a dozen men."

"Thank you so much." A sob caught at her throat, distorting the words.

"God bless you, ma'am," he said as he mounted then rode away.

It seemed unreal that fun-loving, boisterous Seamus was dead. Nelda put her face in her hands, bowed her head, and wept. She wanted to believe that Allen was invincible—but she knew better.

There was a tug on her sleeve. She looked up into Sarah's troubled eyes. "T-t-teacher," she stammered. "Wh-whaa-what's the matter?"

"I just lost a good friend. He died in the battle."

With silence and compassion, the child patted her arm. Nelda kissed Sarah's forehead. There was no one else to share her grief, no close friend or family nearby to offer comfort. But Sarah would suffice. Sarah's sympathy was heartfelt.

Sarah looked up at the clear blue sky. "Do you reckon your friend has already met Mama and Papa in heaven? Likely they're already friends," Sarah concluded.

Nelda smiled through her tears. "More than likely they are." She smoothed back Sarah's dark hair. "Sarah, do you realize that you didn't stammer just now."

The girl's eyes widened. "I never did, did I?" Then she added cautiously, testing each word to see if the hesitation was gone for good. "I never used to stammer—not before I came here. Reckon I'm healed?"

"I hope so," said Nelda. She pulled the child into her arms and held her tight.

As Nelda lay in darkness, tears rolled down her cheeks. They were not accompanied by sobs. Instead, they were an unhurried stream that silently wet her pillow. She grieved for Seamus. She also grieved for Allen. Because of the estrangement with his brother, he would take this death extra hard.

With that thought, depression pressed against her chest, threatening to crush her. After Fred's death, Mama's death, and then Papa's, she had wrestled that monster and had no desire to be overwhelmed again. She must keep very, very busy.

Perhaps she would try sending a few articles north to Captain Tory's uncle. He had mentioned it again that afternoon when he brought her word that Allen was not among the dead or wounded. He had even given her the address of his uncle's paper in New York.

She reached to hold Papa's gold watch. It had never been off the chain around her neck since Allen regained it from that villain Bull Smith. It was a tangible reminder of Papa's love and encouragement. He would be pleased with her decision.

"Reverend Springer?" When Nelda spoke, the chaplain looked up, took off his spectacles and laid them on the oak roll-top desk. "Sir, I'd like to interview the rebel prisoners sentenced to be executed. Could you arrange it with the authorities?"

He had surprised her earlier by agreeing to print her editorial about the stolen uniforms. It had emboldened her to try again.

He frowned. "The execution will be tomorrow. If you're intending to write an article for the paper, I think I should tell you that I plan to write—"

She hesitated. "I'd still like to do the interview. I've been thinking of sending some articles to papers up north. I talked to an officer recently who told me they are paying well for eye witness accounts from the south."

Reverend Springer's frown deepened, and he regarded her with a look akin to pity.

His tone mellowed. "I think perhaps there's a better outlet for your talents, Miss Horton. You've done a good job with your assignments, and I'm especially pleased with your work with the orphans. I've been meaning to discuss an idea with you. On my last trip home, I raised funds for orphan relief. We plan to rent a building soon to house and school as many of them as possible." He went on, "It's only a stop gap measure until real homes can be found. As you know, we're sending them north as fast as we can find homes and accommodations on outgoing wagon trains. But there's always an influx of new children." He sighed. Worry and stress etched his tired face. "I'm hoping you'll consent to overseeing the girls at the new facility. They all seem to admire and like you."

She was astonished. "I know nothing about caring for—mothering—children." She bit back the words on the edge of her tongue—neither do I wish to learn! She was glad to teach them for a few hours, had even enjoyed it. But it was neither her wish nor intent to be a nursemaid.

"I'm sure you'll learn. It's a natural, God-given instinct for a woman." He smiled. "You'll do a wonderful job."

She smiled stiffly. In her opinion, there were females aplenty with no more nurturing instincts than alley cats. Being politic, she kept that opinion to herself. Granted, she believed she possessed more compassion than that; however, nurturing was not her strong suit!

"I'm not interested in the position," she said, trying to sound gracious. "May I suggest Mrs. Hanover. She's a motherly soul and a fine Christian. Just this morning, she was bemoaning the fact that her grandchildren live too far away to visit. I know she needs extra money.

The boarding house rent barely pays for the groceries. I think she would love the position."

"Hmmm," he said, still looking displeased.

Nelda hurried on, "About the interview?"

He rubbed his eyes and put the spectacles back on his thin nose. His words were clipped. "I'll speak to the District Provost Marshal, Captain Judson. Come back at noon. I should know something by then."

"Thank you." Nelda turned to go.

"Miss Horton, if you want facts, I advise talking to prisoner Rowton or Norwood. Copeland loves the sound of his own voice, but I doubt the veracity of all he says."

She nodded.

"It ain't fitten'. Woman ought not be doin' no interview." With the muttered protest, the jailer left Nelda seated in the narrow room serving as the guardhouse entryway. Scowling, he soon returned with a prisoner. Mr. Rowton had refused the interview, but Norwood arrived, wearing iron hobbles and manacles. He was nineteen, broad-faced, and stoutly built but without fat. His dark hair was shoulder length and straight. The armed guard in the doorway kept keen eyes and rifle ready.

"Thank you for agreeing to see me," said Nelda. She pointed to the straight-backed chair opposite. "Please sit."

He glanced at the locked door. The guard stood straighter. Norwood sat down.

Nelda placed a tablet on the small cluttered desk and pulled a pencil from her pocket.

"Mr. Norwood, as I said in the message, I'm writing articles for the northern papers. This is a chance for you to tell your story."

He swallowed and stared at the floor. For a while, she wondered if he would speak at all. Finally, he began slowly.

"I had a good, Christian upbringing. My mother was a God-fearing woman who taught us children the straight and narrow." He gave a sad smile. "Only thing is, I didn't listen so good. I admit doing some wicked things." His eyes suddenly grew hard. "But what I'm being shot for isn't part of 'em. I'm telling you this to set the record straight." He paused. "Do you promise to tell it straight, like I tell you?"

She looked him squarely in the eyes. "I promise to quote you exactly, Mr. Norwood."

He nodded. "Good, that's good." There was moisture in his eyes, and his Adam's apple bobbed as he swallowed again. Silent for a moment, he seemed to collect his thoughts before going on.

"I joined the Rebel Army when I was sixteen. I fought at Pea Ridge and Prairie Grove and in dozens of skirmishes." He sat up straighter. "I swear I had nothing to do with the killing of Mr. Brown. We went up to him and asked if he had any arms. When he turned and ran, like he was going after weapons, one of our boys shot him. I don't think that is against the rules of war." Raising his manacled hands, he wiped his nose on a sleeve. "About stealing and wearing the uniforms...gosh-durn, it's war. A body does what he can to trick the enemy. If you don't kill them, given half a chance, they'll darn sure kill you." As if seeking approval, he looked askance at her. But with pencil busy, she wrote and then waited for him to continue.

His jaw jutted. "We're fighting for our rights. It's fine for folks up north to run things their way up there. We're not trying to take them over. This is our land, our homes, and we have a right to run things our way. The other day, I stood at the window of that cell"—he jerked his head toward the back of the building—"and heard some words read that say we have that right. So I don't see how they can call us traitors."

That whenever any form of Government becomes destructive of these ends, it is the Right of the People to alter or abolish it, and to institute new Government...

The words danced in Nelda's brain. She recalled Allen saying much the same thing—rule of the people over their own affairs, a constitutional guarantee. It was a troubling thought if one got right down to it...

Norwood went on, "I die true to the cause and hope and pray for victory."

He drew a deep breath. "I reckon that's about all I have to say… except I've made my peace with God. If my mother and sweetheart don't get the letters I wrote, maybe someday they'll read what you write. You can add that I love them and hope to see them in heaven, because Jesus has forgiven my sins."

He stood. She sadly watched him shuffle away and wondered what a man pondered his last night on earth.

He turned back at the hall doorway. "If you see Preacher Springer, would you tell him that all the prisoners would like a word with him?"

Nelda nodded. It was a sad outcome for a young man with a loving family and sweetheart waiting at home.

A large throng edged both sides of the Texas Road, all eyes glued to the procession wending its way south. The morning air was still and hot, but chills laced Nelda's arms as the solemn group neared.

Captain Judson and his staff led, followed closely by the military band playing a somber air. To the slow cadence marched the firing squad, sixty-four men of the Thirteenth Kansas Infantry. Unhurried, two wagons rolled past. Reverend Springer sat alongside the driver in the first. Two other ministers rode in the second. Every eye in the crowd fixed on the condemned men, two in each wagon, each sitting atop his coffin, now free of the iron manacles that had been removed earlier by a blacksmith. Three were grim and silent. Norwood, however, was weeping. His lips moved in inaudible prayer.

Nelda swallowed. Although the condemned all professed loyalty to a just cause, there was little doubt they deserved the sentence—at their hand, eight loyal soldiers and even a civilian lay dead—and not in the accepted manner of warfare. However, the harsh reality that these young men would soon die made a lump in her throat. Norwood's agony especially caught her heartstrings, as with lagging steps, she followed the crowd heading south out of town.

Suddenly, she picked up her pace. After a few quick strides, she reached out and grabbed William's shoulder.

Her voice was stern. "Young man, you get right back to town. This is no place for children."

His jaw jutted, and he waved his hand toward the crowd. "There's dozens going," he argued.

Nelda's eyes widened. He was right. What were people thinking, allowing youngsters to view such a heinous sight! She recalled Fred's mangled body riddled by bullets. For months, the image had invaded her dreams.

"Well, you're not going to be one of them," she insisted. "Now scat!" William scowled.

"I mean it. If I catch you sneaking after us, I'll tell Reverend Springer." William's gray eyes narrowed as he considered the ramifications. "All right," he grumbled. "But I bet ya I'll be the only one of the fellows not there."

Nelda glanced back a few times. William appeared to be keeping his word. At least he was not in sight.

Less than a mile out of town, beyond the rifle pits, the procession halted. Infantry formed to keep the spectators at a proper distance. With pencil and tablet in hand, Nelda gained permission from the lieutenant in charge to step closer. She had no morbid desire for a better view. In order to record the event accurately, she must be able to see.

It was a beautifully situated spot. Sloping ground fell away from the wide flat where they stood down to a small stream bordered by trees. A few leaves on a nearby clump of sumac had already reddened in anticipation of autumn.

The judge advocate, in a clear loud voice, read the charges and the finding of the military commission. With haste, Nelda scribbled the names of the condemned—A. J. Copeland, James Rowton, William Carey, and John Norwood—and the specific charges.

At the reminder of Citizen Brown and the eight men of the First Arkansas, now dead and about to be avenged, a murmur swept the crowd. The condemned stood with heads high and eyes forward until Reverend Springer requested the men kneel for prayer. His prayer was short and to the point, asking the Lord to forgive any repentant soul and damn any who were unrepentant.

All along, Norwood's face had been a mask of misery. Now, as the four men stood, they showed equal distress. A line of chaplains and officers shook their hands and bid a final farewell, Carey shook the Judge Advocate's hand.

"Judge, I hope to meet you in heaven." His voice wavered on the last word. He swallowed. Then with great force, he began praying aloud. Soon Copeland joined in. Rowton remained silent, however, his jaw twitched. Norwood softly began a hymn while two soldiers went down the row tying each man's hands with short lengths of rope. Norwood began to tremble

Nelda's eyes filled with tears. She looked away. When she looked back, it was a relief to find the men's anguished eyes bandaged. She drew a deep breath and steeled herself.

As the firing squad stood ready, no soldier knew if his gun held a deadly ball. Half held only a blank cartridge. Forty-eight muskets clicked. Simultaneously, they fired.

It was over in a moment. Four lifeless bodies lay in pools of blood.

Nelda covered her mouth. She could not keep back a sob. In an instant, she relived Fred's death—all the violent deaths she had viewed—and all the tragic suffering at Helena. With tear-rimmed eyes, she spun around and hurried away.

At home, she went to bed and asked Mrs. Hanover not to call her for supper. All afternoon, she tossed and turned, sinking deeper into depression. Finally, she fell into a fitful doze, filled with bad dreams. When she awakened, she chided herself over giving way to such self-pity. Papa would be ashamed. If he were alive, Papa would be doing something to help instead of wallowing in misery. Then she wondered, If he were here what would he do?

Aloud, she muttered, "Of course, Papa would write, and try to end the madness. Hadn't his motto always been, "The pen is mightier than the sword?"

In a flash of revelation, it came to her. The desire to write was embedded in her bones. But not just mindless trivia!

Her eyes widened at the idea. President Lincoln claimed a book had started the war. Nelda had no illusions that she could produce a novel to equal Harriet Beecher Stowe's work. However, there was always a place in history for capturing reality in print.

She sat up in bed. She could do it! She could write a book—a true story of the war and her part in it. The war was winding down. Everyone said it couldn't last much longer. Of course, there were bound to be many books. But didn't she have a unique story to tell, a unique perspective? Through it all, she had remained loyal to preserving the Union, and yet because of Allen, she had been able to avoid the prejudice that blinded so many—such as Reverend Springer—to any understanding of the Confederate cause. If she was able to convey the good and noble ideals held by both sides and depict the ultimate sacrifice each had paid, it would be a noteworthy work that might help bring healing to a shattered nation.

She drew her knees to her chest and hugged them while recalling all the tragic things she had seen, all the loved ones lost. Mama and Papa...and Fred.

Jim Loring and Seamus had died for the Union cause, and Jim's poor wife and children left to fend for themselves. Although it was bushwhackers and not the army that had taken Old Tom, he would likely be alive if not for the war.

Her Confederate friends and relatives had fared no better. Uncle Ned was dead—how she had grieved last winter upon finally hearing that news. Cousin Elijah might be dead, too. She had had no word in ages.

George Garrison, Red Matthers, and Bo and Drew Morrison were all gone. To this day she shuddered recalling the suffering she had witnessed in the aftermath of the Battle of Helena—the awful mangled stumps that should have been Drew's hands. After hours of anguish and suffering, he had paid the ultimate price for his belief in the Rebel cause.

It would be a daunting task to capture reality as she had lived it. As her heart beat faster, she knew she had to try. She had the notes on the execution. It was a start. She would begin immediately keeping a journal and interviewing more people. She bit her lip, wishing she'd done it sooner. With ideas swirling, she got up, lit a tallow candle, and began scribbling notes. It was growing light in the east when she blew out the candle and climbed back into bed. In spite of her sorrow over Seamus, for the first time in a very long while, she felt a glimmer of anticipation.

Nelda sat up and rubbed sleep from her eyes. Light coming through the bedroom windows was faint. It must be very early, she realized, and wondered what had wakened her. Then it came again, the rapid report of gunfire. The memory of the firing squad returned and she shivered.

"Yes, Mrs. Hanover, come in," she called at the tapping on her door.

"Miss Nelda!" The sturdy woman gasped. She was wearing a robe, along with a nightcap on curly brown hair streaked with gray, and she held a lamp high. "We're under attack. I knew you'd want to be up and about to find out what's going on." She turned away but called back, "I'll make a quick breakfast—if we're not blown to smithereens first."

Nelda jerked on clothes and shoes and hurried from the room. She swiftly returned to grab a tablet and pencil. The firing was distant and sporadic, but she stopped on the stairs and threw up her head to listen when it suddenly erupted from another direction. It seemed the Rebels were simultaneously hammering different locations.

"Don't bother with breakfast for me," called Nelda.

"Oh, I wish you'd take time to eat. I'm just now getting some flesh on those bones of yours."

"Not this morning, thank you. I'm in a hurry to get to the office and see what I can learn."

"Let me know as soon as you find out," Mrs. Hanover answered. "I'd like a few minutes warning if I'm to pack up sixty years of my life and flee."

"With all our fortification, I don't think we have much to worry about."

Mrs. Hanover's head poked from the kitchen doorway. "I've lived long enough to expect the unexpected. Now, you be sure and hurry right back. I'll keep your food warming on the stove."

They both jerked as a loud boom rattled the windows. "Think I'll throw a few things into my valise just in case," muttered the woman.

Nelda closed the door, went swiftly down the walk and out the gate to join men rushing down the street toward town in early dawn. Yellow lamplight gleamed from windows. Doors stood open as people still dressed in nightclothes stood listening.

Upon drawing near the main thoroughfare, a mounted cavalry troop sped by. In answer to one man's shouted question, the captain called back.

"Don't worry. We'll drive the bastards back."

Nelda arrived at the New Era office to find the door still locked and Reverend Springer nowhere in sight. She waited a few minutes, watching the sunrise, her ears cocked toward the river where firing was steady in the Poteau bottoms. The tattoo of rifles also drifted from the south. Indecisive, she looked toward the fort. It was unlikely she would be allowed inside the walls, but she might glean information from the sentry.

With that in mind she wended her way along Garrison, between pedestrians and conveyances, the street now as busy as a typical noontime and much more chaotic. The panic increased equal to the increased firing near the river. As she had assumed, the sentry stopped her outside the gate.

"Ma'am, no one comes in today without special orders from General Thayer or Colonel Judson."

"Could you at least tell me if perhaps Reverend Springer is inside? I work for him and—"

The ground shook from a cannon blast.

The soldier turned for a moment to glance toward the river. Worry was keen on his face.

"That was close," he muttered. Then he recalled her and answered the question. "He was here earlier, but I heard him say he'd be down at the refugee camp. The colonel says they're in danger of taking a shell and has ordered them away from the river."

Nelda thanked him and hurried away toward the frenzied camp where lean-faced men and gaunt women with fear-filled eyes hitched mules to decrepit wagons. Reverend Springer was not there; however, she learned he had taken some of the orphans into town to a building being renovated for them.

Although it was early, hot sun baked the trail as she retraced her steps along the road where dust now hung in low clouds behind passing wagons. She tried getting farther off the road; nevertheless, the fine powder settled on her dress and filled her nostrils. By the time she arrived in town, it had mixed with sweat, making dirty rivulets down her hot face.

CHAPTER 6 ⟋

In afternoon sun, Allen hunkered on the riverbank in Indian Territory and stared across the river at Arkansas. The smell of honeysuckle hung thick in humid air. Sycamores growing on the ridge beyond already had a few yellow leaves, and the seedpods on sumacs near the bank were as dark as bottomland dirt.

Allen figured a big snow must be melting in the Rockies. The water in the river was unusually high. The Arkansas had looked just so the day Seamus had swam his horse across the Spadra Crossing with Sheriff John Hill right on his tail. It had been more prank than lawlessness. Seamus had shot out a few windows in the Johnson County courthouse on a dare from Drew Morrison. John Hill had not found it humorous. Seamus had spent his first and only night in jail and had to borrow money from Allen to replace the window glass.

Allen groaned and dropped his head into his hands. Every sight these days held a haunting memory. Nights were worse. Seamus haunted his dreams. But no nightmare compared to the reality he faced upon jerking awake. Why hadn't he died instead?

He looked up as footsteps approached and then stood as a smooth faced private in a gray cap came into sight. The youth swept off his cap and twisted it in his hands while he stumbled through his greeting.

"Mr. Matthers, sir. First off, let me say, I'm mighty sorry about your brother. I hate to bother you, but you're needed back at camp. The generals want you."

Allen glanced at the river once more before mounting his horse and heading back to camp.

General Cooper bent low over the map and frowned as his finger traced the Fort Towson Road. "General Gano, although your victory at Massard Prairie was brilliant, if we storm those fortifications, we'll be slaughtered like sheep. The Federals have enclosed the fort and this entire area with batteries and rifle pits."

He saw Allen. "Matthers, sorry about your loss," he said. "Damned shame."

Allen swallowed warm bile rising in his throat. He was spared a reply when General Cooper abruptly got down to business. "You've been inside the fort. What do you think?"

"They'd cut us to pieces."

Cooper nodded. Then decisive, he said, "I just won't risk it."

Gano, also frowning, studied the map. "We could make a demonstration, sting them some and perhaps round up some more livestock and those isolated units outside the town's defenses."

"My thinking exactly, General," Cooper concurred. "Perhaps we can create a diversion so Confederate families can leave without being followed." His finger once again traced the map. "I think a four pronged attack best with you leading one force over this ridge of hills. A second party can move up the west bank of the Poteau, here, where the stream converges with the Arkansas and fire right into the garrison. I'll move the main body in two columns up the Fort Towson and Line Roads."

He turned to a broad faced Cherokee with shoulder length white hair, beetled brows, and deeply lined face. "General Watie, you and your men will lead the main thrust."

Allen was not surprised. Stand Watie had earned the respect of every Confederate officer present.

In acknowledgment, General Watie dipped his chin once. The Cherokee was not talkative. However, when he spoke, Allen found him to be articulate, well educated, and shrewd in the ways of war.

"Colonel Folsom, I'd like your Choctaws held in reserve here,"—he pointed out the spot on the map—"to be a nucleus of support should the need arise."

"Matthers, stick around," ordered General Cooper. "I've something else to discuss with you." When the others left, he went on, "I need a favor. You're not under orders and you can refuse." General Cooper waited for a response. When Allen nodded, he continued. "My Cousin Emma thinks the authorities at the fort are getting suspicious. She's seen soldiers watching her house. The general may know we're related. Before the war, I visited her a few times."

He went on, "Since you're her contact, she already knows you. During the chaos tomorrow, it might be possible to slip through the lines and bring her out."

"All right," agreed Allen. "Where should I take her?"

"Her daughter lives on a farm in Newton County. I suspect she'll want to go there."

Allen considered for a moment. "After crossing the river, I know a back trail that won't be guarded. It's too narrow for a wagon, but horses can make it. Right now, though, soldiers are thicker than fleas on a hound between here and the river. That'll be the tricky part."

"We'll be keeping them busy to the south and west. I suggest you ride due east and cross the river at the narrowest spot. You can't risk a ferry. But Emma can ride. When she was young, she was good with horses."

Allen's brows rose. "That was a long while back. Do you think she can swim a horse across the river at her age?"

General Cooper laughed. "If I know Emmy, she'll do it or die trying."

Allen didn't argue, but he had grave doubts. For himself, he welcomed the danger. Risking her neck was a different matter.

While the sun slipped low, billowing clouds rose like pink tinged mountain peaks as brilliant coral washed the sky. Allen watched it fade and die. At that moment, he was tempted to start riding west and never come back. There was nothing for him here, nothing but pain and misery. Of course there was nothing for him out there either, he admitted with cold knowing. He was not about to kill himself, but he would welcome a bullet tomorrow. He pulled a flask from his saddlebag and took a long, burning pull.

"Ma'am," he said softly. "Are you alone?"

She jumped and spun around. "My word, Mr. Matthers! You scared me to death. Yes, I'm alone."

"Sorry. The general said they were watching the house so I had to slip in." He pulled back a white curtain just a bit and peeked out at bright day. "I didn't see anyone around."

"No, I imagine not. They're probably all involved in the ruckus. Did you have any trouble getting through the lines?"

"None to speak of," he said without telling her of the picket, now with a lump on his head. He should have killed the soldier. He would wake and spread the alarm that a Rebel had slipped through the lines. And yet, Allen had no stomach for killing, especially a kid hardly old enough to shave. "We need to get you out of here. I have a horse for you out back. Take only necessities and dress for some hard riding." He paused and then added, "It'll be a hard trip, ma'am. We'll even have to swim the river."

Much to his surprise, her eyes sparkled. "An adventure is it? Well, at my age they're few and far between, so I intend to enjoy it to the fullest." Her lips pursed and she tapped her chin with a finger. "But I should leave town in my buggy. The neighbors won't pay much attention to that. If I climb on a horse, they'll all have twitching noses."

"All right. I'll hitch your horse to the buggy while you get ready."

She spoke to herself, "I'll put on a pair of Elmer's pants under my skirt. When I'm out of town, I'll wear that old slouch hat he always wore hunting."

Allen kept silent. Miss Emma wasn't exactly fat, but she was stocky and men's clothes would never camouflage that full chest.

On the way to the carriage shed, he was cautious and saw no one. Soon the horse was hitched and stood waiting near the backdoor. Allen, taking a bandana from his back pocket, wiped sweat from his brow and then paused to listen. A redbird trilled, sounding strange in the midst of cannon and rifle fire that was steady but distant.

After his tiny rap on the back door, Miss Emma exited, a valise and a parcel in hand. Allen stowed them in the buggy alongside the saddle and bridle. Just then an elderly neighbor called a greeting. Without answering, Emma climbed into the buggy and whipped up the horse.

"She's all-fired up and anxious to leave," muttered Allen. "I've not even told her where we're going." With a regretful glance back, he mounted and hurried after. He hated leaving town without even a glimpse of Nelda.

He spurred the sorrel, caught up with the buggy, and then rode alongside until he had given directions. At the end of the street, they turned down another side street and away from town. The roads were deserted. Occasionally, a curtain fluttered and he knew someone peered out. After another turn, the houses began to thin and soon only open country with grassy fields was in view. He halted.

"Wait here until I have a look-see. I won't be long."

Forehead furrowed, she glanced back. "I'll feel better as soon as we're far out of town and across the river."

"We're not crossing the river yet. It's too high. We'll head east awhile before we head north."

He left the road and trotted the horse toward a line of trees. No breeze stirred the branches but it was cooler in the leafy shade. After riding about half a mile just out of sight and parallel with the road, he pulled up. Just as he had suspected, at a fork in the trail was a sentry outpost. Four blue-coated men guarded the road. They sat or leaned languidly against trees and one sat on a stump near a signpost for Fort Smith.

The terrain was too rough to get the buggy through the woods, across a creek, and around them. He pulled the rein and headed back.

"You'll have to ride from here on," he told her. "Head into the trees and we'll leave the buggy out of sight.

She exited the trail and without hesitation climbed down and shed the long skirt. The old britches bagged, held up only by suspenders and a too long belt that hung down twelve inches past the buckle.

She slapped on a big floppy hat. "I know I'm a sight," she said with a laugh.

He took a knife from his pocket. "You can tuck those pant legs into your boots but I'll have to cut down that belt before you trip on it."

She smiled. "Elmer was rather hefty. But he was a fine-looking man. We were married forty wonderful years. I miss him."

"Been dead long?"

Her eyes shadowed. "Just two years. He was a riverboat pilot. I always feared a treacherous shoal or an exploding boiler. Instead it was a crazy, drunk man shooting at another passenger. Instead, he hit Elmer who died two days later." Her voice caught on the last words and broke.

Allen grimaced. His own pain was too raw to be unmoved. "I know it hurts like hell." He quickly amended, "Begging your pardon, ma'am."

She waved a hand. "I've heard it before. Being married to a riverboat man, there's not much I haven't heard. You're right. It hurts like hell." She eyed him closely. "You've recently lost someone dear?"

"Yes," he said and led the horse near. "Need help mounting?"

"I didn't a few years ago," she said ruefully. "We'll see."

She mounted with slight difficulty. "There now, if I could reach the stirrups, I just might be able to ride."

He adjusted the stirrup length. "I'll lash your valise to the back of the saddle.

She pointed to the parcel lying on the buggy seat. "I packed a little food. Don't forget it."

He got the parcel and realized he was hungry. He hadn't eaten in three days. He had thought he would never want to eat again.

They avoided main roads and even most trails. They passed river bottom farms and empty plantations overgrown with weeds, the small yellow flowers carpeting fields once lush with corn and cotton. Tall grasses spiked with seedpods overflowed dooryards abutting skeletons of burned cabins. Allen knew from personal experience the sad stories—

people driven from homes, from the land they had plowed, sweated over, and loved that were abodes now only to mice and squirrels.

The sun was straight up when he called a halt. It was only then that he noticed how wilted Miss Emma was. He chastised himself for pushing so hard. He should have paid more attention. She practically fell into his arms when he helped her dismount. Her red face glistened with sweat. He gave silent admiration. During the ride, she had not complained one peep.

"This is a right fair spot and well out of the way," he said, glancing at tall oaks near a clear gurgling stream. "We'll have a bite to eat and rest a bit before going on."

She removed the floppy hat and fanned her face. "We better not sit too long," she said. "Otherwise, I might stiffen up like a poker. Don't know if I can climb back on that beast as it is."

He was solemn. "You'll feel worse before you feel better."

She hobbled to a rock and sat down. "Don't I know it." She sighed. "It's been ages since I rode, but some things one never forgets. I just hope I don't slow you down. I know the general needs you back."

Allen's hands stilled from unwrapping the paper-covered parcel. It was the first time he had given it conscious thought but he had no intention of going back. He had no plan, but he was not going back to Fort Smith…maybe never back to the army.

He handed a piece of cornbread stuffed with fried salt pork to Miss Emma and took one for himself while thinking of the mountains of cornbread he'd eaten in his life—some good, some fair-to-middlin', and some downright nasty. He took a bite. This tasted a lot like Ma's. Miss Emma was a good cook.

While they sat in the shade, he took a few swallows from his flask and then screwed on the lid. She leaned against a tree and closed her eyes. After a short break, she stood. "Let's hit the trail, Mr. Matthers. As the cowboys say, we're burning daylight."

"Yes 'um." He did not add that he intended to set an easier pace for the afternoon.

They rode slower but steady. As the sun slipped lower, dark blue rain clouds began forming in the west and soon overspread the sky. Near a tiny stream, Allen called a halt.

He got the wooden canteen from his saddle and walked down the grassy bank. A doe bounded away into the brush. With the exception of a few darting minnows, nothing else stirred. After careful perusal, upstream and down, he dipped the canteen into the clear, cool water and capped it and then returned to water the horses.

As the sorrel drank and blew a satisfied snort, Allen patted the sweaty neck and pondered where he would go after Miss Emma was safely with her kin. His thoughts came full circle and ended at home. There was no one there, and yet, he felt an aching need to see it again, to walk the old trails, to sit on the porch, to envision things as they once were—all the family together and carelessly happy. Of course it was useless. Those times were over and done. Longing overpowered reason. Yes, he would go home.

He raised his head. Wind trembled the leaves, and with it came the sharp scent of a distant downpour. He gave a silent groan. It was going to rain. A distant rumble confirmed his fear.

"Oh, my," said Miss Emma. "And me without a parasol." Seeing Allen's distressed face, she gave a dry chuckle. "Mr. Matthers, I was joking. I'm made of neither sugar nor salt. I won't melt."

"I think we'll see if we can find a roof anyway."

By the time they had left the creek bottoms and moved into open country, the rain was a deluge. Allen had given Miss Emma his slicker—in spite of her sharp protest. Now he pulled the wide brim of his hat low and felt rain soak the shirt and run down his broad back. It was a warm rain and not unwelcome in the afternoon heat; however, it did slow progress. He knew it didn't take much wetness to turn these trails into soup. Miss Emma should not sleep out in the damp, not after the hard day she'd just had.

As he recalled, there was a barn a few miles away on the main road. The house had burned, but the last time he'd ridden through, the barn was intact. It was dilapidated but the curling shingles would still turn water better than a tree limb. There were still a few hours of daylight, and leaving the back roads was a bit risky. One glance at Miss Emma's gray face solidified the decision.

They intersected the main road a mile beyond the barn. He hated to backtrack but extra riding was worth a night in dry quarters.

"Ma'am," he called through the gush of rain, "there's a barn back that way. We'll stay the night there. The storm won't last long, but the ground will be wet."

She nodded. He had seen bedraggled wet hens with the same drooping sogginess. He wondered how he'd manage if she got sick. Worry blunted his diligence. The line of blue-coated, mounted men blurred into the tree line.

It was too late to run. They had been seen. He began concocting a plausible lie of who they were and where they were going. The column, led by a wary major pulled up and halted. Allen's hands tightened on the pommel as he resisted the urge to palm his pistol. He would not put Miss Emma in harm's way. His eyes widened when she abruptly rode forward, waving her hand.

"Oh, Major!" she cried, "Thank God I've found you! I have an urgent message for General Thayer at Fort Smith. I've ridden hard for two days to warn him. I've had a terrible time dodging Rebel patrols."

Breathless, she went on, "I've news of Shelby. He has a large command—at least a thousand. Right now he's near our post at Dardanelle and plans to attack all our posts along the river." She looked vexed as the major tugged a long mustache and weighed her words. "The general is my cousin," she quickly added. "Tell John," she pretended to stumble over the name. "I mean tell the general, I'm returning to the fort. I'll see him soon."

In spite of the peril, Allen gave an inward smile. She was as spunky as Nelda. Smart too. The officer straightened in the saddle. He spoke loudly through the rain. "I'm sorry, but you'll have to take the word yourself. My orders take me the opposite direction."

Emma's eyes snapped. Her voice grew higher pitched and louder. "Did you not hear me? We stand to lose all our posts along the river. I'm exhausted. At the rate I can travel, you could get to the fort hours ahead of me. Don't just sit there like a ninny," she scolded. "John needs to send reinforcements immediately."

The major's face reddened. He turned to consult a lieutenant.

In spite of the rain, Allen overheard the low words. "Yes, I've seen her at the fort, sir. She was at the Fourth of July celebration, and I've seen her around the post on several occasions."

The major, still unconvinced, pinned Allen with sharp eyes. "Why didn't he ride on ahead?"

Miss Emma snorted. "To leave me to the tender mercies of rebels and bushwhackers? I think not! John would skin him alive." She nodded toward Allen. "Barnabas was paid to guard me on the way to my daughter's farm. He's stuck close in spite of my decision to turn back." She pursed her lips while eyeing the major with displeasure. "I am most perplexed by your hesitation, sir. Lives hang in the balance. It won't look good on your record. Rest assured—I shall report this the very second I arrive."

The idea of a negative record unsettled the major more than her snapping dark eyes did.

He gave a slight bow. "I need every man I've got, but I'll get word to the general as quickly as possible." Then, looking over his shoulder, he turned to the lieutenant again. In quick order, a man was selected to ride back to the fort.

She called after them, "Tell John that Barnabas is still with me."

The major gave a curt nod and continued down the trail.

As hoof beats drowned in the rain, Allen's eyebrows rose. "That was quick thinking, ma'am...but Barnabas?"

"It was the first name that popped into my head." Her eyes dropped as she adjusted the slicker. "He was an old beau." She looked up, and in spite of strain on her face, her eyes twinkled. "He was gallant, brave, and handsome...a true Galahad."

Allen eyed her. "Did Elmer know about him?"

The deep blush on wrinkled cheeks surprised him.

"No. No, he did not." She adjusted the slicker.

Allen looked down the road. "I hate to do it, but in the morning, we better cross the river someplace near here and put as much distance between us and them as we can. Sure wouldn't want to catch up with the major and us headed the wrong way. This is sort of a bad stretch, but maybe we can find a decent crossing." He looked at her with concern. "That old barn isn't too far away."

She seemed to read his mind. "I'll be fine," she assured. "Press on, Mr. Matthers." However, after a few rods, she stopped. "I wouldn't want you having the wrong idea," she began. "Elmer was not my first love. But after I met him, he was my only."

In acknowledgement, he dipped his head and wondered what had happened to Barnabas. He had enough manners not to ask.

CHAPTER 7

When Nelda entered the dark, cavernous building that was once a warehouse, cool dimness was a welcome relief. Her eyes had hardly adjusted when Sarah flew into her arms.

"Oh, t-t-teacher, I'm s-s-so glad you're here!"

"Miss Horton," called Reverend Springer. "Thank God you've come. You can supervise the children. I must hurry back to the office." He did not seem perturbed by the commotion, merely anxious to be away and tending to other matters.

"But I can't—"

Slamming on his hat, he interrupted her protest. "You'll do fine." He glanced at the children. Compassion made his face a mask of worry. "Calm them." He called back over his shoulder, "I'll bring food and water soon."

Aggravated, she watched him disappear. There was no getting out of it—she must play mother hen to two-dozen or more orphans huddled like frightened chicks near the back of the room. They ranged from toddlers to a few taller children who might be nearing twelve or thirteen. Some had come to her makeshift school. Most she had never seen.

Concern replaced aggravation when Nelda heard loud sobs from a tot, not yet two, perched on a youngster's hip—likely her brother—who was hardly more than seven. She wondered what horrors these children had endured…and what awful things yet awaited. Her brows knit. She had no earthly idea what to do now.

"Children, it's going to be just fine," she began. Another deafening boom seemed to contradict her. The tot took fingers from her mouth and wailed. In spite of the boy jostling and shushing, the wails continued, growing steadily louder.

A cannon blast jarred the miniscule windows and widened Sarah's eyes even more.

"Reckon th-th-they're gonna cross the river and k-k-kill us all?" Sarah's fingers pressed deeply into Nelda's arm and fearful dark eyes sought the doorway as if assassins might enter at any moment.

Nelda patted the clutching hands. "I think General Thayer and his troops are a match for all the rebels in Arkansas."

She hoped it was so. Even if the rebels overran the fort, they wouldn't harm orphans. Then, recalling the New York orphan asylum, she sucked in a quick breath. These orphans were not Negroes. But they were, for the most part, children of Union sympathizers.

She shook her head. No southern man would raise a hand against these children.

Then like an almost forgotten nightmare, she recalled a mob in the front yard, a flaming torch, shattered glass. It had been southern men who set her house on fire—and not trash either. Bo and Drew Morrison had been cultured, educated; and yet resentment and the war had made them heartless fiends.

Nelda gave an inward cringe. Hadn't she turned away Mary Beth and Tabbatha Morrison? As they had trudged away in the snowy night with nowhere to go, she had watched hardhearted without calling them back.

There was no telling what an invading army would do.

She crossed the room and took the howling tot into her arms and smoothed the damp blonde curls away from a finely molded brow. Although her handkerchief was soiled and damp from mopping her own face, she used it to wipe the runny nose. For the moment, struck dumb by Nelda's ministrations, the tot drew a shaky breath and quieted.

The little girl was exquisite, with bright blue eyes, long curling lashes, and high cheekbones in rounded angelic cheeks. The fair-haired brother was equally handsome. Some of the children were not. The three Hermans, standing tightly together, were marked by a distinct lack of chins in narrow, rat-like faces with grime deeply embedded in every pore.

"There now," Nelda began. "We'll all just…" Her voice faltered. Bewildered, she had no idea what they should do.

William emerged from the shadows where he, apart from the rest, had been leaning on the wall near the front door. "Teacher, my ma always said keeping busy was the best cure for fretting. You could read us a book."

"That's a wonderful idea, William. If I had one…"

She looked around at the clutter. Sawed lumber and shavings lay in piles near the half-finished construction of a new partition dividing the single room into two. Cots were piled in one corner alongside a collection of mismatched chairs and two scarred tables. Several kegs and barrels stood against one wall.

"I can run to your house and get one," he offered. "I know the way. It's not three streets from here."

Distant shots were continual, but cannon blasts were sporadic.

"I don't think that's a good idea—"

"Aw, those cannons you're hearing are ours. The Rebs are still a long way from here, way down on the Towson Road, and the others haven't crossed the river yet." He headed for the door. "I'll be right back." Before she could call him back, he was gone.

Then Nelda brightened. Mrs. Hanover would know what to do. She was fond of children and experienced in their care.

Nelda rushed to the door and called, "Borrow a broom and some dust rags from Mrs. Hanover. Ask her to please come back here with you."

He waved before disappearing around the corner.

While awaiting his return, Nelda busied the children with moving tables and chairs.

William was right. The children were soon preoccupied enough to stop jumping at every sound. He returned safely—almost before Nelda had begun to worry. He carried books, also a broom and rags. For the first time, it occurred to her to wonder what books he had picked.

"Here's a couple of books." He held out two volumes.

One was a worn copy of Moby Dick, and the other was stories by Washington Irving. Nelda moved the toddler to her other hip and reached for the books. Moby Dick would please the boys; however, it would likely make the girls and younger children fidget. She decided Rip Wan Winkle or The Legend of Sleepy Hollow were better choices.

William interrupted her musing. "Mrs. Hanover was gone. The front door was open so I just went in."

"The front door was open?"

"Yes 'um."

Nelda frowned. It was unlike Mrs. Hanover to go away and leave the door open.

"Looked like she left in a hurry," William added. "Drawers were open and clothes were all over the place."

Nelda was truly worried. Had someone perhaps robbed and abducted the good woman? When Reverend Springer returned she would ask him to investigate.

Sarah looked up from dusting a chair. "Teacher, this is like playing house."

William stopped sweeping long enough to glare through dust motes swirling in a shaft of light coming through the open door. "Is not! This is real work. I don't play house."

Nelda intervened. "Of course it's real work. Sarah merely said it was like playing house. You are all doing a fine job."

Instantly distracted, she felt moist warmth on her arm and groaned. Where would she find a diaper? She turned to the brother.

"What's your name?"

"Charlie."

"Charlie, do you have any diapers for the baby?"

"There's some back at the wagon. But I ain't sure where they moved the wagons." He added, "Her name is Susan, but we mostly call her Suzie."

Nelda asked, "What happened to your parents?"

Charlie's face went cold and still. "Bushwhackers killed 'em."

"Do you have any other family?" Nelda asked softly.

"None to speak of…" Charlie's voice trailed away. "Some aunts and uncles in Iowa."

"Maybe Reverend Springer can locate them," she comforted.

Sarah stopped dusting and her eyes grew still with pain. "Bushwhackers shot pa and m-ma, too," she said and her voice caught in her throat. "My m-ma saw them c-comin' and she told me to run fast and hide in the brush." Her eyes filled. She stopped to swallow before adding, "She couldn't run on account of she was g-gonna have a b-baby. I stayed hid in the brush, p-peepin' out. Pa came running from the b-barn…" She shuddered and her eyes darkened with memory, but this recollection remained unvoiced.

"Do you have relatives?"

"I got a big s-sister," said Sarah.

Nelda was relieved. "Where is she?"

"She got m-married and m-moved off. I don't 'member the name of the place."

"What's her name? Maybe we can find her."

"L-Lucille…" Sarah screwed up her face and chewed her bottom lip. "I don't remember her n-new n-name."

"How did you get to the fort?" she asked.

"Mr. Thomas, our neighbor came by and f-found me. He brought me here and left me on the s-store porch. He said he didn't have enough food to keep his own young'uns alive and the army would take care of me." Her lips trembled. "I was awful s-scared waiting on that porch in the dark—almost as s-scared as I was when the b-bushwhackers came."

Nelda wanted to throttle Mr. Thomas. Then she sighed. It would take a miracle to reunite these children with kin. Every time a wagon train left town, orphans were crammed aboard. According to Reverend Springer, it was necessary. Food was increasingly scarce.

By noon the room was free of sawdust piles and the lumber stacked against one wall and the floor swept clean. After looking around, Nelda decided most of the dirt had settled on her and the children.

She knew they were thirsty. Her mouth was dust dry. If the chaplain didn't come soon, she'd have to send William after a bucket, dipper, and water.

She sat down on a chair. "You've all done a good job. Now, everyone find a place. There aren't enough chairs so why don't you boys sit on the lumber stack? I'll read a story."

She had only read a few pages, each line punctuated by distant gunfire, when Reverend Springer arrived in a wagon laden with cots, blankets, bowls, spoons, water bucket, dipper, pots of bean soup, and cornbread. To Nelda, even more welcome was slim, wiry, long-faced Elsie Turnbo, a kind-hearted widow who loved children. Judging by the way the young ones flocked to her, the feeling was mutual. Nelda liked her immediately, and with a huge sigh of relief, she handed over the reins of leadership and began following Elsie's capable direction.

Elsie's laugh was loud, almost raucous, but it took only a short while to detect a heart of gold in a body overflowing with boundless energy. Nelda ladled soup into bowls while Reverend Springer answered questions.

"No, they haven't retreated; but I understand we're pounding them with a furious cannonade on the main roads. Their cannons in the Poteau Bottoms aren't close enough to do us any real damage. I have faith General Thayer's troops will prevail over the rebel scum."

Sarah looked up with wistful eyes. "I wish you'd stay, teacher."

"I'll be back in the morning." Nonetheless, as Nelda opened the door and fled like a bird from a cage, she felt a guilty pang.

Twilight softened the oppressive heat in air fragrant with honeysuckle. Lightning flashed in the distance and there was a rumble of thunder. The streets were almost empty now. Occasionally a lone shot rang out and sometimes a burst of rapid firing. Apparently the rebels had not retreated.

Nelda's steps lagged. She decided nursemaids and mothers had the hardest job imaginable. The throbbing in her head made her sympathize with the horrific headaches that used to plague Mama.

She wanted to lie down and sleep for a week, but first she longed for a good soak in Mrs. Hanover's large metal bathtub. Instead, she would settle for a wash in the basin. It took too much effort to fill and empty the tub. Mrs. Hanover's help—a young pretty Negro—would have gone home by now.

Mrs. Hanover was not home. The house was, as William had said, topsy-turvy. Nelda was alarmed. But after a hurried investigation, it appeared unlikely there was a thief or bushwhacker. Only personal items were missing. There was no note, and the only items on the desk were the glass inkpot, quill with metal nib, and a few sheets of foolscap.

"Perhaps she told a neighbor," muttered Nelda, and then she went outside and down the walk. An elderly woman opened the door.

"She left in a big hurry this morning. Only took one bag, but it was crammed full. I asked where she was off to but she never even glanced my way—just hurried down the back walk after that big red-headed fellow, climbed into her buggy and whipped up the horse."

"Big, red-headed fellow?" echoed Nelda.

The woman nodded vigorously. "Red as could be. He was huge—big as a Texas mule. Right nice-looking, though. He had a fine-looking sorrel horse, too."

There were other large men with red hair in the world. It might not be Allen. And yet, she knew it was. But what was Mrs. Hanover doing with Allen?

Instantly suspicious, Nelda asked, "How long have you known Mrs. Hanover?"

"Years and years." The woman's rheumy eyes narrowed. "Why?"

"Oh, no reason," hedged Nelda.

The woman's eyes abruptly widened. "Upon my word! She was from Mississippi. She told me her cousin was high up in the army. I just supposed it was our army. Do you think she might be a rebel, and she's run off to join that trash?"

"I don't know," said Nelda, and then left as quickly as good manners would allow.

The house was dark. She needed a light. Instead she sat in the parlor and stared at the gathering night. A whippoorwill's plaintive call drifted in the open window.

If only she had been here, she could have seen him! She sat straight up. She was being a fool. Allen was a rebel—and a spy to boot. But he was a friend. She felt so alone. Mama and Papa were dead. She had no siblings, only Cousin Becky and her family—and if he were still alive—an uncle she hardly knew. Yes, she was alone. She supposed that accounted for Allen being in her thoughts so much.

Nelda opened the office door. Reverend Springer was talking to Colonel Judson. She had seen the balding officer with the broad nose and pleasant face at the celebration.

"Francis," said the colonel, "I understand your plight. Believe me I'd love to get the children out of harms' way. There is just no safe way to move them yet. General Thayer has ordered no wagons can leave."

Both men looked around as she entered. "Ah, here's Miss Horton now—the young woman I told you about." He motioned her forward. "Miss Horton, Colonel Judson."

She returned the colonel's nod. "Nice to meet you, sir."

A nearby cannon boomed. It was the first of the morning, and she jumped.

He smiled. "I'd ask how you like our fair city, but lately it isn't so fair."

She grinned. "I like the fort. I enjoyed the Fourth of July celebration very much. It was much livelier than anything we have in Clarksville."

His eyes sharpened with interest. "Horton from Clarksville...are you any relation to Phillip Horton?"

"I'm his daughter."

"Wonderful!" he exclaimed. "We were great friends in Mexico. Excellent soldier—hate that he lost an arm. How is Phil?"

"He's dead, sir. The rebels hung him for treason."

His face stiffened. He took her hand. "Please accept my condolence."

"Thank you." A lump gathered in her throat, and she swallowed.

"Chaplain Springer tells me you are helping with the orphans. I suppose you have business to discuss, so I'll get back to headquarters. Plenty to do there, lately." He gave a slight smirk.

"Before you go, Colonel, I have a question."

He paused at the door.

Nelda said, "I'm boarding with a woman named Mrs. Hanover. I came home last night to find her gone, as well as some of her personal belongings. She simply left, no note, no explanation. Do you have any idea—?"

As a keen, knowing look passed between the men, Nelda looked from Judson to Springer. The colonel took a cigar from his pocket and lit it before saying, "Well, Francis, it appears she's flown the coop, and just in the nick of time. Almost makes me wonder...I had the orders on my desk for her arrest."

"What?" Nelda spun to face Reverend Springer.

The chaplain nodded. "Miss Horton, we've long suspected Mrs. Hanover of feeding information to the enemy. I confess that is why I sent you to board there. You'll recall the warning about sedition I gave the day you arrived. I knew you'd keep your eyes open and report anything suspicious."

The colonel quickly inserted, "Did you see anyone coming and going who might have been her contact?"

Allen! Nelda's mind whirled. But her lips remained tightly shut.

"No?" Colonel Judson patted her shoulder. "Well, just think back, and, if you recall anything, let the chaplain know."

"Colonel," said Reverend Springer. "It appears you might even have an informant inside the fort."

After a few more words with Reverend Springer, the colonel left. Nelda barely noticed. She was beginning to wonder if her lot in life was protecting Allen Matthers...and being protected by him.

CHAPTER 8 ❧

The storm had quickly passed but not before rain had plastered the slick trail alongside the river, making tiny lakes of each hoof print. Allen, wet to the skin, was tired and miserable. He hated to think how wretched Miss Emma must be. He glanced back. She came steadily onward but was hunched under the slicker, exhausted, and dejected.

He was relieved to see the barn looming ahead. Some shakes were missing and the walls sagged like a tired old man, but it would be shelter.

"I never knew an old decrepit barn could look so good." Miss Emma thanked him for his assistance as she hobbled farther inside, sank onto the ground, and leaned against a wall.

"Watch where you sit, ma'am. There's likely to be snakes in an old building like this."

She jerked upright and studied the ground but didn't stand. "Tired as I am, he'll have to be the one that moves." Nonetheless she peered cautiously around. "It's so dark in here I can hardly see my hand, let alone a snake."

"I'll make a fire as soon as I unsaddle the horses. There are enough gaps between the logs and in the roof to let out smoke."

"It'll be hard to find dry wood," she observed.

Except for mouse droppings and spider webs, the dim interior was empty. The few stalls had been robbed of log walls, doubtless by other travelers for quick fires. Only the uprights remained.

"I always carry a bit of kindling and some pine knots in my saddle bag, enough to dry out wet deadfalls."

Without too much difficulty, Allen got a small blaze going and soon returned with an armful of limbs and deadfalls. Rain poured from the brim of his hat as he stooped to add them to the crackling blaze.

He turned. "Sure glad you thought to pack food. I only have a few cans of beans and some jerky."

Miss Emma gave a weary smile as he handed her a piece of bread and meat. "Fire, food, and shelter. Blessings not to be taken lightly," she said.

He glanced around. "That's a fact,' he said. "There's been times I'd have traded my eyeteeth for even this much comfort."

"You've seen hard service in the army?"

"No more than most," he answered. "Nothing about this war has been a picnic—not for folks on either side."

She nodded as her lips drew down. "So true. I can't help feeling concerned for my young female boarder, Miss Horton. She's a Unionist, but such a nice young woman—always busy helping someone, the refugees and the orphans. I fear she'll worry about me."

At the mention of Nelda's name, Allen masked an inward jerk. Miss Emma had no need to know of his connection.

"I'll swan," she said. "I don't remember ever being so tired. But I think I'm aching too much to sleep."

"You'll sleep," he predicted.

After he had arranged her bedroll and she had lain down, he pulled the flask from his pack and raised it to his lips. When it was empty, he rummaged in the saddlebags until he found another.

"Mr. Matthers, I have no idea what is eating your heart out, but that isn't the answer. Believe me—I know."

Stunned he lowered the flask. "What makes you think—"

"I see pain in your eyes," she said. "When you reach for the flask, I see the desperation I felt when my husband died." She went on, "I tried to drink my sorrow away. Take my word for it—drink only makes matters worse. It's leaning on a rotten staff."

He raised the flask and drank deeply before saying, "You're absolutely right." He looked at the flask, glinting silver in firelight. "But I don't give a damn."

After a moment she spoke. "You're not a talkative man, but I am an excellent listener. Sometimes sharing a burden lightens it."

"Thank you, ma'am, but I've nothing to say."

Allen eyed the flask with scorn and, for the first time, rued the fact that he could hold his liquor. Troubled thoughts kept him tossing. After daylight, he arose, tired and groggy.

Miss Emma looked equally tired. She had difficulty mounting the horse, but she rode without complaint. They rode hard, being extra watchful for Union patrols in the steamy morning. By noon, the ground was dry, and, by afternoon, the trail was dusty.

Allen frowned as he studied the swift current of the Arkansas. He glanced at Miss Emma with concern.

"No need to dally, Mr. Matthers. We need to cross, and there's no time like the present."

She shifted wide hips in the saddle and then kicked the horse in the flanks. As it entered the water she called over her shoulder, "Come along, Mr. Matthers."

He gave an admiring grin. Miss Emma was no coward.

Allen estimated it was about midnight when his groggy slumber was shattered by a rasping cough. The small fire he'd built the evening before was dead ash now. He lay tense, listening. It was the deep rasping kind that often preceded lung fever. Miss Emma gave a low moan and coughed again. He arose, struck a match and crossed the ground to touch her. She was burning with fever. He had been fearful of just such a thing when she'd gotten soaked crossing the river. No doubt about it, she'd been spunky. She'd not made a peep, just hung onto the horse's mane for dear life while the water roiled almost to her neck.

He'd wanted to build a fire and get her things dry before riding on. Upon seeing a small Union patrol heading upriver, she had insisted they just keep riding because the Yankees hanged spies. He had agreed.

The Yankees did hang spies. There was a rumor they'd even hung a woman at Dardanelle. For certain the Confederates hung spies. They had hung Nelda's pa and Allen's own friend Jim Loring.

"Damn!" he muttered, racking his brain for a solution to this new dilemma. The only person he knew that had any medical skill with lung fever was Granny Tanner. She had successfully treated everyone on Little Piney for ailments from birthing to snakebite. But she was miles away, even as the crow flies. Miss Emma was too sick to cut across the mountains. No. She needed immediate shelter and care.

He chewed his jaw. Yesterday they had passed Ozark late in the day so Clarksville wasn't too far away. He would take her to Carrie Hackett's. Maybe Carrie was good at tending the sick.

Carrie's wide face was anxious as she eyed the pale woman lying on her bed in the one room cabin. "She's mighty sick, Allen. I ain't much good at doctorin'. Ma was a good hand—she learned from Aunt Bitty... Granny Tanner. When we was ailin' she always took care of us, but I never paid much heed to what yarbs she used. Since she passed, I've kicked myself a hundred times for not learnin'. I'll do my best, but this woman needs a doctor."

The rasping of cicadas floated through the open window along with the perfume of climbing roses that clung to the cabin. Emma's eyes were closed. Her ragged breaths were fast but shallow.

"I know," he agreed. "But there's not one this side of Little Rock and none that would come anyway."

"Aunt Bitty might come," she ventured, "if she's able. She's gettin' mighty old. And I calculate mighty feeble since Bo Morrison burned her feet, tying to get her to tell where Elijah was. I reckon you knowed about that—how Bo was a conscript man?" she asked. "Reckon he took men and boys from all over the county."

Allen's jaws tightened. Yes, he knew about that. Likely it was Bo Morrison who had shot Pa—at least Ma's description fit.

"Yes, I heard," said Allen, his mind still fretting over Miss Emma. "Do you know of anything to do for her?"

"I'll brew some willer bark tea fer the fever, and make a poltice fer her chest." Then her face screwed up in thought. "Best I recollect, mustard plaster is the best. Emmitt Gossett might have some mustard powder at the mercantile. I doubt it—them shelves is bare. But he might. Other than that all I know to do is pray."

"What's the situation in town?" Allen asked.

"A lot happened since you and Roy left last fall. The Yankees took over for a spell—set up a post. But they skedaddled for a bit. Set fire to the town a'fore they left. Burnt some buildings. Would have been worse except some of our men come through and helped folks put it out. After that, the Yankees come back fer a spell. Just last week, they high-tailed it out again. At least that's the last I heared."

Young Isaac, who had been hovering in the doorway, spoke up. "Yep, ain't no army, either side, in town now."

Allen was relieved to hear it. He turned, and while putting on his hat, strode to the door. "I'll be back quick as I can."

Isaac followed him into the yard. "Can I come with ya?"

"Ask your ma."

Face downcast, he returned shortly. "She said no. She needs me to fetch water and build up the cook fire."

Allen reined the big sorrel around. "I won't be gone long anyway." He would fetch back a piece of hard candy if Emmitt had any. It was unlikely. As Carrie had said, most of the store shelves had been picked bare long ago.

Allen covered the few miles rapidly, all the while being watchful. Although the Union Army had been gone only a week, they might return. He had known it to happen. Just now, he had no desire to meet the Confederates either. They were still hell-bent on conscriptions. His situation would take some explaining, and he had no time for that.

As he rode, dust rose to settle on low bushes. The odor of honey-suckle was rank where the trail dipped low alongside the creek. He saw no wild game and only a few birds, mostly crows, feeding in deserted dooryards. In the weedy pastures, cattle were nonexistent.

He turned toward town. The thought of passing Nelda's deserted house caused a dull ache in his middle. He shook his head. He was a fool to keep thinking of her. Even with his mind consumed by Seamus, she was never far from his thoughts.

When the two-story, white house came into sight, he came to an abrupt halt. The shattered windows were still covered with boards—the results of a night raid—but he had seen a woman cross the yard. Tall and slender and dark, she looked like Della, but the last he knew she was in Helena. He kneed the sorrel off the trail and dismounted and cautiously circled the pile of burned rubble that had once been a barn. No one was in the yard. He knocked on the door.

"Who there?"

"It's me, Della, Allen Matthers."

"Mr. Allen!" A dark-skinned woman threw open the door. A wide smile beamed from a lovely but too slender face. "I'm so glad to see you!" She drew him inside. "My Gideon told me you got away at Helena. I was plum glad. I thought they'd hang you sure." Her eyes twinkled. "I was mad as a wet hen at Miss Nelda, and I told her so!"

Allen chuckled. Then he asked, "What are you doing here? Nelda said you stayed at Helena."

"I did for a while," she said sobering. "After the battle, I helped nurse them soldiers. But when the baby come, Gideon made me leave. Helena is an awful place now—full of folks and full of dying," she said with a frown. "I wish Gideon could come away too." She went on, "When some folks was coming this way, he sent me and the baby along. He figured Miss Nelda would be home by now. Do you know where she is?"

"At Fort Smith. I saw her just a few days ago."

"When she coming home?" asked Della hurriedly.

"I don't think any time soon."

"Oh." Della's face fell. "I wish she—" She turned when a loud cry interrupted. For a moment a smile flickered. "That boy yowls like a wild Injun the second his eyes open." She crossed the room to pick up a sturdy boy about a year old with a head covered in tight black curls.

"He's a fine looking lad," said Allen. It was so. Both Gideon and Della were handsome, and so was the boy.

Della smoothed the curls and kissed the moist forehead. "Mr. Allen, you got no idea how much you can love a young'un till you get one of your own. I'd die if anything happen to him."

"How are you managing—making out for food and stuff?"

"Did laundry for the army before they pulled out. Not sure how I'll manage now. But my friends help some."

A plan began formulating in Allen's mind. "Della, I need a favor. You said you nursed the soldiers. There's a very sick woman at a cabin a few miles from here. Could you help my friend take care of her?"

"Yes, sir. I can do that. What's her trouble?"

"Lung fever, I think. She got chilled and caught a cold. Now she's got a fever."

"What you got for medicine?" She asked.

"I'm going to the mercantile now for some mustard for a plaster. I'll stop by for you on my way back."

He figured Carrie would be glad for help. He'd spied a flourishing garden bordered with giant sunflowers behind the cabin. She would need a hand with that as well as the nursing.

The Yankees had burned their brand on Clarksville. The Methodist Church was a blackened shell, and one side of the two-story courthouse was badly damaged. He saw no one on the square or the sidewalks but he felt hidden eyes staring as he turned onto Main Street where most of the buildings were intact, although many of the windows were boarded over.

The formerly sparkling windows of the mercantile were grimy, and, once inside, Allen was greeted with the smell of staleness and dust rather than the heady odor of spices and leather.

Emmitt looked up as the bell above the door jingled. His eyes bulged and then brightened with joy. Quickly he rounded the counter and slapped Allen's back. "Matthers! We heard you got yourself hung." His big belly shook when he laughed. "Hell, this is the best thing that's happened in a long time!" He pounded Allen's back again. "Where in the world you been?"

"Scouting for Marmaduke and, lately, for Cooper."

"Yep," he repeated, "this is the best thing that's happened in a long time! I reckon since Ned Loring came back." Emmitt went on to tell of all the news along Piney, especially about the wonderful reunion of the Loring family when Ned Loring was found alive in a prison camp.

A commotion on the sidewalk drew their attention. Allen's lips thinned. "I see Gill hasn't changed."

Gill Harris, the provost marshal, had just knocked a black boy onto the dirt and began kicking him. The boy rolled under the wagon, trying to avoid the heavy boots. Gill grabbed a leg and dragged him out. He slapped the boy hard. His shrill angry words carried into the store. "You black bastard! I told you to hold that horse—not tie it to the rail," he screeched.

"No," agreed Emmitt, "he ain't changed a lick. Because he's a mean son-of-a-bitch—and a runt to boot—he picks on anything weak or small. Never seen a man crueler to his animals and his darkies. Last month one of his bucks ran off. Gill caught him before he got far, and then Gill and that mean bastard overseer of his chopped off the fellow's toes. Said that should keep him home for a while."

Allen grimaced.

Gill stepped inside and stopped dead in his tracks. "What are you doing back here?" he asked.

Without answering, Allen turned to Emmitt. "You have any mustard powder for making a poultice?"

"None in the store. But I got some back there in my room. Use it myself when I get coughs and chills. Why? You sick?"

Gill stepped closer. "I asked you a question, Matthers."

"What I'm doing here is none of your damned business."

Gill took a step back. "As provost marshal I got the right to—"

Allen cut him short. "Since Hindman appointed you, and he's no longer in command, I'd say you're not anything."

When Gill stiffened, Allen knew he'd struck a nerve. More than likely Gill had feared such an idea might take hold in town. Gill had never been liked. But the position had given him the illusion of the power he craved.

"I've not been un-appointed," he sputtered. "That means I'm still the provost. You'll do well to remember that, Allen Matthers!"

Allen's eyes narrowed. "Ma described the conscript man that came looking for my brothers and shot Pa. It sounded exactly like Bo Morrison. Ma's description of the scum with him that knocked her senseless sounded just like that boy of yours. Tucker better pray to God I don't find out it was him."

When Gill's face paled, Allen's eyes narrowed more.

"Tucker ain't no one to mess with," sputtered Gill, and like a scared rabbit, he bolted from the store.

"Biggest damned coward in the country," said Emmitt.

Allen asked, "Do you know anything about who was riding with Bo that day?"

A look crossed Emmitt's face. Although it had been just a flicker, Allen detected fear. Emmitt looked down and began rearranging items on the counter.

"I don't recollect anything about that."

Just like I figured, thought Allen. His blood pounded. Wish I'd followed my instincts and killed Tucker long ago!

He drew a deep breath, pushing down murderous rage. Now was not the time. Miss Emma was too bad off.

"Loan me some of that powder," he said. "Not saying when I can pay it back, but I need some for a sick friend."

"Sure, Allen." Emmitt started toward the room where he slept at the back of the store and returned with a cloth bag. "I kept me some but there's still plenty here."

"Thanks. I appreciate it. Got any liquor for sale?"

"It's rotgut—not the good stuff your pa made. But it wets a man's whistle better than nothing," said Emmitt.

Allen paid him, and started for the door. Then he turned back. "Don't guess you have any hard candy left?"

Emmitt shook his head. "Not even any for myself." Then he added, "You watch out for Tucker. He ain't spineless like his pa. He's meaner than a she-wolf."

Before Allen had pulled the sorrel to a stop, Della left the house with the baby on a hip and a bundle in her hand. She looked toward the woods. "Miss Nelda's mare, Lily, is hid out in them woods somewheres. That Hadley young'un comes by to check on her. I don't reckon I ought to ride her?" she asked.

"No. We better leave Lily where she is. Any scoundrel—in or out of uniform—would want that mare."

"That's what I figured. Miss Nelda is mighty fond of that horse."

"She certainly is," he agreed. His heart twisted as he recalled her joy when he had returned the stolen mare to her.

Della handed him the bundle, "Just a few things for Moses."

"Moses?" he asked, reaching to take the baby while she mounted behind the saddle.

She settled herself and said, "Gideon is right partial to that name."

Allen stared into solemn black eyes. It's a good thing, he thought, the law considers ownership of a slave child by mother not father.

Otherwise, even though Della was free, Gill Harris would claim this child as his property. By law, Gideon still belonged to Gill. If he learned the child was Gideon's, he might cause trouble anyway. Gill delighted in taking advantage of anyone who couldn't fight back.

Allen handed her the child. "Well, Moses, if you find the Promised Land, I just might come along. I sure as hell ain't likin' Arkansas these days."

They had started down the road before Della asked, "Whose cabin we going to?"

"Do you know Roy and Carrie Hackett?"

"Sure do," she said. "Mr. Roy's in the Confederate Army, ain't he?"

"Yes," Allen admitted, "but they're nice folks." He waited for her response.

After a pause, she spoke. "Until I nursed them men at Helena, I didn't have no use for Rebels." She chuckled. "That was before I knowed you was a Rebel, Mr. Allen. I always liked you. I gotta say, most of them Rebel soldiers was nice and polite and treated me real good."

Allen wouldn't mention Miss Emma's occupation. He doubted Della would be as understanding of a rebel spy.

"Did you know Gideon helped me escape from that guard house back in Helena? If he hadn't, they'd have hung me."

She gave a rich, throaty laugh. "He said he couldn't let them hang no such fine fiddle player. Truth be tol', Gideon is right fond of you, Mr. Allen."

"Truth be told," he answered, "I think a heap of him. You got yourself a fine man."

She sighed. "I sure be glad when this war over, and he come home."

When they rounded a curve, a covey of quails ran from the road to disappear into thick brush. Near the riverbank, turtles sunned on logs, and a fish broke the water leaving a wide swirl. Allen recalled the day he and Nelda had feasted on the carp he had speared from the river. In spite of running from the army, that had been a good time. He wondered if Nelda felt the same. Then he scolded himself. She couldn't make it plainer—she had few, if any, fond thoughts of him!

The muggy heat soon wet his shirt. When mosquitoes rose from a marshy bog near the river, the baby began to whimper. Della shushed him and began crooning a soft song in a low alto.

"I forgot what a pretty voice you have, Della."

She slapped at a mosquito and stopped singing. "Remember them good times we had at Gideon's cabin when you used to drop by and play your fiddle? You're the best hand at fiddlin' I ever knew." Della sighed again. "You reckon them good times will ever come again?"

Allen's face tightened. "Maybe." But he knew, at least for him, they never would.

Isaac met them in the yard. Freckles were prominent on his sunburned nose. "Ma'll be glad to see you. She's a'feard that lady is dyin'.'" While they dismounted, he eyed the baby with delighted curiosity. His eyes grew huge when Della handed Moses to him.

"You hold him while me and Mr. Allen helps your ma. But come on inside out of the heat. If you sets him down, watch close—make sure he don't touch the cook stove."

Isaac was reluctant. "I never held no baby."

"Nothing to it," said Allen.

When Moses took a fist from his mouth and patted Isaac's face, he laughed. "Well, hi there, little feller."

Allen followed Della into the cabin. In the far end of the room Carrie stood from bending over a large four posted bed covered with a bright patchwork quilt. She had been sponging Miss Emma's arms and face.

"I brought Della along," said Allen. "She's had some experience nursing."

"Glad to hear it," said Carrie as she raised the hem of her apron and swiped her sweaty face. "She's bad."

Della lost no time. "Ma'am, you got any flour to mix with this here mustard powder?"

"No, I've been out for ages."

Della's brow puckered. "Reckon we can try meal…don't know as it'll hurt anything."

"Tell me how," volunteered Carrie, "and I'll mix it."

"I always use a big spoon of powders an' three of flour…reckon it be the same for meal. Mix 'em up good and add some warm water—enough to wet it. But leave it thick. You got a big cotton rag we can put it on? Can't put it right on the skin. We got to be kerful to check right often—make sure it don't blister."

"Yes, I've got a flour sack."

Isaac looked up from kneeling on the floor. Moses sat nearby, laughing and grabbing for the string Isaac dangled in front of him with a green-backed June bug attached by the leg.

Della glanced over. "Now, don't you go lettin' him get that bug. He put it right straight in his mouth."

"I won't. I'm a'watchin'," assured Isaac.

Moses grabbed for the bug and gurgled with pleasure as it buzzed near his face in a frantic circle. Isaac laughed and looked at Allen. "He's cute, ain't he? I always wanted me a little brother to play with."

Allen felt a knife in his heart. Della began unbuttoning Emma's blouse. "Mr. Allen, you get on out of here. I'm gonna wipe her down to cool off before we put on that plaster."

Allen was glad to leave. It pained him to hear the ragged, rasping breaths. He turned on his heel, left the cabin, and stepped into the bright sunshine. Out of habit, his gaze traced the surroundings. Through the trees came a shimmering glimpse of blue river in the distance. The cabin sat on a knoll bordered with fields and pastures and shady woods beyond.

After untying the jug from the saddle horn, Allen unsaddled in the barn and then turned the horse into the pasture. He got the jug and headed back to the house. He stopped near the rosebush where a humming bird with a bright red breast drank nectar from a pink rose. Allen lifted the jug in mock toast to the bird, and took a long swallow.

"I doubt that rose is this bitter," he said, "but this dulls the senses." He looked at the jug. Although he'd drunk all his life, he'd never been overly fond of it. But enough of it now did take the edge off the memories.

He eyed the garden alongside the cabin where dead stalks had been stripped of sweet corn, but clinging bean vines still held clusters of shell beans. Tomato plants and okra stalks were loaded with produce that would soon need picking. Allen was no hand in the sickroom or the kitchen, but he could at least help Carrie with the garden.

In the field, a small patch of yellowing corn stalks held the long slender ears used for feed. There might be enough for two animals, but Allen doubted it. The crooked rows covered only a scant portion of ground. More than likely, Isaac was too young to handle the plow and Carrie had plowed by herself.

"Mr. Allen," Della spied him and called from the window, "bring that jug in here. A little whisky he'p break up this here cough."

Shadows lay long in the yard when Allen reached to help Della onto the horse. Isaac, his face woebegone, handed Moses to her.

"You bringin' him back tomorra?"

Della snorted. "Ain't gonna leave him home by hisself!"

Isaac brightened. "See you tomorra, little Moses."

Della held onto the back of the saddle with one hand while cradling Moses with the other. "This chile be asleep before we gone half-way," she predicted.

"Would you like me to tote him? I know you're tired," said Allen. "You've worked hard all day."

"Oh, I got him," she said. "I never got to hold him all day," she said. Then she added, "I hope she be alright. Tonight tell the tale. I was gonna sit the night, but Miss Carrie tol' me to go on home on account of the baby." She drew a deep breath. "I am bone weary, and don't no bed sleep as good as home."

The grass-bordered trail soon intersected a broader road that ran adjacent to the wide river. As low clouds near the horizon became an orange glow, the setting sun made a golden path on the water. An eagle, with its white head shining, swooped low over the water, wide wings stretched and talons protruding forward. Suddenly, the dark wings bent, slowing the bird momentarily as the sharp talons snatched a fish from the golden water. Then, with wings flapping, the giant bird rose and soared away.

Allen and Della rode the rest of the way in companionable silence. Allen was weary too. He couldn't remember the last time he had really slept.

While tree frogs and katydids filled the air with deafening chatter, they turned onto a smaller road that crossed and re-crossed a wide creek with rocky bottom. Along one side rose a tall bluff with moss and lichen covered ledges.

Deep twilight had fallen when they reached the house. After stopping near the picket fence, Allen turned in the saddle, and took Moses while Della dismounted. The baby stretched and then snuggled close. Allen's eyes softened. Then his lips pressed hard together. He recalled being eight and tending the baby for Ma.

Would every image, every action hold a memory of Seamus?

Allen's head jerked up. Something stirred in the edge of the yard. At the same instant he drew the pistol.

Della cried out when a tall slender man walked from the shadows with arms raised.

"Don't shoot, Mr. Allen." His dark eyes grew radiant as Della flew across the yard and into his arms.

Allen smiled and sheathed the pistol. "Glad to see you, Gideon."

Stepping near, Gideon's eyes devoured the baby. His voice was reverent while Allen handed him the baby. "Lordy, jest look how that boy has growed!"

"He's a fine little man," said Allen. Then his eyes traced Gideon's rumpled clothes. "Looks like you've seen some rough riding lately."

He hoped Gideon had not deserted. The Union Army showed no more mercy to deserters than did the Confederates, and he had seen plenty of them shot.

"I been in the saddle most day and night," agreed Gideon. "We was ordered on patrol to Little Rock. I asked for to make a sashay home. I got jest a week—"

"Just a week!" moaned Della, her hungry eyes on his face. He nodded, "Jest one, so I rode mighty hard to have more time."

"Well, I'll get on out of here and let you and your family get reacquainted." Allen gathered the reins. "I never got to thank you proper for helping me at Helena. I owe you, Gideon. You saved my neck. Did you get into any trouble?"

Gideon's black eyes danced. "None to speak of. I think them guards was right glad you got away. I even heared the one you busted his noggin say it would've been shameful to hang such a good fiddle player."

Allen laughed. The sound was strange in his ears. When he turned the horse, Della called, "Mr. Allen…"

"Yes?" He looked back.

"About tomorrow…" she faltered.

"Don't worry about tomorrow. Until Gideon leaves, we'll manage without you."

"I come right after that," she called.

He waved a hand and rode away.

However, the next morning, Allen looked across the garden to see Gideon, Della, and Moses coming down the trail on Gideon's brown horse. He cut another pod of prickly skinned okra from a tall stalk and threw it into a basket atop large red tomatoes.

"Isaac, you got your wish. Here comes Moses after all."

Isaac tossed a pod of okra into the basket and rubbed his hands down ragged pant legs. "Reckon we can finish gatherin' this stuff later?"

"I reckon." As the boy ran to meet the riders, Allen kept working.

Gideon was dressed in a brown cotton shirt and an old pair of civilian trousers that were inches too short. He joined Allen, and pulling a knife from his pocket, began cutting okra. "Fine mornin'," he said.

"It is," agreed Allen, looking up at the fresh blue sky, "but it'll be an oven by noon. What are you doing here? I told Della we could manage without her."

"When she tol' me about that sick woman, I tol' her to come right on out here. We can visit in the evenings. That poor woman needs he'p, and Della has a gift with sick folks."

Allen looked toward the house. "Can't say I'm not glad she came. Miss Emma is a good woman. I hope Della can help her."

Carrie had had a rough night. She had stayed by the bed changing plasters and sponging the sick woman until she looked almost as bad as Miss Emma. Allen had offered to help, but she had shooed him outside. Now that Della was here, he hoped she would take a nap.

"She'll try," Gideon said, "We prayed hard for Miss Emma this mornin'." When Allen gave him a puzzled look, he chuckled. "When you knowed me before, I wasn't no prayin' man—but I done changed, Mr. Allen. Jesus done wash all them sins away." Gideon's face shown with a glad light. "They float right on down that Mississippi where Brother Sam baptize me"—his voice deepened in imitation of the preacher—"in the name of the Father and the Son and the Holy Ghost."

"You appear right happy," said Allen, scooting the basket farther down the row with his foot.

Gideon studied his face. "Yes, suh. But I seen gut-kicked hounds more joyful than you." He hesitated and then asked, "Mr. Allen, is you saved?"

"Saved?" echoed Allen. "I never been dunked in the river, if that's what you mean."

Gideon vigorously shook his head. "Naw, suh. Preacher Sam say water don't save a body—it's the believin' and trustin'."

Allen picked up the basket. "Well, I damn sure know there's a God. I've heard idiots say otherwise, but that's pure-dee hogwash."

Gideon nodded. "They's a officer at Helena who don't believe they's a God. That man mean as a snake. You reckon folks tries to make out there ain't no God so they can do to suit they-self?"

"Could be," said Allen. "Never thought much about it."

Gideon's face grew grave. "Marse Gill, he don't have no use fer religion. His colored folk used to go off into the brush to raise a song." Gideon looked shamefaced. "Course back then, I poke fun. But truth-to-tell, I was sort of wishful of 'em. Seemed like they was happy no matter how much Marse Gill torment." His face tensed. "Him and that overseer takes a heap a'pleasure in tormenting—them men loves laying on the strap. I had me a heart full o' hate. Yes, suh, I did. Then Preacher Sam tole me, the Lord says, I got to forgive."

Allen paused and stared hard. "Have you?"

Gideon gave a slow smile. "I'm a' tryin'." Then he chuckled. "Yes, suh, I'm a tryin'."

Truthfully, Allen had been thinking about the hereafter lately—heaven and hell. He supposed Seamus's death had him pondering such things. But he didn't like the ponderings.

Changing the subject, he asked, "Any war news?"

Gideon pursed his lips and then answered, "Look like the war be over soon."

"What you hearing?"

Gideon gave a slow grin, "You wouldn't 'spect ol' Gideon to tell a gray back like you about Mr. Lincoln's plans, now would you?"

Allen joined him in a laugh. "I guess not. Both sides would rawhide us just for picking okra together."

At noon, when Della called them inside for dinner, Allen stepped near the bed. Miss Emma, he thought, looked a tiny bit better. Maybe it was just because Della had combed and smoothed the heavily gray-streaked, brown hair into a neat braid. She opened her eyes.

"Allen," she rasped, "I'm sorry to cause all this trouble. You and your friends have been pure angels."

He patted her hand. "Don't worry," he said and patted her hand again. "You'll be up and around in no time." He hoped it was true. But the fast shallow breathing did not sound good.

Gideon's brows rose in pleased surprise when Carrie insisted everyone sit down at the table. Allen was certain Gideon and Della were not often offered such hospitality at a white man's table.

The meal of fried squirrel and hot cornbread smelled delicious. Allen supposed his appetite was returning. He remembered the Hackett's custom of saying grace and sat still looking at Carrie. She had started to bow her head when Gideon spoke up.

"Askin' your permission, ma'am, kin I do the prayin'?"

Carrie smiled. "Of course."

"Thank you kindly, ma'am." Gideon bowed. "Lord we thanks you for this food. We thanks you for this beautiful day. We thanks you for family and friends. I ask you to bless them. I ask you to bless this house and the good woman who live here. And Lord Jesus, please be a'healing that good woman over yonder in the sick bed and raise her up from that bed of affliction like you raise Peter's kin—a woman took with the fever."

Allen recognized what must have been a quote from Preacher Sam. Gideon's voice always changed to a deeper timbre when he quoted the man. Allen wondered if Gideon planned to pray an entire sermon. He suspected Della had given Gideon a nudge when the petition came to an abrupt end with a quick amen.

The food was good. Allen ate a good portion, the proof a mound of small bones on his plate. Carrie had arisen to refill his water glass when he looked out the window. "Gideon, quick! Slip out the back door," ordered Allen. "Here comes someone."

Carrie's brows rose as she looked questioningly from Allen to the back door where Gideon had disappeared.

Although Allen didn't know the soldier, he was a friend of Roy's from Shelby's command. He stayed only a few minutes to ask if Carrie had any news of Roy. Carrie was disappointed that the man had no knowledge of Marmaduke's recent whereabouts. Fort Smith, he said, was still in Union hands, and Jo Shelby was somewhere around Brownsville, giving the Yankees fits by tearing up railroad tracks and anything else belonging to the Federals, including five small forts.

Although Della remained silent, Allen was certain she took in every word to repeat to Gideon. He wondered how much vital information had been obtained just so by both sides. Long ago, he had learned to be on guard. A person never knew who was listening.

When Gideon returned late in the afternoon to take Della home, Carrie's eyes grew hard.

"There's no need of you coming back tomorrow. I can take care of Miss Emma just fine."

"But Ma," protested Isaac.

"Hush up," snapped Carrie.

Isaac, face downcast, handed Moses to Della. When Moses reached for him again Isaac's face fell even more, but he remained silent.

Della's face was stiff but Gideon said, "Thank you, ma'am, for that fine meal today. It was mighty good."

Allen followed them to the horse. "Sorry about that, Della. I want you to know I appreciate your help. I think you saved her life." He faced Gideon. "She's just afraid—"

"No need to 'pologize," Gideon interrupted. "I knows about fear." He shrugged. "Don't fear like I used to, though. Reckon when a body sure they goin' to heaven, nothin' ain't so fearsome. Don't you think no more about it, Mr. Allen." Gideon glanced at Della. "Woman, ain't no cause to be sulled up like a possum. Remember what Preacher Sam tol' us. We's Christians. We got to be forgivin' all the time."

When their horse had disappeared down the trail, Carrie's lips thinned. "Allen, I got no liking for runaway slaves. Besides that, giving them food and shelter will get a body into a heap of trouble. I recognized that one—he belongs to Gill Harris. Upon my word, Allen, Gill is the provost! What in tarnation are you thinking!"

"Sorry, Carrie. Gideon is a good man and a good friend."

Her stance softened. "He does seem right nice, and he prays like a good Christian. Heaven knows I got no liking for Gill Harris. But I won't get mixed up with no runaway. You keep them away from here."

Allen convinced a hollow eyed Carrie to get a good night's sleep. He sat by Miss Emma's bedside dozing in a chair. Sometime after midnight, when she threw off the covers, he awakened with a jerk.

"I'm wet as a dishrag," she grumbled.

He felt her brow, and she was covered in sweat. He leaned back in the chair with relief. The fever had broken.

The sun had barely risen when his eyes opened. He stretched in the chair and looked over to find her staring.

"What are you doing in cahoots with a Yankee soldier?" she asked, but without venom.

His eyes widened. "What makes you think—"

"I've got eyes," she said. "I can tell by the way he walks and stands at attention. Besides that, I saw his boots. They're Union Army issue."

Allen grinned. "Glad you and me are on the same side. I wouldn't want you for an enemy."

Her eyes sharpened. "Are we, Allen—on the same side?"

He leaned back and met her eyes for a long moment. "Like you once said, I'm not a talking man. But I'm going to tell you a story that will put your mind at rest about me and Gideon."

She lay still, listening while he told about his friendship with Gideon, about his own rowdy, Irish family, about his decision to become a Rebel scout and spy, about Nelda, about his arrest and escape.

"That's why I intend to help Gideon any way I can," he finished, "and if that makes me a traitor, so be it."

She was quiet. When she finally spoke he was taken aback.

"You love her." It was not a question.

He blinked.

"Does Nelda love you?"

He passed a hand over his face and then gripped them together between his knees and stared at the floor. "No, she doesn't. We're just friends." He drew a deep breath and looked out at the yellow glow reflecting on puffy clouds low on the horizon. "We got nothing in common, not one damned thing. I'm rough as a cob—and I told you about my family. You know Nelda. They don't come any more ladylike."

She gave a faint smile. "That, my dear man, never stopped love."

He gave a half smile. "Guess I didn't mention the fact that she's as loyal as Abe Lincoln and about as well educated. Even the Good Book says something about don't be unequally yoked. I reckon we'd pull in harness about like a show horse and a Billy goat."

"If what you say is true, you'd be right. I see a lot more than that, though. You're no clod. I'd say more a diamond that only needs a little polish. Nelda would be just the one to smooth those rough edges."

He started to rise. She put out her hand and caught his. "Something is eating you alive. Somehow, I don't think its Miss Nelda. Allen, too much drink can make a strong man weak and a wise man foolish. You're too fine for that. If you throw your life away on whisky, you'll never win her."

He snorted. "In that case, I'll be doing her a favor."

He left the cabin, stepping into the warm morning. The air held the promise of a hot, muggy day.

He spent an hour sharpening the ax. Winter would come. Carrie and Isaac would have the devil's own time getting wood with a dull ax and rusty crosscut. Isaac joined him. Allen noted with satisfaction, even without his pa looking on, the boy was a good worker. As fast as Allen trimmed a limb, Isaac dragged it away. By midmorning, they were both soaked with sweat.

Pausing a minute to catch his breath, Allen wiped his brow and listened to crows cawing and the drum of a woodpecker. Below the hill, dark trees and white barked sycamores and a few high clouds reflected in rippling distortion onto green creek water meandering its way to the river. All morning, Nelda had consumed his thoughts. He wondered what was happening in Fort Smith.

"Here's some water."

Allen thanked Isaac, lifted the water jug, and took a long drink. He had left the whisky in the barn—not because of Miss Emma's warning. Once, he had seen an ax head buried in Pa's leg. He would work first and drink later. He cupped his hand and splashed some of the cool wetness on his face and neck.

"I sure liked playing with little Moses," said Isaac wistfully. "Reckon Ma might change her mind—if you was to ask her?"

Allen handed him the jug. "I don't think so."

"Reckon you could help me some with the fiddle after supper?" asked Isaac.

Allen was in no mood to fiddle; however, he felt sorry for the youngster. It must be lonely not having brothers. With the thought, once again, a knife twisted his insides.

"We'll see. You might be too tired to play after this day's work."

"No, sir! I won't be. I'm never too tired to play the fiddle!"

That evening, after supper, Allen was surprised at the boy's progress. Although the notes were uncertain and sometimes squeaked, he recognized the slow hymn "Abide with Me." Isaac's face was screwed up, and his brow glistened from the effort. It was, however, plain to see that he loved playing.

When the tune ended, Isaac flushed from the praise.

"You're doing real good, boy. Better than I figured."

"Ma likes that one," Isaac confided in a low voice. "I ain't much fond of it. I'm more partial to the fast ones...only I can't play any of them yet."

Allen took the fiddle and the bow. "I'll show you one you can work on. He played the melody and then sang out in a fine baritone.

I'm lonesome since I crossed the hill,
And o'er the moorland sedgy
Such heavy thoughts my heart do fill,
Since parting with my Betsey
I seek for one as fair and gay,
But find none to remind me
How sweet the hours I passed away,
With the girl I left behind me.

Isaac clapped. "I like that one!"

Carrie rose from fluffing Miss Emma's pillow. "Now that was a fine tune!"

Even Miss Emma voiced a weak, "Play it again, Allen. A jaunty tune cheers a body."

Allen complied. But he was not cheered. The tune reminded him of Nelda. He would never find a girl who could hold a candle to her.

CHAPTER 9

The next morning Allen sat up on the bedroll, held his head in his hands, and groaned as he squinted at the blaze of sun. A blue jay squawked in the tree overhead. He had overslept. As he pulled on boots, Isaac came from the cabin carrying a water bucket.

"How's Miss Emma?"

"Ma says she's a lot better. She ate a big breakfast. Ma asked if when you woke up you'd mind going into town to see if there's a letter from Pa. She ain't heard in so long. She's mighty worried."

"Sure thing," said Allen. Without even going inside he saddled the sorrel and mounted.

He was glad Miss Emma was gaining. Soon he should be able to take her to her daughter. In the hot sunshine, his thoughts turned to Gideon and Della. She would miss Gideon when he returned to the army today. Allen had promised, as long as he was close by, to keep an eye on Della and the boy. She would have a struggle keeping food on the table.

Ahead, a black-eyed rabbit stopped to stare before hopping from the road. At least Isaac will soon be old enough to hunt, he thought. But it'll be a while before Moses is any help to his ma.

About a mile from town, he tugged the reins. Disheveled and dress torn, Della ran down the trail toward him holding Moses on her hip. The baby wailed with each jostling step. Allen sprang from the horse to catch her as she collapsed, panting.

"Della! What—"

Her eyes were wild. She clutched his arm. "Gideon!" She panted. "Gill Harris is gonna hang him!"

"Where?"

She pointed back down the trail and moaned.

"Get hold of yourself and tell me!" bit out Allen, giving her a shake.

"At the house," she gasped.

Allen sprinted back to the horse and galloped away, lashing the animal with the reins. Dirt flew from the pounding hooves. A covey of startled quails fled with whirring wings.

As he rounded the last curve, he slowed long enough to pull his pistol, but kept it by his side, out of sight.

Horses were tied to the fence. Just outside the fence, near the charred rubble pile of the barn, stood Gill Harris and two men wearing Confederate gray.

From the high limb of a giant oak hung a short length of rope ending in a noose. A body dangled. It was Gideon. No longer handsome, his purple gray face had been beaten to a pulp and was now a death mask of contorted agony.

The men whirled. One was a stranger who did not appear to have a gun. The other was Tucker.

Tucker jerked his gun. A red flash erupted with powder smoke. The shot blended with Allen's, making the two shots one. The shot whirred past Allen's left ear. Behind Tucker, bark flew from the tree.

Gill's eyes widened. His hands dropped to a pistol butt.

Unhurt, Tucker cocked the gun and fired again.

Allen fired. The shot went wide. Low on the sorrel's neck, he kneed the running animal and plunged into the men. Both soldiers were knocked sprawling. Gill, still on his feet, stumbled backwards firing. The shot went wild.

Tucker's gun flew from his hand. In an instant, he rolled over, grabbed the pistol and leveled it at Allen's back. Allen heard the loud cock. A second later a bullet grazed his hat. Allen jerked the reins, turned, and fired. As the horse charged, Tucker got to his knees and raised his arm.

The sorrel stumbled. Tucker's shot had hit its head, spraying blood into the air.

Allen's boots kicked free of the stirrups. He dove off the staggering animal before it collapsed onto the dirt. With a quick roll, he brought the gun up and fired two rapid shots.

Blood flew from Tucker's throat. His gun clattered down onto a rock. His mouth opened, emitting a gurgle of bloody froth.

"Tucker!" screamed Gill. Eyes stunned, he took two steps forward.

Tucker gasped for air and then, with glazed eyes, sank to the ground. Gill's face crumpled with grief.

Allen gave a quick glance at the stranger. The man, who wore no gun, had risen and crouched behind a tree. At the cock of Gill's pistol, Allen turned and fired.

Gill's shot splayed dirt several feet away. Allen pulled back the hammer, but Gill, in a stumbling run, had reached the horses. The three animals, scared by the shots, sidestepped and pulled against the tethers. With a lunge, Gill jerked the reins free and leaped onto the back of a tall gray. Hooves flying, it fled down the road, with Gill lying low on its neck.

Allen spun. He turned the gun on the stranger, but the man's hands were already raised in terrified surrender. "Don't shoot, mister. I swear to God, I had nothing to do with this. I just came riding through and stopped when I saw another man in uniform."

Allen lowered the gun. He let out a held breath. He had fired several times. He thought the chambers were empty. They were. He grabbed up Tucker's gun.

The man wiped a hand over his face. "Gawd, it was awful. That young one beat him and beat him. The darkie kept saying he forgave 'em. That just made the young one, yonder, madder than hell." His face paled again as he glanced at Gideon and shuddered. His voice hushed, and he seemed to be speaking to himself. "I never saw anything like it. Even when they put the rope on his neck, he kept sayin' it."

Allen's jaws tightened as his eyes went to Gideon. He wanted to hunt Gill down and tear his heart out. However, now was not the time. He didn't want Della to witness that battered mess.

He began reloading. "Go tell them at the mercantile that Tucker Harris is dead. If anyone wants, they can come get him. Otherwise, I'm dragging him into that pasture and leaving him to the hogs and buzzards."

The man sprinted to the horse and pounded away. Allen cut Gideon's rope and gently lowered him to the ground. He grimaced. They must have almost killed him before the hanging. He hoped Della did not return until he could wipe the bloody gore from Gideon's face. He stared at Tucker and his lips thinned. He wished he had followed his instincts and killed the bastard months ago. Then Gideon might still be alive

After he drew water from the well, he bent and wiped the battered face. Anger burned in his breast at the injustice. There was, however, a slow creeping sadness pushing it aside. He dreaded the ordeal for Della. With a deep breath, he realized, his promise to Gideon would require much more than an occasional visit to bring food and perhaps cut some wood.

He looked around for a good gravesite. There was a pretty spot on the far side of the pasture under the pines near the creek. Before digging, he would ask Della. He would much prefer to bury Gideon before she saw the beaten body. Ma had wanted to hold Pa's body and say her goodbyes. He figured Della would feel the same, so he lifted him and carried him inside and laid him on the fancy sofa in Nelda's parlor—at least it had been fancy before Bo Morrison and his gang had set the house on fire. Now, that's fitting, thought Allen with a scoff. He'd forgotten that Tucker had been part of that gang.

His eyes traced the room. The red velvet was soot-streaked and dusty now. For a brief second, he recalled the night he had put out the fire and then pulled shards of glass from Nelda's feet. He wished she were here. Della would need a woman's comfort. Carrie was kind-hearted, but she had made it plain; she wanted no involvement here.

The back door burst open. Della, breathless, cried out, "Gideon! Gideon!"

Allen stepped into the hall. Disheveled and stricken, she froze. Her eyes darted toward the parlor.

"I'm sorry…" He stopped. "I was too late."

She sank to the ground and let go of the baby. Moses took a chubby fist from his mouth and began to whimper.

Allen swallowed. "He's in there."

Della stared. Then she gave a loud wail. She bowed, face to the ground, and wailed again and began sobbing. Terrified, Moses took a toddling step and then, wide-eyed, sat down.

Allen waited until she finally rose to her knees. "I killed one of the bastards, Della."

He looked out the back door. Emmitt Gossett and two men stood in the yard staring at Tucker's body. Allen helped Della stand and led her into the parlor. She sank to her knees again alongside the sofa and stroked Gideon's hair. As she wept and moaned, Allen patted her shoulder and then left her alone with her grief. On his way to the door, he stepped around Moses who sat on the floor, crying loudly.

Emmitt looked up. The other two men were unknown to Allen. Both were nervous and kept looking from Allen to the body.

Emmitt's jaws worked. "Damn it, Matthers. Over hanging a darkie?"

"Tucker drew first."

"Yeah, that's how that fellow told it before he high-tailed it out of town." Emmitt shook his head. "Don't know how this will play out, though, with Gill being provost and all. You might be in a heap of trouble."

"Could be," said Allen. "You going to bury him?"

Emmitt took a deep breath. "I'll tote his body over to Whitey Lawrence. He's sort of the town undertaker." Emmitt's big shoulders slumped a bit. "Reckon I'll ride out to Gill's and let him know."

Allen gave a derisive laugh. "He knows."

Emmitt's eyebrows rose. "Was he the other—"

"Yes," said Allen. "This isn't over."

Emmitt nervously shuffled his feet. "No one likes Gill," he said. "They liked Tucker even less. But the Harris's have lived in the county for years. Folks won't take kindly to you killin' him over a darkie—especially since rumor is Gideon had joined the damned Union Army."

Allen gave him a sour look. "Do what you want. I'm going to dig a grave and bury a fine man."

It was mid-afternoon before the grave was dug. Allen leaned on the shovel and stared with dread across the pasture toward the house. Della might be hard to handle. He recalled once helping Pa and Caleb Tanner dig a grave. The grieving neighbor woman hung onto the body of her child until Preacher Simon pried her fingers loose and dragged her from the grave.

In languid heat, twittering birds along the brushy creek bank had stilled. A gray fox stuck his nose from the brambles. Upon seeing the man, it darted back into the thicket.

Allen stood. "Has to be done," he said aloud. His teeth gritted and he muttered, "There's yet Gill to deal with."

All afternoon, he had pressed down rage, black and ugly. His disdain for Gill did not begin today. More than once, Allen had seen Gideon's back split open. Gill was the only man Allen knew who beat his slaves, men and women alike.

Now, because of him, little Moses had no pa. What a struggle Della faced! Every time he envisioned Gideon telling Gill and Tucker he forgave them, Allen's blood boiled. His mind puzzled on the thing—how could a man forgive like that?

With lagging steps, he returned to the house and went inside. He waited a moment, listening. It was still as a tomb. Then from the parlor came the low notes of Della's humming. It was the same tune Gideon had sung a few days ago while helping in the garden—something about heaven and Jesus welcoming his lambs.

Walking softly, Allen stepped through the door. Della sat in a rocking chair drawn close to the sofa. In one arm she held sleeping Moses. The other hand gently smoothed Gideon's hair. She looked up. To Allen's surprise her face was calm.

"You ready?" she asked.

"Yes," he said. "Why don't you stay here until I finish? I'll come get you."

A sob caught in her throat, but she nodded, and left off smoothing the hair. "I got one of Miss Nelda's quilts from upstairs. Don't reckon she'll mind."

"She won't," assured Allen. He lifted the body and the quilt and carried them down the hall and out the door. After wrapping Gideon in the colorful patchwork shroud, he lowered him into the hole and filled it with dark, crumbling earth and wondered how many more graves he would fill. All the while, he was watchful. Gill was a cowardly runt, just the kind to shoot a fellow in the back. On his way to the house, Allen glanced back often at the line of trees rimming the pasture.

He rubbed dirt from his hands onto his pants and then reached for the child.

"Here, let me carry him."

Della stood and followed out the door. They finally stopped alongside the bare mound of soil. A warm breeze stirred the long, yellowed, sage grass beyond. A cardinal trilled and a frog croaked down near the creek. Allen removed his hat and cleared his throat.

"I ain't no preacher, Della. But I know Gideon was a good man and a God-fearing one. Not much doubt Saint Peter will let him right through those pearly gates."

She gave a wan smile. "That man love Jesus." Her face hardened. "I been thinkin' about Mr. Gill and them others." But as she looked at the grave, her eyes grew troubled. She turned away. "If you keep hold of Moses, I'll pick some of them black-eyed Susans and Blazing Stars yonder to put on the grave."

When she returned shortly with a large bunch of wildflowers, Allen studied them. The yellow ones with dark throats were the same as he had put on Seamus's grave. Della bent and laid them on the dirt and then she took Moses.

Allen left her alone at the grave while he returned to the yard. He removed his saddle from the dead sorrel, took the flask from the saddlebag, and took several swallows. Then he got the hangman's rope, and using Tucker's reluctant mare, dragged the dead horse across the pasture and far into the woods. With regret, he gave the animal a final pat. It was a good horse, almost as good as his old sorrel that had been stolen from an army stock pen the second year of the war.

After Della returned to the house, he went inside and stayed with her in the kitchen until the sun was low. He glanced out the window. It was one of the few panes that were not board-covered. Slowly, he pushed back the cup of hot cornbran water.

"You want me to stay?"

"No."

Della kept staring at the wall. He drew a worried breath.

"You gonna be alright?"

She glanced up. "Yes," she said, listless. "Sure hope Miss Emma doin' better."

With a troubled look, he left her staring once again at the bare kitchen wall. He mounted Tucker's brown mare, took another pull on the flask, put it inside his shirt, and started down the wagon road. It was striped now with long, blue shadows. His eyes made vigilant sweeps of the woods bordering the trail. When a rabbit darted from the road ahead, the mare made a skittish sidestep. Allen frowned. He hated a skittish horse. As soon as possible, he'd get a different mount. But one like the sorrel would be hard to find. Emmitt had a big bay he might trade for.

Before dropping into the shadowy ravine, Allen stopped to study the terrain and to listen. Except for the shrill noise of insects and the distant murmur of the creek, he heard nothing. He rode on. Near the creek, each hoof print in the sand quickly filled with water and each step made a sucking sound. His nose flared at the dank odor of rotten fish. The decomposing carcass of a carp lay near long-stem ferns at the water's edge.

He rode forward but stopped to study the far rocky bluff. Stunted elms and willows dotted the ledges and a few scrubby cedars clung stubbornly to the crevices. On the hill above the rocks, the timber thickened. Slowly, Allen guided the mare into the shallow water and kneed her into the deeper pool. She balked, although the green pool was not chest high.

A red flash pierced the high rim. Almost simultaneously, another followed. The horse screamed and reared. Allen dove off, hitting the water. The shots had narrowly missed him and grazed the mare's left shoulder. The horse ran wildly down the trail, taking his rifle along.

Without standing, he floundered to the far bank and hugged the bluff. He left the pistol sheathed. It would do him no good. Both it and the spare cylinders in his pocket were soaked. The wet cartridges would not fire. His eyes narrowed with contemplation. There had been two simultaneous blasts—he figured Gill and at least one more shooter. They had him pinned down. The last thing they would expect was an assault. Nearby, a little dirt crumbled from the ridge.

Allen pulled a short bladed knife from his boot and held it with his teeth as he scrambled up the rough ledge. His wet boot slipped on the rock, but he grabbed handholds of willow and cedar and quickly scaled the rim. Eyes wide and terrified, Gill stood a few feet away. The powder horn in his trembling hands fell to the ground as he turned and fled.

A tall slender man with a pock-marked face stood nearby trying to reload. It was Drake Arden, Gill's overseer. With cold hard eyes, he raised the rifle butt like a club, stood, and watched Allen come. Allen jerked it away. In one swift motion, the knife plunged into Drake's abdomen. He gasped. The blade slashed upward and blood splayed onto his coarse, butternut shirt. Allen pulled out the knife. With a guttural moan, Drake sank to his knees and fell face forward.

Without slowing Allen whirled and started after Gill. Before Gill had gone another rod, Allen caught him. Holding Drake's rifle by the barrel, he slammed it between Gill's shoulder blades. The blow sent Gill and his rifle sprawling. On all fours, he scrambled to escape. Allen raised the gunstock. He remembered Gideon's bludgeoned face. In blinding rage, reason fled. Again and again, he bashed Gill's back and head. Then he rolled him over and smashed the barrel into the narrow face. Through shattered teeth and blood, Gill cried out, begging for mercy. Allen was deaf to pleas.

All the months of suspicion, sorrow, frustration, and anger exploded in his brain. He pounded Gill's face and body again and again. Allen's breath came in pants as he jerked Gill up and slammed him into the jagged boulders. The cries turned to whimpers. Gill fell again, and as Allen kicked him with heavy wet boots, even the whimpers ceased. The bloody visage bore no resemblance to man. Arms and legs dangled, broken and useless. Allen grabbed him by the hair and dragged him to the rim's edge. With a big heave, he hurled the body from the cliff and watched it land in the water with a mighty splash.

Half in the water and half out, Gill's body wedged on a log lying at the pool's edge, where it rocked gently in the slow flowing water. Allen sank on the rocky lip and stared.

He wiped a shaking hand across his sweaty face and then grimaced. His hands were wet, covered with Gill's blood. His eyes never left the body as he wiped them on a clump of tall grass growing near his knee. With a shudder, he expelled a long breath.

"My Gawd!" he whispered. "What's happened to me?"

He had killed before. That did not bother him. In this war, he had beaten men with his fists—but never like this. He had never taken part in cruel torture. It sickened him. As he gazed at the dark lump wedged against the log, his senses rebelled that he had been the maniac that had brutalized it.

Stunned, he scooted back from the rim, leaned against a rock, and dropped his head forward. He sat like a statue as dusk came slowly on. When a whippoorwill called, he raised his head. The sun had sunk from sight. Down the creek, bats circled in the pink streaked dusk. They lowered below the clouds and then disappeared.

He drew the flask from his shirt and took off the lid. It was half way to his lips when he froze. His gaze riveted on the lump of wet flesh still jammed by the log. He eyed the cold metal flask, and with a mighty fling, hurled it. It clattered on the rocks and splashed into the creek.

CHAPTER 10 ✎

"You wanted to see me, sir?" Nelda stood in a pool of sunlight coming through Reverend Springer's office window.

He took off his spectacles, laid them on the desk, and rocked back in his chair. "Miss Horton, first let me say, you've done a marvelous job with the orphans. Widow Turnbo tells me several of the children have formed a great attachment to you."

Sweet, little Sarah Campbell did cling like a burr. Tiny Susan was never satisfied unless sitting on Nelda's lap or perched on her hip. William was not as demonstrative, but he did listen attentively to all she said, and he was never far away when she needed him. Nelda waited. She knew Francis Springer well enough by now to know he had not called her here on a busy Monday morning to pay compliments.

"Uph…" He cleared this throat and went on, "As you well know, the situation here for the children is growing dire. Supply trains are having the devil's own time getting through, and there's no reason to believe it will improve any time soon. I can't in good conscience put them on the latest wagon train getting ready to head north. There are already fifteen hundred refugees in that train without enough food to last a week. However, General Thayer plans to start a heavily armed troop to Little Rock soon with a few empty wagons. I suggested he send as many of the children as possible. From Little Rock, they can be sent by steamship on to Saint Louis or some safe destination."

Nelda hated to think of the children being sent so far away. It was, however, better than starving. "I suppose that's the only thing to do," she reluctantly agreed.

"Yes," he said brusquely. "They will need supervision."

Nelda arched an eyebrow.

He went on, "You, of course, are the logical choice. I told the general I was sure you'd be glad to assist."

She was not glad. It was not what she wanted! Of course, she was the logical choice. Elsie Turnbo was approaching sixty, and the trip would be strenuous.

Her shoulders sagged. "When will we leave?" She capitulated. "How many children will be going?"

"I'll find out the details and let you know. General Thayer did mention he hoped to start them before the week is out."

Nelda drew a deep breath and turned.

"Miss Horton."

She turned back.

"Thank you," he said. "I know the past week has not been easy. I do appreciate your efforts."

She dipped her head in acknowledgement and stepped outside to face the dusty bustle of Garrison Avenue. Every day, more ragged wagons filled with gaunt-faced refugees streamed into the fort. She waited for just such a pitiful cavalcade to pass, and then she crossed the street and headed for the warehouse stuffed with the orphans that had consumed her time.

Reverend Springer was correct. The past week had been difficult, sleeping on a cot and rousing constantly to allay fears and shush crying—washing, ironing, cooking, cleaning, sewing, and doctoring scrapes and bruises. However, that had not been the hardest part. Her heart was heavy. She grieved over Seamus. Her cheeks warmed as she silently admitted that Allen was the real burden.

"Miss Nelda, wait up." Captain Daniel Tory hurried down the sidewalk. "I've been meaning to find you," he said. Suddenly he seemed at a loss for words. He removed his gloves and twisted them in his hands.

"What is it, Captain?"

He drew a deep breath and let it out slowly. "It may be nothing..."

"Go on," she urged.

"I heard some talk the other day." He looked at her and then dropped his eyes to the gloves. "I remembered that question you asked me about the man with red hair."

Nelda's heart squeezed. It seemed an eternity before he continued.

"Some fellows were talking about a strange thing that happened the day Seamus was killed. They said a giant of a man—a Reb not in uniform—picked up one of our dead and toted him away. The way they told it, both men were huge and had red hair. One must have been Seamus."

Nelda sucked in a breath. Tears sprang to her eyes. She put a hand on the brick wall to steady herself.

Daniel took her arm. "Are you alright? Do you need to sit down?"

"No. I'm fine." She wiped tears with her fingers. "The other man was Seamus's brother."

"That's what the fellows speculated. Tragic," said Daniel, slowly shaking his head. "I'm so sorry, ma'am." He offered his arm. "May I escort you somewhere?"

"Thank you, but no, Captain. I appreciate your kindness. Thank you for telling me." She wanted to be alone. She brushed past him and hurried on, stifling a sob.

Poor Allen. What heartbreak to find Seamus dead on the battlefield!

Her steps turned from their course. She could not face the room full of children—not yet. Instead, she walked to the boarding house. It was unlocked and just the way Mrs. Hanover had left it. Nelda entered her room. She went to the window and touched the pane. Allen had stood just there the last time she'd seen him. She threw herself onto the soft bed and sobbed.

Sarah was inconsolable. Nelda bent and took the trembling chin into her hands. She smoothed dark hair off the delicate forehead.

"I should only be gone a few weeks. Mrs. Turnbo will be right here with you, night and day. Sarah, honey, the colonel is right—your sister might come looking for you. Wouldn't it be awful if she came and you were gone? Besides, after we get to Little Rock, these children will go on somewhere else."

Both William and Sarah, along with seven more youngsters, were staying at the fort. They were the ones who had family in the area. The relatives had not yet been located, but the colonel had sent out inquires.

"When I get back, I'm going to make sure you get a new dress. You'd like that, wouldn't you?"

Sarah looked down at the ugly brocade. She fingered the mother-of-pearl buttons. "After I c-came here, my d-dress got c-caught on a nail and ripped. They gave me this one. It was in the m-missionary b-barrel. That lady told me it was way too b-big for me." She looked up. "But these b-buttons are awful p-pretty, so I asked c-could she make it fit."

Nelda instantly repented the uncharitable feelings she had harbored for whoever put the child into the hideous rag.

"We can sew those buttons onto a new dress."

Sarah's face momentarily brightened.

William stood in the open door. "The wagons are loaded. Sergeant Mac says he's ready to roll."

"Thank you, William. Tell him I'll be right out." Nelda kissed the top of Sarah's head, picked up baby Susan, and gave an exasperated sigh. The child was wet again. She picked up the valise and started for the door. She'd change the diaper in the wagon.

Elsie Turnbo met her on the sidewalk. On her face was a concerned frown. "They're all loaded—some in each wagon. That's a lot for you to see after alone, Miss Nelda."

Nelda heartily agreed. Twenty children would be a handful.

Elise cut worried eyes at the two ragged, canvas-topped wagons and the line of two dozen, mounted men. "I supposed the soldiers will give you a hand. But men ain't usually much good with young ones."

A bearded sergeant with bright blue eyes and a ready laugh leaned from the wagon seat. He reached for the baby. "Come on up here, little one. Old Uncle Mac will teach ya how to drive a cantankerous team of hard-mouthed army mules."

William took the valise and held it while Nelda stepped onto the wheel spokes and then onto the high wagon seat. Charles' blond head appeared at the hoop of canvas opening. He reached for his sister. "I'll take her," he said possessively. "She's my sister."

Mac handed her over with a grin. He spoke low to Nelda. "Now I like that. Little man is watching out for his sister."

"He worships her," agreed Nelda in a whisper. "I pray they're never separated. It would break his heart."

She looked inside. On the bench along one side sat the Bradford twins and Emily Bodkins. Sandwiched between were the three Herman children. Their faces had been repeatedly scrubbed with many good washings; nevertheless, the sallow skin retained a dull, dirty cast. The other bench held the four Gilberts, pudgy Henry Jordon, and Charles with Susan on his lap. Piled on the floor between were barrels and boxes and a few wicker hampers of food brought just that morning by Reverend Springer.

"Everyone ready?" She hoped there were no last minute trips to the outhouse. They had already delayed the train past the scheduled leaving, and the bronze-faced second lieutenant commanding the troop was scowling.

Nelda shooed a fat green fly from buzzing in her face and then braced against the hard seat as the sergeant started the four brown mules with a slap of reins. She had chosen the unenviable position of riding in the last wagon and eating constant dust. However, it was customary for a child to hop down, head for the bushes, and then run to catch up. Although she had assigned each little one an older helper, she intended keeping sharp eyes to make certain no one was left behind.

As the secure walls of Fort Smith disappeared and the brick and board buildings of town fell behind, they entered a wide road, faced into the morning sun, and spread out the distance between the wagons. Dust still rose in waves to settle on Nelda's skin and dark brown dress and to lodge as grit in her mouth and nose.

"Will we cross the river?" she asked, seeing a blue shimmer in the distance.

Sergeant Mac, arms resting on muscled legs and reins held slack in brown, callused hands, paused to spit over the wagon box. He wiped his mouth and answered, "We'll stay south of the river—unless we run into trouble. The road over there is better, but one of our scouts reported a big party of Rebs on the other side yesterday." He cocked an eyebrow. "'Course that don't mean they aren't on this side now."

Nelda was disappointed. She had hoped to stop by the house and check on Lily—if the Hadley boy had been able to keep the mare from being stolen. The horse was the only living thing left in Clarksville that she cherished. More than likely, Pa's old hound, Sirius, was dead by now. He had been decrepit with old age two years ago.

She looked ahead and frowned. More than a score of armed men should be reassuring. But they wouldn't count for much if a Rebel force was large.

"How long will it take us to get to Little Rock?"

His face screwed up in thought. He rubbed his beaded chin. "Once I was with a fast-traveling patrol that made it from here to there in three days—but we were on yon side of the river on the good road and without wagons and bony mules to slow us." His eyes twinkled. "And no women and children." The pipe stem held in his teeth shifted. "I figure it'll take at least four times that and maybe more."

One look at the lieutenant's rigid back made Nelda dread the idea of slowing him even more.

They passed empty dwellings and burned houses with stark chimneys left standing. Broad fields, un-furrowed by plow, were carpeted with tall grass and stubble. The only creatures encountered all morning were a few white tailed deer, a skulking coyote, and a black snake that slithered away as they rolled into sight. As the sun rose higher, Nelda pulled at the high neck of the long-sleeved dress and wished for sundown. The children, somewhat awed by the escort and the trip, had talked in subdued tones. Now, amid Susan's whimpers, an argument arose between the boys. Nelda turned.

"Charles, let me hold the baby. I want you and Henry and Toby to get out and walk for a while. Stay close where I can see you."

The boys gladly clamored down. Soon, two boys from the forward wagon joined them. Nelda had forgotten the short one's name, but she thought the tall boy with the limp was Mark.

The stop under the shade of tall cottonwoods at noon was brief. The men ate quickly and washed down hardtack and canned beef with water from canteens. Nelda passed out cornbread and fried salt pork to the children. Their faces fell. It was the same rations they had had for days. There were cans of beans and of beef in the baskets. She was saving those for later when the pork and bread ran out.

Uneventful, the day finally passed. Sergeant Mac kept up constant, lively conversation. He was from Kansas. According to him, the lieutenant, also from Kansas, had little use for Missouri Federal troops, and even less for the ones from Arkansas.

"I don't think much of this Arkansas country, myself. I have to admit, though, I've not seen it under the best of circumstances. Most of the time, I've marched through rain and swamp and cold and heat without enough rations. After a long draw on the pipe, he pointed the pipe stem at the lieutenant. "All the while, I've served under him. He's a fine man, the lieutenant is—no matter what has been said about him."

Nelda wondered what had been said, and she wondered what made the man so dour. At the noon stop, he had not spoken a word to her and hardly a word to any of his men.

"Have there been bad things said?"

Sergeant Mac gave a nod as he looked ahead through a cloud of blue smoke. "Aye. He was accused of mishandling the J. R. Williams affair. But according to my lights, he did the only thing he could. We couldn't retake the boat. There were just too many Rebs and savages."

Nelda had heard of the steamboat full of supplies headed for Fort Gibson in the Indian Territory that was captured by the Rebels back in June. As she recalled, General Thayer had made accusations that one officer had abandoned his post. That must have been the lieutenant.

The sergeant's mouth drew down. "But the general thought otherwise. That's why we get the worst mules, the worst wagons, and the worst details—begging your pardon, ma'am."

Nelda didn't suppose being bodyguard to a bunch of orphans was an enviable detail. She hadn't been thrilled with the prospect herself.

They pressed on until late afternoon. Nelda climbed down, stiff and sore. She dreaded the days ahead of swaying, jarring travel. But nights were almost worse with a bedroll on hard ground surrounded by restless children and feasting mosquitoes. Soon, there were dark circles under her eyes, and in spite of the jostling seat, she developed the tendency to doze in the long afternoons.

The third day, Sergeant Mac pointed to a spot alongside the road. "A terrible deed happened right over there," he said and then as Nelda waited expectantly, he looked as though he regretted speaking.

"Well, what was it, Sergeant?"

He lowered his voice so the children would not overhear. "There's a settlement ahead, name of Roseville."

Nelda nodded. She knew Roseville well. It was only a few miles upriver from Clarksville.

He went on, "We had a small post there that came under attack a while back. Colonel Judson sent a surgeon from the fort and a detail of twenty-five men to tend the wounded."

The sergeant stopped. His eyes grew haunted ,and Nelda thought he shuddered.

"I was with the detail sent to bury them. They had been set upon by the Rebs and hacked to pieces." His jaws hardened. "It wasn't guerrillas."

Nelda's eyes widened. "Regular army? Are you sure?"

"Tracks showed a big force—at least two hundred." He nodded toward the lieutenant. "He was head of the burying detail. None of us ate for days."

Nelda bit her lip. Perhaps the lieutenant had reason to be grim. He had endured some hard things.

Although the miles passed under the creaking wheels, the ill-fed mules set a slow pace. The horses appeared in slightly better shape but they too slowed to keep pace with the decrepit mules. In the simmering heat through the long afternoon, the languid animals plodded even slower.

The wagon lurched as a wheel hit a chug hole. Nelda's head jerked up as she awakened from the light doze. In a sleepy stupor, she heard the twittering whistle of a wood thrush, and as she breathed in the sweet scent of honeysuckle, she heard the gurgle of a creek. They crossed the narrow stream. Mark hopped from the forward wagon just as the lieutenant raised a hand and called a halt. A felled tree blocked the road ahead.

Suddenly, a shot pierced the stillness. "Throw down the weapons, Lieutenant. You're outnumbered." The command came from dense brush alongside the road.

For an instant Mark froze. Then in a running limp he returned to the wagon and dove inside.

The lieutenant, with rifle pointed, hesitated.

"Don't be a fool. You're surrounded and you have civilians along. Throw those guns far away and step down."

Nelda sat straighter on the seat. The lieutenant glared, but threw the rifle onto the ground.

"Do as he says, men."

Fear traced Nelda's spine as she thought of the massacre. This might be the same group of ruthless men. She turned and spoke quickly, "Stay where you are, children."

Rifles and pistols landed in the dirt. Nelda and the sergeant climbed down. The lieutenant's men dismounted. A few gray-coated, armed men stepped from hiding to prod Nelda and the soldiers into a group. Two men held guns on them while the others approached the wagons.

"Good Gawd, Cap'in! This wagon's full of young'uns!"

"What?" A tall man, rifle ready, stepped from the bushes. He was closely followed by at least forty more armed men stepping from the undergrowth into the trail.

An older man with grizzled hair and beard gave a short laugh. "This here wagon, too. Plum full of 'em. Ain't exactly a mother-load of supplies or ordnance, is it?"

The captain's mouth turned down. He was a fine looking man— dark hair and eyes, about mid-thirties. Nelda thought she had seen him before but just where eluded her now.

"No, Levi, not exactly." He walked toward a wagon and looked inside. "Damn!" he muttered. He holstered his pistol, turned on his heel, and approached the lieutenant.

"You have a rather large family," he said with an eyebrow quirked.

"Orphans we're escorting to Little Rock," answered the lieutenant with a snarl. "Do you intend hacking us all to pieces? That seems to be customary for your army these days."

The captain crossed his arms and stared. "I have no such intention. But I might pistol whip a jackass Yankee lieutenant."

"Cap'in," called Levi, "lookie here. This little 'un's cute as a button."

"Don't you touch my sister!" Charles jumped from the wagon and stood on the ground, glowering.

The captain glanced over his shoulder. "Levi, put that child down."

Susan, however, seemed taken with Levi. She patted his face. He laughed and handed her to Charles.

"Young'uns and dogs—they all love me." He joined the handsome captain. "What ya wanna do, now?

The captain glanced around. "I suppose we'll let them go on their way." He tipped his hat to Nelda. "Ma'am. God bless you for looking after all these children." He stared back at the lieutenant and scowled.

"Rest assured. If it weren't for these children, you and all your men would be dead."

Levi smirked. "Now that's gospel. I had you in my rifle site with my finger on the trigger when that young'un hopped out of the wagon."

The lieutenant looked unperturbed, but Sergeant Mac swore under his breath. Levi called to the retreating captain.

"We gonna let 'em keep their guns?"

"Gather them up. We'll drop them in the trail a ways ahead. They'll need them to protect the children."

Nelda let out a deep breath and wiped sweaty palms on her skirt. For the time being, disaster had been averted.

Mac knocked old tobacco from his pipe and began refilling it while he looked at the lieutenant. "That was a close shave."

The remaining journey was uneventful. They encountered no more patrols. Nelda wondered if perhaps the Rebel captain had sent word ahead to allow them unmolested passage. A week later, she finally espied Little Rock, at first from trails of smoke in an evening sky awash with rose and pink. Then came the smattering of buildings on the outskirts of town where the smells of cooking mingled with the odor of smoke.

The sight of the city stirred memories. There were good times spent here with Papa before the war. But the overriding recollection made her stomach queasy. The last time she had seen Papa, he had been a prisoner here. Here was where the rebels had hanged him as a traitor. She wanted away from this place as soon as possible.

Nelda located the correct address of the stately white house fronted by a massive front porch and balcony supported by tall white columns. With great relief—tinged with a moment of regret as she kissed Susan—she turned the children over to two Negro women and a broad-hipped matron who hugged and coddled them as if they were her own grandchildren.

Only Charles ran after her down the sidewalk to tell her goodbye. She kissed his forehead.

"You're a fine young man. I hope you'll take advantage of every opportunity to get a good education and study hard. I know you'll take good care of Susan."

"Don't reckon I'll ever see you again," he said wistfully

She blinked away tears and smiled. "You never know." She kissed him again and hurried down the walk without looking back.

"Lieutenant, what are the chances we could return on the road north of the river?" asked Nelda. "If possible, I would like to go through Clarksville." She had decided to dig up the rest of the money buried under the flagstone near the flowerbed. She intended to buy Sarah some decent clothes. There would be some left over to help the other orphans.

When he gave a surly look, she thought the chances slim indeed. However, he pursed his lips and nodded. "We may as well. Either side seems equally lousy with Rebel patrols."

They left early the next morning, leaving the tired mules and wagons behind. Mac had picked a good gaited horse for Nelda and another for himself. They rode fast and bypassed settlements. A recurring stitch in Nelda's side made the ride miserable. They ate at noon without making a fire. In less than twenty minutes, they had finished the hardtack and salt pork and were back in the creaking saddles. By the end of the day, she was as dirty and drooping as the dust-covered foliage. It took gritted teeth to dismount. After a night's sleep on hard ground, she faced the day with aches and pains and dread.

On the third day, they crossed the Illinois Bayou with white water foaming over slick rocks, and, in a few hours, they came to the east hill overlooking Clarksville. An uneasy feeling pressed down on Nelda as she stared across the long, covered bridge spanning Spadra Creek toward the red brick buildings baking in the noonday sun. "Look sharp, men," ordered the lieutenant. "We've no post here now. Neither do the Rebels, but there's plenty of them here and maybe even some patrols riding through."

The men tensed and sat up straighter. At a brisk trot they crossed the bridge. Nelda and Mac brought up the rear. The streets fronting vacant stores were empty—nothing stirred amidst the shabby buildings. It made a pang in her breast to see the town as neglected as a stray dog left to fend for itself. She wondered if things would ever prosper again.

Then her eyes widened. The courthouse was blackened with only two walls unharmed. Fire had taken a toll on several structures. Her mouth turned down as it always did when she saw Papa's old building, the windows board-covered and dusty. At least it was unharmed by the fire.

The lieutenant halted in front of the mercantile. He waited to dismount until she had come abreast. His eyes traced the streets and then rose for a quick scan of upper story windows.

"This town makes my flesh crawl. I wouldn't be surprised at a pot-shot any minute. Miss Horton, we'll wait here twenty minutes. If you aren't back we'll leave without you."

"I'll hurry," she assured, turning the horse. She thought about going to the Hadley shack first but changed her mind. If there was time, she would go see David and thank him for caring for her horse in her absence. First, she would dig up the money and then search for Lily in the woods near the pasture.

After rounding the courthouse, she abruptly pulled the horse to a stop. She pressed lips together to still the trembling. The little, white Methodist Church was a charred skeleton, the bell tower a blackened ruin. Someone must have torched the town, setting fires at different locations. The burned buildings were random and not abutting. She wondered who had done it—and she wondered if her house still stood. Spurring the horse forward, she left town at a fast cantor, sending dust flying.

Almost holding her breath the whole way, her eyes pierced leafy walnuts and oaks, desperate for a glimpse of the tall chimney and upper story. As trees flew by, she prayed. In one sense, home was no more— everyone she loved was gone. But the dwelling still meant much. She had no idea how much until now.

A ragged sob caught in her throat, and she uttered a glad cry. It was there! Through the green boughs flashed patches of light, reflections from her bedroom window in the second story of the tall house. Home! She wanted to throw open her arms and hug it. Without slowing, she loped the horse all the way to the fence and bounded off onto the ground. For a long moment, she held the reins and stared.

The paint had peeled, and the boarded windows were a sad reminder of evil times. But the sturdy walls and chimneys were strong and solid, as if awaiting happy times again someday.

She sucked in a shocked breath when the front door opened. Della stepped onto the porch and in her arms was a beautiful, bright-eyed boy.

"Della," she cried and ran forward. "What are you doing here?" She embraced the thin, calico-covered shoulders, drew back, and caressed the child's face. "What a handsome child! I knew you and Gideon would have a beautiful—" Joy faded from her voice. "What's wrong?"

Della's eyes were hollow and pained. "Gideon's dead."

"Oh no!" Nelda gripped her arm. "Tell me what happened."

"Mr. Gill Harris and that boy of his hung him." Unseeing, Della stared into the distance. Tears ran down her face.

Nelda groaned. "Why did you and Gideon come back? Surely Gideon knew how dangerous it was!"

Della made a scoffing noise. "He knew. He knew Mr. Gill, all right, and he knew that no account Tucker, too. But I was here with the baby, and he wanted to see us. He had done sent me back here. Helena was awful—you remember how it was. He didn't want me and the baby gettin' sick. Lots of folks dyin' all the time. Back then, the army had done set up a post here. He reckoned I'd be safe. I figured to take in washing and maybe do some cooking for the soldiers. I did for a spell, until they up and pulled out."

Nelda interrupted. "I saw the burned buildings. Was there a battle?"

"Yes 'um. They's been a few fights. But that ain't what burned the buildings. Folks says the Union soldiers done set stuff a'fire to keep them Rebels from gettin' supplies here."

"Tell me about Gideon," prompted Nelda gently.

Della's face crumpled, and she wept great ragged sobs. Through tears and sobs, she stammered out details of the hanging and how she had tried to run for help.

"Then Mr. Allen—"

Nelda's head snapped up. "Allen! Is he here?"

"Yes, 'um. He's staying a ways out of town at that rebel woman's cabin."

Nelda's stomach tightened. She fought to keep her face expressionless.

"Him and some sick woman is both there. I heard them talk. He brung her from Fort Smith, but she took sick on the way. I helped nurse her for a few days until Gideon come, and then Miss Carrie got scared she'd get in trouble. She knowed Gideon had run off from Mr. Gill."

So Allen was here, and apparently so was Mrs. Hanover!

"I prayed you'd come back, Miss Nelda. I don't know what to do. I got no money. No one will let me work. The onliest food we got is what my friends and Mr. Allen brings us."

"I guess everyone is afraid of Gill," said Nelda.

Della gave a dry laugh. "Not no more they ain't—nor of Mr. Tucker neither. I seen Mr. Tucker dead on the ground right yonder under that tree. Mr. Allen shot him." Her lips quivered. "But they had done killed my Gideon."

"What about Gill?"

Della's face hardened. "He dead and good riddance! Few days ago, some menfolk found him and that wicked overseer beat plum to death down yonder by the creek." She drew a ragged desolate breath. "Don't know how we'd manage without Mr. Allen. I ain't been able to find no payin' work. He brings squirrels and rabbits and birds and some garden truck."

Nelda's mind raced. Allen was still around. She would stay, at least until she had seen him. She must tell him how sorry she was about Seamus, and how much she appreciated all he had done for Della.

"Della, do you know if Lily is still hidden in the woods?"

"Far as I know. That Hadley boy come sometimes. He don't stop by the house, but I see him cutting across the field carryin' a bucket."

"Good," said Nelda. "I have to go back to town. I won't be gone long. If Allen should come while I'm gone tell him to wait."

Nelda mounted the borrowed horse and headed for town. She was grief-stricken for Della, and yet she could not deny the joyous beat of heart. Allen! No matter what, it would be good to see him.

Nelda crossed the field and then shaded her eyes with one hand and raised the other to wave at David. She hurried to where he stood waiting on the far side of the pasture.

"Hello, David."

"Howdy, Miz Nelda." He flashed a quick grin. He had grown taller and was still a handsome, smooth-faced boy, but his cheeks were too hollow, and the long legs and arms were too thin.

"How are you, David? And how's your grandfather?"

"I'm tolerable," he said. He swallowed before adding, "Grandpa is dead."

"I'm so sorry." Her eyes went quickly over his scrawny frame. "Are you living alone now?"

"Yes, 'um. I come every day and move Lily around." He stared at the ground. "Miz Nelda, your old hound is dead, too. He died along about the same time as Grandpa. I buried 'em right close to each other."

Nelda's hand went to her throat. She turned away and stared back at the tall white house bathed in afternoon sun. It was silly to cry over an old hound. Sirius, until he had grown too old, had been Papa's shadow. Losing him was like losing a little bit of Papa all over again. She sniffed and wiped at her eyes.

"I took as good a ker of him as I could." David's voice was troubled.

Nelda quickly turned back and put an arm around his shoulder. "Oh, David, I know you did. He was just too old. I can't thank you enough for seeing after him and Jepner and Lily. How is Lily?"

"She's doing good. I was just on my way to move the picket rope. I keep her tied or someone is bound to steal her. I bring grain when I can—which ain't often," he admitted. "But she ain't in too bad a shape, just a mite on the thin side. Old Jepner is thin as a rail, but that mule is just as ornery as ever."

Nelda fell into step alongside him. Yellow and green grasshoppers leaped away to settle again in the tall, yellowed, sage grass that had crowded out the good grasses that used to flourish here. The sun baked pasture was hot, but as soon as they entered the trees near the gurgling creek, the air grew pleasant. Nelda heard a loud neigh.

In a grassy opening near the fence, the white mare, ears pointed forward, strained against the rope. Her head bobbed and she whinnied.

David laughed. "She's glad you're back. She never acts like that when I come—not even when I'm toting grain."

Nelda rushed forward to throw her arms around the graceful arched neck. She buried her face in the long mane and let the tears flow. When the mare turned her head to nuzzle her, Nelda laughed through the tears. "Lily, I missed you, too, girl!" She turned to David. "She looks wonderful. I can't thank you enough."

"Reckon now that you're back you won't need me to tend her no more."

"I'm not sure how long I'll be here. I'll let you know. In the mean time, come to the house with me. Della is making supper, and I want to pay you for all you've done."

"Aw, you don't owe me no money. It weren't no trouble a'tall." He patted the mare's shoulder. "She's a fine animal, and I liked caring for her."

Nelda didn't argue. But she would pay him—and she'd insist he eat a few good meals, too.

It was late the next afternoon before Allen arrived. Nelda saw him through the kitchen window as he rounded the house, coming to the kitchen door. Her heartbeat quickened as she reached to smooth her hair and then pulled open the door at his rap.

"Nelda!"

Allen's eyes widened, but no more than her own. He had the same wide shoulders and powerful build, but the drawn face and dull eyes bore scant resemblance to the jovial man she knew.

Momentarily, his blue eyes brightened. "What are you doing here?"

"I traveled with an escort from the fort to take some orphans to Little Rock. On the way back, I stopped off here and found Della." Her voice broke. "Oh, Allen, I'm heart-broken about Gideon." She rested a hand on his arm. "About Seamus, too."

He stiffened, his face granite. He handed her a basket heaped with okra and purple hull peas, and then held up two plump quails. "I need to tend to these."

When he turned away, she bit her lip. Her hands trembled as she put the basket on the table. Although she knew he didn't want to talk, she had to let him know she shared his pain.

He paused, turned back, and said, "Come with me while I dress 'em. Better bring along a bowl."

As he walked to the well, he asked, "So, how are you?"

"Me...I'm fine—other than being sore in every joint and muscle. I haven't ached like this since we made our long ride together. Remember how stiff I got?"

He stopped and met her eyes. "I remember everything about that trip."

She glanced away from the tender look. But she knew his probing gaze held. She relaxed only after he began walking again.

"So how does one clean a quail?"

"Nothing to it," he said while he moved aside the well cover and let the wooden bucket descend. The squeaking pulley echoed in the silence. There was so much Nelda wanted to say, and yet, she stayed mute, wondering where to begin.

"First," said Allen, "you cut off the head, wings, and feet, like this." Using the dull side of the knife blade, he first cracked the bones and then with the sharp edge, he made quick work of the task. After putting the knife down on the rock ledge, he used strong fingers to part the tender skin in the middle. His movements were smooth and decisive—and as she had noticed before—without wasted motion. "Then you pull down and strip off the skin, sort of like a fellow shucking his clothes." When he pulled downward, the skin slipped off the breast and then the legs. "I used to ask Pa why they called it dressing game instead of undressing it."

She gave a brief smile. "That looks easier than plucking a chicken. We never skinned them; Mama wanted them dipped in scalding water, plucked, and then singed to get off every last speck of feathers." Her eyes grew sad. "Before the bushwhackers took every living thing, we had a big flock of leghorns and all kinds of bantams. I loved the chickens, but I hated the butchering. Sometimes, I managed to get out of it—but never the cooking. Mama claimed I was a better hand at frying than she was."

He stopped and looked up. "I thought you couldn't cook."

"Oh, I cook," she said with a chuckle. "When I told you I couldn't, I was jesting. Actually, I'm a good cook. You know how particular Mama was about everything. She made certain I mastered all the housewifery skills."

"Well, I'll be damned," he muttered and then turned the bird over and proceeded to strip the skin off from the neck to the tail. He picked up the knife again, cut off the tail knob and then he held the legs, pulled the breast forward and removed the entrails. After he had tossed the refuse over the fence, he eyed the small fowl as he washed it in the pan of water. "When you get one dressed, there's not much left. If I'd known you were here I'd have shot a few more."

A small breeze had sprung up, stirring the sharp scent of marigolds in the flowerbed. It ruffled Allen's hatless hair and the shirt un-tucked at his waist. It hurt her to see how much he had aged. Unless he was smiling, his face was haggard. There were even a few gray hairs at his temple. He turned and caught her staring. Their eyes held. She was the first to look away.

As he proceeded to clean the second bird, in the silence that stretched, she sat down on the ledge and brushed at imaginary lint on the brown skirt. "It was tragic about Gideon," she said. "Della is sick with grief." She eyed him before adding, "She says something happened to Gill Harris." Nelda wondered if Allen had killed him.

His knife stilled. "A man reaps what he sows." Then his eyes shadowed and grew far seeing. He muttered, "I sure ain't looking forward to all of my crops."

Nelda arched her brows, instantly haunted by visions of Mary Beth and Tabbatha Morrison as she slammed the door in their faces. "Me neither." She rubbed at a sudden chill lacing her arms. "I suppose there are still some people in this town who would like to help the Almighty mete out my justice. Gill was one of them. He hated me for my Union sympathies."

He faced her. "It still isn't safe for you here. Folks hate Yankees worse than ever. Those bastard soldiers have done some wicked things."

"Well, they're not the only ones!" she shot out. She stopped cold when she noticed the tiny grin. She drew a deep breath and then let it out. "There I go again."

Allen faked a strong brogue. "That, me love, is the Nelda I know and love."

Her mouth opened and closed.

He chuckled. "What are you going to do now?"

"I'm really not sure. I know Della needs me. But so do the orphans. Especially one little girl named Sarah Campbell—"

"What?" His eyebrows rose into high arches. "Am I hearing right—you cook and you're maternal?"

"It shocks me, too," she said with a shrug. "At first I didn't want anything to do with caring for orphans. Oh, I enjoyed reading them stories well enough and even the little teaching I did. But I have to admit Sarah has wormed her way into my heart more than I thought possible. She's the sweetest thing—tiny as a wood mouse and just about as timid. She has a terrible stutter. But she's smart and pretty. She's very attached to me."

She shook her head. "Things are awful at the fort—not enough food or anything. After the battle, so many refugees poured in." She stopped for a moment and bit her lip again. In the silence that stretched, she finally said, "I am so very sorry about Seamus."

He grimaced.

She reached for his arm. "Oh, Allen, I know how much you loved him. We had become good friends. Did you know he took me to a dance at the fort? I cried for days when I found out he'd been killed." She paused and then softly added, "It was you who removed his body from the battlefield, wasn't it?"

His face was tight. "Yes."

"A soldier told me that a big man—a rebel—moved the body. How awful it must have been for you, finding him on the battlefield."

His jaws worked.

"Does your ma know yet?" she asked gently.

"No." For a long moment he stared at her hand clasping his arm. "I figure one of these days—after the war ends—I'll head for Texas and bring her back home."

When he had finished washing the knife, dried it, and returned it to his pocket, Nelda stood. They walked side-by-side toward the house, each lost in thought as the setting sun washed the low sky yellow. Puffy clouds, higher up, reflected hues of brilliant pink and coral and then melted into pale blue.

"What a beautiful sunset," she said, pausing.

He smiled, and for the moment, his face grew young. "I never see a pretty one without thinking of you."

She looked back at the sky. "Allen, I know it pains you to speak of Seamus."

His face darkened as if a curtain fell across a bright window.

She drew a deep breath and tired again. "Sometimes keeping the hurt inside only makes it worse. I made that mistake once…" She let the words drift away. Allen hardly needed to hear of her heartbreak after the death of Fred Reynolds.

Without a word, he started on again and then stepped aside to let her enter first. She sat down at the kitchen table in the darkening room and invited him to sit.

"Get a bowl," he said, "and I'll help shell these peas. We had some for supper last night and they were mighty tasty."

While Nelda searched in the cupboard for a bowl, she called over her shoulder. "How is Miss Emma? Della told me you brought her here,"—she turned and added with a mischievous grin— "although, I'd already figured it out. She was a good spy. Even as suspicious as I've become, I never guessed—not until she flew the coup. When the neighbor described the man who drove the buggy, I knew it had to be you."

He gave a low chuckle. "I figured you'd put it all together. You always were way too smart."

She made a scoffing sound. "Apparently not. You fooled me for a long time and so did Miss Emma. I never dreamed she was a spy. It's downright disturbing to never know who you're talking to these days." She sighed and sat down after handing Allen the bowl. "Do you think the war will ever end? Just about the time I think so your side comes back with a vengeance. I heard back in July that a general named Jubal Early marched his forces to within five miles of Washington."

Hands busy shelling peas, Allen nodded. "Yep. But he got driven back to Virginia. If Sherman takes Atlanta, I reckon it'll hurry the end, especially since Atlanta is our munitions center."

"I keep thinking what a tragic waste it has all been," she said and then stopped. Although she did not agree with his cause, she did not want him to think she belittled it.

"The South will be a long while recovering," he said. "Are you planning to leave soon?"

"I really should get back to the fort and help with the orphans. But I'm not sure about Della and me traveling without an escort. The patrol I traveled with left two days ago."

He was adamant. "Don't try it, Nelda. It's too risky. It would be bad enough traveling with a patrol, but it would be downright foolhardy to go all that way alone." He held up a hand before she could comment and added, "Now don't go gettin' Irish on me. If you'll hold off awhile, I'll take you. It may be a few weeks before I'm free to go, but a little delay is better than not getting there at all."

She stopped stringing a hull to stare at him. "You never cease to amaze me."

His eyebrows rose. "How so?"

"Fort Smith is the biggest Union post around—and yet you'd just sashay back there with me." She shook her head. "Allen Matthers, sometimes I question your sanity."

He gave a half grin. "A man in love is apt to be a bit foolish."

Her eyes dropped. She was saved a reply when Della came through the door, holding Moses perched on her hip, his hair damp and face shining. The boy reached for Allen with a happy gurgle.

"Howdy, Mr. Allen. I had done put this boy to bed, but he heard you and set up a howl to see you."

Allen smiled and took him. "We've become pretty good comrades, haven't we little fellow? I'll miss you when you're gone with your mama and Miss Nelda."

"I ain't goin' to Fort Smith," said Della.

Nelda was surprised. Although they had not spoken of it, she had assumed Della would want to go with her.

"Gideon and me had made plans. We was goin' north. I ain't going no other direction." She lovingly smoothed the child's damp hair. "I can get a good payin' job, and Moses will have a fine life there."

Nelda recalled the burning of the Negro orphan Asylum in New York. The North was not the Promised Land for Negroes. She opened her mouth to protest but Allen spoke.

"I'll leave you two to talk that over." He handed back the baby. "It's getting dark, and I need to get on back. I'll come back tomorrow. I would suggest that you both stick close to the house."

After he stepped into the dusk, Nelda remained seated. It was good to see him…and yet it was troublesome the way he persisted in wooing her. It would never work. He should be smart enough to see that. She wished he would stop. She desperately needed a friend.

The breeze gusted, fluttering the curtain at the open kitchen window. Amid loud, cheeping frogs a dog barked near the creek. Another answered from a far ridge. A mosquito hummed near Nelda's ear. When it alighted on her arm, she mashed it.

She sighed, picked up a pod, and as fat, gray-green peas rolled into the pan, her brow furrowed. Poor Allen. He was taking Seamus's death extra hard. More than likely, he was feeling guilty over their estrangement. If that was so—and if he would let her talk about it—she would tell him she had assured Seamus he was no longer upset at him for joining the Union Army. That should comfort Allen. Her shoulders squared. Whether or not he wanted to talk, the next time he came she would tell him.

CHAPTER II ⌒

Allen stopped and turned in the saddle to look back at the white house shrouded in blue shadows. He drew a deep breath and let it out slowly while his shoulders drooped and desolation pressed on his chest like a giant fist.

It was good seeing Nelda—and yet he felt gut-kicked. He fidgeted with the reins. Although he knew she would never have him, it hurt like hell each time she turned away.

The bay he had gotten from Emmitt dipped its head, tugging on the reins. Allen patted the sweaty neck. "So you want to get back to the barn and some feed, do you? I figure they're waiting supper on me too." With another glance back at the house, he kneed the horse and started down the road.

By the time he reached the river, the trees were black silhouettes and the sunset a mere line of silver blue reflecting on dark water. He could just make out the white markings on a nighthawk, swooping low in graceful circles as it almost skimmed the water. The squeaking notes it emitted seemed a stark contrast to its graceful flight. He stopped to watch as the bird settled on the bank to roost for the night.

Allen had just turned off onto the trail when he heard horses. He turned his head to listen. There were several, and he heard the squeak of a wagon. He reined the bay off the trail and into the woods. He dismounted and put a hand over the horse's nose and mouth. A whinny at the wrong time could cause a man's death.

"I tell ya, cap'n, the bone around here has done been picked clean. We've rid twenty mile without getting a wagonload."

"I know it, Levi, but tomorrow we'll keep trying. I'm not going back to the colonel empty handed. That is one man who doesn't accept excuses."

Allen helloed before stepping onto the road. "Reeves, don't shoot. It's Allen Matthers."

The captain and the eight riders with him pulled rein. "Well, I'll be damned. Matthers, I never expected to see you again. We heard you were dead." He quickly dismounted and shook Allen's hand. "Sure is good to see you. What are you doing here? Scouting I suppose."

"Something like that," Allen said, returning the firm handshake. "Good to see you, too, Reeves. Kind of late in the day to be foraging." He nodded toward a rickety wagon.

"We're putting a little distance between us and the last house we visited. There was a young rooster who didn't take kindly to us raiding the garden. We took his musket, but he was such a little hothead I figured he might come after us with a butcher knife. I don't want to have to kill a snot nose kid."

Allen straightened. "Was that kid a towhead with a gap between his front teeth."

Captain Reeves' eyes widened. "You know him?"

"Yeah, I do. You might not want to rob those folks."

"Aw, come on, Matthers—we aren't robbers. You know the army has to eat. We have no choice but—"

Allen cut in, "Did you see that sick woman?"

Reeves nodded. "She gave us quite a tongue lashing. She claimed she's related to General Cooper…" He stopped and gave a low whistle. "You mean she really is?"

"General's cousin," avowed Allen.

Reeves looked over his shoulder back down the trail they had come and muttered, "Oh, Lordy." Then he faced Allen. "There wasn't a lot to begin with. Now there isn't a tea cup full of anything left on that farm." He shuffled his feet uncomfortably after seeing Allen's hard stare. "They won't starve. You know all these people have enough hidden to make out."

"I don't know any such thing," said Allen, his voice brittle.

Levi chuckled and spoke from atop his horse. "Cap'in, yer damned if ya do and damned if ya don't. Cooper will skin you alive for taking her stuff, and Brooks will skin ya alive if you come back empty handed. Then ag'in," Levi pointed out, "a general outranks a colonel."

"Hell, I know that," Reeves snapped. "But Cooper isn't here, and Brooks is."

"Why not give back half of it," suggested Allen. "You can raid some other poor family tomorrow."

Reeve's face reddened. "Damn it, Matthers," he snapped. However, after he looked at the ground and reconsidered, he said, "All right. We'll return some of it. Maybe not half, but some."

"Good. I'll bet Carrie might even cook your supper. You can bed down in the yard. If you're real nice, she might even make breakfast. She's a fine cook."

When they rode into the yard, Isaac bolted from the door, red-faced with fists clenched. "You done took everything we—" He stopped, eyes wide, when he saw Allen.

Allen dismounted, smothering a chuckle. "Isaac, these fellows got to thinking you'd make a bad enemy, so they decided to bring back some of the stuff."

Carrie stepped through the door. Her eyes and face were puffy from weeping. She eyed the riders skeptically. "Are they really going to give it back?"

"Yes, they are," Allen assured. "I told them, if they did, you might cook us a fine meal."

Her eyes became narrow, angry slits. "I got no hankering to fix for thieves. But since you want me to, Allen, I reckon I can throw somethin' together."

"I'd appreciate it," said Allen. He turned to Reeves. "It might be best if you waited out here."

Reeves gave a snort. "Don't worry. I intend to."

Allen entered the cabin to check on Miss Emma. She sat up in bed, propped high on Carries' plump feather pillows. Her face was white and drawn. Allen suspected the day's drama had taken a toll.

"I'm weak as a kitten," she avowed with a nod toward the door, "but very relieved that you persuaded those boys to bring back the food. I'd like to know how you did it," she said with a wan smile.

He gave a slight grin. "Nothing to it. When I mentioned you were the general's kin, they got downright contrite about taking all those vittles. I better give Carrie a hand with peeling potatoes."

After the horses had been fed and corralled, the soldiers hunkered in the yard, awaiting supper. Allen finished helping Carrie and then joined them. Soon Isaac, somewhat mollified, drifted among them carrying his fiddle.

He stopped in front of the soldier named Levi. "Mister, how'd you get that scar on the side of your neck?"

Levi, his long, gray-streaked hair pulled back and tied with a leather thong and his wrinkled face covered with a long grizzled beard, squinted at him through pipe smoke. Then he tilted his neck sideways and ran a thick finger down a long puckered white scar.

"Got this 'un at Wilson's Crick from a Yankee saber. It don't amount to much. But I got a doozy on my stomach from a Injun skinin' knife. He pret-nigh gutted me. Didn't think I was gonna make it through that one. Reckon the good Lord just weren't ready fer me yet."

Isaac's eyes widened. "You've fought Injuns?"

Levi nodded. "Mex, too." He puffed on the pipe and then talked around the stem. "I used to be a great one for a scrap. Don't look forward to 'em as much now. Reckon I'll be right glad to see this one end."

Isaac drew a deep breath. "Me too. Then my pa can come home. You know Roy Hackett? He's my pa. He's in General Marmaduke's cavalry."

"Don't reckon I know him, son. Until just lately when my feet give out I was infantry. But I knowed Marmaduke. He's a damn fine officer."

He pointed the pipe at the fiddle. "You play that there thang 'er just wag it around?"

Isaac grinned. "I'm learning. I ain't much good at it." He nodded toward Allen. "He plays real good."

Levi cut his eyes sideways. "Play us a tune."

As a chorus of agreement rose, Allen reluctantly took the fiddle. It was the last thing he wanted to do, but he'd play them a quick song and then be done with it. Lonely men hungered for music and a break in monotony. He tucked the instrument under his chin and raised the bow. It was a song he had composed but never given a name. As his sadness melded with the bow and poured into the night, he fought back tears and a lump in his throat. Seamus had loved the tune.

When he finally lowered the bow, Levi's voice was hushed and reverent as he pulled the pipe from his mouth and said, "That there puts the birds to shame."

Allen, ignoring the unanimous requests for more, handed the fiddle to Isaac. "I better go see if your ma needs any more help."

The men ate hardily and with enough good grace to thank Carrie for the fine meal of the fried potatoes, black-eyed peas, and cornbread.

The next morning Allen was gratified to see Captain Reeves had unloaded almost all the plunder from the wagon. Carrie beamed as she stood on the porch and waved them good-bye.

Before riding from the yard, Reeves turned in the saddle. "Matthers, are there any more of your friends we should avoid? I'd just as soon not waste my time again loading and unloading supplies."

Allen grinned. "Now that you mention it, there's a tall white house on the edge of town with boarded-up windows. As long as you don't bother the young woman who lives there and as long as you stay away from Little Piney Creek, I don't reckon I'll have any beef with you."

Levi pulled rein. "Little Piney Creek," he echoed. "I know a young feller from there. We fi't lots of battles together, all the way from Pea Ridge to the White River. He left a few months back and headed home. Name of Elijah Loring. Would you be knowing him?"

"Lived close, neighbors," said Allen, surprised. "I knew he'd been conscripted, but I didn't know he had gone home. Haven't been home lately myself."

"He shore is a fine lad," said Levi, "and a damned fine soldier. If you see him, tell him old Levi asked after him." His eyes twinkled. "Tell him one of these days, I just might take him up on that there offer to come fer a visit."

"I'll tell him."

When they rode away, Allen looked north, toward home. It had been a long while since he had been back. As soon as Miss Emma was safely delivered, and as soon as he had taken Nelda back to the fort, he would head there. Right now, he wanted to see Nelda. He drew a deep breath. Of course, seeing her was bittersweet. He felt like a poor kid in Emmitt's mercantile eyeing the candy jar and knowing he couldn't have any. He rubbed the stubble on his jaw and decided to shave.

In the garden, Nelda glanced up and then stood from kneeling. The basket on her arm held collard greens. She smoothed back her hair and dusted off her skirt at the knees and then shaded her eyes against the low sun to watch as Allen dismounted and tied the bay.

"Della must have second sight," she called with a smile. "She told me to pick lots of greens. She's frying fish. David Hadley brought us a fine mess of perch a while ago. You'll stay for dinner?"

"Never could resist a good meal," said Allen as he joined her and immediately took out his knife and began cutting the broad green cabbage like leaves, making sure to cut away the thickest stems.

Nelda stooped alongside. "These are all that was left in the garden. Thank God for perennials."

"Haven't had Della's collards in a long while," he said. "She makes 'em better than anyone," he said. "I didn't come empty-handed. There's sweet potatoes in my saddle bags, and Carrie sent some butter."

"Oh my goodness!" exclaimed Nelda. "What a treat! That was certainly kind of her."

"I think she feels bad over telling Della to leave and not come back. She was afraid because of Gideon being a run-away. But she was mighty sorry to hear about the hanging. So was Miss Emma."

"How is Miss Emma?"

"Still weak. At her age, a body doesn't bounce back fast. But she's tough-minded and determined, so I figure she'll get well. In the meantime, I hope you'll stick around. I sure don't want you heading out on your own."

Nelda's lips pursed and then she spoke slowly, "I don't suppose you could take me and then come back for Miss Emma?"

"She is weak yet to be traveling," he slowly considered. "But nights are already growing chilly. I'm worried about her traveling in bad weather." He scratched his jaw. "I am under orders. The general won't take it kindly if I get myself caught heading back to the fort before I've carried them out."

"I don't want you getting into trouble," she quickly asserted.

Allen smiled. "Well, that's an improvement," he joked.

Nelda groaned. "You won't ever let me live that down, will you?"

"I'm hoping you'll feel contrite enough to behave yourself and stick around. I figure Miss Emma will be able to ride in a week or so."

Nelda frowned. "Two or three weeks—and then more while you escort her to her daughter's. I don't know Allen. All those children at the fort—"

"Those orphans have other folks to look after them for a little while, don't they?"

She could not erase visions of little Sarah's doleful face, and yet Allen was right. It was foolhardy to attempt the journey alone.

"I supposed they have," she finally agreed.

His eyes grew grave. "You haven't forgotten what a close shave you had with that bushwhacker gang, have you? Now the country is lousy with such as them."

She shuddered. "No, I haven't forgotten Jess or his vile partner Heavy. If you hadn't come along, I'd have suffered worse than death and then probably died too." She drew a deep breath. "All right. I'll acquiesce on one condition—that you bring your fiddle next time you come and play some music. You know how I love—" Her brows drew together. "Why, Allen, what's the matter? You look as if a mule kicked you in the stomach. If you're not feeling well I'll finish—"

"No," he said, bending to cut a few more greens, "I'm fine."

After a while, he stood and turned to look at her. "Nelda, I have an idea. Miss Emma is still mighty weak and could use some looking after on the trip. I can't do things for her like a female could, especially if she gets sick again. Why don't you come with us?"

Nelda's eyebrows rose. "My word! Miss Emma is a rebel spy. Have you forgotten I'm a Unionist?"

"Hardly," he said with a dry laugh. "I'm not askin' you to help her spy—I'm just asking one good woman to help another in a time of sickness. Truth be told," he added, "you and Miss Emma are cut from the same bolt of cloth. You're both brave ladies fighting for what you believe in."

Nelda's lips drew down. "You're asking me to aid the enemy, Allen Matthers."

He chuckled. Then his brogue grew thick. "Nelda, me love, wouldn't you be thinkin' you've broken that sacred commandment more than once already?"

Her face reddened. "And lived to regret it," she sputtered.

With a calloused finger, he tipped up her chin and stared into her eyes. His probing look was serious. "Really? Do you regret helping me?"

Her heart skipped and then beat faster. His eyes were bluer than the sky, and although she wanted to, she could not tear her own away. She hated the weakness in her knees. Finally she said, "No. Considering all you've done for me, I haven't done nearly enough for you."

"Is that the only reason—because of how I helped you a couple of times?"

"A couple?" she began, but as his gaze held steady, she stopped and swallowed. Then her shoulders squared. "Please don't spoil our friendship, Allen. There's just too vast a difference between us to ever be anything but friends." As his hand dropped, she hurried on. "To be perfectly honest, you're the best friend I've ever had, and I'll always treasure our friendship."

"At least that's something," he said with a hint of bitterness.

"Please, don't ever stop being my friend," she said.

He looked surprised. "Of course I won't."

"Good." She briefly looked away. "Even if I agree, Miss Emma might object. Remember, she knows I'm a Unionist. Do you honestly think she'll want me along?"

"If I asked her to, she will."

"But—"

"You don't have to decide right now. Just think about it."

She chewed her lip a minute. She would like to help Allen, but there were so many other considerations.

"I'll think about it," she said.

"Good. Now let's give Della these greens. I smell fish frying, and I'm hungry.

When the table was set, however, and the crispy brown fish and succulent greens set before them, he ate little. Nelda barely touched her food as Della looked on with troubled eyes. Allen left immediately afterwards.

"Somethin' wrong betwixt you and Mr. Allen? You done had a fight about somethin'?"

Nelda shook her head and then pondered. Della had a wise head. It would be good to hear her opinion.

"Allen asked me to go along when he takes Miss Emma to her daughter's."

"That be good," said Della. "Sick as she is, Miss Emma gonna need some he'p on a hard trip like that."

"I don't think it's a good idea," said Nelda.

"Now don't you be frettin' about me and Moses. I got friends here. We be just fine."

After a moment's hesitation, Nelda blurted out, "But I'm afraid if I do go, he'll keep on with a foolish notion of courting me. that would only hurt him worse."

Della was so long in responding, that Nelda's brow puckered. "Well?" she finally asked. "What do you think?"

Della crossed her arms and gave a hard stare. "You done asked, so don't go gettin' mad."

"Go ahead," Nelda urged, but she drew up on the inside. She probably would not like what Della had to say. The woman was brutally honest.

"You is a foolish woman, Miz Nelda. Anybody what Mr. Allen cast his eyes on, is a mighty blessed woman. That man been lovin' you for years—but you keep pushin' him off, and one of these days, he just likely to go."

"But Della, we're so different. I mean…his family and…" Her words trailed away. Della's world was too simple. She could not understand the dynamics of the situation. "You just don't understand," she finished lamely.

"I understand your mama thought herself better than a lot of good folks."

"I'm nothing like Mama," Nelda shot out.

Della's eyebrows rose. "You a lot more like Miz Louise than you knows."

Nelda's mouth fell open. She had always despised Mama's high hat ways. How could Della think… She spun around and left the room.

CHAPTER 12 ❧

A llen tucked a few more items into the wagon alongside the small feather mattress. "Carrie, I sure do thank you for the loan of the wagon. I'll bring it back as quick as I can. But, like I said, there's a good chance it might get stolen or conscripted by either army."

With arms crossed over her chest, Carrie shrugged broad shoulders. She wore a calico dress that may have once been blue but was now of nondescript gray from many washings.

"Old thing is about to fall apart anyway—canvas top is 'most rotten," she said, "and it's fer certain Miss Emma can't ride horseback all that way, weak as she still is."

Allen eyed the contraption. It was true. The ragged top would hardly shed rain. But he had tightened every part possible and greased the wheels. Hopefully it would make the journey without leaving them stranded, for it was equally true that Miss Emma was in no condition to ride.

Miss Emma opened the door and stepped into a bright patch of morning sun bathing the porch. She wore the same outfit, baggy trousers and shirt. Now they hung loosely on her big frame, and the floppy hat shaded a much thinner and newly wrinkled face. She was draped with a shawl against the crisp morning air. She took Carrie's hands.

"How can I say thank you for all you've done—how can I ever repay you for nursing me night and day, feeding me, fussing over me like a mother hen?" She looked at the wagon. "As if you hadn't done enough, you took the mattress right off your own bed." She shook her head. "There's just no way I can ever thank you enough." Tears glistened in Emma's eyes.

Carrie patted her shoulder. "Aw, there now, don't go makin' so much out of it. I still got two good ticks left, more than enough fer a good soft bed." She chuckled and smoothed the worn dress over wide hips. "There's always my own good padding," she said with a smile. "I'm just praising the good Lord you pulled through. Hit was nip and tuck there for a while. Truth be told, I was dyin' of loneliness myself till you and Allen showed up. Visitin' with you has been a pure pleasure. Allen has done enough work since he come to more than pay fer your keep. Hit'll be downright lonesome after ya leave."

The bay snorted and shook its head as if trying to shake off the harness. Allen patted its rump. "I know you got no liking for being hitched to a wagon. But you behave now like Miss Emma's nice mare. See there, she ain't raising a fuss."

Isaac rubbed the mare's nose. "She is a nice horse. We got to be pretty good friends. She even let me ride her without a bridle." Then he cut his eyes sideways and grew red to the roots of his fair hair. After glancing nervously at Miss Emma, he mumbled, "Reckon I should have asked—"

Allen thought any boy worth his salt had done the same thing. Aloud he said, "You ought to have asked. A body's horse is a valuable possession."

"Reckon I ought to tell her?"

Allen nodded.

Although dread washed Isaac's face, he climbed the steps. "Ma'am." He shuffled a bare foot, stared at the porch, and swallowed. "I rode your mare around a few times. Hope that was all right."

Miss Emma shook his hand. "Young man, thank you so much for exercising that lazy animal. If allowed, she's too much like me and gets fat and lazy." She reached into a pocket of the baggy trousers and pulled out a silver dollar. "This is for all the extra water you've had to draw and for all the fetching and toting you've had to do on account of me."

Isaac's eyes grew almost as large as the dollar held in his palm. He looked at Carrie. "Kin I keep it, Ma?"

Although earlier Carrie had refused Miss Emma's coins, now she smiled. "I reckon so."

Miss Emma tousled his hair and then she hugged Carrie. Still holding Carrie's shoulders, she drew back and stared into her eyes. "A friend loveth at all times, and a brother is born for adversity," she quoted. "Carrie Hackett, in the truest Christian sense, you've been both a friend and a brother to me. I'll never forget you."

Allen's teeth gritted. He looked quickly away at the bitter reminder that he had been no such brother to Seamus. Every day held a thousand such barbs. He supposed someday he'd get used to them.

"Mr. Matthers, I'm ready when you are."

"Back of the wagon or up on the seat?"

"I'll try sitting for a while. It's too glorious a morning to lie in bed— even if it is in a wagon bed," she said with a sunny smile.

"All right, but when you get tired, sing out. I don't want you overdoing."

She took his hand and climbed up and looked back toward the porch where Carrie and Isaac stood, both looking dejected. "Isaac, bring your mama to see me up in Newton County one of these days."

He flashed a grin and waved as they drove from the yard. "I sure will, ma'am."

Miss Emma sighed and stared ahead. "Good folks, your friends, the Hacketts. I hope her husband survives the war." As the trail intersected the wider road and the canopy of timber opened to show a wide blue sky, she pointed at the eagle circling overhead. But when she spoke, it was of another matter. "So, you trust Miss Nelda with your life, and yet she's just a friend, you say?" She gave a cryptic smile.

Allen stared ahead with the reins held loosely in big hands. "Sharp as you are you'll figure out quick enough—if I had my way, she'd be more."

"Ah," said Miss Emma. "So the young lady doesn't share your ardor?"

"Nope. She is a good friend, though. Even took a bullet intended for me. She claims there's just too much difference between us, and I reckon she's right. Before the war her pa owned the town newspaper." He shrugged. "Me—I'm a hillbilly from a rowdy clan. Only good thing the Matthers were ever known for was our music." He added with a sour smirk, "Pa made fine moonshine."

Deep in thought, Miss Emma pursed her lips. Finally she spoke. "That is a good bit to overcome," she admitted. "Before the war—considering the social disparity—I'd say you're chances were slim to none. But things are different now. This war has leveled many a social barrier. You said yourself she's just about destitute and living in a rundown house with boarded windows. You are anything but ignorant, Allen. I'm constantly surprised at your knowledge. You must be an avid reader. Personally, I think any woman who wins your affection is lucky indeed."

"Too bad you can't convince Nelda," he said with a dry laugh as he chirruped the bay, which had begun lagging to steal a bite of tall grass alongside the road.

Miss Emma smiled. "It will be a long trip. One never knows what might happen."

The pleasant September morning held the gentle promise of fall. Leaves fluttered onto the trail. Cooler air, filled with happy bird song, had replaced the blazing heat of preceding weeks. Miss Emma pointed to an overgrown field dotted with bouquets of tall white yarrow and yellow and brown coneflowers.

"I love wildflowers. Do you know the legend of the yarrow?"

Allen shook his head. "Don't reckon I do. All I know is Granny Tanner—who is a sort of herb doctor back home—uses 'em to stop bleeding. Once, when Pa cut himself real deep with an ax, she used 'em on the wound."

"How interesting," said Miss Emma. "That medicinal quality just might be how the myth started. They are said to owe their origin to Achilles. Supposedly, they sprang from some metal scrapings of the great warrior's spear."

Allen gave a quick smile. "Granny wouldn't approve of that myth. She's strong on Bible and hell-bent against anything with a taint of heathen."

By the time they reached the edge of town, Miss Emma's usually straight shoulders were slumped and her jaws were taut. Allen gave her a worried look. "You all right?"

She grimaced. "I'm pathetic as a newborn kitten. It's disgusting to be such a weakling."

"I don't think you know how close you came to the pearly gates. I probably shouldn't have let you talk me into going this soon. You sure you're up to this?"

"No, please, let's keep going. I have the strangest premonition that something is wrong with Dorcas and her family."

He frowned. "All right. But don't push yourself. Yonder is Nelda's. After we pick her up, why don't you get in back and lay down—at least for a few hours."

"I just might do that."

When he slowed the team, she tipped back the hat to stare at the two-story house with boarded windows and a white picket fence in need of paint. "So this is where your sweetheart lives."

"This is where my friend lives," he corrected. "Miss Emma, I get the feeling you're a romantic."

"Guilty. Every woman I know is. So is your Nelda—in spite of all her noble protests."

Allen shook his head. "No, she's different. While the other gals flirted and danced, she'd be with her pa and the other men discussing the happenings in Little Rock and Washington City. Even before the war, she was keen on politics." He quickly added, "Oh, she loves to dance, too. We've had some grand swirls around the floor. But for the most part, she ain't like most females."

"I dare say, she's not that different in matters of the heart," Miss Emma said with finality. "A man never truly understands a woman."

"You'll get no argument from me on that," he muttered.

Nelda exited the front door, valise in hand, as Allen pulled the team to a halt. Della stepped out with Moses perched on her hip. She also held a dishtowel-covered lunch basket. Allen stepped down to assist Miss Emma.

She climbed down, smiled, and held out both hands to Nelda. "Miss Nelda, it is a pure pleasure seeing you again."

Nelda scowled. She felt anything but friendly. She had been betrayed yet again, and she'd never learned to like it. However, Miss Emma's wan face and timid, hopeful smile began melting resentment. Maybe Allen was right. Maybe she and Miss Emma were cut from the same bolt of cloth. At least she was willing to be civil if not friendly. She kept hold of the satchel and briefly shook one of Miss Emma's outstretched hands.

"Glad you're finally able to travel. Allen, would you kindly stow my satchel?"

He put the satchel in the wagon and then helped Miss Emma climb into the back. Before she disappeared under the ragged top, she called, "Della, thank you so very much for all you did for me. I'm very grateful."

As soon as she was situated on the mattress, he took Moses into his arms and held him while Nelda hugged Della. "Take good care of this little man," he said as he handed him back to his mother. "I'll be back soon and we'll see about getting you north. I have a plan, but I'll have to check on some details when I get back."

"That be real good, Mr. Allen. You take care of yourself"—she nodded toward the wagon where Nelda now sat on the seat—"and them. Likely you have your hands full with that. I be prayin' for all of you."

"Thank you, Della. Like I said, with any luck, I'll be back soon."

Before climbing onto the seat, Allen stared up at Nelda. "I figure it would be a good idea for you to stay out of sight until we're out of town. Yesterday I saw a lot of Rebel troops in town, and you never know who might recognize you and remember what you did at Helena."

Without argument she climbed into the back and found a perch on a bundle lying alongside Miss Emma's mattress. She peeked out and gave a final wave as Allen steered the team back onto the road.

"We make unlikely traveling companions, do we not?" asked Miss Emma with a tired chuckle. "Three spies. Sounds like the title of a story." She cut her eyes to Nelda. Since you like to write, you ought to write a book about your adventures someday. From what I've heard, you've had some."

"Perhaps I will," she murmured.

When they passed the courthouse, she pasted eyes to a rent in the canvas to look out. There were troops and horses everywhere and a regular tent city near Spadra Creek. Although she recognized no one, she was glad to be out of sight. Instead of turning right onto Main Street and crossing the covered bridge, Allen faced north. At the far edge of town, he whoaed the team.

"I think you can come out now if you'd like."

She climbed out and settled back onto the hard seat. "I've been wondering if we'll pass close to Aunt Becky's on our way to Jasper."

He shook his head. "We'll head through the mountains, but closest we'll come to her would take an extra day's travel."

"Oh," she sighed. "I would so love to see her."

"I wish you could, too," he said. "Maybe on our way back. Emmitt told me the news about Ned."

She sat up straight. "What about Uncle Ned?"

"Reckon you knew they thought he was dead?"

"Yes."

"He's not dead. He was a prisoner. But he's home again and doing fine—so Emmitt says. It seems Elijah's wife Cindy and Caleb Tanner went down to Shreveport to fetch him."

Nelda's eyes shone. "That's wonderful news about Uncle Ned! Aunt Becky must be overjoyed! I had no idea Elijah had married."

"He did. Cindy Mason. She's a fine girl. Her pa is Preacher Simon, a good friend and neighbor of ours on Piney." He guided the horses across a small creek and kept heading north. "Sad thing, though, about Caleb. He got killed on the trip."

"Poor Granny Tanner," murmured Nelda. "He was her only son, wasn't he?"

"Yep. At least she has Ned back now. You must not have heard any of what happened this past year." Then, as the town disappeared behind them, Allen kept her enthralled with the horrible tale of Granny's torture at Bo Morrison's hands. He ended with the gristly facts of Bo's death. By the time he finished, Nelda's knuckles, gripping the seat, were white.

"Bo was just plain wicked," she said with a shudder. "When we were children, I considered the Morrison's my family—but even as a child, Bo was mean."

"Well, he's dead now," said Allen grimly. "If Lew hadn't finished him, I would have."

"Before the war, I'd have been appalled to hear you say such a thing. Now I understand all too well."

They lapsed into silence. The wagon creaked past wide fields overgrown with wildflowers and red tinted sassafras sprouts. Near scattered farm houses and cabins were a few vegetable gardens and patches of feed corn with mature ears hanging down, hard and ready for gathering. The sun shone bright and yet the air remained crisp. Soon the fields gave way to hilly ground, and, before long, they crossed a rocky-bottomed creek. Yellow, fallen leaves floated on clear water that reflected overhanging bushes, willows, and white-trunk sycamores. Soon, they pulled a steep incline. From the top Nelda saw overlapping, blue, flat-topped ridges in the distance. Dogwood trees edged the trail, their leaves a light reddish pink. Black gums were a dark shade of red, and oaks, with trunks as wide as the trail, wore a mixture of green, yellow and brown foliage.

A young buck with perfect antlers stepped from a thicket. He threw up his head and stood statue still for a brief moment. Then, white tail raised, he bounded into the woods.

"Nice buck," said Allen. "He's lost his velvet."

"His velvet?" questioned Nelda.

"Along about May when they start sprouting antlers, their horns are covered with a soft fuzzy stuff like velvet. It lasts awhile and then they scrape it off by rubbing their horns on branches and bushes."

Nelda looked through the trees to where the buck had stood. "I know so little about animals and the woods. Papa never hunted, and we rarely went anywhere outside of town."

"Reckon it would be impossible to hunt with only one arm," said Allen.

"I think he was happiest inside the newspaper office anyway." Nelda gazed at the far mountains and drew a deep breath. "I sure do miss him."

"I didn't always agree with him on politics," said Allen, "but he put out a good newspaper. After this war is over, Clarksville is going to miss him too."

The morning passed without incident. Nelda noticed Allen's vigilant eyes scanning the surroundings. Often he even searched the trail behind. When they reached the foot of the mountains, he stopped to give the horses a rest. Miss Emma climbed from the wagon to join them under tall trees to eat lunch of fried fish and cornpone from the basket Della had packed.

The afternoon passed as they made slower progress on the steep, rough trail. The sun was low when they reached the top. Nelda was already weary of the jolting. She even felt sympathy for Miss Emma who stayed inside the wagon when Allen stopped where a spring ran from the hillside to make a pool below.

"We'll stop here to water the horses. It's not far to where I aim to spend the night."

Abruptly, he handed Nelda the reins and reached for a shotgun. A rider approached, slowing at the sight of the wagon. He wore a long, ragged beard and a slouch hat atop shaggy gray hair.

"Matthers!" he called. "I thought that was you. No one else around here big as you with hair that color. Good to see you!"

Nelda relaxed as Allen propped the shotgun back against the seat.

"Howdy, Elton, good to see you too. Where you headed?"

"Going home. I been over to Lewisburg checkin' on Ma's kin. She's been right worried ever since she heared her sister took sick. Berthy did might-nigh die, but she's doin' better now."

"Glad to hear it."

"Where you headin'?"

Nelda could read the curiosity in the old man's eyes as his gaze kept sliding to her.

"Taking a friend to her people," said Allen briefly, without adding details.

"Heading back any time soon?" asked Elton as he let his horse drink from the rippling spring. He quickly added, "I ain't prying. Just thought you ought to know they's a big Union force headed fer Fort Smith. I seen 'em at Lewisburg, several hundred of 'em. They'll be in Clarksville by tomorrow. I figure lead will be flyin' hot and heavy—what with Brook's cavalry in town."

Allen's eyes flashed. "Does Brooks know?"

Elton shrugged. "No idea. I cut across country and never rode that way. I figure he'll have pickets out." Elton pulled his mount back onto the trail. "I better get along home before dark catches me. You go ker-ful. They's a sight of bushwhacking varmints in these hills, and they're bold as brass these days." He tipped the battered hat to Nelda. "Ma'am."

When he rode away, Allen's eyes did not follow. Instead he looked into the far valley toward Clarksville.

"You're thinking about riding back to warn them," Nelda speculated.

"The thought crossed my mind," he admitted and then climbed onto the seat, "But Elton's right. These woods are full of two-legged varmints. No way I'm leaving you and Miss Emma alone on this trail. "

"Good," said Nelda. "That saves me a long, hard ride to warn the Union troops that Brooks is in Clarksville."

Allen chuckled. "Reckon we'll just call this hand a draw."

"Reckon so," said Nelda with a drawl.

They camped alongside the trail in a flat surrounded by small knolls. A trickle of water ran down a small creek bed, enough to cook supper and fill the canteens. Nelda sat near the campfire, squinting at occasional puffs of smoke, while listening to wind sway tall pines on the ridge above.

Allen handed Miss Emma a steaming cup. "It's not as good as coffee, but parched corn water is better than nothing when you're chilled."

"Thank you." She reached shaking hands and took it. "I am chilled. It will help warm me."

Nelda and Allen exchanged worried glances. Miss Emma's pale face looked ghostly in the flickering light.

Finally, Allen spoke. "You sure about going on? It's only a day back to Clarksville."

Her head snapped up from bending over the cup. "Most definitely I want to go on. Something is wrong with Dorcas. The sooner we get there the better."

Nelda slept in the wagon on the pallet alongside Miss Emma. The woman's frequent coughing kept her awake. Allen threw a bedroll on the ground near the wagon. His sleep also seemed restless, for often, deep in the night, Nelda heard him stirring about.

"Allen," she said in the morning, "have you been having nightmares?" She sat alongside him on the hard seat in warm sunshine.

Surprised, he faced her. "Why do you ask?"

"Last night, you called out in your sleep."

His face tensed. "What did I say?"

"I couldn't hear from inside the wagon, but you sounded…well, anguished." She searched his eyes. "I'm a good listener, if you'd like to talk."

He faced forward. She could see his mouth had drawn down.

"Like any man who's ever fought a war," he finally said, "I got my ghosts to deal with. Most times, when I'm awake, I can sort of blot things out. Don't reckon there's any way to control a body's dreams."

She gazed at the far blue hills. "I have my ghosts. And my nightmares," she added. "The bad dreams haven't tormented me as much lately, but there was a time I dreaded falling asleep."

He nodded. "I know what you mean."

She prodded again. "Sometimes it helps to talk—to share one's burdens."

His mouth opened. Then without speaking, he shut it.

In silence, she waited.

"I appreciate what you're trying to do," he said. "I know I can talk to you. When I'm ready, maybe I will. Right now, I just need to sort things out on my own."

She said, "Fair enough. You know I'll always want to help if I can."

When he said no more, she added, "I sometimes wonder what life would have been without the war." Then she gave a playful smile. "More than likely, you'd be married to Mary Beth Morrison and have a couple of red-headed sons by now."

He made a scoffing sound. "Mary Beth was easy on the eyes. But I'd not have her for a wife. She's like a filly that looks good in the pasture, but isn't much use for anything. Anytime the going got hard, Mary Beth didn't know what to do except sit and cry." He went on, "Besides, after the way she treated you—turning her back on a lifelong friend, I lost any liking for her. I won't marry a woman I don't respect."

With nervous fingers, Nelda made imaginary pleats in her skirt. She did not want to be diminished in his eyes, and yet she felt compelled to confess. She drew a deep breath and said, "After their house burned, Mary Beth and Tabbitha came to me for help. It was the day Mama died. I slammed the door in their faces." She kept her eyes averted. "All that resentment and bitterness just boiled over. After they had treated my family like lepers, I thought, How dare they come to me for help. It was cold and snowing, and I had no idea what they would do, but I slammed the door anyway. I know it was heartless. I'm even shocked at myself. I suppose now you'll think I'm horrible."

He took one hand from the reins to gently lift her chin.

"No. I don't think you're horrible. I think you're human." He let her chin go and toyed with the reins. "After the things I've done, I've no right to cast stones at anyone," he said. "I don't fault you. I've had a good bit of bitterness for the Morrison family myself. I've been thinking on that a good bit lately—bitterness that is." He looked down and brushed at a fly trying to light on his wide, brown hands. "There was a stranger, a soldier, at Gideon's hanging. He said even after Tucker and Gill beat him and put the rope on his neck, Gideon kept saying he forgave them."

"Oh, my," whispered Nelda. How could Gideon? It was beyond comprehension.

"Hard to figure, ain't it?"

"Yes."

He added, "I reckon when Gideon got religion, it was the real article."

"I'd say so," agreed Nelda. She was not charitable like Gideon. She hoped Gill and Tucker were roasting in hell. As a chill laced her spine, she silently admitted how unchristian her reaction was. Quickly she changed the subject. "We seem to be traveling in a huge semi-circle," she observed.

For days, the trail had edged the lip of a vast canyon of intersecting hollows and hills rimming a wide valley where distant farms resembled squares on a checkerboard. Nelda never tired of the majestic view or the deepening colors of vibrant foliage.

"We are," Allen agreed. "As the crow flies, Jasper isn't so far, but we have to go around this canyon. Country is too rough to go straight across." He looked at her. "But I'm glad. It gives me time to be with you. That's the only thing that gives me pleasure these days."

Not making a response, she merely fidgeted. She could not meet the piercing blue eyes. She was walking a tightrope—wanting to be his good friend and yet keeping him at arm's distance. She feared Della was right. If she weren't careful she'd lose even his friendship.

In the days that followed, Nelda felt growing respect for Miss Emma. Although the ailing woman's face bore the traces of suffering, she never complained. In the conversations they shared, her wit and charm finally earned Nelda's admiration and liking. Allen, on the other hand, was often silent and morose.

When he stepped away from camp one evening, Miss Emma turned to her. "Something is eating that man alive. I'm worried about him."

Nelda nodded. "I am too. He never used to be like this. Allen was the most happy-go-lucky person I knew. Of course, he's heartbroken over his brother's death. Still, he wasn't like this even after his father was killed. I suppose finding Seamus's body on the battlefield was an extra shock."

"Which battlefield?" Miss Emma quickly asked.

"Massard Prairie—the battle near the fort a few weeks ago. Didn't you know?"

Miss Emma's eyes rounded. "I had no idea. Oh my!" she breathed. "I heard a rumor at the fort—the day after that battle. I never even considered it until just now—"

"What?" asked Nelda, sitting up straighter.

"One of the privates swore he saw a Rebel shoot a Federal soldier and then cart the body off the field on his horse. I wonder—"

Nelda sucked in a breath. Her stomach knotted. "Dear God, no!" she muttered and covered her mouth in horror.

Surely it wasn't true! Yet it made sense. Her sorrowful eyes sought him in the darkness.

Allen had killed Seamus!

Desperately, she wanted to help, but there was no way to undo such a tragedy. It grieved her to realize he had not confided in her, turned to her for comfort—then again, why should he? She had—as Della said—pushed him away, again and again. Her arms longed to reach out and console. She dared not. Allen wanted to keep his secret.

So far as Nelda could see from a distance, the tall, regal young woman standing in the cabin doorway bore no resemblance to Miss Emma. As the wagon drew near, the woman's hard face crumpled into tears. She sprang forward. The butcher knife hidden in her skirts fell from her fist and clattered to the porch.

"Ma!" she cried. "Oh, Ma!" She flew to the wagon, reaching open arms as Miss Emma stepped over Nelda and climbed down. It's the miracle I've prayed for!"

After a tearful greeting, Miss Emma drew back to eye the threadbare dress and mussed hair. "Dorcas, what in the world has happened?" asked Miss Emma, taking her daughter into her arms again and smoothing the hair off her brow. "What's happened?"

"Wallace," she stammered.

"What about Wallace?" asked Miss Emma.

"Oh, Ma, he's dead!" She talked around sobs. "I got the word a month ago. He was killed at Vicksburg. Since then, I've almost lost my mind. We have almost nothing left to eat, and my milk has almost dried up. The baby cries all the time. It breaks my heart," she sobbed.

"I knew something was wrong," muttered Miss Emma.

"It's terrible." Dorcas bowed her head into her hands and wept.

"There, there." Miss Emma leaned on her arm. "Let's all go inside so I can sit. I'm weak as branch water."

"Oh, you're sick!" she cried. Her eyes grew desperate.

"No, no." Miss Emma shushed her. "I'm getting well. Just tired from the trip. These are my friends, Allen Matthers and Nelda Horton. We all need to rest a bit after that rugged ride."

Dorcas' face flushed. "I don't have much to offer guests," she explained when they were inside the near empty cabin. "Bushwhackers hit a month or so back and cleaned me out of all our food and some house plunder. If it hadn't been for some kind neighbors who shared their little, I suppose we'd have starved.

She turned woeful eyes on Miss Emma. "Ma, the villains took all our nice stuff—the mahogany sideboard, Grandma's little desk. They even took Papa's sea chest."

"That's all right," comforted Miss Emma. "We're here. Things will be better now."

What good will that do? thought Nelda as she spied the bare shelves on the kitchen wall. The cabin was one large room, holding a table, a few chairs, a long bench at the table, and two beds, one in each corner. Only one had a quilt atop the mattress. The other was bare.

Dorcas raised a shaky hand to smooth thick honey-colored hair gathered into a loose knot. "I'm sorry to be such a sight." She apologized in near whisper. "But for the last few weeks, things have been terrible."

Two small girls retreated, big-eyed, to the far side of the room. One, no older than five, held a wailing baby on her hip. The other, about four years old, sought comfort in a thumb crammed into her down-turned mouth.

Allen stepped outside and soon entered with their food basket. Nelda joined him to quickly put bread and meat onto a tin plate. With a little urging, the girls left the corner, sat down, and soon were shoving food into their little mouths. It took more urging to convince Dorcas.

"You need to, hon, for the baby's sake. Sit down and eat," pleaded Miss Emma. "There's enough for all of us, isn't there, Allen?"

"Sure is, ma'am. I can shoot some more game when this squirrel is gone."

"Thank you," whispered Dorcas. At first she only nibbled. But after a few bites, she too, ate ravenously.

Nelda, from the corner of her eye, studied her. In spite of obvious suffering, she was lovely, with a porcelain face and full-busted, erect carriage. She glanced up to see Allen studying Dorcas also.

That evening, Allen asked Dorcas, "Ma'am, do you have any salt, enough to cure meat? I'm going hunting in the morning. If I have good luck, there'll be enough to eat fresh and some to cure."

She looked up from caressing the whimpering baby in her arms. "That's about the only thing I do have. When it started getting scarce around here, I hid our salt keg in the barn under the hay. The marauders never found it."

The next days passed in a whirlwind of activity. Allen killed a fat doe and several rabbits and squirrels to preserve with hickory smoke and salt. He built a fish trap and caught a good supply to salt down as well. While Nelda and Dorcas helped prepare the game, cooked, and cleaned house, Miss Emma sat in a chair and visited with her grand-daughters and tried to pacify the fretting baby.

Near dark, a mist began falling, and by nightfall it was a cold pouring rain. Allen built a fire in the fireplace. After supper, they drew near the cheery blaze to warm before bedtime.

Dorcas had brightened more each day since their coming. Tonight she was cheerful, laughing and chatting while she combed out the girls' hair and braided it for the night.

"Ma," complained the oldest, "I wish you wouldn't always braid my hair at night. It's lumpy to sleep on."

"You'd like it less if I didn't. It would be a tangled mess in the morning and then I'd have to pull out the snarls."

Allen reached a hand to his own hair, hanging long on his collar. "I don't get a haircut soon, I'll have to start braiding my hair."

"I'll cut it—" began Nelda.

Eagerly, Dorcas interrupted. "Oh, let me cut it, Mr. Matthers. I'm a good hand at cutting hair. I always cut Wallace's. I'd love to repay you, at least a little, for all you've done."

"That's mighty nice of you, ma'am."

"Good! Off to bed with you, girls. Mr. Matthers, sit right here while I get my scissors."

She draped a cloth around his shoulders and combed through the thick mane. "If you don't mind me saying so, you have beautiful hair. It's almost a shame to cut it."

"I reckon you can just braid it, if you're a mind to," he jested.

She laughed and began to snip.

Nelda stood. "Good night," she said. As she made her way up the ladder into the loft where her pallet was spread alongside the girl's beds, she failed to see Miss Emma's sly smile.

One morning Allen rose from the table. "That was a fine meal, ma'am."

Dorcas smiled. "I'm glad you enjoyed it, Mr Matthers. There would be no food on this table if not for you. I hope you know how much I appreciate all you've done."

"Call me Allen, ma'am. It's my pleasure to help any way I can." He went on, "As soon as I finish splitting that wood I snaked in yesterday, I'm going after more. I doubt I'll be back until late this evening, so if you don't mind I'll just take this piece of cornbread along. "

"Please call me Dorcas," she insisted. "Of course take the bread." She reached for another piece. Her eyes were soft as she handed him the bread. "Take another. There's plenty of meal now, thanks to you."

He wondered how hefty Miss Emma, with her bright blue eyes, could have had such a slim, green-eyed daughter. He figured Elmer Hanover must have had green eyes. As Miss Emma had claimed, he must have been handsome. Miss Emma wasn't ugly. But she was by no means a handsome woman like Dorcas; although, there were tracks of sorrow on Dorcas's face, the same kind he saw when looking into a mirror. He recognized sorrow.

As he stepped outside, Nelda, with a shawl around her shoulders, followed him into the yard. He strode toward the pile of logs he had dragged in behind the mare.

"When do you plan to start back?"

He raised the ax and took a swing before answering. "I figure to cut a good bit of wood, and then see if I can scrape up a few more supplies. I'll need to take the wagon, and I figure I'll be gone about a week. I know some folks near Harrison that might be able to help get together enough to get these folks through till spring." He looked back at the house. "I know you're in a hurry, but Dorcas and her family are apt to starve if I don't."

Nelda's brows rose. He took another swing, severing the log. Then he propped it on end and with two more swings, split it into smaller pieces. He tossed the severed wood into a nearby pile.

"I'm sorry if the delay makes you mad," he said.

"I'm not mad."

"Then why are you scowlin'?"

"I am not scowling." She looked away, but after a moment she looked back. "Of course, I'm anxious to get back. Who knows what is happening to Della or the orphans at the fort?"

"There's children right here to worry about. Dorcas needs help—" He stopped short when she whirled and stalked away.

His eyes followed her until she slammed the door. He shook his head and began chopping again. Didn't she realize he couldn't ride off and leave this family to starve? Lately she had been hard to figure. She had acted half mad at him since they arrived.

After pondering a bit, he decided it was small wonder she was put out. He was sorry company. If he stayed busy, sometimes an hour passed without a thought of Seamus, but each evening, while the women sat in front of the fireplace chatting and trying to quiet the cranky baby, he— in spite of mentally vowing not to—slipped into brooding silence. Last night, he had looked up to meet Dorcas's eyes. In the exchanged glance, he had felt and returned her sympathy. Then, with hardly a word of leave taking, Nelda had stood and gone to bed. He would suspect she was jealous if she hadn't already made it plain that he was not for her. She was right. These days, he was not fit for any woman.

CHAPTER 13 ⌒

Allen returned with a load of supplies, food, a few blankets, and a worn wool coat that must have belonged to a large man, for other than being a bit snug in the shoulders, it fit him. He offered no details, and Nelda asked no questions. She suspected his connections were in the Rebel Army. Most of the supplies were the same as soldiers received.

Miss Emma's strength began to rally. She began cutting apart one of the wool blankets to make coats to fit the children.

Weeks became a month. Nelda, in spite of silently chaffing, could not disagree over Allen's decision to stay. In spite of Dorcas having more nourishment, the baby continued to decline. Loud wails had become the pitiful mews of a kitten. Nelda thought its pale skin was as thin and translucent as Ma's Spode china.

In dim light coming through clouds, Dorcas sat near the window, urging the baby to nurse. It refused to grasp the full, blue-veined breast as she studied the tiny, pinched face while her own was the image of pain. She lowered her voice so the girls playing at the far end of the room could not hear. "She's dying, isn't she, Ma?"

Miss Emma pursed her lips tight and swallowed. "Yes, darling, I'm afraid so."

Dorcas stifled a sob. Then as silent as stone she held the child and stared out the window.

Nelda grabbed her shawl and headed outside. She could not bear to watch such misery. Pain, suffering, death, and misery. She had seen enough to last a lifetime.

Wind whipped brown-leafed oaks in the yard and fluttered a loose shake on the roof. The heavy skies did nothing to lighten her mood.

She walked slowly toward the sound of hammering where Allen was repairing a shed. A few days earlier, he had found a milk cow wandering in the woods. It was thin and had the frayed end of a picket rope attached to a worn halter. He suspected someone had hidden it from bushwhackers and then something had befallen the owner. Until someone claimed it, he had assured Dorcas it was right to keep and milk the animal.

Nelda stopped and leaned on the barnyard fence. Allen glanced up. "Liable to get wet if you're going for a walk," he commented.

She looked at the low gray sky and sighed. "I couldn't stand it inside another moment." She looked at him. "You know the baby is dying."

He slammed the hammer onto the nail with a fierce, angry blow. "I know. There's not a damn thing I can do about it." He propped an arm on the board and leaned his forehead against it. She watched with pity. Some things, she thought, were hardest on a strong man because his physical strength was useless. When she put a hand on his arm, he looked up. The grief in his eyes tore her heart. No doubt, he was upset about the baby. However, she was certain the anguish was over killing Seamus. She longed to wrap her arms around him, but she dared not. He would mistake her motives. She dropped her hand and stepped back. His jaws tensed. He began hammering again.

"I've cut enough wood and begged enough food from the army to get them by until spring—if they're frugal," he said. "I figure to stay around to help bury the baby and then we'll head back. I doubt it will live out the week. If it does, we'll have to leave anyway. If we wait much longer, bad weather could be a real problem."

She pulled the shawl tight and nodded. There was already a sharp edge to the wind cutting leaves from the trees. She had no heavy cloak.

He paused and looked around at the wide fields ending at a sloping creek bank. In the distance rose gray stony bluffs and the tree line bordering the Little Buffalo River. "Damn shame her husband got killed.

This is a fair place. Bottomland like this grows good crops. They could have had a good life here."

Rain washed the windows in torrents. The young sisters sat subdued and reverent, playing with rag dolls, but silently questioning why Ma said their baby, who was lying in her cradle, had gone away to heaven.

Dorcas, hollow-cheeked, looked through the watery glass. "Our burying place is across the creek. Even when the rain stops it will be days before we can cross."

Allen donned a slicker and stepped outside. Even louder than the drumming rain came the creek's thunder. He walked to the edge of the rushing torrent and frowned. Churning, muddy water carrying sticks and limbs parted at a large boulder and sent spray high into the air. It was at least two feet deeper than it had been the day before. Dorcas was right. It would be days before it could be crossed.

He went back inside. He met Miss Emma's eyes and shook his head.

She gently said, "Daughter, I know you want her buried there— alongside Wallace's people and little Aaron, but it would be far better to go ahead and let Mr. Allen prepare a place on this side."

Dorcas' head dropped. Then she nodded.

It was late afternoon before the rain stopped. With grim jaws, Allen went alone to dig a hole that he knew would immediately fill with water. He would have to weight the body with rocks. Before the women came outside, he intended to have the grave filled and smoothed.

The shovel sliced the soft mud easily. It was the easiest digging he had ever done for a grave. However, every spade full was as heavy as his heart. He hoped it was the last such hole he was ever called upon to make. Surely he'd done his share of grave digging in this life.

When he returned for the baby, Dorcas, her eyes brimmed with tears, reluctantly handed him the tiny bundle. His eyebrows rose when he saw the tiny body wrapped in a large square cut from a quilt.

With a defiant look, she squared her shoulders. "Since we're so short of covers, I suppose you think it wrong that I ruined the quilt." Then her shoulders dropped and her lips trembled as she whispered. "I couldn't bear to put her into cold, wet ground wrapped in an old scratchy blanket."

"The quilt is just right. Glad you thought of it." His comforting words were rewarded by a trembling smile.

The damp evening was bone chilling. All the women stood huddled inside shawls. Allen was relieved that Dorcas had told the girls to stay inside by the fire.

He stood with head bared as Miss Emma voiced a prayer. Her words were too soft to be heard clearly over the creek's roar. Dorcas stood silent—tears mixed with the rain pouring down her cheeks. When she asked to be left alone at the grave, reluctantly they returned without her to the house.

Allen looked back and frowned. He hated to desert these women in their grief, but it was high time he and Nelda headed back to Clarksville. The weather was an issue, of course, but he was more disturbed by a report he'd heard in Harrison. General Sterling Price and thousands of troops—with Marmaduke's, Shelby's, and Cabell's among them—had left Arkansas for a foray into Missouri. They had been gone for weeks.

With so many troops gone, marauding would be rampant. If defeated, Price's army might come running back any day now with Yankees on their tail. He would feel better when Nelda was safely at the fort.

The bay blew an impatient breath and shook his head protesting the harness. Allen sat on the wagon seat, holding the reins while Nelda made her final goodbyes. He didn't like the idea of Nelda traveling in such miserable weather. Fog was so thick he could hardly see past the horses' ears. But it had been unthinkable to just go off and leave Miss Emma and her daughter in such terrible straits.

He'd much prefer leaving the wagon here. They would make better time on horseback. But, he had promised Carrie he'd return her wagon if possible. She would be surprised at Miss Emma's generous gift of the mare. It was true there was no fodder here for the horse. Just feeding the cow would be a strain. But Miss Emma could have sold the horse to the army. Instead she insisted he give the mare to Carrie, and he figured the Hacketts could make good use of it.

Allen wondered how Roy and the rest of Marmaduke's men were faring. It seemed a foolish thing that Sterling Price had left the state to go raiding in Missouri. Even if Price was successful in retaking Missouri, it was probably futile. On his last visit to the army camp, he had learned that, back in September, Atlanta had fallen to Sherman's forces. Since it was a major supply depot, Allen imagined it was a deathblow to the Confederate forces in the East. He was glad he was well out of it. If he had his way, he'd seen his last battle.

Dorcas interrupted his musing. She stood alongside the wagon and handed him a gray knitted muffler. "Allen, I can't thank you enough for all you've done. Please take this. It isn't much but I want you to have it." Her soft eyes met his. "Please come back to see us."

He took the scarf. "That's mighty kind of you, ma'am. I'll wear it. I will come back and check on you the first chance I get."

She smiled. Her eyes went over his face. "I'll be looking forward to it." She stepped back. "Goodbye to you too, Miss Nelda."

"Goodbye." Nelda gave a stiff nod, climbed up, and sat alongside him, ramrod straight.

When Nelda settled back against the seat, Allen gave her a puzzled look. Then he nodded to Dorcas and gathered the lines. He slapped the reins on the horses' rumps. As the wagon began to roll, he glanced over.

"What you scowlin' about? I thought you were raring to leave?"

"Why do you keep accusing me of scowling? Of course, I'm anxious to leave. But it seems I'm the only one. It's plain you can't wait to come right back. I'm dreadfully sorry that taking me home is such an inconvenience."

Taken aback, he started to speak. His mouth opened and then closed. Something had miffed her. It was probably wistful thinking on his part, but she seemed jealous of Dorcas's attention to him. Maybe it was just the way of women. Even if they wanted no part of a fellow, maybe they just couldn't stand it that another woman did. Hell, he couldn't figure out the female race, and he didn't intend to get his hopes up where Nelda was concerned. He'd only get disappointed again.

He turned back once to wave at the women standing on the porch. Wrapped in fog, they were barely visible.

Since Nelda was in no mood to be reasonable, he decided to change the subject. "If we stop anywhere or meet anyone, I reckon we ought to say you're my wife. It will make it a mite less awkward."

"I suppose so," she said, but her spine stiffened even more.

He figured the idea didn't sit well with her, so he added, "Of course maybe that isn't a good idea, after all. Pretty woman like you, maybe I ought to take a lesson from old Abraham and say you're my sister."

Nelda scoffed. "One look at the both of us and no one would ever believe I'm related to you, Allen Matthers. Since I'm not beautiful like Sarah, I greatly doubt any man would want to kill you just to get me."

He spoke slowly. "Reckon, I disagree. Seems I remember a time when I wondered if I'd ever draw another breath because of that very thing."

She dropped her eyes to stare at her lap. "Me too." She looked at him. "I haven't forgotten how you saved me from that gang, and I am eternally grateful." She drew a deep breath and looked straight ahead. "Let's just say I'm your wife."

They rode for a ways in silence. The bay, although still unhappy with being hitched to a wagon, kept pace with the mare and plodded along in the sticky mud with only a few attempts to leave the path. Fog dripped from trees that had shed their brilliance. Leaves lay in wet drifts alongside the trail while low clouds wrapped the morning in tomb-like quiet.

Nelda shivered and drew the shawl tighter. "Such a damp, dreary morning!"

Allen reached back into the wagon and drew out a large wool coat. "Here, put this on."

"Thank you." She put it on and then laughed at the way the garment swallowed her with the shoulders sagging to her elbows and the sleeves hanging far past her hands. "A bit large," she said. "But it feels wonderful." She took a deep breath. "It smells like you, too."

He looked quizzical. "Is that good or bad?"

Her cheeks pinked. "Let's just say, I'm not offended by the odor."

"That's good," he said. "At times, army life makes a fellow ranker than a polecat, but I am fond of a good bath and a shave, and I wash my clothes as often as I can."

"You do your own laundry?" she asked, surprised.

"Sure do. Some men bring their slaves along to wait on 'em hand and foot. Since I don't have slaves or coin enough to hire it done, I pound mine on a rock in the creek or the river, and nine times out of ten, let them dry on my body." He went on, "In summer I've seen the Arkansas sudsy from fellows bathing and doing laundry. A lady better be careful not to come too near camp any warm winter day. If the air is warm—even though the water's ice—most of us head for the river and peel our clothes. Lice and filth are the worst scourges of an army."

She shivered again. "I hate filth as much as anyone, but I'm not sure I'd have the stamina to bath in ice water. I hate being cold—almost as much as being hungry."

"When it's necessary, a body can do a lot of things they never thought they could." He glanced over. "But I hope you never have to find out. If I have my way, you'll never go cold or hungry."

When she didn't answer, he hunched forward on the seat and frowned. Since it wasn't up to him where she went or what she did, he had little control over those things.

"I been thinking," he said, "about you helping those orphans. It's a good thing. A body ought to help when and where they can. In the spring, I figure I'll head back here."

"Oh," muttered Nelda.

"They're gonna need help getting a crop planted. I figure that's as good a way as any to spend my time."

Finally Nelda looked over. "Dorcas is a nice woman—and deserving of your help, I suppose," she said. "I'd never have thought it possible, but I consider Miss Emma a good friend."

"She thinks a heap of you," Allen said.

"Really?"

"Yep." He didn't add that Miss Emma's parting words to him had been to lasso that girl and marry her. She declared that after the wedding, Nelda would come to her senses and realize she loved him. He hadn't bothered to answer such a ridiculous notion.

"What do you plan to do after you've deposited me at the fort? I mean after you go back and check on the widow."

He glanced over, surprised at the poison tip on her words. Before he could comment, she went on, "I suppose you'll return to the army?"

He sat up straight. "No. That's one thing I'll never do again."

"Of course," she murmured.

"I aim to go home for awhile. There's no one there now, but..." His words died away. It didn't make sense, even to him, but somehow he felt as if he'd be close to Seamus again—as if his spirit might be there in the hills and hollows where they'd roamed as boys.

Preacher Simon would scoff. He asserted when a body died he went immediately to heaven or hell. He was probably right. Allen was no theologian, but he recognized Simon's expertise in such matters. In spite of no formal training, the country preacher was a Bible scholar, and besides that, he had a heap of common sense. Allen's brows furrowed. He suddenly decided it might be a good idea to go talk to Simon. Maybe he could even share the burden of what had happened. Sometimes he felt as if he'd burst keeping it to himself.

"Do you have any plans after that?" asked Nelda.

He shook his head. "Not really."

"No hopes or dreams?" she pressed.

"No," he said. After a bit, he admitted, "I used to have."

"What? Tell me."

He shrugged and flipped the reins again to encourage the lagging horses. "Oh, it seems foolish now, but once upon a time, I wanted to study law—be a lawyer. Reading that book of Blackstone's years ago, I reckon."

Her eyes rounded. "Why, Allen, I had no idea—"

"I've long since given that up. I can tell by the look on your face you find it a foolish notion, too."

"You misunderstand," she said defensively. "I just never pictured you with such ambition. It's not foolish. It's wonderful. Papa said that reading Blackstone is exactly how Abraham Lincoln became an attorney." She gave a little laugh. "Of course, being a Rebel, you probably don't find Mr. Lincoln a great role model."

Allen pondered. "I ain't overly fond of his politics. There's no doubt he's smart. I've read some of his speeches and debates."

Nelda hurried to add, "You're smart, too, Allen. After the war, when things get back to normal, you can get training—perhaps in Little Rock."

"At my age!" He scoffed.

"Thirty-one is not old. Many men don't start careers until they're your age. Papa had a friend who was a country doctor. After his own health failed, he became an attorney at fifty. He said lawyers weren't called out all hours of the day and night." She withdrew her hand from the enveloping coat and touched his arm. "Honestly, Allen, you should consider it. I'm certain there are attorneys who'd love to have such an intelligent man for an apprentice."

He started to dismiss the idea out of hand. Then, from somewhere deep inside, the buried longing raised its head. Abruptly, he shook his head. It was too foolish to even contemplate. He was a backwoods hillbilly—a bit self-educated because of his love for reading, but in no way qualified to even consider such a scheme! Nelda's shock was proof of the absurdity.

Nelda grew extremely quiet. From the pucker between her brows he could tell she was deep in thought.

"What are you thinking?" he finally asked.

"Oh, nothing," she said.

Allen's lips drew down. She was probably pondering how crazy the idea of him as a lawyer was. He fell into morose silence.

As the day lengthened, the cold worsened. In late afternoon, Allen felt a cold wet drop on his face. He looked up from watching the road. Scattered white flakes dotted the air.

Nelda held out her hand and caught a flake. "Surely it's too early to amount to much," she worried aloud.

"I've seen it snow heavy in November, but you're right. Usually it doesn't amount to much. I'd feel better, though, if we weren't up so high. Winter can come early in these mountains. There's a cabin a few miles ahead where I figure we can spend the night."

On the way to Jasper, in the mild weather, camping had been fine. This trip was different. Nelda needed shelter. They had only two thin blankets between them.

CHAPTER 14 ❧

At first, the hawk-nosed old man stood in the cabin doorway, gripping a rifle. When he espied Nelda on the wagon seat, he eyed them both critically for a minute, and then his eyes went over the team.

"Get yer woman in out of the wet. You can put the team in the barn."

To express appreciation, Allen dipped his head and gave a quick tug on his hat brim. "Thank you kindly."

When Nelda stepped through the door, the old man moved to the fireplace but propped the rifle near while he poked at smoldering logs. Red sparks crackled up the chimney as blue and yellow flames burst forth. Even while he worked he kept an eye on her. Nelda didn't fault him. One never knew how far to trust a stranger.

She was very grateful for the shelter and the warmth reaching out to embrace her and for the wonderful aroma of food rising from the pot hanging from a tripod. As her eyes adjusted to the dimness, she glanced around, relieved to find although the cabin was not clean, neither was it filthy.

He turned sharp eyes on her. "Poor weather fer travelin'."

"Yes, it is," she agreed and then related how they had taken a friend to see her daughter. When she explained how they had been delayed to help the widow and her children, his face grew skeptical. "I seed you pass by about a month 'er so back. Thought I recognized that mismatched team. That big bay don't look like no draft animal."

"He's not. He's..." she hesitated. "He's my husband's saddle horse. But we needed a pair to pull the wagon."

After taking a pipe and a pouch of tobacco from his pocket, he began to pack the bowl. He picked up a taper, lit it in the fireplace, and then held the burning twig to his pipe. He drew until smoke filled his mouth. Exhaling a deep breath, he removed the pipe but kept the stem near his mouth. "These days a body has to make do ever-which-way he can."

Nelda wondered where his sympathies lay, but he said no more. Instead he pointed to a stack of wooden bowls on a shelf before he bent to stir the bubbling pot. "Fetch them bowls." He ladled generous portions of what appeared to be a stew of pork and potatoes. "What's yer name?" he abruptly asked.

"Nelda Hort—" Caught off guard, Nelda blinked. "Matthers," she corrected the blunder. "My husband's name is Allen. And your name?"

"Perdue," he said.

"I'm glad to meet you, Mr. Perdue. We're from Johnson County," she added.

He said. "I've heared the name Matthers. Ain't that the bunch what plays fer all the parties?"

Relieved, she nodded. "Yes, that's Allen's family. Do you know any of them?" she asked.

His face instantly hardened. "Nope," he said and then squinting against the smoke, he swung the pot forward and ladled stew into the bowls.

Nelda took the filled bowls and sat them on the table.

Allen came inside, bringing a cold blast of air before he quickly shut the door. "Wind is picking up out there, and it's starting to snow pretty hard. Good thing you invited us inside. It's a poor night for camping."

"I've slept on the snow before," ventured the old man. From the looks of ya, I reckon you have, too. In the army, ain't ya?"

"I was." Allen looked him squarely in the eye.

"Well, pull up a ch'ir and set. This here stew is gettin' cold."

Nelda noticed both Allen and the man neglected to share political preferences. At least he had not turned them out.

They ate in hungry silence. The stew was good, and so was the corn-bread he had withdrawn from a spider buried in coals.

"This is a fine meal," said Nelda.

Allen paused between bites. "It is. Not many lone men cook such a feast for themselves," he observed, giving the old man a penetrating look. "Especially these days."

Before answering, Perdue took another slurping spoonful. "I keep a big pot on the fire. Never know but what ya might have company."

Allen said no more. However, Nelda noticed his eyes searched the cabin. It occurred to her that he must suspect the old man of something, but she wasn't sure what. When darkness settled and the old man lit the lantern on the table, she realized Mr. Perdue was not as old as he had appeared in dim light. Although his hair and beard were gray, there were few wrinkles on his face. Nelda judged him to be about sixty.

"You're mighty lucky to still have coal oil to burn."

She detected an undercurrent of suspicion in Allen's remark.

He went on, "Most folks have been using candles for a couple of years."

A sour look was the old man's response. In the tense silence, the crackle of the fire seemed loud. Then his eyes narrowed. "I live careful," he said. "Could be some folks ain't as sharp as me at managin'."

Nelda dipped another spoon of stew. It never reached her mouth. Allen shoved the table. She jumped as Perdue toppled backwards. It was then she saw he had pulled a hidden gun to shoot Allen under the table. Perdue fired as he fell, but the shot went wild. The window behind Allen shattered. The old man gave a shrill cry when he saw Allen looming over him. His head ducked like a turtle trying to return to the shell. Even then he raised his gun.

Nelda jerked from the loud boom. Her horrified eyes saw the top of Perdue's head was gone and his face was a bloody pulp. She gagged. Even so, she could not tear her eyes away. Her startled mind seemed frozen.

Allen looked up, his head wreathed in powder smoke. "I'm sorry you had to see that," he said, "but I had to kill him. In another second, he'd have killed me."

"How did you know—"

"I was watching close. I heard the hammer click." He reloaded as he talked. "We have to get out of here, quick."

Nelda blinked and then looked at him. "What's going on?" she asked. Why would he want to kill you...us?" she added, instinctively knowing the next shot would have been for her.

"When I was putting up the team, the bay got rambunctious when I tried putting him into a stall. He kicked up the hay and I saw a trap door. Since most folks don't have a trap door in the barn floor, I decided to take a look-see. There is a pile of loot down there." He picked up Perdue's rifle and examined it. "This carbine of his is a fine weapon— a Spencer. It's a repeating rifle that shoots copper cartridges—mostly Federal Cavalry issue, and much too fine for a poor farmer."

"But we have nothing worth stealing."

Allen stepped to the window and looked out. "The horses. I saw him eyeing the bay. I figure Perdue was in cahoots with some bushwhackers."

Her eyes rounded. "No wonder he has plenty of food."

Holding the gun, he walked to the door. "That's the way I figure it. That barn has been used by several horses and not that long ago. I'm betting he was expecting someone, if not tonight then soon. Stay here," he ordered.

With extreme caution he opened the door. A cold draft flickered the blaze in the fireplace. She shivered and held her arms across her chest to stop the trembling. Her whole body was shaking, and she couldn't stop. She avoided looking at the body. She was no stranger to gore. After the Battle of Helena, she'd bandaged men's mangled flesh. She'd seen Bull, the riverboat captain, with his throat slit. Somehow this seemed worse—perhaps because Perdue was an old man or perhaps because she had witnessed the shooting. Whatever the case, she felt sick.

It was only a few moments until Allen reappeared. After taking a blanket from the bed, he draped it around her shoulders. He opened the door, and, peering around, he took her hand to steady her on the frozen porch, and then his big hands circled her waist and lifted her over the slick rock that was the doorstep. When her feet touched the ground, he pulled her forward, running through the darkness. Icy wind whipped her skirts and blew wetness into her face. Once, she slipped, but he grabbed and steadied her. She marveled that he could see where to put his feet. She could not see a thing. She bent her head against the gale and blindly followed where he led.

Allen threw open the barn door. When they were inside, he shut it and cupped his hands and struck a match on a post and lit a lantern hanging on the wall. The mare nickered and the familiar scent of horse and hay and barn brought a touch of normalcy to the surreal night. Nelda was surprised to see the horses already hitched to the wagon.

He answered her inquisitive look. "I figured we'd be leaving in a hurry." He helped her onto the seat. "Can you drive a team?"

"I never have, but I've driven a one horse buggy lots of times."

He looked around and then got a saddle from atop a stall partition and threw it into the back of the wagon. After a quick search of the tack room, he returned with a second saddle and added it to their load.

"I figure we'll have to ride," he explained.

After Allen blew out the lantern, she heard the barn door open. As he led the team from the barn and the wall of wind hit, she hunched over and pulled the blanket tighter. In the black, cold darkness, she was thankful to have Allen near. She was surprised when the wagon halted near the dark hulk of the cabin, and she felt the reins being pressed into her hands.

"Just hang onto them. I'll be right back."

It seemed an eternity, however, before she heard him near the back of the wagon. It sounded as if he stuffed some more things inside. She felt his weight settle alongside her.

"Here's a coat," he said.

Her stomach tightened at the thought of putting on the dead man's coat, but she took it and was instantly grateful for the course wool. When Allen sat an unlighted lantern in the seat between them, the faint scent of coal oil arose. The horses did not go willingly. If not for Allen's strong hands on the reins, no doubt they would have returned to the barn.

Suddenly, she saw a flicker of light and looked back. A blaze danced inside the cabin, flashing through the windows. She gasped and whirled to face him. "You set the cabin on fire?"

"Yep. The snow will soon cover our tracks. I'm hoping Perdue's cronies will think he died in the house fire. I don't want them following us. But the hair on my neck is standing straight up. I'll feel better when we're long gone from here."

Nelda, shivering, looked back just as a window broke and flames shot out. Soon, the whole cabin would be burning like a torch.

Allen seemed to regret the hasty words. "Nelda, it ain't likely they'll be traveling on such a night. I'm just being cautious. Bushwhackers prefer the dark, but I reckon even they don't like freezing."

"I'm not scared. Not really." It was true—astonishing but true. She always felt secure with Allen.

"Let's be as quiet as we can. I need to listen. If I hear horses we'll pull off the road and wait until they pass." They rode a long while through the darkness in silence. Finally he spoke.

"We have some hard traveling ahead," he said. "Why don't you get in back and sleep if you can. I piled some more blankets back there."

"I couldn't sleep a wink," she argued.

"You'd at least be in out of the wind."

"I'd rather be out here to help you listen. I have good ears. Besides, the wind isn't as strong now." It was not. Either a hill had blocked it, or it had begun to abate.

"All right," he capitulated. "But if you get tired, get inside and take a nap. I'll wake you if I hear anyone coming."

They drove for an hour. Cold crept through the blanket wrapping Nelda's feet and legs. Finally it even crept through the rough wool coat. Several times, Allen halted the slowly plodding horses to cock his head and listen, but each time, after a few minutes, he drove on. Several times the wagon jolted over rocks when the team wandered from the trail. A few times, Allen climbed down and walked ahead to make sure they were not missing the road. Nelda's stomach tightened with memory of deep canyons alongside the trail. A misstep in the dark, and they could plunge to their death.

"You're freezing," Allen noted. "I can feel you jerking. You ought to get inside and get warm under that pile of blankets. We've come a good ways. I feel better about our prospects. You need to get some sleep if you can."

"All right," she agreed.

He stopped the horses while she crawled back.

Tense as a bowstring, she doubted she'd sleep; however, she was freezing, and protection from the gale would be welcome.

She lay for a long while embraced by the swaying wagon and jarred by the bumps each time the wheels landed in a rut. Her mind replayed the events of the last few hours. The thought of Perdue's hidden gun under the table aimed at Allen made her queasy. If not for Allen's keen insight, they would both be dead.

Allen's skin crawled, and although he was willing the slow horses to run, he held them to the steady plod. Even though his eyes had grown used to the night enough to detect dark shapes alongside the trail, it was too dangerous to go faster on the dark, slick road. He dared not light the lantern. They were not out of danger yet—not by a long shot. He wanted no one to give a report of them passing. Although he had not wanted to alarm Nelda, it was unlikely their presence in Perdue's barn would go unnoticed, at least not if there was an observant man in the gang. The horses had left fresh droppings, and although he'd scattered hay over the floor, it wasn't hard to see the hay had been disturbed and the trap door opened.

More than likely at least some of the gang were Perdue's kin. If they—like most mountain folk—still lived by the unwritten code of the feud, they'd not rest until he was dead. Even if revenge was not a motive, he figured they would go to great lengths to stop him from telling the army.

He wrestled with the notion of going on in the wagon. It would be easier on Nelda. But his better judgment spoke against it. They'd make faster time and could hide their trail a lot better on horseback.

Suddenly he stopped the horses. The sound of hooves was faint, but unmistakable. "Damn!" he muttered.

"Nelda!" He hissed. "Wake up."

Almost instantly her head popped through the opening. "What is it?"

"Horses coming."

She quickly crawled out and sat on the seat. Allen jumped down, and taking the horses by the bridle, he led them off the road and into the woods. Tree limbs scraped against the canvas top. When one slapped Nelda's arm, she ducked her head to shield her face and eyes. The horses stopped.

Allen strained to listen. They had barely exited in time. In moments, the horsemen were upon them. From the sound, there were at least five or six men, riding single file. He held the horses' noses as they passed. The first hoof beats were fading when the mare gave a muffled whinny. Allen stiffened.

"Hey, Bill," called a man. "Wait up. I heared somethin'."

Horses turned back. "What's the matter?" asked a deep voice.

"I thought I heared somethin' in the woods yonder."

"Like what?"

"I donno—hit was just a funny sort of sound."

They all seemed to listen. Seconds passed. Allen gripped the bridles, every nerve straining.

"Hit was likely just a critter. Damnation, Curly. Ain't no one crazy enough to be out tonight but us. Come on. We're hours late already. Uncle Perdie will have et all the stew if we keep dallying."

"He's right," said another voice. "My mouth's watering for some of Pa's cornbread, too."

They began to ride on.

"Hell, I'm more interested in a warm bed and some sleep," grumbled another. "This night riding stunt is crazy."

"Aw, shut up yer belly-aching. It's made ya all rich men."

"Not lately it ain't. I wouldn't cross the road for the piddling little haul we made tonight."

The voices grew fainter. "I reckon you've fergot that sack o' money the old woman dug up last month. Ain't no tellin' how many more..." Finally they faded.

Allen expelled a loud breath. Nelda waited to speak until he approached the wagon.

"I thought we were goners," she said.

"I did too," he admitted. "I had hold of their noses but trying to hold both of them didn't work so good."

"Well, they're gone now," she said. Then she stiffened. "After they see the cabin, do you think they'll come back?"

"All depends. If they notice the wagon tracks in the barn they might. I'm hoping there'll be enough snow to hide the rest. Even if they get suspicious, hopefully they won't see the direction we came and will just get their loot and scatter some other direction."

"But we can't count on that," she said.

"No, we can't," he admitted. "That's why we're leaving the wagon. We'll make faster time, and we can hide our trail a whole lot better. If we're lucky, snow will cover the wagon tracks and anyone following won't know we're on horseback." His eyes were grave. "This is going to be unlike any riding you've ever done. I wish you had better clothes for it. Your long skirt won't work too well."

She took his hand to alight. "At least that icy wind has stopped, and Mr. Perdue's coat is warm. It smells like an old boot, but it is warm. I do hope that mare is easy gaited. It's been far too long since I've ridden."

Allen's brows drew together in a frown. He dreaded the misery in store for her. It would be a hard ride for him, let alone for her. In spite of the hardships, he knew she would doggedly follow wherever he led. They'd traveled together before.

More by feel than sight, he unhitched, and, drawing a pocketknife from his trousers, he cut the reins the right length for riding. Then he tied both horses to a tree.

"We'll travel light. I'm taking nothing but the blankets and food. More than likely, we'll be sleeping on the ground. I'll put my shotgun in your scabbard and I'm taking Perdue's carbine."

She hated leaving her satchel behind, but it was too bulky to carry. Besides, her other dress was worn almost threadbare as was the extra pair of stockings.

After lighting Perdue's lantern inside the wagon, Allen drew out blankets along with the sack of food, and then he pulled out a pouch and opened it. "Here's Perdue's pistol and some extra cylinders. Can you shoot a handgun?"

"Yes, Papa taught me."

"Put them in your pocket." He hesitated. "Nelda, if need be, shoot to kill. Those men are Perdue's kin. Their kind doesn't play by the rules. It's them or us."

"I hope it doesn't come to that," she said. Her face was a pale oval in the dim light. Snow fell gently on the scarf covering her head.

"Me either," he agreed. "Hell, I don't like killing. As a matter of fact, I hate it. It wouldn't bother me to never point a gun again—if things were peaceable, which they ain't."

Without a word, she took the gun. To feel the heft, she aimed it at the dark shape of a pine tree, and then put it into the coat pocket.

At a muffled sound, Nelda jumped. Immediately, she shoved a hand in the baggy pocket to grip the pistol.

Allen smiled. "It's just wet snow falling from a limb," he reassured her. Then he blew out the lantern and smiled to himself. She was game.

"Stay close," he said. "We'll have to ride slow. Don't want you dropping off a cliff. There's a settlement a few miles ahead. We'll rest there, somewhere out of sight until daylight. If that gang does follow, hopefully, our tracks will be lost among the others. Then I aim to leave the main road and take a shortcut across country."

He loaded the provisions and then untied the mare and held her steady. The saddle creaked while Nelda mounted. He handed her the reins.

Nelda was grateful for the saddles. Riding bareback was hard.

The bay snorted as Allen's weight settled. "All set?"

"Ready," she said.

Wet leaves muted the thud of hooves, but Allen knew they would still leave tracks. The snow was not nearly as deep as he had hoped. He had seen patches of bare ground under the trees. At least they should have a few hours head start.

He turned onto the trail and waited to make certain Nelda followed. With a nudge to the flank, the bay stepped out and the mare followed.

Frigid air bit Nelda's nose. With a free hand she rewrapped Dorcas' muffler, thankful that Dorcas had insisted she take it and the knitted gloves on her hands. Soon she adjusted to the horse's gait. The mare was shorter than Lily but her gait was smooth. Ahead in the blackness was the dim outline of Allen's broad back. For the next two hours, he kept a slow, steady pace, turning occasionally to glance behind. Nelda stayed close. She remembered the steep canyon alongside the trail. If Allen intended cutting across that rugged country, it would indeed be a rough ride.

It surprised her how quickly she felt the saddle. She was out of shape.

Off the trail a short ways loomed the outline of buildings. A dog barked. Allen rode on, but, after passing the farm, he reined and waited until she drew alongside. He spoke low. "That little settlement is just ahead. On the far edge of town is a deserted blacksmith shop. I happen to know the smithy is in Marmaduke's cavalry. We'll hole up there until daylight."

She would be glad to rest. It must be long after midnight. Her eyelids were grainy. She'd gotten no rest in the wagon. After being tense for so long, she felt drained.

With stealth, they rode silent and careful past dark buildings. Finally, Allen turned off the road. Right at his heels, Nelda followed as he rode toward a log structure. She stayed mounted as he got down and opened a wide door.

"Wait here just a minute," he whispered. He led the bay inside and returned shortly to take the mare's bridle.

Nelda eased stiffly from the horse's back and stood still. The room was dark as a tomb until Allen struck a match just long enough to get his bearings. Then by feel, he led the horses to the far end of the room, unsaddled, and took down bedrolls and the food bag. With Nelda's help, he spread both rolls on the dirt floor.

His voice was low. "You hungry?"

"No. But sleep sounds good."

"Don't take off your boots," he cautioned. "In case we have to leave in a hurry."

"Are you going to get some rest?"

"I'll nap for a bit, but I want to be awake come daylight. If they do come riding through, I want to see them."

Grateful for the chance to stretch out, even on the hard earth, she soon heard Allen's deep even breathing a few feet away. He must have fallen asleep the minute he lay down. It was her last thought before slipping into slumber.

A noise awakened her. She propped on an elbow. Allen stood near the wide door. It was opened just a crack, barely enough to let in the dim light of an overcast sun. As she stood, he turned and put a finger to his lips. She slipped to the door and looked out. She stiffened to see two men riding slowly down the road studying tracks.

"There's been enough traffic already this morning to sully our prints," assured Allen, speaking close to her ear. "Three more of them passed by a bit earlier, studying tracks. I figure they split up to keep from looking like a gang. From the voices we heard last night, I figured there were five of them."

Nelda eyed the men who had just passed. Both were medium build and wore heavy coats and hats. One rode a buckskin, the other a nondescript brown mare. They had stopped, turned onto a trail branching off the main road, and, still looking down, ridden from sight. Soon, however, they reappeared and continued heading away from town.

Allen put on his hat. "That's what I was hoping for," he said. "They think we either stayed on the main road or took another fork a ways on down the road. If we hurry, we'll get a good head start before they realize their mistake and circle back. Come on. We'll eat later while we ride."

The horses were already saddled, and his bedroll packed. It only took a few seconds to load hers, and while she mounted, he cautiously opened the door. Smoke rose from nearby chimneys, but no one was in sight. He also mounted and urged the bay quickly across the road. Skirting the fork in the road, he headed for a few rods into the woods before making a wide loop and, on a patch of stony ground, entered the trail leading down into a deep, wooded hollow.

Snow clung to the road in melting patches. In spite of the frigid air, the ground was too warm to hold the white blanket. After a few yards, the rocky surface gave way to mud, easily churned by the trotting hooves. Nelda glanced back to see the muddy hoof prints. The gang would have no trouble following that.

Huge trees, iced with snow—virgin oak, hickory, and black gum— lined the trail and filled the deep hollow that fell sharply away on the left. The trail wound steeply downward with numerous switchbacks on the descent.

Allen pushed on without a backward glance. When the trail occasionally leveled, he trotted the bay, and Nelda followed suit.

Five hardened criminals chased. It was never out of her thoughts. She had once seen Allen best five such men. However, then he had had the advantage of surprise. This time was different. If they could keep far enough ahead of the bushwhackers, they might escape. Or perhaps they could reach Little Piney where Allen had friends who would help. This was certainly a lonely, isolated place. She would feel better when they reached another settlement.

They had gone several miles when a big valley appeared on the right. Allen pointed and spoke over his shoulder.

"Limestone Valley over there."

Soon, she spotted a creek and, miles away, distant blue ridges. It was a beautiful land, one she would have relished seeing at a leisurely pace. They held to a lope until the trail grew steep again and then slowed. She silently groaned when Allen set the bay trotting. Already, her side hurt with the old familiar stitch. She set her teeth and nudged the mare's flanks. The pain became agony. It took great effort not to cry out with each jolting footfall.

The pale sun filtering through leaves was overhead. Nelda estimated they had come at least ten miles. Tall white-barked beech trees towered over one side of the trail, and bordering the other were tall layers of shelf rock. On the hills beyond were jagged outcroppings of bluffs. The trail grew so steep, she had to brace against the saddle horn to keep from sliding forward.

When the trail finally leveled, Allen began to trot again. Nelda bit her lip and started to knee the mare. She could not do it. The knife in her side was red-hot and searing.

"Allen," she gasped. "I'm sorry but I have to stop."

Abruptly, he turned back. He dismounted and held the reins while she limped to the side of the trail and sat on a large rock. "I'm so sorry," she began.

"The horses can use a breather," he said.

But she noticed his concerned eyes strayed back the way they had come.

"Give me just a minute," she said, "and I will at least walk."

"Rest a bit," he said. "We'll take a break and eat." He opened a saddlebag and drew out jerky and cornpone.

She took a bite and grimaced. "I wish you could have saved Perdue's stew."

Allen shook his head and laughed. "You're quite a lass, Nelda, me love."

She stopped chewing. "It's been a long while since I've heard you use that thick Irish brogue," she said. "I've missed it."

"Have you?"

"It reminds me of happier days."

"Like the day I kissed you?"

Her face reddened.

"Nelda, I'd given up hope—but lately I've begun to wonder. I mean could you...do you care for me at all?"

"Allen, this isn't the time or place—"

"It's as good a time as any. You know the old saying. We're not promised tomorrow." His look was probing.

She averted her eyes. "Please, Allen, don't. Not now."

He stiffened. "All right. Don't worry, I won't ever ask again."

She didn't know what to say. Her thoughts had been a jumble ever since Allen had made known his ambition to be a lawyer. In her mind, that shocking revelation had narrowed the vast social chasm between them. Of course, the chances of him actually doing such a thing were slim—but the idea was unsettling. She needed more time to think, to sort out this new view of things. She admitted her mind kept skittering away from the notion. She had once trusted him implicitly and been betrayed. In spite of that duplicity, he had proven faithful, time and again. To be totally honest, she recoiled from being hurt again.

There had been Fred. She had truly loved him. She never wanted to feel that pain again.

She looked at Allen's rigid back and drew a deep breath. He was a good man. He deserved happiness. Perhaps Dorcas could make him happy.

She stood. "I don't think I can climb back on that horse just yet, but I will try to walk."

When he turned around, his face was emotionless. "We need to hurry. Near where we'll cross Big Piney, there's a trail that enters this road. If they took it, they could head us off. I want to get there first." He took the reins of both horses and started down the trail.

With a silent groan, she followed.

The afternoon sun broke from the clouds and bathed the muddy road, melting the patchy snow like magic. It was not long before she began to sweat. As she struggled out of the wool coat, Allen paused long enough to help. He took the coat across his arm and strode on. Nelda eyed him with wonder. After the way she had hurt him, it was a miracle he was even civil.

After a few minutes, he looked at the sun and then turned worried eyes back down the trail. "Think you can ride?"

The pain in her side had eased, but she was not fooled. It would return the minute she climbed back into the saddle. She gritted her teeth and did it anyway, and, after three seconds, she was accosted with another jab in the side which bent her double. Her backside was dreadfully sore.

Allen's brows knit with concern. "You gonna make it?"

She nodded but set her teeth to keep from moaning. The pain was excruciating; however, it paled in comparison to being gunned down by bushwhackers. "How much farther?" She gasped.

"A few miles yet. If you can stand it, we need to lope here where the trail is flat. It won't hurt as bad as trotting."

It was not the answer she had hoped for. She prayed for strength and held on as the mare began to run.

The terrain changed. A ridge with big rocks loomed on the left, shutting off the distant view. On the right, the land fell away, almost straight down to a bench almost a hundred feet below. Heavy ropes of grapevine twisted in the tops of leafless trees.

The trail abruptly began to twist again, and soon a huge formation of rocks beetled over the trail. Scraggly cedars poked from the crevices of gray, pitted stones that were streaked with blue and brown. Melting snow trickled from a deep recess between the rocks to puddle on the road.

She breathed a short-lived sigh of relief when Allen slowed to a walk. Then the ache returned, taking her breath away. She longed to cry out, to beg him to ride on without her. He would not. She could not bear the thought of endangering him more than she already had. If not for her, he would already be at the ford. No, she must hang on and endure the torture. Surely she would survive a few more miles. At the thought, cold sweat beaded her brow.

Allen pointed. "See that valley. That line of blue down there is Big Piney. Little Piney is over that next mountain range."

Far off, at the base of the ridge, stretched a wide, roomy valley, cradling small farms and fields and a meandering stream that, from this distance, was only a thin blue line. Nelda could not stifle a groan.

"It's not far, now." He encouraged her.

To her it appeared a very long ride. She put a hand to her low back. "We must have come twenty miles. At least my poor body feels like it."

"It's been a hard, fast ride, I know." He sympathized. "I wish we could stop, but I doubt they've given up—not that easily. Either they are behind us on this trail or they took the other fork and plan to head us off near the creek."

"Then, what are your plans?"

"With any luck, we'll get to the ford first. We'll cross the creek and camp for the night. There are some bluffs not far from the ford, a pretty decent place to camp. I'll get you set up with a small fire, and then I'll go back and watch the ford."

"For how long?" she asked. "I mean, we don't even know for sure that they're following."

"They are. We killed their kin, and we can identify them—at least we can identify their hideout—and it won't be hard to prove who they are. They know as well as I do that the army has sworn to clear out the bushwhackers around here, and they won't want anyone carrying tales. They don't want to hang." He looked at the sun, now low on the horizon. "I figure they're only a couple of hours behind. Even if dark catches them, they'll be after us early in the morning."

As the sun settled through the trees, the next miles passed in a blur of pain. She silently vowed, if she lived over the ride, to never climb on another horse.

Her drooping head bobbed up with a jerk when Allen spoke.

"Wait here. But stay mounted. I want to scout ahead. That other trail they may have taken to cut us off is around the bend yonder. If you hear shooting, head off into the woods toward the creek. Go until you come to a farm. Wait until I come for you."

He dismounted, tied the bay to a bush, and removed the shotgun from her scabbard. "You ever use a shotgun?"

"No, just a rifle and a pistol."

After pulling both hammers back to half cock, he placed a cap on each nipple. "When you're ready to fire, you pull the hammers all the way back. Front trigger fires the right barrel and the back one the left. If you have to use this, don't take time to aim. Just point and shoot. If you're close enough, it'll do the trick. You'll only have two shots so don't waste 'em."

"I'll remember," she said and took the gun.

He then took the Spencer from his saddle scabbard and filled his pockets with extra shells.

"Allen," she said, and he looked back. "Please be careful."

In acknowledgement, he dipped his chin. "You, too." Then he slipped through the trees and was gone.

Although it was good to sit still, her nerves were as raw as her backside. Her ears, straining for every sound, heard only the trickle of water running alongside the trail and the tiny patter of melting snow dripping from branches.

At the same instant, the mare's ears went forward and a rifle shot rang out, quickly followed by two more. Nelda froze, listening. For several seconds all was still. Abruptly a series of blasts shattered the calm.

She looked toward the woods. Allen had said to ride toward the farms. That was what she had intended to do. However, after only a moment's hesitation, she dismounted, tied the mare, and pulled the shotgun from the scabbard. She was not leaving him alone to face five armed men. With white knuckles gripping the gun, she started through the woods.

She paused often to look and listen, and then slowly, carefully, circling wider, made her way through the trees. Ahead, near a giant sycamore, the low sun glinted off something metal. She stopped, hugging a cedar tree and waited. A loud report and a puff of smoke proved there was a shooter straight ahead. Circling even wider, she intended to slip far enough to end up a few yards behind.

Suddenly, a man yelled, "Curly, grab the woman! She's coming yonder through the trees."

Ahead a man lurched from behind a tree, heading straight for her. By the time she raised the gun and cocked it, he was only a few steps away. Even in the dim light she saw his eyes widen as she fired. The blast slammed him back into a tree. He slid down onto wet leaves in a pool of blood.

The firing gun knocked her a step backwards. Even though she dropped the gun, the jolt saved her life, for a spattering of bullets hit a tree near her head. She dove for a pile of rock a few feet away just before another blast rang out. She bit her lip and looked at the shotgun. She dared not reach for it. Cold sweat trickled down her armpits. She gasped and lay against the rock. She had killed Curly, but his partner had almost killed her. How easily it could have been her head! Where was Allen?

Crouching, she drew the pistol from her pocket and sat still with her heart beating wildly. From the sounds, she discerned two more shooters. Both seemed to be concentrating on a large boulder near the base of the slope. First one and then the other sent shots toward the spot where Allen must be hiding. So far as she could tell, Allen had not fired a recent shot. She prayed he was unharmed. Her eyes scanned all directions. There should be five marauders. So far she had accounted for only three. She bit her lip wondering if she should risk a peep. Some man might even now have her in his sites. The woods were deathly still. She endured the dearth of action a few agonizing minutes longer. Her heart beat loud in her ears. She doubted she could hear anyone slipping close.

Is Allen hurt?

Suddenly a volley of shots split the air and someone shouted.

"I winged him, Denver! I seen him jerk!"

The shout crystallized her decision. She looked out in time to see a man edging closer to the large boulder directly ahead. Surprised at her steady hands, she braced the pistol on top of the rock, placed the site on the man's back, and as Papa had taught, squeezed the trigger. He jerked. He gripped his side, and there was blood on his shirt. But she had only wounded him.

A shot sent rock dust into her face. She ducked. Her eyes darted all around. Another shot sounded, and a man cried out. Nelda scooted to another spot near the far edge of the stone and risked a quick peek in time to see a third man lying, arms outstretched, on the ground far to the right of the boulder.

She ducked back behind the rocks. Two men were dead. But where was the wounded man? Where were the other two marauders? When Allen remained hidden, she assumed he must have the same questions.

A cry rang out. "God mister, I'm hit bad. You've done killed my friends. You gotta help me. I've throwed away my gun."

Allen made no move. Neither did she. The woods were growing dark. She wondered if they would remain here all night afraid to move. She was almost afraid to breath for fear of missing a sound. It was surprising how many noises now reached her straining ears. They must be very near the creek. She could hear running water and even smell the odor of creek bottomland.

A rifle fired followed by deathly quiet.

Minutes passed. At a slight whisper in the leaves, she tensed and raised the gun. She almost jumped out of her skin when Allen spoke. "Don't shoot, Nelda, it's me." Out of the gloam, he stepped into sight. He hunkered nearby, cradling the Spencer. Her eyes widened to see a long gash on his cheek and a hole in his hat.

"Are you all right?"

"Yeah," he said. "You?"

"Fine." She looked toward the dead men. "You killed him?"

"He was hit but not bad. He threw out a rifle, but he had a handgun, hoping I'd step out."

"So there's three dead, now. You thought there'd be five. Where are the others?"

"I found where the horses were tied. I don't think the other two are here yet. You wait here while I go careful back to our horses. They might be waiting to ambush us there. I'll whistle if it's safe for you to come. If I don't whistle you stay right here till morning."

She let out a long held breath and nodded. When he disappeared, she kept a hold on the pistol. She wished for a fully loaded cylinder. There were still a few shots left in this one. But right now a full gun seemed imperative.

Her straining ears were soon rewarded with a long low whistle. She struggled to her feet and hurried under the dark trees toward the road. Allen held both horses. Nelda took the mare's reins and put her foot in the stirrup; however, her body refused to cooperate. Her feet were lead. As she held to the saddle horn and struggled again, Allen's hands encircled her waist and lifted her.

"Sorry," she whispered. "My legs just won't seem to work."

"You're lucky you aren't dead." His voice was gruff. "Pretty soon, we're gonna have a long talk about that stunt you just pulled."

She was too tired to argue, so she stayed quiet and followed as he mounted the bay and started down the trail. Since the sun had disappeared, the air had grown colder. She reeled in the saddle and prayed he wouldn't ride far before making camp. As they passed the fork in the trail used by the marauders, she glanced up the hill and shuddered. That ambush could have easily ended differently. At one time, the idea of killing a human had appalled her. Two years ago, when she had shot a bushwhacker out her kitchen window, she'd been nauseated. This time, her emotions were hardly stirred. It surprised her how callous she had grown. Or perhaps, she reasoned, she was simply too tired to feel.

The water was not deep at the crossing. By the light of a pale moon reflecting silver on water and gray rocks protruding from the flow, Nelda could see the moss-covered, rocky bed just below the surface. Beyond the crossing, however, were deep shadowy pools bordered by large shelves of rock and shaded with overhanging trees. She was thankful the crossing was shallow. A wetting would be more than her exhausted, sore body could handle.

Then, she groaned when Allen turned midstream and headed up the creek. Nelda raised her feet as the water grew deeper and splashed onto her skirt and boots. They rode slowly on the rocky bottom. Finally, after what she judged to be a mile, he left the water, walking the bay out at a rocky spot. Soon, Nelda dodged limbs and wound under tall, virgin timber in the dark, barely able to keep Allen's back in sight. He halted and climbed down. She sat still. Her wet feet and legs were ice, and her legs were jerking until she doubted they would hold her. She didn't protest when he drew abreast and lifted her.

He spread a blanket on the ground. "Sit here and rest while I spread the bedrolls. Here's another blanket. Wrap it around you under your skirt to keep the wet off you. I know you're wet and cold, but I don't dare make a fire. You can't even hang your clothes to dry. Those other two could be anywhere. Sleeping with boots on ain't comfortable, but it is necessary. I know. I've done it many a time in the army."

She knew he was right, but the thought of wearing wet socks and shoes all night made her teeth chatter even more. With cold stiff fingers, she lifted the wet skirt and petticoat. She was thankful only the lace edge of the pantaloons were damp.

She called through chattering teeth. "I'm decent, Allen."

He soon appeared to hand her a piece of cornpone and a hunk of cold meat. "It's cold, but filling. You need to eat."

"Thank you." To her surprise, the food tasted good. She supposed as Ma used to say, hunger was the best sauce.

They ate in silence. Occasionally, Allen looked all around and turned his head to listen.

After they finished, he shared the canteen and spoke, "I know you're no coward—and as you once told me—you go toward a fear and not away. But what you did today, coming out there after me, was downright foolhardy. And—"

She interrupted. "Allen Matthers, if you think I could just ride off and leave you to face what I thought was five armed men in ambush, you have another thing coming!"

"I should have known you'd argue," he muttered. His jaws hardened. He traced a finger along the bloody crease on his cheek. "Do you see this? The closest I came to getting killed today was your fault. If they had caught you, they'd have used you to get me. When that fellow went after you, I stepped out to take a shot and almost got my own head blown off."

She gasped and covered her mouth with a hand and went cold to the marrow of her bones imagining him lying dead on the ground because of her. Her next words were truly contrite. "I am so sorry."

"Sorry won't help if I'm dead. We're likely to have another showdown before this is over. I want your promise to do exactly what I say—and exactly when I say it."

In the past, when he had asked for her promise to forgo spying for the Union, she had refused. This was different. Although it went against the grain to bind herself with such a vow, she knew he was right. She had put him in mortal danger.

She drew a deep breath. "All right. I promise. But I'm not a helpless child. I did kill one of those men and wounded another. Surely that counts for something? Please don't just ask me to run away and leave you in danger."

Before speaking, he slowly considered. "It did count for some- thing—it counted a lot. It was a brave thing. Your spunk is one thing I've always admired." He faced her. In the moonlight, his eyes looked grave and serious. "What it comes right down to is if anything hap- pened to you, I'd rather be dead."

Her stomach tightened. She stifled a sob, hoping he wouldn't hear it. This was not theatrics. Allen was telling the truth. He loved her that much. Unable to meet his eyes she looked away.

He stood and walked to the horses. "I'm leaving them saddled. I'll loosen the cinches, but if we have to run, there'll be no time to waste." Then, carrying the carbine, he walked into the darkness and left her alone with her tumultuous thoughts.

For the last two days, she'd been sucked up in a raging tornado, spun around, and spat out. Every muscle and nerve in both body and emotions were raw and throbbing. She bowed her head into her hands and cried.

By the time Allen returned, she had finally regained some composure. His next words, however, sent her reeling.

"I know it goes against all propriety—and I know you set great store by propriety—but we'll both sleep warmer if we sleep close and cover up with all the blankets. It's up to you, though. I've slept on cold ground with only one blanket many a time."

Her cheeks grew warm. It was appalling to think of lying close enough to share blankets. Mama would be turning in her grave. But he was right. They would both be warmer.

"Nonsense," she said brusquely. "It's best to be practical and both stay warmer. We have a hard ride ahead and maybe a fight. We both need a good night's sleep."

"All right," he said. "I'll spread the bedrolls together. You keep wrapped up in that blanket," he added. "The others will be enough for covers."

When he called, wrapped like a squaw in the wool coat and blanket, she slipped under the covers. Quickly, she snuggled under the blankets and shivered. Her cheeks grew warm again as Allen lay down and scooted under the blankets. She eased as far away as possible.

He chuckled. "Nelda, you're plum off on the ground. I'm gonna turn over. You ought to snuggle up to my back and get warm. I won't turn over—promise."

At first she only drew a little closer. However, soon his breathing was deep and even. It was astonishing that he had gone immediately to sleep. Hesitantly, she scooted closer and soon lay cradled against his wide warm back. Her own eyelids grew heavy. He stirred a bit and she jumped.

"Be still," he ordered. "You're lettin' in cold air."

She lay still.

Sometime during the night she awakened. Even her cold feet had warmed. She sensed Allen was also awake. Then she wondered what had wakened them.

Still groggy, she whispered, "Is anything wrong?"

"No. The horses were stirring, but it was only a howling coyote. Go back to sleep."

She nestled against his back and was soon soundly asleep.

CHAPTER 15 ⌖

Allen slipped from the blankets. He turned and watched her sleeping. Curled into the perfect shape of his back, her dark hair fanned around her head like a halo. In the moonlight, her face, free of cares, looked like an angel's. Again he relived the nightmare of seeing her gliding through the woods. He had expected to see her killed any second. He'd never endured worse agony—except for seeing Seamus lying dead from his own bullet.

No doubt she was still exhausted. He toyed with the idea of leaving her asleep while he checked downstream to see if they were being followed. The risk was too great. He let her sleep while he reloaded the cylinders for the pistol. Then he felt in his pocket, drew out the box of cartridges for the Spencer, and studied them. The copper bullets were a wonderful improvement. A man had no worries about damp powder with them. He just wished he had more boxes. Likely Perdue had plenty stashed, but there'd been no time to find them.

The sun had not risen when he shook her shoulder.

"Nelda."

Her eyes flew open.

"I'm going to head back a ways and see if they're trailing us. If they are and if I'm lucky, I can waylay them while they're crossing the creek. Keep your gun handy."

She sat up. "Let me come."

He shook his head. "I won't risk it."

For a split second her jaws squared. Then her eyes grew calculating. She pointed toward the woods. "They might be right out there watching us now. I'd rather be with you than here all alone. Besides, if you do get a chance to ambush them, two guns are better than one." As his mouth opened in protest, she quickly added, "I'll do exactly what you say, when you say it. If you tell me to hide and stay down, I will."

He frowned. The idea of taking her back to the crossing went against the grain, but she had a point. He had no idea where the men were. Leaving her here alone could be dangerous as well.

"Promise?"

"Promise."

She started to rise. With a groan, she sank back. Then, as if fearing he would change his mind, she sprang up again. Allen could tell the effort this cost by the whitening of her face.

When she had finished eating the hurried, cold breakfast, he tightened the saddle cinches. "Need help mounting? You'll get used to riding again in a few days. For now, no need to suffer more than you have to."

She eyed the mare and drew a deep, shaky breath. "Oh, I think I can—"

His hands circled her waist. He swung her up and into the saddle. He almost expected a tongue-lashing but her voice was subdued as she arranged her skirts.

"Thank you."

With a tug to the hat brim, he said, "My pleasure."

In truth it was torture. He longed to hold her. To him, she weighed no more than a feather, and he longed to forever help and protect her. At every opportunity, she made it plain she wanted no part of that.

He stared at her pale face. "Remember, just what I say and when I say it."

"I remember."

The morning was chill but not bitter. This time Allen did not enter the creek. With the rifle across his lap, he rode along the bank keeping watch nearby and on the woods across the dark water, always aware that a few steps behind, Nelda followed. Occasionally, he stopped to listen. With the exception of a few birdcalls, all was quiet.

Finally, he pointed ahead. "The crossing is right around that bend. While I go check, wait here."

He handed her the bay's reins, and, circling wide up into the woods and slipping from tree to tree, he made his way to the bank. Shallow water rippled dead grass near the water's edge. Relieved to see no fresh tracks on either road or bank, he found a good hiding place nearby and hunkered to wait.

Half an hour passed. All was as still as the yellow dawn streaked the sky. If they were coming, it should be soon. He shifted his weight to ease a cramp in his leg. Then he tensed at a sudden noise in the leaves. Slowly, his head turned.

A few yards downstream a large bobcat, black-streaked and spotted, sprang onto a rock. Front legs standing, it sat back on haunches. With ears pointed forward, it fixed gray slanted eyes on him. After only a glance, Allen's eyes left the animal to probe the woods across the creek. Only rabid cats attacked humans. This one was only out for a morning hunt.

Soon, the sun sparkled on the water and edged its way into the woods to lay stripes on naked trunks and moss-covered rocks. Allen decided the marauders were not coming, but to be certain, he waited a bit longer. At last he stood.

The cat remained fixed, only moving its eyes to stare. Suddenly its ears perked, and the gray eyes grew fixed across the creek.

Rifle ready, Allen quickly hunkered just before riders appeared and stopped at the water's far edge. The two men gazed across the creek and then lowered their eyes to study the tracks. One was young, still in his teens. His high-pitched voice carried across the sun-flecked water.

"They crossed here, all right. Look, here's the prints of the heavy horse, and right there's the light ones of the kid or the woman."

As he started forward, Allen raised the rifle.

"Damn it, Ray, hold up. I tell ya, hit's stupid to keep trailin' 'em. Man, woman, or boy, they done kilt three men, and every one of 'em crack shots. I say let's go back, get them other horses, load the bodies, and head home. I know Curly was your kin, but hell, look at it like this, if we go back now, there's a whole lot of loot to split between the two of us. If we go on, apt as not, we'll get a bullet in the head. You seen from Zearl's wound, that feller that made the big tracks must have Perdie's gun—and he damn well knows how to use it. Let's cut fer home and live to enjoy all that money."

As Ray hesitated, so did Allen. He had a clear shot. Without a doubt both men were bushwhackers. But the smooth young face was too reminiscent of Seamus.

Allen's jaws tightened as did his grip on the gun. If they came on, he would shoot. If they turned back, he would let them live.

"Hit rankles to just let 'em go," said Ray. However, he pulled the reins and turned the horse.

Allen waited until they were out of sight. Then, in case Ray changed his mind, he waited a while longer. Finally, he stood. The bobcat had disappeared.

Nelda's face brightened as he rode into sight. "They aren't following?"

"Not now. I overheard their parley at the crossing. Both of them decided it was wiser to gather their dead, head home, and divide that loot." He gave a quick smile. "From your boot tracks, they weren't sure if you were boy or woman. Either way, they were afraid of you. They could tell you killed Curly."

"Good," she said. "I'm glad we're rid of them. Now we can stop looking over our shoulders."

He reined the bay toward the trail. "I'm glad we're shed of them, too, but never stop looking over your shoulder, Nelda. It ain't healthy."

In spite of the lack of pursuers, he set a fast pace. Although Nelda was likely suffering the tortures of the damned, he knew it wasn't permanent. She'd be good as new with a few days rest. He'd feel much safer once they reached Little Piney. She was being quiet. He wondered what she was thinking. Then again, he decided, maybe he was better off not knowing. She was probably cussing him for riding so fast.

He pushed on with Nelda staying a few rods behind. Occasionally, he stopped until she rode abreast. Her pale face bespoke misery, but she did not request a halt. At midmorning, he stopped near a fork in the trail.

"You making out all right?"

She didn't bother to speak but gave a brief nod.

He dismounted. "We'll stretch our legs a bit."

She eyed the ground and stayed seated. "I think I'll stay where I am."

"Afraid you can't stand up?"

"Yes. If I climb down, I'll never get back up."

He smiled, lifted her down, and handed her a canteen. "We'll go a bit slower from now on. We're getting closer to friendly territory."

Her brows arched. "Whose friends?"

"Yours and mine. By sundown we'll be a few miles from your Aunt Becky's."

"Oh, I'd love to see her."

He studied a minute. "If we pushed hard, we might get there today, but it would mean riding farther than I intended today. We'd not get there until after dark."

When her face blanched, he went on, "I don't think we ought to try it. I have friends closer by where we can spend the night and then head on tomorrow. If you want, you can spend a day or two at Becky's and rest up before we head on to Clarksville."

"I'd love that," she said brightening. The idea seemed to revive her, for after a short trip to the woods on unsteady legs, she returned ready to go. Once again, she made no protest when he lifted her into the saddle.

In late twilight, they arrived at a small cabin belonging to an old woman who was Allen's acquaintance. Nelda practically fell into his arms. "Thank you," she whispered and limped toward the door, leaning heavily on his arm.

The next morning, Nelda awoke more rested but extremely disappointed when Allen decided to head straight to Clarksville. He was right, of course. Since the old woman had warned them of a Federal army patrol headed up Little Piney, Allen should not risk it. Nonetheless, she felt dismayed over once again being so close and yet unable to see her kin.

The trail ran parallel with the creek, occasionally twisting and turning away to shortly reappear alongside the rock-strewn crystal clear water. Nelda was too sore to appreciate the fine morning, but she was grateful for the slower pace. She wondered if it was out of deference for her or because Allen watched for patrols. He was silent and morose this morning. She suspected being this close to his home held too many reminders of Seamus. She also was busy with her own thoughts. The last time she had made this ride, she had been captured by bushwhackers. If not for Allen, that would have ended in disaster. She recalled meeting his family and the delightful evening of music as she sat on the sagging front porch listening to the guitars, fiddle, mandolin, and Seamus's harmonica. That seemed years ago. So much had happened since then—Big Red Matthers and Seamus were both dead. Kate and the boys had gone who knows where. Nelda had endured Mama's and Papa's deaths...and Allen's betrayal. Without question, he had redeemed himself from that. Although, occasionally, the memory still reared its ugly head.

Finally, she urged the mare alongside the bay. "Have you been thinking any more about what you'll do after this?"

He looked over. "I'm going home for a while. I miss the place. First I aim to see you safely to Fort Smith, if you're still a mind to go."

"I am," she said. "I feel obligated." She went on, "I've been giving a lot of thought to your idea of becoming a lawyer."

He made a scoffing noise.

"Don't do that." She went on, "It's exactly what you should do. I've been thinking about how I might help."

His eyebrows rose.

"Papa has a friend who is an attorney. He used to live in Fort Smith, but I heard he lives in Little Rock now…of course he's also a Unionist, but after the war, that shouldn't matter, should it? Papa said he was a brilliant man—just the sort you'd want to apprentice under." She frowned. "Now, Allen, stop scowling. It's a great idea." She studied him a moment. "You're not afraid to try, are you?"

He looked away. Then he shrugged. "Who knows—maybe I am."

She drew an exasperated breath. Of course he wasn't afraid. So far as she could tell, he wasn't afraid of the devil himself. She had only been trying to jar him out of lethargy. She feared moroseness over Seamus might stop him from attempting anything of value. That worried her.

"It pains me to think you might not try," she added. "It would be such a waste—"

"A waste? Reckon my whole life has been that," he said.

"Now you're being ridiculous. Just think of how much good you've done—how many people you've helped."

"And hurt," he said.

She knew what he was thinking. "We all have regrets, Allen. I certainly do. What really matters is doing the best one can. Papa always said each new day is a gift from God, and He's watching to see how we unwrap it. Lately, I've thought a lot about that, too. I suppose that's one reason I'm returning to the fort. In the past I've been mostly a selfish creature. But I know I can do some good there for the orphans."

As a gray rabbit darted across the trail, he steadied the shying bay. "I reckon that's understandable. What about after that? You have any plans? Any dreams, like you asked me about?"

"Actually, I do." She glanced at him then added. "After the war, I plan to write a book—a book about the war from my perspective, a southern woman with Union sympathies, but also with a view for better understanding the Confederate cause." She went on, "If the North wins, there will be a lot of animosity against the South. I suppose it's a lofty ambition, but I hope to bring some reconciliation. Thanks to you, I believe I have a better understanding than most Unionists."

For the first time that day, he smiled. "I reckon you must—seeing as how we're traveling together."

She joined him in a chuckle.

Then she grew serious. "No one may read it. I might fail, but I have to try." She waited a moment and then gently added, "So should you. An attorney can do a lot of good. Something tells me the Southern people will be desperate for good representation after the war."

He stared down the trail. "I reckon you're right. But I doubt I'm the right man for it."

Encouraged, she urged, "At least give it serious thought."

He pondered and then slowly nodded. "I will."

She was delighted with his response and left him alone to think. She hoped—if Allen agreed—that she would be able to convince Mr. Baylor to take him as an apprentice; however, that gentleman might take a dim view of a Confederate scout turned spy.

Her shoulders squared. If Mr. Baylor wouldn't, they would just find someone who would! Her brows suddenly drew together.

Why was she so passionate about this?

Clouds rolled in, covering the sun. Along with them came a stiff wind that rattled bare trees and tore at Nelda's scarf. As the trail wound steeply downhill, she gazed west with unseeing eyes, hardly noticing the majestic scenery of the rugged Seven Devils, steep craggy ridges as ribbed as a washboard. The long morning passed with her thoughts in a whirl. She had slammed the door on a future with Allen, and yet, as she tried to imagine going her way and possibly never seeing him again, her heart gave a strange twist. She tried pushing such thoughts aside. Of course, she was too cold and miserable to be rational. Later, when she was alone in her bedroom, she would unravel all the twisted emotions. In spite of increased misery from biting wind and pain from the plodding gait of the mare, the thoughts refused to abate.

Allen raised his voice above the wind. "You all right?"

She lowered the muffler enough to answer. "Yes. Except for freezing to death and dying of soreness."

"If you're too bad off we can stop for the night."

"By all means press on. I'll make it." The thought of her own bed and cozy bedroom did revive her enough to grit her teeth and endure.

He shook his head. "I don't think so. You're white as a sheet. I know a place up ahead where we can make camp out of the wind alongside the creek. We'll camp there tonight and ride on tomorrow."

Nelda silently admitted she was glad for the decision. She could barely stay in the saddle.

The next morning, Allen let her sleep late. The sun was high by the time she arose to eat a cold, tasteless breakfast. He helped her mount and then searched her face. She knew she must be a fright.

"Feeling better?" he asked with concern.

"Yes. I'll be fine when I get home."

They left the main road to bypass the small settlement of Hagarville, and after a brief halt near tiny Minnow Creek, they rode on. Once, they left the road to wait in the trees as a caravan of three wagons pulled by gaunt mules passed. It wasn't army, rather a few poor families heading north, probably refugees trying to escape the war.

Nelda felt more dead than alive by the time they crossed the bridge over Spadra Creek and entered Clarksville. In deep dusk, the false-fronted store buildings and the tall courthouse were dark shapes. As they rode on, facing the cold wind, she saw a few flickers of candlelight coming from windows.

They finally stopped. Nelda sat still, wondering why no light came from the two-story white house. Allen dismounted and lifted her down.

She pulled aside the muffler. "Since we were gone so long, do you think Della gave up and headed north?"

"I doubt it. Traveling with a baby in wintertime would be downright foolish, and Della's no fool."

However, the house was locked. While Nelda felt for the key always left hidden under a certain rock near the back steps, Allen pounded on the kitchen door. Her fingers closed over the key just as Della called. "Who there?"

"It's Allen and Nelda."

The door opened. "Praise the Lord! I had done give you up comin'. I figured somethin' bad had happened." She stepped aside to let them enter, and then hurried to light a candle on the table. She wore a long white gown and shawl wrapped around her shoulders. "Miss Nelda, you's froze stiff. Warm yourself by the stove while I poke up the fire and make you a hot drink. They's some rabbit stew left from supper—reckon enough for you both to have a bite or two. Mr. Allen, you get on over here and warm up, too."

Nelda held her hands to the warmth as Della opened the damper, poked sticks into the firebox, closed the door, and pulled a pot onto the stove eye. The stew was soon simmering and sending out a wonderful aroma. Until then, Nelda had not realized how ravenous she was. Her mouth watered, and as Della dipped two steaming bowls to the brim, she was relieved there was plenty for both of them.

"Sorry we were so long in coming," explained Allen, around mouthfuls. "Miss Emma's family had troubles and needed help. How are things around here? You and Moses making out all right?"

"We fine," she said and then drew a quick breath. "I most forgot to tell you—that Hackett young'un come by lookin' for you Mr. Allen. His ma is right bad sick. She was wantin' you to go fetch her kin, that granny woman in the mountains who does the doctorin'." She pulled the shawl tight around her shoulders. "Miss Carrie had done said she didn't want me and Gideon settin' foot there no more, so I never went to he'p." Della glanced away and grew shamefaced. "Likely, if he was alive, Gideon would have gone anyway. I been feelin' right bad about it."

"Don't," Allen admonished. "It's Carrie's fault. She asked you to stay away and you did." He finished the last bite and stood.

Nelda paused with spoon in mid-air. "You're not leaving already?"

He picked up his hat hanging on the back of a chair. "The Hacketts are good friends."

She blinked. Of course he would go. She should have known. Allen would never stand idly by when a friend needed help. Hadn't he proven that with her, time and again?

"You'll come back soon?"

"As soon as I can. If she's bad enough, though, I'll have to go after Granny. That could take a couple of days. You try to get rested up and ready for the trip to Fort Smith."

She stood and walked alongside him to the door.

He paused, and as if memorizing her face, gave her a long steady look. He donned his hat. "Goodbye, Nelda."

When he opened the door, the candle flickered and went out. He stepped into the night.

She relit the candle and slowly climbed the stairs to her room. After setting the light on the dressing table, she sat down to stare at her image in the mirror. Abruptly, she groaned and buried her face in her hands.

What would life be without Allen? Cold, dark, and dead.

The thought was unbearable. Denial was useless. She had deceived herself far too long. She loved him. She loved Allen Matthers with every piece of her lonely heart. Just having him near made her alive in a way she had never known before.

Once, she had fallen in love with Fred. But she had grown into love for Allen, a deep and abiding love. Not the fluttery schoolgirl thrill she had felt with Fred, rather a deep respect and caring—a feeling of being incomplete and half-alive without him.

Allen was a man worthy of any woman's love. In every way he had proven himself a gentleman. How had she ever thought him too rough, too crude, beneath her in any way? He was noble in the truest sense. From the first, he had been her champion. Like vivid pictures, scenes flashed with new clarity on her enlightened mind. Allen facing Jess's evil gang—for her. Allen fighting and killing—for her. Allen risking death on the retreat from Helena—for her. Allen sitting by the sickbed, night and day—for her. Allen risking discovery at Fayetteville—for her. Allen braving a Union fort to bring a warning—for her. Had any man ever done more to prove his worth, his love? It was a selfless love, a love to cherish.

Why did he love her at all? She had done nothing to deserve it. Unlike him, she had been a selfish creature. It was she who was not good enough. She was not worthy of such a man. She had been a fool not to see it long ago.

Della was right. She was like Mama—blinded by prejudice and caring too much what others thought.

Now that pretence was ashes. She would tell him. She would ask him to stay.

She had no idea how they would manage such a relationship. It would be easier, of course, now that he was no longer in the Rebel Army and she was no longer spying for the Union. But she still felt an obligation to the orphans. A myriad of problems sprang to mind, but she pushed them aside, content for now to simply hug to herself the wonder of knowing she loved Allen Matthers and he loved her.

Early the next morning Nelda awakened to knocking on the door. Her heart sang when she saw Allen standing on the porch. Before opening the door, she smoothed at tousled hair and retied the sash on the long white wrapper over her nightgown.

He kept his voice low. "Sorry to wake you. I'm on my way to fetch Granny."

"Oh, no. Can I help? I could look after Mrs. Hackett while you're gone."

He hesitated and then said. "It isn't Carrie—it's Roy. He was wounded in the hand on Marmaduke's raid into Missouri. When they got back to Arkansas, he deserted and made his way home, running and hiding. He's in bad shape. The wound has festered and he's almost starved to death."

"Oh, no!"

"Don't mention this—not even to Della. If anyone questions her she won't have to lie. They'll shoot Roy if he's caught."

"Of course, I won't say a word.

"I'm sorry I can't take you straight to Fort Smith. I will as soon as I can, but it all depends on Roy."

"I understand," she said. As he turned to go, she called, "Allen."

"Yes?"

She hesitated. It was not the time to speak—not yet.

She added, "Be careful."

"I will," he assured her and climbed onto the bay.

She stood in the doorway and watched until his broad back disappeared from sight. She hoped he hurried back, and she hoped he saw any army patrols before they spied him.

Two days later, she answered a rap on the door. Her heart sped up as she peeked though the curtain, expecting to see Allen. Instead, it was a stranger. The gaunt woman clutched a worn shawl tightly and stared with scared eyes.

"Are you Miss Horton?"

"I am." Nelda stepped back. "Won't you come in out of the cold?"

"Thank you, kindly." The woman stepped in but refused the offer of a chair or anything to drink. "I can only stay a minute. I have to get back to my children. I live a ways out on the Wire Road. I have some important news—" She tensed when Della entered the hall.

"That's my hired girl, Della," explained Nelda. "You may speak in front of her."

The woman drew a deep breath and began again. "I didn't know where else to turn. I remembered you and your pa wrote articles against secession." Her eyes searched Nelda's face. "I assume from that, that you're still loyal to the Union?"

Nelda nodded and the woman continued. "A soldier from Little Rock is at my house now with a gunshot wound in his side. He's in the same outfit as my husband. He was a passenger on a steamer loaded with supplies headed for Fort Smith. The boat was grounded on a sandbar and sank downriver a short way from here. Sergeant White was riding overland to take the message to the fort when guerrillas shot him. He's lost a lot of blood. I'm not sure he'll survive. But he's frantic to get word to the fort so they can send a train to salvage the freight before the Rebels discover it. He says the fort is desperate for supplies. I was hoping you might know someone who could take the message."

Nelda bit her bottom lip. "I might."

"Wonderful!" she exclaimed. "But warn whoever it is to go careful. Sergeant White says he's the third man to fail trying to get through. One got killed yesterday. The other made it back to the boat after he got wounded, too." As soon as the woman had thanked her again, she hurried on her way.

Nelda made a decision. She would go. She'd ride night and day.

"I'm going myself."

Della gasped. "Miss Nelda, that plum crazy. You done heared how three growed men never made it."

"All the more reason for a woman to try. Perhaps the guerrillas will let me alone."

Della's bottom lip stuck out. "Mr. Allen ain't gonna like it. He done tol' you to wait till he get back and can go along with you."

"Della, I have to go. That boatload of supplies might make the difference in people starving. Maybe this is providence. As you're so fond of pointing out—the Lord works in mysterious ways. What would be the chances that I would learn about the boat getting grounded and that I would need to go anyway, and that I have a good mare like Lily to get me there? Don't you think the Lord might have had a hand in this?"

Only slightly pacified, Della turned away and sat Moses down on the floor. "Ain't no changin' you. You is the stubbornest creature ever was, so reckon I best get some food ready to take along. Likely you'll freeze to death 'fore you get to eat it."

Nelda hurried up the stairs. She opened drawers and began pulling out woolen petticoats. Suddenly she stopped, turned on her heels, and went to her parent's bedroom. With a quick intake of breath, she paused for a moment on the threshold. The room evoked so many memories. She hadn't been there more than a couple of times since Mama's death, not even to pack away their belongings.

She opened the drawer and saw Papa's clothes neatly folded. Upon taking his heaviest coat from the closet, she caught a faint whiff of pipe tobacco. For a minute she sat on the bed and let tears fall. Then she squared her shoulders, got up, and drew on heavy underwear, pants, shirt, and old hat. She tucked the too-long pants into her own old work boots, and, carrying the wool coat over her arm, she descended the stairs.

Della glanced up. Her eyes rounded. Nelda expected loud protest over the indecency of a woman wearing men's clothing. Instead, Della nodded.

"Least you got sense enough to go lookin' like a boy 'stead of a woman, and maybe you keep from freezing plum to death in them warm duds."

Nelda stepped to the mirror. "I wish I'd had them on the trip back from Jasper. This is certainly better than the smelly, old, wool coat I wore—not that I wasn't grateful to have it. Before that, the only coat we had was Allen's. I'd have frozen if he hadn't lent it to me."

"Reckon he froze then," observed Della with hands on hips. "That man do love you."

Nelda left the remark unanswered. "Do you have the food ready? I want to leave right away."

Della handed her a cotton bag stuffed with bread and meat. "Good thing I baked cornbread this morning and fried plenty of that wild hog my friend brung."

Nelda took the bag. "Thank you, Della." She started for the door but abruptly halted. "It just occurred to me that you might be gone by the time I return." Abruptly she put the sack onto the kitchen table and gathered Della into her arms. Della returned the hug with a hard squeeze. "I want you to know, no one ever had a better friend. I love you."

Della wiped her eyes on her apron. "I love you too, Miss Nelda. Oh, I know I scold and find fault. But you is a fine lady. Don't seem like I can stand to not see you no more."

"When you get settled send me a letter addressed to the New Era Newspaper office in Fort Smith, and address another to here. I'll get one of them. Perhaps someday, you can come back for a visit or I'll come visit you." She wiped a finger across her own eyes. She leaned and kissed Moses on the forehead. "Take good care of little Moses."

Della gave a soft smile. "One of these days he be takin' good care of me—just like his pappy."

"I'm sure he will," Nelda agreed.

"I be praying real hard for you, Miss Nelda—that you get there safe and don't have no troubles."

"Thank you." She began hesitantly, "When Mr. Allen comes, tell him…tell him that…"

Della waited expectantly.

"Oh, never mind. I'll tell him when I see him." With another quick hug for Della, she picked up the food, hurried out the door, and headed for the woods to find Lily.

Chapter 16 ⟡

A llen got off the bay, stamped his feet, and pulled off gloves to blow on his hands. Since noon the temperature had been steadily falling, and it was beginning to snow. The horse wasn't thirsty, so he remounted, crossed the swift creek, and headed up the trail past flat, overgrown pastures and fields. Sorrow almost overwhelmed him as he approached the rambling cabin that had been home. He pulled the bay to a stop while his eyes went over the weed filled yard and ramshackle buildings, the decrepit old barn and smoke house and the wide, low cabin with tall rock chimneys at each end. It looked like a thousand other deserted places he'd seen since the war began. But this one put an ache in him.

Seamus's sweet harmonica filled the honeysuckle air, and laughter, good-natured quarreling, and music echoed from the sagging porch where Ma sat fanning alongside Pa while he tipped a jug, drank, and declared it the best batch yet.

In reality, the music was only Little Piney Creek and the wind in tall pines. Allen swallowed, pulled the reins, and rode on. He left the trail and made a beeline through the woods. Daylight would soon be gone. If Roy were to survive, he'd need Granny Tanner's expert care.

The bay's hooves sank into soft loam making no sound. Allen kept a sharp watch but saw only a few wild hogs with long snouts rooting near the ice-crusted edges of a spring. They scattered and fled at his approach. Through the light snowfall, he soon saw a curl of smoke rising above the trees and heard the ring of an ax. He slowed, cautiously weaving his way through the trees, but came on when he recognized Elijah Loring's lean frame near the chopping block.

Elijah put down the ax and reached for a rifle propped nearby. Then he grinned and put the gun down as his voice traveled across the yard. "Howdy, stranger. Where you been keeping yourself? We feared you were dead."

Allen rode in and stepped down. "I'm alive. At times, just barely." They shook hands.

Elijah's dark eyes dimmed. "Sure was sorry to hear about your pa."

Allen nodded. "I know you folks have had your troubles, too. Emmitt told me about Caleb—a damn pity. He was as fine a man as ever wore shoe leather. Sure was glad to hear about Ned, though. Best news I've had since the war began."

"For a fact," agreed Elijah. "Hey, did you know Cindy and I got married and have a young'un? He's a strapping little fellow who looks just like Pa."

"That's mighty fine," said Allen. He glanced at the cabin. "You living with Granny now?"

"No. We're staying at Pa's until we can get our cabin finished. Pa and I work on it every chance, but it's sort of slow going with just the two of us. Now that Caleb's gone, I stop by every day or two to check on Granny. She can't lift big logs into the fireplace now so I keep plenty of split stuff handy." He gathered up the rifle. "Come on inside. She'll be glad to see you."

Allen followed him toward the neat cabin. The tiny woman gave a glad cry and hobbled forward on rag-covered feet to wrap him in welcoming arms. Once again he silently cursed the memory of Bo Morrison, the fiend who had tortured her by burning her feet. In spite of wrinkled skin, she had always seemed ageless. Now, Allen detected a weakening of the frail body, although the jet black eyes still danced with spirit.

"As shore as I'm born, if hit ain't Allen Matthers!" She stepped back and looked him up and down. "Honed down a bit, but jest as handsome. Shore is good to see ya. Tell me, what about yer family?"

He had dreaded the question and made as brief an answer as possible. "I've not heard from Ma since she left for Texas. I saw Dillon a few months back. He and Shawn had joined the army. Patrick and Mack headed west." He paused a moment. "Seamus got killed."

She gripped his arm. "Oh, no! Not Seamus!" Tears glistened in the black eyes. "That boy was a plum joy. I never heared anyone could sing so sweet."

Allen's jaws tightened as he looked away and then quickly changed the subject.

"Elijah, your cousin Nelda is back in Clarksville. She's fine and anxious for news of all of you."

Elijah's handsome face lit with a huge smile. "That's wonderful! Ma will be glad to hear it."

Granny pointed to a chair drawn near the fireplace and a roaring blaze. "Sit yerself down by the fire and warm. Hit's bad weather fer travelin'."

Viola Tanner, Caleb's widow, sat nearby, hunched over and wrapped in a quilt. She had always been a spindly, querulous woman. Now she was a skeleton with down-turned mouth and vacant eyes. Emmitt had said that after Caleb's death, she had lost her mind.

"Yes, it is," he said. He sat down and hurriedly explained his mission. "I hate to ask you to go out in such weather, Granny, but Roy is barely hanging on."

"Course, I'll go!" she said. "Lige, we'll have to borrow yer wagon. We'll leave first thing in the mornin'. Send Cindy over to he'p me get ready. She'll need to get my yarbs down from the loft."

After Elijah left, she hobbled over to a large pot swung over the fire and began dipping a bowl of good smelling stew and handed it to Allen. He ate, grateful for the filling warmth.

Before nightfall the news of his arrival brought visitors flocking. Along with Cindy and the baby came Becky and Ned. In spite of Union sympathies, Simon Mason arrived with heartfelt gladness and the offer of a pair of mules to pull the wagon.

They left the next morning, just after daylight. The wind had lain, and although the day was cloudy, only a dusting of snow powdered the frozen ground. Granny sat bundled in a warm cloak, scarf, and mittens, and a heated rock placed at her rag-covered feet. Allen drove Simon's red mules hitched to a wagon with the bay trailing behind.

"Hit ain't as cold without that awful, sharp wind," said Granny. "Yesterdee, the way my bones was aching, I knowed it was gonna snow. But thank the good Lord hit never amounted to much." She went on, sharing local gossip and news of the neighbors.

Allen, not inclined to talk, listened as they headed out of the timbered hills and finally into flatter country checkered with pastures and fields. Then she surprised him.

"Allen Matthers, I he'ped bring you into the world—I tended yer ma every time one of you come. I've treated yer hurts, from stubbed toes to snakebite. I kin tell there's a deep-down sickness in you now, eatin' at ya. You're keepin' shut tighter than a steel trap, but a burdened soul will sicken ya to death. Many is the heart that's been bared to me, and I've yet to break a confidence. Rest assured hit won't go no further than these old ears of mine."

He frowned. Then he fiddled with the reins and stared at his feet. He was soul-sick. For months he had endured the guilt like an anvil pressing on his chest. Although he had put no stock in Ma's religion of praying to saints and confessing to a priest, he sometimes felt he would explode if he didn't confess to someone. There was no one he trusted more than Granny. However, the words stuck in his throat.

He began slowly. Finally, the story poured out. She sat silent with lips pressed tightly together as he relived the agony. At last she expelled a deep breath.

"Fer a fact, hit's a sad tale, Allen. But you ain't the first to bear such a burden. I've done so myself."

He stared at her.

She nodded. "Gospel truth. Ain't no one living now who knows my story. When Pappy Tanner and I was young—back in Tennessee—we had a little black-haired girl, pretty as a angel. Eight months old and crawling. Usual, I raised the bedposts and put it on her dress tail when I went to the spring to fetch water or outside to stir the wash pot. That particular afternoon, she was napping. I needed a bucket of water and never wanted to wake her. So I left her alone on the bed, fast asleep. When I got to the spring I seed some ripe blackberries and commenced to pick a few and put 'em in my poke bonnet, thinkin' to make a pie fer Aaron's supper." Her face gone gray, she stopped for a minute before going on. "Crossing the door yard, I heared awful cries. I run fast as the wind but it was too late. She had crawled to the fireplace. Her gown was a'fire and her pretty black hair all in flames." Granny stared straight ahead as she paused again. Finally, she went on. "We buried her under the big walnut tree in the back yard, loaded the wagon, and never looked back. I couldn't live in that cabin thick with the smell of her burned flesh." She looked at him. "So, ya see. I know the tortures of the damned, too. Hit was my fault and mine alone that my baby died."

"How did you stand it?" he asked, his voice choked. "Some days, I think it'll drive me crazy."

"I know," she said, patting his leg, "I know." She thought for a bit and then said, "Fer a time, I did lose my wits. Even tried to take my life, but my Aaron nursed me like a helpless child. For the longest time, I hated God. Yes, Allen, I'm plum ashamed to name it, but I did. I knowed it was my fault. But God could have stopped it."

Allen silently admitted to such thoughts. Deep down, he also had faulted God.

"Then one day, I was sittin' in the rocking ch'ir and there on the table was my dusty Bible. Always before, I had read it every day. I picked hit up and it fell open of it's own accord to the Book of Job. Right there on the page hit said our days is determined by the Lord and the number of our months. That part about the months, jest jumped out at me. God knowed all along how short her life would be. Life and death is in the hands of the Lord. Right then and there I started to fergive myself. I had to let go. Hit goes ag'in the grain, but when ya think on it right and proper, everyone dies—some sooner and some later. I've outlived all my young'uns—little Sally and Reeda May and Caleb, my last. I don't know why God's left me here fer ninety four years and took them. But I reckon that's his business. Mine is jest to trust. I've said, time and again, this here life is one big test, to see if we'll turn toward the good Lord er away from him. Allen, you got to leave this go and fergive yerself. Seamus was a growed man, a soldier gone off to shoot and to kill. He'd not fault you none fer doing yer duty. You got to think on this rightly. This were an accident to you, but still and all, the Lord is the one determined Seamus's months and years."

He drew a deep breath. "I don't have your faith, Granny."

She put dark eyes on him. "A body is as close to God as he wants to be."

He pondered. "Reckon that's true. I read the Bible and pray sometimes. But not like you."

"Ain't too late to start," she admonished.

He gave a half smile. "Thanks for listening. I think it helped to get it off my chest."

"I believe it done me good, too, to talk about little Sally. I've not spoke her name for many a year." She gave a tiny chuckle. "I reckon Reeda May and Caleb was right vexed at me when they got to heaven and found a sister they never even knowed about."

When the mules' ears perked forward, Allen reached for the shotgun. Around the bend came a mule with a heavy rider overlapping the saddle. Allen relaxed as he recognized Tom Sorrells.

"Hit's fat Tom Sorrells," muttered Granny. "That ne'er-do-well won't stir his stumps fer nothing but to get to the table 'er to collect gossip. Must be somethin' going on fer even him to be traveling in this weather."

Allen shared Granny's opinion of Tom. He was an idle man and more gossipy than a woman, but a good neighbor so long as it required no effort.

Tom's round face was a wreath of smile. "Why, howdy, Allen!" He doffed his hat. "Granny." Tilting his head to the side, he eyed them with curiosity. "Must be something big to bring you out in such weather?"

Granny's lips turned down. "I was just sayin' the same about you, Tom."

"Oh, I've been to town fer Laveney. She was hoping fer a word from Todd. She's not heared since his company rid off to Missouri again. Weren't no word from him. But he still ain't on the dead er missin' lists."

"That's good," said Granny.

Allen recalled that plump Laveney Sorrells had married a local boy named Todd Dougan who had joined Marmaduke's company.

"Emmitt says Marmaduke got captured. No way of knowin' yet about Todd, but Laveney will swoon fer shore. She drops over if ya even say boo." His eyes suddenly lit. "Granny, you got any salts to bring her around?"

She gave a disgusted snort. "I ain't some ninny given to the vapors. So, no, I don't carry no smelling salts around in my apron pocket. Throw some cold water in her face. She'll come around quick enough."

Tom looked crestfallen, but only for a moment before turning his attention to Allen. "A feller Emmitt knowed come in while I was there. He'd just come from Spadra Landing off the Little Rock boat. He says Abe Lincoln has done ordered 'em to abandon Fort Smith. Ain't that somethin'?" He slapped his leg in glee. "Jest when we thought we was whupped, the Yankees is skedaddling!"

Allen frowned. It made no sense. The Union had repulsed every attack on the fort. "Did he say why?"

Tom shrugged. "Too hard to supply, and too many guerrillas, I reckon." Then curiosity prompted Tom to press on. "Ya'll heading in fer supplies, are ye?"

"Ya know darn well, I ain't," snapped Granny. "Why don't ya just come right out and ask our business?"

Tom's face never reddened. Allen supposed he was used to Granny's brusque ways. She was famous for them.

"Then where you headin'?" he abruptly asked.

"To London to see the Queen." She poked Allen in the side. "Hurry up, Allen, er we'll miss the boat."

Allen drove off and left Tom staring.

Granny chuckled. "His shirttail won't hit his back till he finds out. Bet ya a round silver dollar he stops to ask Ned 'er Elijah."

"No bet," said Allen.

"Good thing," she said with a smile. "I've not even seed a dollar in four years."

Allen's mind was on weightier matters. If the fort was being abandoned, Nelda must not return. The town crammed with starving refugees would be chaos after the army retreated. He was glad to get the news in time to stop her, and he was glad she would stay in Clarksville. At least he could see her occasionally and bring her supplies.

Although he worried about Granny's stamina, she never uttered a word of complaint. With only a few short stops, they pressed on and arrived near town in late afternoon. Allen was tempted to drive to Nelda's, but they would make better time bypassing town and heading straight for the Hacketts'.

Isaac met them on the trail. "Ma is sure gonna be proud to see you. Pa is awful sick." He scrambled aboard the tailgate to ride the short distance to the cabin where Carrie, wrapped in an old shawl, stood on the porch.

She hurried down the steps. "Aunt Bitty, I've done all I knowed, but his hand is festerin', and he's a burnin' up with fever."

Granny leaned heavily on Allen's arm as she went up the steps. "Calm yerself, Carrie. I'll do what I kin."

Feverish eyes open, Roy lay pale and still on the pillow. Allen frowned when Carrie uncovered the wound. It was worse. Red streaks ran up the arm. While Granny studied it, she removed her wraps, and then drew a tin box of snuff from her apron pocket and placed a pinch between her lower lip and gum.

"Hit ain't good, fer a fact." She paused in thought. "A surgeon would take off the hand. But I ain't no surgeon."

Carrie drew a scared breath. "Maybe Allen—"

Granny shook her head. "I've seed folks try hit, but never but what the person died."

"No," said Roy, weakly. "I live er die a whole man."

Granny nodded. "We'll try somethin' else. He may not make it, Carrie, but hit won't be no worse than sawing his hand off and then him dying."

Allen silently agreed. In amputations, even surgeons lost more than they saved. He had seen such heroics attempted on the battlefield when there was no doctor—never with success. The agonizing cries of torment still rang in his ears.

Granny began digging in her satchel. "I brung some good yarbs and Epsom salts. Fetch me some warm water. First we'll soak it good in salts water and then lance it to draw out the poison and pack hit with a strong yarb poultice." She looked at Allen. "Get yer knife sharp."

He had seen Granny work miracles before, so he did as bidden and began putting a fresh edge on his knife.

CHAPTER 17 ⌒

L ily seemed glad to be on the road with Nelda on her back. She stepped out brisk and willing. It would be a long trip of fifty miles, so Nelda, resisting the urge to cantor, held her to a fast walk. The day was cold, but the sun shone brightly and the few high, patchy clouds were not the ominous kind that threatened snow. Dressed in heavy wool, Nelda was too warm until she unwound the muffler and pushed it back.

She supposed it would be safer to take back trails. With the necessity of speed, she decided to risk the main road. With luck, she could head into the woods to avoid patrols and travelers.

Della was right. Allen would be angry when he returned to find her gone. She regretted that.

He was never out of her thoughts. Now that she had faced her heart, she longed to tell him. Her thoughts stayed so busy, she hardly noticed the miles that passed under Lily's steady hooves. It was an uneventful day. Without incident, she passed through several small settlements and the larger town of Ozark. The few travelers she passed were civilians and mostly old men and women, bundled against the cold and in a hurry to reach their destination. About noon, she passed two young men riding bony nags. Although they eyed Lily with appreciation, neither made a move to take her. Nelda wore the pistol in plain sight. She hoped it was enough deterrent to keep them from turning to follow. Nonetheless, she ate in the saddle and stopped only to walk a bit to keep from growing stiff.

For a long way, the wide band of river was in sight. Once, she saw a small skiff poled by a boy who was fishing. He must be hungry, she decided, to be fishing on such a cold day. She waved, and he waved back.

On the trip from Jasper, her body had grown more hardened to riding; however, by late afternoon, she longed for rest. But she pushed on. Eventually the moon rose, and Lily doggedly followed the path. Nelda's eyes refused to stay open. She dozed in the saddle. She awakened once to find Lily had stopped but with only a nudge the mare started forward.

The night grew colder. Near morning, she grew so cold her hands were numb. Exhausted, she climbed down and walked again to warm the blood flowing to her hands and feet. Intending to rest for only a moment, she sat down and leaned against a tree. She awoke with a start, and then was relieved to see the moon had not traveled far. Lily stood with head drooped and eyes closed.

"Sorry, girl," said Nelda as she climbed stiffly back into the saddle. "When we get to the fort, if there's any grain to be had, I'll beg the general for an extra ration for you."

The rest of the night passed in a miserable blur. Uncertain of how much she had slept, she gave Lily's neck a pat and blinked at the rising sun. Her grainy eyes felt full of sand.

It was possible, she knew, to ride a horse to death. She studied Lily. The mare was tired but didn't seem to be in distress. Nelda wondered what she would do if the horse gave out.

The next day crept with agonizing slowness. Nelda, dull and stupid and much of the time in the mode of a sleepwalker, passed the day in a surreal fog. Because of Lily's determined plodding, late in the evening, she reached the ferry across the Arkansas River at Van Buren. Across the murky water, the shoreline was lost in dark shadow. Reeling, she stayed in the saddle by clinging to the saddle horn. She didn't think Lily could go another step.

There was a sentry guarding the ferry. When she blurted out her errand, he called to another sentry.

"Take over while I escort this woman to headquarters."

Nelda added, "Can you tell me where I might find a place to stable my horse and get some sleep?"

"Not any boarding houses open that I know of, but seeing as how you almost killed yourself to bring us that message, I'll bet they'll put you up at the Drennen House. Army is using it now. That's where we're headed." He pointed. "It's that white house up on the hill."

She thanked him, and with a deep, shaky breath, turned the mare and followed. She eyed the long white frame house situated high on the bluff above the river and breathed a prayer she could stay in the saddle long enough to get there.

It took some urging to get Lily to climb the steep hill. Finally, they reached the long, white frame house with two smaller rooms at each end. Judging from the tall chimneys and numerous shuttered windows, it belonged to a prosperous family.

Almost falling from the saddle, Nelda dismounted, tied Lily to the hitching post, went to the door, and followed the sentry through the door.

The soldier who ushered them inside took one look at her pale face and quickly offered a chair in the entryway before he hurried off to find a superior. Nelda glanced around at the gracious surroundings. Off from the blue-walled entryway opened a large parlor with a fireplace at the far end. Along each sidewall hung huge twin mirrors with ornate gold-colored frames. Except for a wide desk littered with papers, the room was almost void of furnishings. She wondered if the family had taken the contents or if—as was constantly reported—some disreputable officer had confiscated them for his own use and sent them to Kansas.

Across the hall was another room, but the door was shut. She hoped there was a room for her.

A tall, gray-haired major soon entered, digested her story, and abruptly instructed the orderly to escort her to a room, stable the mare, and give her a generous amount of grain. The orderly had barely gotten a cot set up before Nelda, fully clothed, fell upon it. Undisturbed, she slept the clock around. Evening shadows slated the room when she awoke.

She stiffly arose and went directly to the stables to check on Lily. The horse was in the stable yard, contentedly munching hay. With a glad whinny, Lily came to the fence and nuzzled Nelda's hand as if hoping for a treat.

She rubbed the velvet nose. "I wish I had an apple for you, girl. You certainly earned one. As soon as I have a bite to eat, we'll head out to the fort."

It was, however, necessary to wait until morning. The ferry had stopped running for the day, so after a simple meal of beans and canned meat eaten on the wide front porch, she returned to the cot, and to her surprise, slept the night through and awoke feeling greatly refreshed. Lily, curried and fed, was also ready to travel and rode the ferry across the rippling water as if she did it often.

Sarah flew into her arms. "M-miss Nelda! I thought you weren't ever c-coming back!" She squeezed with all the might in her frail arms.

Tears sprang to Nelda's eyes as she pushed the dark hair off the child's face and kissed her forehead. The girl still wore the hideous black brocade with the mother-of-pearls buttons.

"I'm sorry I was delayed, but it couldn't be helped." Nelda glanced up as a boy approached. "Why William, you've grown a foot." His gangly arms and legs had outgrown both sleeves and pants.

He did not rush to embrace her, but his eyes were glad.

Nelda looked around at the crowded room in amazement. There were almost as many children as before. Most looked under the age of twelve, and there was a tiny baby in the arms of a haggard-looking Elsie Turnbo as she hurried forward.

"Miss Nelda, you are a sight for sore eyes. I'm just about done in." The woman's cheeks were more hollow than ever, and the gray knot of hair, usually tight and high on the back of her head, was hanging limply on the base of her neck. "We feared you'd been killed."

"No, just delayed," said Nelda. Her eyes swept the long, barn-like room. "I can't believe there are so many more."

Elsie sighed. "I know. It's a good thing we sent some north or there'd be no room now. We're strapped to keep them fed. To be honest, some days there's not enough."

"Oh my." Nelda breathed. She was thankful she had come. Perhaps there would be enough supplies on the boat to keep them from going hungry.

Elsie lowered her voice. "Things are worse than ever. Last week, the reverend printed a report from a soldier who escaped a Reb prison camp in Texas. Took him twenty-six days to get here, living on corn and acorns. He says the country south of here is empty of folks. I can believe it," she said with a shake of head. "Most of 'em came here. That's a lot of hungry people to see after." She added, "There's hardly a day but what more orphans come—Oh, ever so often, someone shows up to claim one of 'em. But even if these still have any kin, it's not likely they'll get back together. The Reverend does all he can, but the poor man has worked himself sick."

Nelda thought it was no wonder! Already, the weight of responsibility settled heavy on her chest.

Elsie shifted the baby to the other arm. "Now that the army's been ordered to evacuate, law, Miss Nelda, I don't know what we'll do. Likely, we'll all be murdered in our beds."

"What?" Nelda was incredulous.

"You hadn't heard? Well, it's true. Abe Lincoln himself ordered all the army in the whole district to leave."

Nelda's legs went weak. She walked to a chair and sat down. What would they do with all these children? She must find the reverend and ask.

Sarah still held her hand and only let it go reluctantly upon the assurance that Nelda would be right back.

The reverend did look ghastly, with hollow cheeks and dark circles under deep-set eyes, red from lack of sleep. Despite this, he greeted her joyously. "Miss Horton! Wonderful to see you. General Thayer related your heroic deed. It is nothing less than a miracle that you got through unmolested."

"Yes, it is," she agreed, and then got right to the problem. "Reverend Springer what are we going to do with all those children? Elsie says the army has been ordered to evacuate the district—surely she's mistaken?"

"I wish she were," he said gravely. "It's all too true. There's great panic in town, people throwing what little they can into carts and wagons and leaving everything else behind. Some are even building rafts to float the river." He shook his head. "Of course, we have to leave or face the wrath of the invading army or mobs of guerillas and bushwhackers." He handed her a copy of newsprint strong with the smell of ink. "This is probably our last edition. For the lead, I've printed a letter written by Elijah Leming. Although he's not addressing the people of Sebastian County, it certainly applies to us as well."

Quickly, she read the letter addressed to the Union people of Scott County.

> Last February I wrote to you from this place advising the women and children to remain at home as long as their provisions lasted. I was then watching General Steele's forward movement, the result of which was contrary to my anticipations. I would now advise you to come out and go north as fast as possible. You cannot remain in a desolated, uncultivated country. You must go to the rear of the Army and the bow of hope will light up your way as you go.

Reading on, she wondered where the army would find the wagons promised for transportation to the fleeing families, and what they would do for food. The article ended with the dire words, "…in the land of the stranger, you must ask shelter from the pelting storm." and was signed, "I remain yours, Elijah Leming."

Her eyes were wide. "How soon do we leave—and where will we take the orphans?"

"I'm working out details with the general. For now, he's sending a detail to get the supplies from the grounded boat. We're going to need every bite of food it holds and then some. In the mean time, we must make do with what food the general can spare and with donations from the public."

Nelda left the office with few answers and a splitting headache. She stepped from the office and gave a groan to see snow sifting down. As a child, she'd loved snow. Now it was only an added burden. Most of the children had holey shoes, and some had no socks.

The days passed with the drudgery of hard work, little sleep, and never enough food to fill hollow, hungry bellies, and still no word came from the reverend with plans for their departure.

They had developed a routine of work sharing. Older children had charge of the younger, and everyone who was old enough shared chores. William kept the wood box near the potbellied stove full of split wood and kindling. Sarah did any chore well and cheerfully. Her favorite pastime was entertaining the tots with games and stories. During the telling, she seldom stuttered. Nelda gleaned the girl's mother or father had had a love of reading, for Sarah knew and related several of the classics with accuracy.

One snowy morning Nelda's hands stilled from buttoning a small boy's ragged coat.

"What we gettin' fer Christmas?" he asked.

Over the top of the boy's head, Elsie's worried eyes met her own. Nelda had given Christmas no thought. Judging from the look on Elsie's face, neither had she.

"Christmas presents are surprises," she hedged.

Instantly, she determined every child would get some token on Christmas morning. It was only ten days away, but surely the reverend could help come up with something!

Later, when the children were busy with chores, Elsie approached. She wiped the baby's runny nose with her apron and then whispered, "Miss Nelda, what in the world are we going to do about Christmas? I hate to see them disappointed."

"Is there anything left in that barrel of stuff people donated?"

Elsie nodded. "A few clothes that were too large for the children and some odds and ends."

That night, after the children were tucked in on cots lining the walls, Nelda lost no time in perusing the contents. Two full skirted, large cotton dresses, one with a pink stripe pattern and one with small yellow flowers on cream background, would make nice aprons for the girls and perhaps rag dolls for the younger ones. She put aside the last item, a dress of deep maroon with a rent but with fabric of excellent quality. It would be the perfect shade for Sarah's olive skin and dark hair and eyes.

The boys would be a bigger problem. There was nothing left in the barrel but a broken fan and one pair of worn high-topped ladies shoes minus a few shiny buttons. She would appeal to Reverend Springer tomorrow. For now, she took the scissors Elsie had borrowed, and using an old apron for a pattern, she began snipping.

A few times they were interrupted by muffled crying, some homesick child longing for mother. Nelda felt inept and dreaded such encounters, so she left them to Elsie. She appeased herself that Elsie was better at consoling.

It was after midnight when she and Elsie finally ceased sewing. Nelda rubbed a stiff neck and blew out the candles. Her eyes ached from working by the poor light. When the war ended and there was coal oil to be had, she vowed never to take it for granted again.

Even after the candles were extinguished and Nelda lay on the hard cot, sleep was elusive. She worried about the children. She worried about Della and little Moses. But most plaguing of all were visions of Allen staring down into Dorcas's beautiful eyes.

She thrashed about and groaned and put an arm across her eyes. If only she had had a chance to speak to him. When he returned and found her gone, he might leave and never come back.

For the next week, sleep became a rare luxury. Both women went about with bleary eyes and lagging steps. Oblivious, the children ran, played, and anticipated Christmas as if there were no war, and as if on Christmas morning they would awaken and magically be once again in the bosom of loving family.

Reverend Springer solved the problem of gifts for the boys. He appealed to the soldiers. Although preparing to evacuate, the men drew cherished items from packs—socks, scarves, and trinkets. Then they scoured the fort for wood to carve into whistles and toys. A few women, also packing to leave, offered cast off toys. When the troops returned with supplies from the marooned boat, they would have a bountiful meal without scrimping. All in all, Nelda was pleased with how things were shaping up.

When the aprons were finished, she turned all her attention to making Sarah's dress. It was showing favoritism, and she worried about how it would appear to the other children. Nonetheless, the horrid black brocade was sufficient incentive to risk it.

Nelda, though not an expert seamstress, could ply a needle with a degree of efficiency. The style was simple—a scoop neck shirtwaist, long sleeves, and a skirt gathered onto a band at the waist. She planned to remove the mother-of-pearl buttons from Sarah's old frock late on Christmas Eve and sew them to the new dress and hang it on the nail at the head of the girls' cot in place of the old one. Nelda knew the joy in Sarah's eyes would be her own Christmas gift.

Reverend Springer arrived one morning with nothing more than a bag of cornmeal and two small tins of canned beef. Nelda took one look at his long face and asked, "What's wrong?"

He drew her aside out of earshot of the children. "I just spoke to the colonel. He received a dispatch. The troop train going after the supplies reached the boat." He paused a moment. Then with compassion in his eyes, he said, "They've been delayed by bad roads and high water. But the boat was loaded with only forage."

Nelda's face blanched. "No food at all?"

"None."

She sank into a nearby chair. There would be no extra food for the children. That terrible journey had been for nothing more than a boatload of forage. She had left Allen for a boatload of cornstalks or hay!

"Reverend, what are we going to feed these children? There's Christmas…"

Strain washed his face. "I don't know, Miss Horton. But I'm sure the good Lord will make a way."

Elsie took the news in stride. Talking low she said, "We'll eat mush every day, and save the beef. I'll make a special gruel out of it on Christmas morning—maybe enough to stretch for Christmas Dinner."

Nelda admired Elsie's spunk. She herself wanted to cry. Reverend Springer put on his hat and hurried away, but Nelda thought there were tears in his eyes too.

"M-Miss Nelda." Sarah stood nearby.

"Yes?"

"Is anything wr-wrong?"

"No, Sarah."

Unconvinced, Sarah went on, "M-my m-mama and I always p-prayed about t-troubles.

Elsie's head snapped up. "Now Sarah Campbell, I call that a right fine idea." She looked at Nelda. "It's a fine idea. Won't hurt a thing to let them pray about this. Besides, we been neglecting the spiritual training of these young'uns. Could be the very thing to do just now—what with Christmas celebrating the birth of the Christ child."

With Nelda's nod, Elsie wasted no time. "Children, gather round." With more candor than Nelda had intended, Elsie made the children aware of the need for food and gathered them into a circle.

When every head was bowed, the heartfelt pleas arose. Nelda had no idea how God felt, but she was moved to tears. They poured down her cheeks.

To her astonishment, Elsie thanked the Almighty for the food He would send before Christmas and then gave a hearty, "Amen," and raised her head.

"Elsie," she later managed to whisper. "What if it doesn't—"

"Never you fear, Miss Nelda. God ain't gonna turn a deaf ear to that. Here, Sarah, hold little Nettie, whilst I get this mush on to boil."

For the next two days, Nelda, who had given up the habit of regular prayers, prayed without ceasing. Nonetheless, she was amazed when Reverend Springer arrived on Christmas Eve with a beaming face and loaded arms.

"Greetings all! A very Merry Christmas!" He waved a hand toward the window. "Look outside at the bounty. The Lord has richly blessed!" As he dumped the armload of bundles onto the table, Nelda rushed to peer out the frosty glass at a wagon filled with boxes and barrels.

"A train arrived from Fort Scott. There were enough supplies for the troops here for two weeks and the general has been exceedingly generous with us. He sent a dispatch to Saint Louis begging for more to be sent immediately by boat." The chaplain added, "I sent along a written plea to my dear friend and former neighbor, Mr. Lincoln, asking that he please countermand the orders to abandon the district."

William tugged on his sleeve. His voice was awed. "Reverend Springer, did you for real and honest live neighbors with the President?"

He gave a wan smile. "I certainly did—for real and honest—right across the street." He went on, "Of course, he wasn't the president then, just a struggling attorney."

Elsie was busy inspecting the bundles. "Canned beans and beef and oats and… laws-a-mercy!" she exclaimed. "Bless me, if it ain't honest-to-goodness wheat flour and even some saleratus!" She turned beaming. "We'll have real bread for Christmas." She waved the children forward. "Now come on. We prayed and the Lord answered. Won't be mannerly not to thank Him. Preacher Springer, would you voice the thanksgiving?"

Christmas morning dawned cloudy and frigid. Although their breaths rose in cold vapor, the children arose with excited vigor and began dressing behind the curtained partitions that separated girls from boys. Nelda stood out of sight peeking around the curtain when Sarah arose.

The girl reached for her dress, gasped, and withdrew her hand. Then she reached again and caressed the fabric before spinning around and running into Nelda's arms.

"I...it's the p...prettiest dress in the whole world! Oh, t...thank you!" Nelda hugged her. "Well then," she said with a laugh. "Go put it on."

Sarah pulled the dress over her head and her eyes grew even wider as she fingered the buttons. "You remembered." The shining eyes were sufficient reward for Nelda's late night work.

The other children were equally pleased with their gifts and with the wonder of beef and gravy and wheat flour bread for Christmas Dinner.

Three weeks later, Nelda entered Reverend Springer's office. Shivering, she pulled the shawl tight. It was almost as cold as outdoors.

"Miss Horton." He stood and offered her a chair near the potbellied stove. "Forgive the chill. I got so busy, I neglected the fire. It's just now catching up again." He sat down behind the neat desk. "Thank you for coming. I wanted to speak to you without the children overhearing."

His face was graver than usual. Her stomach tightened.

"Although boats arrived from Little Rock, no foodstuffs were onboard. In another week, things will be dire again. As you know, the district is to be vacated. General Thayer has come up with a plan—and I think a valid one—to load the boats with refugees and send them to Little Rock. I agree with him that we must move the orphans."

The reverend continued, "The boats are docked now and will be leaving day after tomorrow. It's short notice, but I hope both you and Mrs. Turnbo will accompany me and help look after the children."

Nelda's mind was spinning. "Of course, I'll go. But where?"

"I'm making arrangements with an orphanage in Cairo, Illinois, where I have close connections. It's a wonderful establishment, and the children will be well cared for."

Nelda nodded, but she suddenly felt ill. Poor Sarah and William! They'd be sent off to live with strangers.

Elsie agreed to go and arrangements were made for transportation to the boats. There was one advantage to having so few goods mused Nelda. There was little to pack.

In the cold dawn, after a hurried breakfast of hominy grits, the children, with freshly scrubbed hands and faces, stood at the river's edge alongside Nelda and Elsie and hundreds of other refugees. Most had weary, gaunt faces and were dressed in tatters. Some wore rags for shoes on the frozen ground.

Although Nelda held the hands of two young children, Sarah kept hold of her sleeve and stared wide-eyed at smoke pouring from the stacks of four large riverboats.

William eyed the water. "The river sure is rolling. Must of come a big rain upriver."

Sarah's eyes were large. "Is it s-safe?"

He answered with a scoff, "Course it is, or the reverend wouldn't be putting us on it. The Annie Jacobs is a good boat." He nodded toward a boat moored farther downstream. "Yesterday, the Chippewa outrun the whole Reb cavalry."

Nelda did not find that comforting. Hopefully, the Rebel cavalry would be otherwise occupied while they slipped past.

Reverend Springer arrived carrying a large satchel. He smiled at the children. "Is everyone ready to board?"

The chorus of answers ranged from Sarah's timid, "Yes, sir," to David's hearty, "You bet!"

Then David nodded toward the Annie Jacobs, "How many of us you reckon will fit on there? If this one's too full, I'll ride on the Chippewa."

"No, son. We'll all stay together. I understand from the captain there's room for five hundred on this one." The reverend looked at the teaming crowd of soldiers and civilians carrying bundles, hampers, baskets, and bags of every size. "From the looks of things, it will still be crowded."

David looked wistfully at the Chippewa, but said no more.

Nelda hoped they would board soon. The wind blowing across the gray water made standing miserable. None of the children had enough warm clothing—although the reverend had managed to scrap together, albeit ill-fitting, coats, hats, and wool stockings for the ones that had none.

As if in answer to her wishes, a member of the crew removed the heavy rope blocking the gangplank, and they began surging forward.

"Sir." A private stopped Reverend Springer. "Begging your pardon, but General Thayer suggested you travel on the Chippewa. There's better accommodations for the children."

William's face glowed.

"Keep together now," cautioned Nelda as Elsie, like a frantic hen with chicks, herded them toward the Chippewa and aboard. The paddle wheel was on the side of the ship, and there were two decks with a pilothouse on top situated between twin stacks rising high into the sky and bellowing smoke. Without enough seating to be found, most men and boys remained standing. A kind soldier ushered the children and Elsie to a backless bench situated on the bottom deck near a wall and out of the cutting wind.

Nelda, along with David and the older boys, found a place near the rails to watch in fascination as people clamored aboard—a hodgepodge of soldier, civilian, young, old, black and white and red.

One black man stood head and shoulders above the rest and carried a huge barrel on his shoulder. For a moment, Nelda's mind darted to Allen when he had spied at Helena and acted as a stevedore.

"Step smart, Noah," ordered a skinny man with a permanent scowl embedded on his face, "and don't you dare drop that barrel. It's full of the missus's dishes."

Noah answered cheerfully, "Yes, suh. I won't drap nothin'."

Reverend Springer stood nearby. "A vast multitude. Rather like the children of Israel fleeing Egypt," he said with a shake of the head. "Fleeing in hopes of a better life elsewhere."

But there is no Moses, thought Nelda, and no promised land.

Finally, a shrill whistle announced departure, and the boat, with a great shudder, backed from the dock, and, after gaining the middle channel, turned slowly and headed downriver with a slow, steady throb of the engine. The Chippewa had the lead. Behind came the Annie Jacobs followed by the Lotus and the Ad Hines. Van Buren soon disappeared behind.

By noon, tired of the novelty of watching the dead landscape slide by, the boys wormed their way back to sit on the cold deck near the bench. Elsie reached into a hamper and pulled out cold biscuits to pass around. Even without butter, jelly, or meat, they were a treat. Nelda didn't care if she ever saw another grain of cornmeal. She quickly amended the thought. Cornbread was certainly better than no bread at all.

The young children became fretful. Nelda hardly blamed them. She longed for a nap in a bed piled high with warm quilts. It suddenly occurred to her that the boats would pass Clarksville. She wondered if they would stop there. They might. By that time, it would be late in the day, and they must moor somewhere for the night. The Union Army had reoccupied the town. Captain Judson, the colonel's son who had been the provost marshal in charge of the execution of Norwood and the other young rebels, was now stationed there. If they stopped, she hoped it would be long enough to see Della and to send word to Allen of her whereabouts.

She turned to the reverend. "You mentioned that Mr. Lincoln was once your neighbor when he practiced law."

"That was long ago, back in Springfield."

"I have a friend. He's an intelligent man who wants to study law, but he has no real connections in that field. Would you have any suggestions?"

"I have very good connections in Springfield. I'll be more than glad to arrange an introduction to some of the finest legal minds. You say this man is a friend?" He smiled. "Ah, Miss Horton, do I detect pink cheeks?"

She gave a brief smile. "Yes. He is…very dear to me."

The reverend patted her arm. "I'm glad to know you have—shall we say—a special friend."

Lowering her voice, she changed the subject. "Reverend Springer, you will make sure Sarah and William find good homes, won't you— where they'll have love and an opportunity for a good education?"

"I'll certainly try. In these difficult times, it may be hard finding homes. There are so many war orphans. But, believe me, Miss Horton, the place they're going is a fine establishment, not at all like the dreadful asylums of storybooks. The children are well cared for. It's spacious and sunny and—"

Nelda jerked from a deafening boom. She spun around to face forward in time to see a huge plume of water spray into the air.

"What the—"

A soldier cursed. Then he and a dozen more uniformed men ran toward the starboard rail and raised rifles as another volley of shots sprayed the air and a large projectile splashed water high in front of the boat.

The next shot landed even closer. Men shouted. Women screamed and children cried out in terror.

"They'll sink us!" screamed a frantic woman. At the same instant, more shots rang out. A man leaped overboard and began swimming toward the far bank. Two more men clamored over the rail.

"No! Stop!" yelled Reverend Springer. He grabbed another by the sleeve. "The water's too cold. You'll never make it."

As musketry on the bank rained shots onto the hull and splintered wood on the deck, the man shook him off and jumped. The first man still flailed water, only half way to the shore. His head went under. For a moment, it popped back up. Then the swirling water swallowed him. Nelda watched, horrified. None of the men got further than mid-stream.

Elsie, with the baby in one arm, had already begun herding children against the wall and under the benches. Both women then knelt, acting as shields against the flying lead ripping the deck apart.

The giant black man, Noah, grabbed his leg and collapsed, moaning. In a rain of musket balls, the reverend rushed to the man, took hold under his arms, and began pulling. He was too large. Nelda stood and in a hunkering run started forward. She had only gone a few steps when William darted past and also grabbed a shoulder and pulled. Noah struggled to help, and, together, they managed to reach the wall. The wounded leg left a bloody trail across the deck.

"Thank you, suh, bless you," he repeated over and over. "Lord bless you all. Thank you."

The wall shielded Nelda's view, but the constant thunder and the spray of lobbed shells left little doubt that the Rebels could sink them.

"Damnation," cried a soldier as a screeching cannon ball hit near the center of the boat. A woman fainted at Nelda's feet. Tongues of flame began licking away walls on the bottom deck. Everything was flame and smoke and panic. Crazed people, like stampeding cattle, ran and plunged into the frigid water. She watched in dismay as a woman's head disappeared under the rushing gray water. For a moment Nelda felt strangely detached, like a spectator at a tragic play, until the terrified cries of the children snapped her back to reality.

Nothing she had experienced compared to the terror of the cannonade as giant shot ripped apart wood and water and human flesh. If the boat went down, the dark cold river would swallow them alive. Helpless, all she could do was huddle, shielding the children the best she could. If she tried to speak, they could not hear her.

Giant plumes of black soon joined the smoke pouring from the stacks. The boat abruptly changed course and began heading toward the south shore. The cannons quieted, and the shooting ceased.

In the surreal calm, Nelda's voice seemed loud. "We're surrendering!" she exclaimed.

Reverend Springer looked up from tying a kerchief around the big man's leg. "I don't think the captain has any choice."

Sarah reached from under the bench to clutch Nelda's arm.

"It's all right, Sarah," she whispered. "The Rebels aren't devils. I know some who are actually very nice."

Terror lessened in the girl's dark eyes; nonetheless, she kept a death grip on Nelda's arm.

With a violent shudder, the paddle wheel reversed course and finally stopped.

"Throw down your weapons!" barked a loud voice. "All of you get your hands in the air. If anyone moves we'll shoot."

Soon, a troop of men, some in gray uniforms and some in worn trousers and butternut shirts, overran the boat. One stopped nearby. He prodded Reverend Springer with a musket. "Get them hands in air!"

"No. I must staunch the bleeding, or this man will die. Shoot if you must."

The soldier glared but said no more. Then he spied the children under the bench and swore. When he ordered them out, Elsie fuzzed up like a setting hen. "Leave them alone!"

"I ain't gonna shoot 'em, lady. I got orders to clear you all off this tub." He gestured with the musket toward the fire. "Course you can stay if you like and get roasted."

Reverend Springer interrupted. "I'll need help to move him."

As Nelda and Elsie began gathering the children, the soldier called to a group of men being herded forward by more armed men. "Hey, you men. Get over here and help this man off the boat." With sullen looks, they complied to help Noah hobble along with the crowd pressing down the gangplank.

In the confusion, children coughed and cried. Grown women wept aloud. Nelda tried to steer the children away from the wounded and groaning and a man with sightless eyes lying face up in a pool of blood.

Through smoke-blurred, watering eyes, she saw a large group of hard-jawed men on the bank watching them disembark. Soldiers were abruptly separated from civilians, and, in separate groups with the exception of men forced to unload supplies from the smoldering boat, all were moved farther up the bank.

The far shoreline was almost lost in smoke. Mists hovered over the river, glazing bushes, rocks, and grass along the bank with a thin sheet of ice.

"Search them," ordered a captain. "Take any valuables and put them in a pile right over there. Keep a sharp eye for hidden weapons."

Papa's watch! As person after person gave over trinkets and jewelry, Nelda gripped the gold watch on a chain around her neck. She had lost it once before to a murdering thief. She had no intention of doing so again. Barely moving, she inched her way to hide behind Elise, reached inside her blouse between the buttons, and turned the chain until she felt the clasp. With cold clumsy fingers, she finally managed to unhook it. "My papa's watch," she whispered in Elsie's ear and then furtively reached under the baby's blanket to wedge the watch between it and the baby. Elsie clasped the blanket tight.

"I got no valuables a'tall," insisted Elsie, "except this baby that needs changing mighty bad."

The soldier wrinkled his nose and went on down the line, patting down both men and women to search. Nelda hardly breathed until he had passed on.

A commotion up river drew all eyes. Artillery had opened again. This time the Annie Jacobs was the target. The boat was still a long way off and making a valiant effort to escape by turning around midstream. Shell after shell shrieked through the air. Wood and debris blew into the sky. The stack in front of the pilothouse toppled. Smoke boiled into the air.

"Look there. More damn fools jumpin' overboard."

Nelda glared at the old, leather-faced soldier. "If you'll stop firing, they'll stop jumping."

He chuckled. "Cap'in, this one has a mouth on her." He looked closer. "I've seed her a'fore. Wasn't she with that bunch of orphans in the wagon train?"

The captain glanced over. "Yes, she was, Levi. Ever since then, I've been trying to remember where I'd seen her before. It finally came to me—she was at Helena tending the wounded. She bandaged my head. She was the one General Fagan arrested for spying." Then his lips pursed. "Take all of them back to camp, but, Levi, watch her closely. I need to talk to the colonel."

They were rounded up again and forced at gunpoint away from the bank. Nelda and Elsie gathered the children, all white-faced under the smoky soot. Tears had washed white trails on Sarah's smudged face.

Nelda tipped up her chin. "We're going to be fine, Sarah. They won't harm us." She prayed it was true.

"I'm not s-scared," denied Sarah. "I ripped my new dress." Fresh tears slid down sooty cheeks as she moved her hand to reveal a rent where the bodice joined the skirt.

"Oh, that's easily fixed," comforted Nelda. "The fabric's not torn. See, the seam just gave way. I can mend it in no time."

She was rewarded with a tiny, relieved sigh.

The soldiers gathered them into a tight knot. "Stay together. Don't try running. We got orders to shoot."

A guard pointed toward Noah. Blood still seeped through the big man's bandage.

"What about him?"

"Leave him," said Levi. "He's too big to tote."

"You can't just leave my darkie!" protested the skinny man. "He's valuable property!"

"Then you tote him," Levi snarled.

As they were prodded away, Nelda called back, "Noah, if you can make it across the river to Clarksville, then go to the Horton house—a tall white house close to the Methodist church. There's someone there who will help you."

He nodded. "Horton house, close to da church. I remember. Thank you, kindly ma'am. You too, suh," he called to Reverend Springer. "You all done saved my life."

The camp was a mile away. When they arrived, two-dozen campfires emanated welcoming warmth and tripods held large kettles of steaming food. Nelda wondered if they would be fed—although it was doubtful there was enough for all of them. They must number several hundred. She hoped they would at least feed the children. After all the terror and the long walk in the biting cold, they needed warm nourishment.

Heavy guns thundered in the distance, punctuated with the constant rattle of musketry. Over leafless trees, smoke roiled into the afternoon sky.

"Sit or stand, as it suits ya," said Levi, "but don't get any bright ideas about running off. There's a dozen guns on ya."

The sun was slanted low in bare treetops when hundreds of mounted men rode into camp. Union guns had done some damage. There were several wounded and one dead soldier was draped behind a saddle.

Grimy faced soldiers piled off horses, and quickly devoured the hot food that cooks ladled into tin cups. Then, to Nelda's relief, what was left was distributed to the prisoners.

A guard pointed at them. "What we gonna do with all of 'em, Cap'in?"

"I have no idea. There comes the colonel. He'll tell us."

Nelda's eyes widened. It was Colonel Brooks, a man she had once spoken to at the courthouse in Clarksville.

He sat on a fallen log, took a cup of beans, and thanked the cook. After a few hurried bites, he wiped his mouth with the back of his hand and addressed his aide. "Escort the prisoners back upriver until they can be seen from the other bank. We ran two more boats aground on the north shore, but the other one got away. It won't be long before this whole place is crawling with Yankees."

"The soldiers too? You turning them loose?"

"They'd just slow us down. I don't shoot prisoners."

"Excuse me, sir." It was the rebel captain. "You might want to speak to one woman before releasing her. She was our prisoner at Helena. General Fagan arrested her for spying, but on the retreat she escaped."

The colonel spoke around a bite of food. "Bring her here."

Nelda dreaded the encounter, nonetheless, she walked with head high and shoulders straight. The colonel stared. Then his eyes registered recognition.

"You're that Clarksville woman who was searching for her uncle— you claimed his name was Brooks. Of course that was probably a lie."

"No, it wasn't. I do have an uncle in the Confederate Army and his name is Tap Brooks." Her chin came up. "I am not spying. I'm taking care of children that you and your kind helped orphan!"

He gave a slow smile and then lifted the cup near his mouth and watched her over the rim as he ate. Handing the empty cup to an aide, he wiped his mouth. "Take her with us."

"No, please. The orphans—"

Reverend Springer stepped near to intervene. "Colonel Brooks, I'm Reverend Francis Springer, Chaplain of the First Arkansas Infantry. Miss Horton is telling the truth. She is helping conduct these orphans to Little Rock. Surely that poses no threat to you or your army."

"Reverend, you and your orphans are free to go. I figure your services are needed across the river where there's plenty of dead and dying. But she's coming with us. I'm taking her to General Fagan. If he says she's no threat then she'll go free." His eyebrows rose as Sarah darted forward and stopped right in front of his face.

"M-mister, p-please don't t-take M-Miss Nelda!" She had been crying and now spoke through hiccups and stutters.

The colonel's face softened, and he reached to gently take the child's shoulders.

"What's your name?"

"S-S-Sarah"

"Well, Sarah. I have to take her, but I'll make sure she isn't harmed. And as soon as the general gives the word, I'll turn her loose, and she can come to you."

As Sarah dissolved into tears, Nelda gathered her close. "Sarah, I will come to you if I possibly can." She bent to look into Sarah's eyes. "Until then, Reverend Springer and Miss Elsie will take good care of you."

"So will I," said William. After giving the colonel a belligerent stare, he stepped past and took Sarah's hand. "I'll look out for her good, Miss Nelda."

Nelda could hardly see through the tears. "Thank you, William," she whispered and hugged him too. "God keep you both."

Elsie, holding the baby in one arm, stopped to hug Nelda. Soon the weight of the watch pulled in her pocket. Her eyes thanked Elsie as she said, "Elsie, please see to mending Sarah's dress."

"I'll do it. Miss Nelda, God keep you."

Sarah held William's hand as the guards herded them away. She looked back as long as possible.

Nelda went to the campfire and sat down on a nearby rock. Shortly, Levi brought a horse and told her to mount. Surely this couldn't happen again! She had lived this nightmare once before. Perhaps she was destined to hang as a spy—just like Papa.

She was dazed but angry. Would the rebels never give up? Why did they keep inflicting misery and suffering for a cause that was lost? Abruptly her eyes widened.

What if their cause wasn't lost? After all, the whole district was being abandoned. Perhaps they weren't in the dire straits she had been led to believe. Colonel Brooks certainly had plenty of men and fire-power—granted, they looked like tattered scarecrows and the horses and mules were bony. But the men fought to win.

What if they did? What if the rebels won? Her mouth drew farther down at the thought while they rode quickly downriver.

Nelda slept little on the bedroll with no tent to block the frozen black sky. She worried about Sarah and William and Elsie and all the children. It was a cold night. Hopefully, they had found shelter.

She thought about Lily and hoped the mare would fall into good hands. Likely, some officer would claim her when the post was deserted.

The sun had barely risen when Levi handed her a cup of steaming water and sat down on the ground.

"Ain't got much flavor," he said, "but it warms a body." He took a sip from his own. "So yer from Clarksville," he said.

"Yes. I've just been helping out with the orphans at the fort."

"Morning Colonel," he said as the colonel stopped nearby to watch men repairing a wagon wheel.

The colonel also sipped from a steaming cup.

"Levi, come lend a hand," called a man lifting the wheel.

"Hey, Matthers!" shouted Levi.

Nelda gasped and spun around.

"Come he'p. Yer the only one big enough to lift a wagon."

Nelda's heart leaped in her chest. Across the way, a big man with red hair stood from hunkering near a campfire and started forward. As he drew near she knew it wasn't Allen. It was Dillon, his younger brother. He was broad shouldered and tall, but leaner now and wearing a full beard.

"Colonel," she said, "I need to talk to that man."

"You know Matthers?" he asked.

"I'm engaged to his brother, Allen."

The colonel's eyes narrowed. "A Union spy engaged to Allen Matthers?"

She gave a scathing look. "I'm no spy, but I am engaged to Allen Matthers." She didn't add that Allen didn't know it yet. She fabricated another quick lie. "We planned to marry just as soon as I returned from escorting the orphans to Little Rock."

"Matthers," called the colonel. "Come here a minute."

Dillon turned. His face split into a huge smile when he saw Nelda. "Well, howdy, Miss Nelda." He greeted her warmly, taking her hand.

"So it's true," said Colonel Brooks. "She is engaged to Allen."

Dillon blinked and then sizing up the situation, he said. "Reckon so. Allen never looked at another woman after he met her." He faced the colonel. "Why? Something wrong?"

"The captain says she was arrested at Helena as a Union spy."

"Aw, Allen told me about that. That was all a mix up. She ain't no spy."

The colonel chewed his jaw. "Well…" He eyed her again.

Levi interrupted. "Like she said, she has been taking care of orphans. A few months back, we stopped a supply train. She was on it and had a whole slew of 'em in tow."

"Maybe it is a mistake," said the colonel. "I respect Allen Matthers as much as any man I know. I'll feel better if I speak to him, personally. Do you know where he is?"

Dillon looked at Nelda.

"He's at home—at your cabin."

Dillon nodded. "With your permission, Colonel, I'll go fetch him."

"All right. You can catch up with us. We're heading south until the grass greens. If you don't catch up before, tell Allen I'm heading for Danville."

"I'll catch up quick as I can. I'd like to take my brother Shawn with me." He pointed across the camp to another broad shouldered man eating breakfast.

"All right, Matthers." The colonel added, "The river is too high. You'll have to find a boat or a ferry."

Dillon nodded.

Nelda caught his arm. "Tell Allen..." she hesitated. "Tell him I love him with all my heart."

He smiled and then strode on to speak with Shawn. Shawn flashed Nelda a big grin and a wave. In less than five minutes, both men had ridden from camp.

CHAPTER 18 ᶜᵘ

A llen stretched his feet toward the cavernous fireplace. Night after night, he'd watched ghosts dance in the flames. Tonight, as the howling wind rattled shakes on the roof, he watched again. He held a steaming cup. Finally he took a sip.

Life seldom turned out the way a body plans, he thought. Just look at Della. She'd lost Gideon, and yet that hadn't stopped her from picking up the pieces and going on. She was determined to make a good life for little Moses. And she would.

He supposed as soon as the weather permitted, he'd head for Jasper. He could at least do some good there.

Suddenly, he reached for the repeating rifle. Someone was outside. Even in the wind, he'd heard heavy boots on the porch. A fist banged on the door.

"Allen! Open the door!"

It was Dillon. Gun in hand, Allen hurried to the door. War had made him cautious, and that had kept him alive. He lifted the bar and stepped back, ready for trouble.

Dillon stood in dim light coming from the fireplace. He held someone slumped against him. "Shawn's been shot," he panted. "Just a few miles back someone fired while we were crossing the creek. He's lost a lot of blood."

Allen put down the gun and helped him to the large bed at the far end of the room and stooped to examine the wound in Shawn's side. He raised the coat, and as gently as possible, lifted the kerchief Shawn pressed over the wound.

"He's bled like a stuck pig," Dillon added again. Worry etched lines in his face. "Yeah," said Allen, "but the bullet went straight through and there's no organs there. The main thing is getting the bleeding stopped. Look in that chest over yonder and see if Ma left any sheets."

Dillon fumbled with the clasp. "Fingers is so damn cold I can't do nothing. Yep. Here's one."

"Tear it into strips that we can bind around him." Allen took a jug from a shelf and splashed liquor into a cup. "Shawn," he said loudly, shaking Shawn's shoulder. Shawn's eyes were closed, and his face was deathly white. "Take a drink of this." Allen put the cup to his lips. "I'm gonna pour some whisky into the wound. It'll hurt like hell, but it's better than water for cleaning a gunshot."

As Allen poured the whisky, Shawn's teeth gritted and he moaned. Sweat popped out on his forehead.

When the bandage was finally in place, Allen sat back to wait. After a bit, he spoke with relief. "It's not bleeding through."

Dillon hovered. "You think he'll be all right?"

"I do. Just to make sure, in the morning, we'll fetch Granny."

"You think I ought to go get her now?'

"No. It's a bad night out. I'd hate to drag that old woman from her bed. I would if I thought it was necessary, but I don't. I think he'll be fine with some rest."

Dillon let out a relieved breath. "Damn, that was a close shave. We been a while gettin' here, and rode all that way without trouble—except for diving into the brush a few times to hide from Yankee patrols. Here we was almost home! Now ain't that a pretty come off!" He shook his head. "I never even got a shot off before the varmit rode off, crashing through the brush."

"Didn't get a look at them?"

"Not even a peek. I think there was only one. At least there was just one shot and it sounded like only one horse."

"You look beat," said Allen. "Why don't you spread your bedroll over by the fire? I'll sit up with him."

"I am whipped. Not much sleep for the past week." Dillon gripped his shoulder. "Thanks, brother. We'll catch up on news in the mornin'."

Dillon's heavy breathing soon filled the cabin. Allen sat in a chair drawn near the bed. Catch up on news. He had some to share. He dreaded the telling.

Shawn was restless. Near morning, Allen felt his brow and frowned. It was hot. Before the sun had risen, Allen shook Dillon's shoulder. "Go fetch Granny."

Dillon sprang up, shoved on boots, coat, and hat, and bolted out the door. Allen held a cup of water to Shawn's lips. He drank very little.

In a short time, Granny hobbled through the door with a cloth bag in hand. "Strike me a light," she ordered, while heading toward the bed. "Can't see nothin' in this here dark corner."

While Dillon lit two candles, Allen unwrapped the bandage. He flinched hearing Shawn's rapid breathing. Holding the light near, Granny frowned. She minced no words.

"Wound don't look bad. Must be somethin' inside—and that kin be worse." Using her tongue, she moved a pinch of snuff to another spot in her bottom gum. "Bullet might have nicked a bowel."

"What can you do for him?" Dillon's voice was shaky.

"A poultice and some yarb tea. Ain't sure hit'll he'p."

Dillon sank into the chair with a groan. "Granny, ya can't let him die!"

"Livin' and dyin' is in the hands of the Lord. If it ain't Shawn's time, he'll not die." She patted Dillon's hand. "I've knowed folks to get over sech. We'll do all we kin and then trust the good Lord." She eyed the brothers. "I don't hold with prayin' to no saints like yer ma done, but I reckon if that's yer way…"

Allen had already been praying. But he had faith in Granny, too. She had pulled Roy Hackett through. Although the hand would always be stiff, Roy was alive and mending.

She stayed until the sun was overhead, and then after giving strict instructions on administering tea and poultice, she left. "No, no need fer neither of ya to come. I kin handle the mule and wagon," she insisted.

Dillon hovered the bed. "Damn, he looks awful, don't he?"

Allen didn't answer. He looked up as Dillon added, "Hell, I forgot to tell you why we came—Brooks has Nelda. He's taking her along until you come get her."

"What?"

"We fired on some Yankee steamboats, and took one of 'em. She was on it—wet-nursing some orphans or some such. Anyway, one of the fellows recognized her and told Brooks she was a spy who got away on the retreat from Helena. The colonel wants to ask you about all that. He headed south, down to Danville."

Allen scowled. Nelda Horton had a talent for getting into hot water. Of course, he'd go. But, he wasn't leaving Shawn at death's door. He knew Brooks. No harm would come to her. Just as soon as Shawn was out of danger, he'd go then.

Shawn's eyes opened. "Git out 'a my face, Dillon." His voice was faint, "I ain't gonna die just so's you can have my rifle."

"Glad to hear it," said Dillon with a relieved laugh.

In spite of the jest, Shawn hovered near death. Day and night while he tossed and raved out of his head, they sat with him and although they followed Granny's instructions to the letter, Allen had almost given up hope.

They were running low on food. Allen intended to go hunting, but was loath to leave the sickroom. As was customary, neighbors soon came with generous offerings from their own meager stores. Becky and Ned Loring brought turnips and a squirrel stew. Elijah and Cindy Loring along with their fine baby boy came bringing potatoes, cabbage, and cornbread. Even fat Tom Sorrells came toting a big pot of hominy.

Simon Mason brought a basket of meal and two freshly skinned rabbits. He doffed a shapeless hat long enough to offer up a prayer—one

Elijah supposed Granny would consider a proper one without mention of a single saint.

The offerings were heartfelt and accepted the same way. Allen had to swallow a lump in his throat each time before saying thank you.

"Dillon, come away from the bed and get some sleep. You've not left him all day. I'll take a turn."

Dillon wiped a sleeve across his eyes and shook his head. "I don't think he'll last the night, Allen. It's pitiful the way he's suffering. If he ain't gonna get better I hope he goes ahead and dies."

"Reckon there are worse things than dying," agreed Allen.

Tears spilled onto Dillon's face. "It's my fault. I asked Brooks if he could come. If he'd stayed, this wouldn't have happened."

"Maybe not, but he might have caught a bullet heading south. I reckon Granny's right. I've been giving it a heap of thought—life and death ain't up to us."

"Well, it'll kill me if he don't make it," said Dillon, blowing his nose. "No it won't."

Allen started to say more, but closed his mouth. He'd wait for a better time to break the news about Seamus.

They both sat near the bed. Near midnight, the room grew quiet. Allen jerked awake. He rubbed his eyes. There were no mutters or thrashing. With dread he lit the candle.

Shawn lay still. His eyes were closed. Allen reached a shaky hand and touched him.

Shawn's eyes flew open. They closed again. "Glad you're awake," he muttered. "The way you two snore, a body can't get a lick of sleep."

Allen grinned. He kicked Dillon on the leg. "Hey, get to bed. This ornery cuss is gonna make it, after all."

Allen's horse was saddled and his gear was stowed behind the saddle. The collar of his coat was turned up against the cold wind blowing off the creek. Dillon waved from the cabin doorway. "Be careful, brother. Give that gal a kiss for me."

Allen lifted a gloved hand. He swung into the saddle. Then he lowered his head and groaned. There had not been a good time to tell them. But there never would be. With jaws set, he dismounted and went back inside.

Dillon paused from handing Shawn a plate of breakfast and looked up. "You forget something?"

Allen removed his hat and stood for a minute. "I've been trying to tell you for days,"—he stopped to swallow—"Seamus is dead."

"Oh, hell," muttered Dillon and sank into the chair near the bed. Shawn's face turned whiter, but he stayed silent.

"When?" asked Dillon. His eyes had filled.

"Back in July—battle out on Massard Prairie near Fort Smith."

"Hope he went quick," said Dillon. "Don't reckon you'd have any way of knowing."

Allen's jaws worked. "I...I—"

"Aw, hell, Allen. Seamus knowed soldiering was dangerous. I tried to talk him out of going—especially out of joinin' the Federals. Patrick and Mack tried too before they headed west. But he was crazy upset over Pa gettin' killed. You know how headstrong he was. Just like all of us Matthers."

Shawn spoke, "Allen, don't take on so. It wasn't your fault."

Allen stood like a statue. "Yes, yes it was. I shot him. I killed him myself."

In stunned silence Dillon and Shawn exchanged incredulous looks. Then Dillon stood. "If you did, it was for sure and certain an accident. You always looked out for us all and even fought for us." He wiped a sleeve across his eyes and gestured to the chair. "Come on over here. Sit down and tell us what happened."

Allen dropped into the chair. He stared at the hat clasped in his hands. It was a while before he could speak. "It was a cavalry charge," he began slowly, reliving the scene in his mind. "I was riding with Gano's command. We swept across that prairie like wild fire—the Feds didn't even have time to round up their stock. Even caught unaware like that, they fought like banshees." He stopped for a long moment before going on. "Fight hadn't been going long when I saw a rifle sticking from some brush. I fired. We advanced, and, when I went to make sure the man was dead... ." his words trailed away.

Dillon grimaced. Then he gripped Allen's arm. "What else could ya have done? Not one damn thing."

Shawn's words came through tears. "He's right, Allen. It was a terrible thing, but ya had no choice."

Slowly the logic penetrated. Allen had relived the gristly scene with crystal clarity, over and over again. Never before had he actually asked himself that question.

What else could I have done? Dillon and Shawn were right. Not one damn thing.

CHAPTER 19 ⤳

Nelda sat on a cot and stared at the bare wall. Although it wasn't a jail, just a room on the bottom floor of a house in Danville, it was reminiscent of Papa's cell, and he had left it only to be hanged. With a silent groan, she wondered if the same fate would soon be hers.

The officers here had not looked kindly upon her involvement at Helena. They had, she admitted, not been cruel. Neither had they been solicitous of her comfort. The sagging cot was decrepit. In the cold room, her breath made a cloud. Along with her coat, she wore the lone, thin blanket to keep from freezing. They fed her, but the fare was poorly cooked.

There was nothing to occupy her mind—no books, no diversion, no companionship, no one to talk to except the grizzled old man who brought her meals. He smelled so bad she was glad he never tarried.

Morbid thoughts were her company. She was plagued with worry—worries for herself, worries for Allen, worries for the children. If only she could hear they had made it to safety! Reverend Springer would do his best. But it was war and there were more rebel guns to pass on the way to Illinois.

She had expected Allen to come in a day or two or, at the very most, a week. As time dragged on, she imagined every possible scenario—he never got the message; he was ill; he was killed or captured on the trail. Or he had decided to leave her to her fate because she had spurned him once too often. Her fevered imagination painted cozy scenes of him sitting in the firelight with Dorcas, her beautiful eyes shining with adoration.

It was a silly notion. Allen loved her. He would not forget her so quickly. But, in the lonely room, Della's words rang in her ear. "You keep pushin' him off, and, one of these days, he just likely to go."

A key rattled in the lock. There was a rap on the door. As usual, a stooped old man with a ragged tobacco-stained beard brought a tasteless lunch of cooked dried peas without enough salt and cornbread that was half bran.

"I tol' the major ya wanted somep'in to read. His woman sent ya this here Bible."

"Thank her for me. Is there any news?"

"None ta speak of." With that, he shuffled away.

Nelda forced herself to eat. After three bites she stopped and angrily dashed away tears. She wasn't going to be a weakling. Not even if Allen never came—not even if they hanged her. She would die a patriot to the Union.

Since her arrival, there had been a bright spot of news. Ulysses S. Grant lay in front of Petersburg less than twenty miles from Richmond, and he had vastly superior numbers to Lee, who was only hanging on to the city by the skin of his teeth. Grant was bound to conquer, and then, surely, the end would come quickly—no matter what Brooks and his Confederate Cavalry did in Arkansas.

She grimaced. Of course, the victory might be too late to save her. The old man who brought her meals was taciturn, but she'd wormed enough out of him to know they had given up on Allen coming and were discussing her fate, which was to be decided as soon as word arrived from some general—he wasn't sure which one.

She sat the bowl aside and picked up the Bible. In spite of vowing bravery, her tears dripped onto the cover. It was a stark thing to know she might soon meet her maker and judge. What if—just as she had done with Allen—she had pushed him off once too often?

With shaking hands, she opened the book. "Doth he not leave the ninety and nine, and goeth into the mountains and seeketh that which is gone astray?"

She held the book open. Staring at the bare wall, she envisioned the storybook picture of a lamb draped on the good Shepard's shoulders. Suddenly, she felt a deep longing to be carried on shoulders that were more than human. Her tears fell harder, and she didn't try to stop them.

Her head jerked up. That was Allen's voice! She'd know it anywhere! Her heart pounded as she rushed to the door and waited. It seemed forever before a key grated and the knob turned.

She flew into Allen's arms and kissed him. His eyes widened, but the young, handsome major standing nearby merely smiled.

"Oh, Allen, I was so afraid something had happened. Why were you so long in coming?" She laughed and cried and touched his face. It was covered with a short beard, and his eyes were bloodshot.

"I'll tell you all about it on the trail," he said.

Her grateful eyes sought the major. "You're letting me go?"

"Colonel Brooks said you could be released into Mr. Matther's custody with the understanding that, right after your honeymoon, he will bring you back if General Fagan wants to question you."

Allen spoke up. "I promised—right after our honeymoon."

The major grinned, but Nelda was crestfallen.

Would Allen actually do such a thing? Would he bring her back to face an inquisition?

"Get your stuff together."

She wasted no time in complying. There wasn't much, a comb and an extra pair of stockings given by the major's wife. She already wore the coat and muffler.

When they had mounted and ridden away, she looked back, glad to see the two-story white building disappear. She wouldn't feel safe until they were far from the place. However, after only going a short way, Allen stopped at a store and swung down. He tied the reins to a hitching rail.

"I need to get a few supplies if they have 'em. You coming in where it's warm?"

She looked back down the road. "Personally, I'd rather we just hurried on away from this town. Allen, you wouldn't actually bring me back would you?"

He gave a rueful smile. "The chances of that are just about as good as the chances of us ever going on a honeymoon." With that he abruptly turned and entered the mercantile.

Nelda blinked. What did he mean by that? He was acting strange. Why, he hardly seemed glad to see her. Come to think of it, he didn't even kiss me back. Her brow furrowed. He loved her. She had no doubt of that. Perhaps she had wounded him one too many times. Perhaps he doubted her declaration of love. Surely he didn't think I said that only to escape the rebels?

Just then, he exited the store and stuffed a few parcels into his saddlebags. She patted the side of her mount. "This is a nice horse. Where did you get it?"

He glanced over. "It's Shawn's. He won't be riding for a while. He took a bullet just before he got home. That's why I was so long in coming."

"Oh, no!" She dropped her head. When she looked up he had mounted. "I am so very sorry. Is he going to be all right?"

"I think so. I'd like to push on home as fast as I can. Dillon is with him, but he needs to get back or Brooks will think they've deserted. We'll cross the river at Dardanelle, and I'll take you close to home, but I won't go all the way. Clarksville is covered with Federals, troops coming and going all the time. They're trying to salvage the other boat that Brooks ran aground."

"Oh." She was stunned. She had declared her love, and yet he was just going to dump her off and ride away. So be it! She silently fumed. Her jaws squared. They rode from town in cold silence.

As the first flush of anger cooled, Nelda wilted. She loved him. It was impossible now to imagine life without him. Then her shoulders straightened. I won't beg. I have my pride!

The word suddenly rang in her ears. Pride. Papa had called it the deadly sin. She had certainly suffered from Mama's pride—the whole family had. For years Aunt Becky had been ostracized for marrying Uncle Ned. She herself was constantly forbidden activities and friends that didn't reach Mama's exalted standards.

Nelda looked over at Allen sitting straight and tight-jawed. If pride ruled, she would lose him. Hadn't Della claimed she was like Mama?

He felt her eyes and turned. "You warm enough?"

The pale sun filtering through bare trees did little to warm the still morning. Yellowed, dead grass glinted with frost and puddles on the road were ice rimmed.

"I'm fine."

They rode the rest of the morning in silence. Finally Allen stopped and stepped down. He drew a parcel from the saddlebag.

"We'll eat and rest a few minutes, but like I said, I want to push on."

She got down unassisted and took the piece of hardtack from him but held it un-tasted in her hand. "I know you're worried about Shawn, but…" she hesitated, "you don't seem like yourself. What's wrong?" While waiting for his answer, she took a tiny nibble. The hardtack was stale.

His lips thinned as he tipped his hat back off his forehead. "That little scene you pulled back there wasn't necessary. The major had already said you were free to go."

Her eyes battered as her mouth opened and closed. It took a moment to find her voice. "Little scene?"

"Hell, it was good acting," he said. His eyes were bitter. "For a second there, I almost believed it myself."

"That wasn't acting." She met his stare. "Didn't Dillon give you my message?"

He frowned. "He said Brooks had you, and I was to go fetch you—stand good for your character or some such."

She put a hand on his chest. "I told him to tell you I loved you. Allen Matthers, I do love you. With all of my heart."

His big hand covered the small one resting on his chest. "For true?"

Her hand slipped around his neck. She drew his head forward. The kiss was long and slow.

"For true and always," she breathed. "I have for ages. I just didn't have sense enough to admit it—even to myself."

He sat on a rock and stared. She chuckled. "You look like someone punched you in the belly."

"That did sort of knock the wind out of me." He shook his head. "You ain't foolin' me, are you?"

She shoved his hat back again and bent to kiss him. "I ain't foolin'."

He pulled her down alongside him and put an arm around her. With the other hand, he held her hand. "Reckon this changes my plans. You're not going back to Clarksville—not until I put a ring on this pretty little finger. You will marry me, won't you?"

"The sooner the better."

His smile began soft and slow and then overspread his face. She never remembered feeling so happy in her life. Judging from the shine in Allen's eyes, she thought he felt the same.

"I reckon women like big weddings and fancy dresses—"

She interrupted. "I'll settle for quick and simple."

"Preacher Simon at his cabin?"

"Preacher Simon? Yes, but I think Aunt Becky will want it at her house."

His smile was radiant. "Aunt Becky's it is. But maybe not so simple—let's invite everyone on Little Piney."

Her laugh rang out. "First, we have to make it there alive. Mr. Matthers, let's go home."

At first, Nelda had argued against the delay, but Allen had insisted on making the Matthers' cabin fit for a bride. She had enjoyed the time at Aunt Becky's, getting reacquainted with loving family.

On her wedding morning, Nelda sat on a stool in her aunt's bedroom and peeped out the window to see the sunny yard full and overflowing. People stood elbow to elbow. For one sad moment, she thought of faces that would be missing today—Papa and Mama and big Red Matthers and Kate…and Seamus.

On the porch, chairs held the elderly, including Granny Tanner, who leaned to spit into a flowerbed before saying. "Yonder comes fat Tom and May." A comical looking couple sat on a wagon seat—an obese man and a twig thin woman. He carefully steered the mules across the fast-flowing creek "Tom ain't missed a wedding er a free feed in his whole life," avowed Granny.

Near the catalpa tree was handsome cousin Elijah, Cindy, and the bright-eyed baby. Elijah's black-haired cousin Jenny and two children Nelda didn't know and her own broad-shouldered Uncle Tap, who had only returned two weeks ago from being a prisoner of war were also there. Uncle Tap was middle-aged, but he was still a well-built man though his stomach had a slight paunch and his hair was thinning. She thought from this angle his profile was very like Mama's.

Near him stood a tall man. Nelda's eyes widened. Why, it was big Noah!

He had survived the wound and looked supremely happy holding little Moses in one arm and Della's hand with the other. Nelda's heart overflowed.

Her eyes sought and found Allen. Big and bold and smiling, he stood alongside Brother Simon. She gave a tender smile. How like him to surprise her like this! He knew how much she had missed Della.

"Don't fidget." scolded Becky, but her blue eyes danced with joy. "There." She stepped back and laid the hairbrush on the dressing table. "Perfect. You always did have beautiful hair." Then her eyes misted. "I wish your mama were here to see how beautiful you look."

Nelda smoothed the skirt of the borrowed dress. "I'm not sure she'd be happy about this," she said.

"Oh, I think she would. According to Ned, Louise did a lot of changing before she died."

"She did. But I would marry Allen even if she were alive and didn't approve."

Becky smiled. "He's a fine man—one of the finest I know."

"We have a lot to overcome," said Nelda, "so many differences."

"No more than your Uncle Ned and me. I don't think there is such a thing as a perfect marriage. But there's joy in sharing a life with a man you love and who loves you back. You and Allen will have problems a'plenty. But together you'll overcome them."

A lovely young woman rapped on the door and then stepped inside. A chubby, dark-eyed baby was perched on her hip. "They're waiting," she said. Then as Nelda stood, she exclaimed, "The dress fits ya perfect—just like it was made for ya."

"It does, doesn't it?" said Nelda, eyeing the long-sleeved, high-neck tailored gown of white satin, mellowed by age to a soft cream. "Aunt Becky is a miracle worker with a needle. Thank you so much for lending it, Cindy." Then she frowned. "I'm afraid it will never fit you again."

Cindy chuckled. "Don't reckon I'll ever have need of another wedding dress. Elijah is stuck with me forever and enduring."

Nelda smiled. Forever and enduring. It had a wonderful sound. She hoped Simon used it in the ceremony.

Becky adjusted the tapering tip of the long sleeve on Nelda's arm. "The dress was Cindy's mama's," she explained. "I only removed the gore Polly added to make it fit Cindy." She turned loving eyes to her daughter-in-law. "Of course, I hope and pray she never needs it again." She looked back at Nelda. "You ready?" With Nelda's nod, Becky stepped to the door and motioned to a fine-looking, bearded man. "She's ready, Ned."

Love shone in Ned's eyes as he stepped into the room and offered his arm. "Allen is a mighty lucky man."

Nelda took the arm and squeezed it. "Since I can't have Papa, there's no one else on earth I'd rather have give me away." She smiled her thanks as Becky pressed a small bouquet of white blossoms into her hand.

In the main room, delicate dogwood and white sarvice blossoms, like the ones in her bouquet, filled the mantle and numerous bowls and jars on shelves and tables. A gentle breeze fluttered white curtains at the cabin windows that sparkled from a recent scrubbing.

When they stepped into the doorway, the crowd quieted and parted, making an aisle. Allen turned. His eyes found hers. In his expression, pride and joy and love blended. Nelda could not suppress a happy laugh. Everyone within earshot chuckled.

Granny's voice carried on the flower-scented breeze. "Happy bride—hit's a good omen."

Nelda was happy. A bride, she'd heard, should be nervous. She was not. If she lived to be a hundred, she doubted any day would contain as much pure joy. Allen Matthers stood a few yards away, and soon she would be completely and totally his.

Ned led her forward, and without a word, placed her hand in Allen's. Then Simon, tall and thin and humble, spoke words that for centuries had joined males and females until death did them part.

Her vows were clear and true. Allen's were strangely soft, spoken to her and her alone, his eyes tender on her face.

Simon beamed. "Then I pronounce ya, man and wife."

The hush lasted only until Allen bent and they exchanged a lingering kiss. The air filled with deep-voiced hoots and yells from men and sweet congratulations from women. Children, suddenly freed from restraint, chased about, and a small black dog barked and ran among them.

A man took her hand. "Nelda Jean, you're as pretty a bride as I ever saw. Louise would be proud."

"Thank you, Uncle Tap. I'm so thankful you got to be here. A bride wants her kin near." She tiptoed to kiss his cheek. She barely knew the big smiling man, but he already held a special place in her heart.

His eyes twinkled. "Reckon a groom does, too. I asked, and Miss Jenny said yes."

"That's wonderful," she cried and hugged a happy-faced Jenny.

When Jenny took Tap's arm and turned away, Della stepped up to hug her. "Your papa's smiling down from heaven."

"Oh, Della! It's so good to see you, and to see you looking so happy," she added with a smile.

"Noah a good man, Miss Nelda. Moses done worships the ground he walk on." For a moment, her eyes dimmed. "I hope my Gideon—"

"I think it is exactly what Gideon would want. I'm very happy for all of you."

Noah gravely shook her hand. "Missy, I wants to thank you for savin' my life—and for sendin' me along to Della. I gonna take real good care of her and Moses, too."

"Then, I thank you. They are very dear to me."

With a wide smile, he stepped away.

Nelda accepted, with equal grace, kisses from rough, bearded faces and ribald remarks that made her blush. Elijah kissed her cheek and slapped Allen's back.

"I see you've not let go of her hand. Afraid she'll run off?"

Allen's eyes twinkled. "I'm taking no chances."

Plank tables set under newly leafed trees held pots and kettles of all shapes and sizes with offerings from the festive crowd. Scarcity made the meal an odd hodgepodge of wild game, fresh polk greens, dried peas and beans and corn prepared in various ways—but that had become normal in recent years. Nelda knew the children here could not conceive of a wedding feast of bygone days. Nonetheless, it was a gay crowd that filled plates and found places to sit on quilts spread on the ground.

Simon had quieted everyone and bowed to say grace. Suddenly every head jerked up and turned toward the road. A rider galloped across the creek, sending water flying. He shot a pistol as he came. Nelda's mouth went dry. But the shots fired harmlessly into the air.

"That-there man used to ride with Simon's Yankee troop," muttered someone.

"What's that he's a' shoutin'?" asked Granny loudly.

"Something about the war—"

"It's over!" came the drunken shout. "The war is over! Lee done surrendered."

Nelda's heart leaped. The crowd, however, was deathly silent. There was no jubilation. She realized many here had fought for the Confederacy and many had lost loved ones to the cause.

The man rode on up the creek road shouting and shooting and weaving in the saddle.

"Dang fool," said Granny. "Drunk as a lord. Most likely fall off his horse and drown—er else shoot hisself."

As a murmur of opinions swept the crowd, Simon held out long tapered hands. The voices stilled again.

"If it's true," he said, "we got even more to thank the Lord fer. Hit's been a terrible costly thing—tha war has. Not one here but has lost someone. Some of us several." He swallowed. "We've fi't on different sides. But we put aside them differences as trouble and sickness come among us. Today we done it again fer a happy occasion. Makes sense to keep it up. Neighbor to neighbor, we ought to all pitch in and he'p build back all that's been tore down. Now let's pray." His gaze swept the gathering. Every head bowed.

The meal was subdued. By mid-afternoon, people began leaving. Nelda awaited Allen on the wagon seat when Granny hobbled up with a gunnysack bundle in gnarled hands. "Here's a wedding gift fer ya, Allen."

He took the parcel. His eyes widened when she added, "Hit's Caleb's best fiddle. He'd want you to have it. Billy ner Ned ner Elijah never took to playin'. When Caleb was learnin' you to play, he said you had a gift like none other."

Allen struggled for words. When none came, he stooped and kissed her forehead.

She hugged him fiercely and then pushed him back. "Get along with ya now, a'fore that new wife gets jealous." She winked at Nelda.

He laid the fiddle carefully under the seat, climbed onto the wagon, and started the mules forward. Nelda took his arm. He smiled but remained quiet.

Trees soon hid the cabin from view. Nelda snuggled closer. "You're mighty quiet," she finally said. "What are you thinking?"

He drew a deep breath and fiddled with the reins. "If it really is over, the boys will be coming back, and maybe even Ma. I'll not ask you to share a cabin with all of them. Do you really think that chaplain will help me find a place to study law?"

"I do. Reverend Springer should have gotten my letter by now. I'm expecting an answer soon. Allen," she said, leaning on his shoulder, "what would you think about adopting a couple of orphans?"

"That little Sarah and William you're always talking about?"

She nodded. "They're such special children. I would love to give then a good home and a good education."

"A ready-made family, eh?" He tilted up her chin. "I'd not be opposed to it." His blue eyes glinted with mischief and with something more. "But first, Nelda, me bonnie lassie, I intend to make some babes of me own."

Her heart pounded, and her eyes dropped. Perhaps she was a little nervous after all. "There's nothing to stop us from going to Springfield soon, is there?" she asked.

His white teeth flashed. "Not a thing—except a shiveree and a honeymoon."

She sat bold upright. "A shiveree!"

He chuckled. "Yep. They'll get over the shock of war news soon enough to come tonight, beating and banging on pots and yowling like a yard full of wildcats."

"Oh, no!" Such a thought had not entered her head. Oh, she knew of the custom and the horrible stories—brides and grooms pulled from the bed and subjected to all sorts of coarse teasing and sometimes rough treatment for the groom. The idea was mortifying!

"Don't worry," he said "It ain't as bad as it used to be since most of the young rowdies are gone. The last shiveree I went to was downright mild." He tweaked her nose. "I won't let 'em get out of hand. They sure as hell won't be riding me on any rail." He grinned. "Even if Tap and Noah both come, there's not enough man power to hog tie me."

She leaned back, only a bit mollified. For the shiveree, she would change from the white satin into the pretty soft blue house dress that was a wedding present from Aunt Becky and made from the last piece of gingham in Emmitt's mercantile.

Then she sat up again. Her cheeks burned, but she went on, "I am not going to bed until they have all gone. I don't care if I have to sit up all night."

"All right. I'll sit on the porch and fiddle." He cut his eyes sideways. "Hadn't planned on doing anything else, anyway." Then he laughed aloud at her red face.

Allen was right. The crowd was small. With the racket of thunder, they came just after dark, ate and drank and danced a few Irish tunes from Allen's fiddle. By the time the moon had risen, they departed with happy jests and good wishes.

As the last guests walked away down the silvered trail, he changed the melody to the haunting tune he had composed. Nelda had first heard it at Mary Beth's party and next here on this porch surrounded by his wonderful family. That had been a lifetime ago.

Once again her heart ached at the lovely sound. Across Little Piney, liquid notes echoed off high rocky bluffs and then died away on the sweet evening air. In imagination she heard all the Matthers clan, playing and singing, the moonlit porch a shrine to wonderful memory. Someday, her strong sons would sit here, making wild and beautiful music.

Allen laid the fiddle down and gathered her close against his chest. "Your hair smells sweeter than Ma's lilacs."

She retuned the ardent kiss. Then her finger traced his strong jaw.

"I love you, Allen Matthers. Forever and enduring."